NO REST FOR THE WICKED

NO REST FOR THE WICKED

A Novel

Rachel Louise Adams

MINOTAUR BOOKS
NEW YORK

This is a work of fiction. All of the characters, organizations, and events portrayed in this novel are either products of the author's imagination or are used fictitiously.

First published in the United States by Minotaur Books, an imprint of St. Martin's Publishing Group

EU Representative: Macmillan Publishers Ireland Ltd, 1st Floor, The Liffey Trust Centre, 117-126 Sheriff Street Upper, Dublin 1, DO1 YC43

NO REST FOR THE WICKED. Copyright © 2025 by Rachel Louise Adams. All rights reserved. Printed in the United States of America. For information, address St. Martin's Publishing Group, 120 Broadway, New York, NY 10271.

www.minotaurbooks.com

Designed by Gabriel Guma

The Library of Congress Cataloging-in-Publication Data is available upon request.

ISBN 978-1-250-36211-7 (hardcover)
ISBN 978-1-250-36212-4 (ebook)

The publisher of this book does not authorize the use or reproduction of any part of this book in any manner for the purpose of training artificial intelligence technologies or systems. The publisher of this book expressly reserves this book from the Text and Data Mining exception in accordance with Article 4(3) of the European Union Digital Single Market Directive 2019/790.

Our books may be purchased in bulk for specialty retail/wholesale, literacy, corporate/premium, educational, and subscription box use. Please contact MacmillanSpecialMarkets@macmillan.com.

First U.S. Edition: 2025

10 9 8 7 6 5 4 3 2 1

For my mother, with whom sharing this book has been absolute magic.

And for my twin, who never needs a gun when it comes to demon-slaying.

One

NIGHTMARE

Some people count to ten to wake up from a nightmare, but Dolores always counted the bones of her head instead. *Sphenoid, frontal, lacrimal.* Her muscles relaxed, like she had glided into a warm bath. On the one occasion her ex-husband dragged her to his yoga class, she used those words as a mantra.

"If you learned how to focus on your body," Max said, "you'd sleep better."

Dolores had laughed this off. She didn't need to sleep better, she needed to sleep faster.

Back then, she could see herself keeping the pace of this mad merry-go-round until retirement. Twelve-hour days? Just munch vitamins in between meals, drink enough coffee to turn her blood black. But as forty came a little closer to knocking, Dolores started to see a lot of things with fresh eyes.

Coming home to find Max with his pants down and his yoga coach spitting out some of his pubic hairs probably played a part in that.

"Dolores?"

Temporal, ethmoid, orbital.

Her date, Guy, was staring at her. Of course, any technique to wake up from a nightmare worked better when she was *actually having one.* Not when she was sitting on a moist vinyl seat at a diner where she bet the cooks squashed cockroaches during slow hours.

"Sorry," she said, "you were telling me about your sisters?"

A stiff look flashed over Guy's face. Yes, he had definitely talked about his sisters. Dolores's brain fell off the wagon when he mentioned the youngest getting her wisdom teeth pulled out, because that was apparently context she needed for their first date.

"Yeah," Guy said. "Like, ten minutes ago."

Dolores licked her lips, fishing for a rebound, before Guy released a sigh–exactly like the one he'd given the waitress when he sent his steak back. *Overcooked. Can you believe these guys?*

She smoothed over her bare ring finger with her thumb. It was yet to tan back to its sun-kissed L.A. shade. Why was she bothering with Guy again? If she and Max had broken up in a less humiliating way, she would have steered clear of men at least for a few months. Not so much because she needed closure, but because on some days she barely scraped together the time to wash her hair, let alone date.

But the cheating–

Just admit it. It hurt your pride.

She didn't think it would, and part of her knew Max was the cheating type from their wedding day, when she cut the cake and he licked buttercream off her finger with his grandparents in the front row. But it did hurt, and now she was left looking for crumbs of her dignity in all the dirty corners.

Was that how she would find it? With Guy?

Dolores bit back a smile. What a fool she made. "You know what? I'm gonna call it a night."

He made a show of checking his watch. "It's half past seven."

"Yeah, well."

Guy caught the drift. "Oh, that's it? You think there's plenty of fish in the sea for separated women who handle dead bodies all day?" He slammed a twenty on the table, so hard their plates shook. "Good luck."

Since he looked so intent on it, Dolores gave him the satisfaction of storming out while customers eyed her. When sifting through viscera was your bread and butter, you stopped caring so much what people thought about you. Dolores waited a few minutes before she got up, heels sticking against the floor. She fished a ten-dollar tip out of her bag, stuck it under Guy's empty beer glass, and headed out.

The streets sparkled with cars whizzing by. Storefronts dribbled with fake blood, cottony cobwebs, and grinning pumpkins. Halloween was still a few days away, yet its anticipation pebbled the entire city.

Dolores zipped up her jacket, more against the Halloween spirit than the night air, and got into her car.

Her phone rang as she sat at a red light. "Hello?"

On the other end, she heard Amy sigh. "What are you doing?"

"Uh–"

"This is a trick call, Dolls. You know, like trick questions, where there's a right and a wrong answer?"

"What's the right answer?"

"The right answer is no answer. You don't pick up, because you're having dinner with Guy."

"Right. Amy, I love you, but you do know Guy is run-for-your-life boring?"

Amy snorted. "That sweet mouth of yours, Dolls. He's a decent lay, though."

"Maybe if you never let him open his mouth."

"Your divorce isn't even final yet. You aren't looking to meet the love of your life."

"No, and I'm not looking for someone so obnoxious I wish I hadn't kicked Max out."

"I thought we didn't mention Evil M anymore."

Dolores rolled her window down, whipping fresh air into the car.

"Is he the only one of your friends who volunteered to take me out?"

"*Well*"–Amy shifted into diplomatic mode–"you've got to admit as far as blind dates go–"

"I know, I know." Dolores quoted Amy. "My front yard is paved with red flags."

"I love you, Dolls, but if I didn't know you? You don't have an Instagram account, your profile picture on Facebook is a cityscape, and you haven't posted in like four years. If that doesn't turn men off, there's the *coup de grâce*."

"My job?"

"It would help if it didn't have the word 'pathology' in it."

"Huh," Dolores said.

She and Amy had been roommates a few years before Dolores started her residency. Though they'd always been an odd match, their cohabitation was one of those things that made no sense but worked, the way salty French fries inexplicably bring out the sweetness of vanilla shakes. After their workdays, they found common ground by dropping on the couch and watching soap operas.

They stopped being roommates when Dolores moved in with Max, and their relationship mainly came down to phone calls now. L.A. was such a big city, and twelve-hour days left little time for Dolores to socialize.

"If you want to meet someone," Amy said, "do it face-to-face. Get out of your apartment. Breathe a little, for goodness' sake. Why don't you come to my Halloween party? I know you hate Halloween, but you'll barely have to dress up."

That still left other people's costumes, lychee-eyeballs punch, and Marilyn Manson songs. More Halloween than Dolores could stomach.

"Thanks, but I'll pass."

"Up to you, Dolls."

Dolores hung up. It took her over an hour to get back to her apartment, and she thought of all the ways she could have filled that precious dose of spare time instead of going out with Guy. Once she got home, she kicked off her heels and darted for the shower, ignoring the dirty dishes spewing out of her sink, the laundry she hadn't found time to wash.

Her phone rang just as she was stepping into the shower. *Damn it.* Why couldn't she have a normal job and let calls go to voicemail like everybody else?

She slipped inside a robe and trotted back to the living room, where her phone buzzed on the coffee table. Unknown number. Then, she almost *did* let it go to voicemail, because if someone tried to sell her something right now, she would scream.

"Hello?"

"Dolores Hawthorne?"

Goose bumps broke down Dolores's arms.

Not because the man sounded so grave–but because of what he'd called her.

Eighteen years since someone last called her by her father's name. *Dolores Hawthorne.* Eighteen years since she left that name behind in Little Horton.

"Yes, this is she."

"I'm Special Agent Wyatt Holt, with the FBI."

Dolores almost hung up.

She did *not* have time for phone pranks, and this was a prank, surely, because why would an FBI agent call her, ever? But something—that name, like a stranger's now—pushed down her throat the certainty that this wasn't a joke.

In a split second, Dolores's apartment turned into a hostile environment. The too-full trash cans smelled like rotting bodies; the sharpness of every object narrowed into focus.

"Miss Hawthorne?"

"Yes."

Agent Holt cleared his throat. She appreciated that second of humanity, like she'd appreciated the genuine horror on Max's face when he'd said, "*Oh Doll, oh shit, oh shit.*"

"Look, there—there's no right way to say this. I'm afraid your father was reported missing early this evening."

The words punched air from her lungs. She had been so sure he would say *Your father is dead.*

What did a missing person crime scene look like? Dolores dealt in dead bodies, not missing ones. If her father had left his body behind, it would have at least given her answers. Time of death. Cause of death. The *certainty* of death.

Her breath hitched and she pictured the ivory-white bones of her head against the phone.

"I know this is delicate," Agent Holt said. "But it would help if my partner and I could talk to you in person. There's a few things you might help us shed light on."

Silence.

The thought of leaving Los Angeles, of taking a flight back to Wisconsin, to her hometown, caused a flash of nuclear white to radiate through her forehead.

"Miss Hawthorne, I don't want to alarm you. But it's important you realize there's evidence of foul play." Agent Holt paused. "Of course, we can work from a distance. This is a difficult situation, I understand."

There it was, her window for flight. Though she longed to take it, Dolores couldn't bring herself to say the words out loud.

Yes, yes, thank you. My father is missing—evidence of foul play—but we'll work from a distance. I have so much work to do, you see, divorce papers to sign. I just can't be bothered right now.

Hang up the phone, and then what? Hop back into that shower? Go to work tomorrow morning like nothing happened?

Her father's sparkly blue eyes set her memory ablaze—he was one of those people who smiled with his eyes. How he used to look at her, like she was a piece of sunshine.

He's your father, Dolores. He's the only parent you have left.

"I'll come," she said.

Agent Holt sighed. "Thank you, Miss Hawthorne. I appreciate it."

Dolores didn't answer.

The scar across her belly burned like hot tar.

She didn't say that the last time she had seen her father was eighteen years ago. That she had left her hometown in tears and spent the whole flight vomiting into a Delta Air sick bag, vowing to herself all the while—*I'll never go back, I'll never go back.*

Two

UNDERWATER

Dolores crammed a fistful of clothes in a suitcase and slipped back into the dress that hung from her bathroom sink. She slammed the door behind her, rushed down three flights of stairs, then climbed them again to fish for her coat, buried in a pile of junk inside her closet. She'd need it in Wisconsin.

The Uber she called was waiting outside her building when she finished packing, so just ten minutes after she hung up with Agent Holt, Dolores was on her way to LAX. She called the hospital, promised she'd be back to work in a few days, and hated how hackneyed the words sounded–*family emergency.*

Tears didn't spring to her eyes. Her voice didn't crack. *I can do this,* she thought, and she really could, so long as she had things to do. Carried by the rush of the airport as businessmen and women hurtled into her, coffee splashed out of go-cups, kids bellowed from exhaustion. Just finding her way around the circular, maze-shaped airport occupied her brain for half an hour.

It was only when Dolores boarded and dropped in her seat that the reality of the situation smashed into her.

I'm on a plane back to Little Horton. My father is gone.

The plane took off and Dolores dragged in deep breaths, leaving moon-crescent nail prints on the arms of her seat.

"You don't like flying?" her seat neighbor asked.

He had a gray-and-black beard, not salt-and-pepper, but with the colors divided into neat halves. From his accent and utter lack of tan, a Wisconsinite flying home, not an Angeleno flying out.

Dolores shook her head. *He's trying to distract me, being a nice guy.*

Right now, she didn't really care to talk to some guy whose beard looked like a vanilla-chocolate Dixie cup. But if she didn't take the distraction, there was a real chance she would throw up.

"No, I don't."

"Well, don't give it a second thought. Chances of crashing are close to none. It's the safest way of getting anywhere, and you don't think of dying in a car accident every time you get behind the wheel, do you?"

Actually, Dolores did think about it. A symptom of handling dead bodies all day. When she showered, her mind wandered to soapy floors and cracked skulls. In the streets, when a man's eyes lingered on her, she couldn't stop herself from picturing torn underwear and bruised throats.

She'd explained this to Amy when she got her job at the hospital. "Being around dead people all the time–it becomes *how* you think, not just what you think about. Like you, with Instagram. If you see a donut next to a steaming mug, you'll jump to how wonderful it'd look in a picture. You can't *look* at the donut without your brain working on what angle you'd photograph it from, what filter you'd use."

"So," Amy said, "you can't do anything without thinking about how it might kill you?"

Amy made it sound macabre, but Max had liked that about her. When Dolores turned forks upside down in the dishwasher and said, "People fall and impale themselves on those things all the time," awe dribbled from Max's gaze like melted butter. That she saw death every day, and that death didn't scare her, maybe allowed him to feed off the deluded lie that it didn't scare *him*.

Max was thirty-seven when he met her, already very aware of his mortality. She caught him in front of the bathroom mirror sometimes, tracing the lines across his face, as if he could erase them if he spotted them on time. If anything, Dolores blamed those wrinkles for Max's infidelity–for his inability to refuse an opportunity to feel eighteen, to feel alive.

She closed her eyes, half expecting to see her father in the brief lapse of darkness. Instead, a warm glow enveloped her, one she only felt when her father was looking at her. Dolores used to think the glow came from her. It took moving to Los Angeles for her to realize that that special shine dripped from her father's eyes—that she was like the moon, reflecting the sunlight, and that without him her whole being was blunted and blind.

"Why wasn't there a body?" she let out.

"What?"

Dolores jerked back into focus. The plane. The bearded stranger.

The words almost streamed out of her. *My father is missing but really I'd rather they had found a dead body.*

"Nothing," she said.

A cabin crew member perched on impossible heels wheeled by with a trolley, and Dolores refrained from grasping her arm in despair.

"I'll have a drink, please."

IN FACT, SHE HAD three, and after she ordered a second, Pixie-Beard pretended she didn't exist. Her eyes squeezed shut in exhaustion. When she opened them, she found the plane completely empty, the lights dimmed. A glance out the window confirmed she was dreaming: either that, or it was perfectly normal for domestic flights to cross the ocean, and to fly inches from water.

"Don't worry."

Dolores gasped. Pixie-Beard had disappeared from the seat next to hers, and in his place sat a seventeen-year-old girl, legs crossed, flipping through a magazine. She had chestnut hair and dark eyes. A smile that split all the way to her cheekbones. If her eyes had been a few inches closer to the bridge of her nose, her chin less pointy, she could have been Dolores's twin.

Kristen Horowitz. Dolores had gone to school with her, but they hadn't been friends until the summer before Dolores's senior year. Her last summer in Little Horton.

"It won't hurt," Kristen said.

"Sorry?"

Kristen looked up from her magazine. She hadn't aged, although she must be in her mid-thirties now, like Dolores.

"When we go in."

Dolores's gaze darted to the window. The surface of the sea zoomed in as the plane plunged. She closed her eyes–*lacrimal, ethmoid, orbital*–but somehow she could still see the plane going into the water behind her lids. A dark blue-green flooded the plane, and Dolores's breath hitched as she waited for the water to enter her lungs. But everything just went very quiet. Fish drew near the window and scattered when Dolores touched her hand to the glass.

"Told you," Kristen said.

Dolores nodded. Suddenly, she didn't know just what she was doing on a plane back to Little Horton, except that she was going to see her father. Yes, and she hadn't seen him in a very long time–why, she couldn't remember, either. An ache bristled to life deep inside her, smelling of mahogany and whiskey, shaped like a tall old man who smiled with his eyes and loved her more than life itself.

Her father felt so close to her she could almost make out the brush of his fingers against her cheek.

She turned, and her mouth went dry when she saw the young man sitting across the aisle, his hair gleaming like asphalt on a hot day.

Jacob.

Her high school sweetheart looked coldly at her. "What? Am I supposed to say hello, Dolores? After you left like that, all those years ago. Would it have killed you to say goodbye?"

Terror trickled down to her toes.

Dolores pictured the bones of her head screwing tighter together, like she could seal the vision of Jacob away.

She longed for some snappy comeback.

Why would I have said goodbye to you?

Do you think you deserved it after what you did?

But her tongue stayed glued to her mouth.

She had not managed to speak a word to Jacob, after he'd shattered the trust between them and trampled the remains.

Apparently, Dream Jacob was having the same effect.

"Let her be, will you?" Kristen winked at Dolores. "A girl can't disappear anymore without men losing their shit."

Dolores glanced back at the window and shuddered. A shark scuttled by, beady eyes meeting hers.

Sweat broke down her neck as she looked at Jacob. His seat concealed the lower half of his face, so she couldn't see his smile. Yet he was smiling. It glinted in the jades of his eyes.

"Don't worry," he said. "I hear they don't bite."

Dolores woke with a cry, and Pixie-Beard put effort into frowning his disapproval. Sweat pasted dark locks to her forehead. Everything had been so clear, but as she opened her eyes, the dream blended into the murky ocean of her life in Little Horton, dark, impenetrable. Jacob had been there. And a girl Dolores used to know, a girl whose grin was so wide, you could see her missing back molar.

Typical Dolores, Max would say. Great at having nightmares, greater at forgetting them.

Three

HALLOWEEN TOWN

"Little Hortwhat?"

Dolores shifted in the backseat, eyes on the sheet of Plexiglas that divided the backseat area. "Little Horton."

The driver scratched the stubble on his chin. "Oh, that's right. The Halloween town?"

A pebble jammed Dolores's throat. "Yeah."

"Not much of a crowd goes there aside from October 31. You're a little early, aren't you?"

In L.A., the driver would have just tapped the address into his phone and they'd be rolling right now. One of the things Dolores had struggled to get used to in a big city–how people were so caught up in their lives, they looked at you like you were part of the furniture. She could have used that tonight.

"It's not exactly next door," he pointed out.

"If it was next door, I wouldn't need a cab. I could walk."

His eyebrows shot toward the roots of his hair.

"Sorry. I'm having a day."

A beat of silence. Drizzle whipped against the windshield, and Dolores clutched her fist over her coat collar. She should have worn a scarf. And a sweater.

"Is it your first time in Little H?" the driver asked.

Dolores was happy enough with the truce to overlook the touristy nickname. "No. I grew up there."

"Tourists tell me there's no place like it for Halloween. Maybe I'll give it a try this year. You'll still be in town?"

"No."

The landscape flashed by, a dark waste of blue deserts. In the daylight, azure skies would loom over green pastures, trees plump with orange foliage and lakes like the ocean.

"Isn't it a shame to come all this way and leave before the Halloween celebrations?"

"I don't like Halloween."

"You don't say! And you're from Little H? Well, I guess you tire of it eventually."

In fact, a lot of people did. Tourist fatigue was the kind of thing you pictured for sunny paradises. Hawaii, the Bahamas. Not a town that could barely squeeze out two thousand souls, three-quarters over sixty. Most people who stopped for gas would gape if you told them the average rent for a house. Travel guides listed Little Horton in the top ten "Most Expensive Small Towns in America."

But if you took Halloween out of the picture, Little Horton was not much to write home about. True, it had looks on its side, with Queen Anne-style houses and a quaint city center that featured a library, local souvenir shops, and a total of five restaurants.

If Little Hortoners tired of anything, it was having their town raided by tourists on Halloween and ignored for the rest of the year.

"It didn't help that my stepmother was a Halloween fanatic," Dolores volunteered. "When you have to dress up the house and bake sweets for a whole week, it takes the fun out of it. I wouldn't bother if I were you. It's not worth the gas."

"Come on. *The* place for Halloween, right?"

"Two hundred people crammed into diners meant to hold fifty. A pumpkin-carving contest, which I assure you is as exciting as it sounds. And drunk, *very* drunk people that holler throughout the night."

"What about this great spooky tour–"

"The Little Horton Halloween Tour." The name didn't wrench one drop of nostalgia from Dolores. "It's tacky, and kind of in bad taste."

The driver stayed silent, so she went on. Every minute she chatted was a minute she didn't need to think.

"Little Horton's famous for its history of violent deaths. Hence the Halloween vibes."

"Violent deaths?"

"Really, there hasn't been a murder there in seventy years. Just freak accidents that spawned urban legends about the town being haunted, because they happened on Halloween."

"What freak accidents?"

She sighed. "October 31, 1886, a bridge collapsed during the town fair. Twelve people died. Two horses. 1902, a circus was in town for the celebrations. The juggler threw five knives into the air, caught four with his hands, and the last one with his forehead. The whole town saw it."

"Holy Moses."

"1934, a restaurant burned down. 1959, a man fell off a ladder in his garden holding a chain saw, sliced himself in two."

"What was he doing with a chain saw?"

Dolores shrugged. "Trimming a tree? Little Hortoners are fanatical about their gardens."

"And these accidents only happen on Halloween, do they?"

"No. Freak accidents happen all year long, like in any town. It's purely coincidental that a lot of them took place on Halloween—and City Hall obviously saw a way to cash in."

Dolores looked at her shoes. Talking about City Hall without mentioning her father had been the town's mayor for years tasted one teaspoon away from a lie.

"How d'you know all that?"

"You can't grow up in Little Horton and not know it. School teaches it, the kids make up songs about it."

Eighteen years since she last stepped foot in this town, and she still remembered the rhymes. *One night at the circus the juggler looks blue. A knife lands in his head: it's nineteen o' two.*

"Damn. If you hate it so much, what brings you back?"

Her thumb hit the bare skin of her ring finger. "Family," she said.

A sigh heaved out of her.

Tomorrow, she'd be back in L.A. The police would find her father and Little Horton could go back to being a place no realer than Neverland or Bluebeard's Castle.

Four

LITTLE HORTON

As the cab's headlights illuminated the "Welcome to Little Horton" sign, a maniacal beat entered Dolores's heart. What was she doing here? Did she expect she could cruise to her hometown, knock on the door of the family house, and everyone would welcome her in?

Familiar sights sent jolts of adrenaline through her body. Diners where boys had taken her out for ice cream, the bakery where she'd bought breakfast on her way to school. The houses flashed by, though the car couldn't be going faster than twenty miles per hour.

She heard herself say, "Take a right."

The cab squeezed into a cramped street and before she could brace herself, the Hawthorne house loomed over her. Its red-and-black bricks gleamed, burning coals in the night. Time stopped the way people say it does when you're falling in love or about to die.

"You can stop here."

The driver craned his neck to glance at the house. "Christ! This is your place?" His eyes narrowed at her. "You famous or something?"

"No."

He could google who the house belonged to if he liked, and decide for himself whether being the estranged daughter of a former senator made Dolores famous.

She tipped him, and thanked him for the ride.

"Bye," he replied, his friendliness vanished behind a wall of Plexiglas.

Predawn hit her with an icy drizzle as she stepped out.

The path that led to the front door was paved with white pebbles that drank in the moonlight. She checked her phone. Five thirty in the morning.

I haven't even called anyone to tell them I'm coming.

Should she check into a motel, wait for a more decent hour? She could use the wait before she stumbled back into the life she had torn out of, rupturing the fabric of family and trust.

But light beamed through the burgundy drapes at the living room window. Someone must be awake.

Dolores thumped on the door. Something brushed her leg and she swiveled, half ready to see a man pointing a gun at her.

L.A. reflexes.

It was just a cat. Scrawny, with about half an ear chewed off, he mewled as he rubbed against her bare calves.

Footsteps sounded in the hallway and the cat scurried into the night.

The door flung open.

A man stood in the hall, mid-twenties. Hair the color of oatmeal curled down his forehead. Cheekbones so high, she could cut her hand slapping him.

Dolores took a step back. The last time she'd seen Asher, he was five years old, a blond cherub with fat cheeks who smelled like warm caramel when she hugged him. Today, he was such a clear-cut product of the Hawthorne brand, tears welled in her eyes.

"Who the fuck are you?" he said.

But from the flash of thunder in his robin's-egg eyes, Dolores knew he recognized her. "It's me."

"It's you?" Mock confusion, an undertone of anger.

"Dolores," she said.

"Right, right. Dolores. Who barges in before sunrise in the middle of a family crisis but Dolores?"

She hardened against the cracks in her voice. "He's my family, too."

Her brother stepped aside to let her in, eyes drilling holes in the back of her head. A crystal chandelier burned bright in the hallway. Most families saved them for the living room or the dining room, places where they invited people over. But chandeliers adorned every hall and every room at the Hawthornes'.

The air smelled of firewood and antiques, a merger between home and a museum. In a flash, Dolores knew she could make her way around blindfolded, hands tied. She had crawled these floors as a little girl, rug-burns on her knees and palms–had turned this castle into her playground.

As a reflex, she hung her coat on the rack by the door, and Asher snorted. "Make yourself at home."

"Where's Charlotte?"

"Asleep. Doctor gave her forty milligrams of temazepam."

"And Josie?"

An invisible shield slammed between them. "You don't get to mention Josie. You never even met Josie."

Dolores chewed on her tongue as she studied Asher. Part of her had expected he would still be a boy, whenever she was ready to leave room for him in her life.

Sprinkled on the walls were diplomas, awards; Asher and Josie's entire childhood had no doubt conquered the house. They were the true heirs–Hawthornes to the backbone. What remained of Dolores's life? A few pictures at the beginning of a dusty album? A box in the attic?

Just like my mother.

She broke eye contact with Asher. She deserved his anger. Just because she had grown up in this house–did it give her the right to return out of the blue and act like she belonged?

She grabbed her coat. "I'm sorry. I shouldn't have bothered you."

Asher stopped her wrist. His touch was icy-firm, yet she melted into it. Five-year-old Asher, squeezing tiny fists in excitement as he read his homework to her.

"Mom will kill me if I let you stay at a motel. Come on."

He led her to her old room. None of Dolores's stuff remained, yet everything about it felt familiar. The way the mattress gave under her weight as she sat down, the smell of cherrywood soaking out of the walls.

"You should get some rest," he said. "The feds want to talk to you."

"You knew they tried to reach me?" Silence trickled between them. "Why did you pretend you didn't know me just now?"

"Can we not do this?"

A sour taste filled Dolores's mouth. "Shouldn't we talk about Dad?"

The mention of their father might have softened Asher. Instead, his face tightened.

"I just thought–"

"Oh. You want to talk about Dad? Do you wanna start with the phone calls you never made? The letters you didn't write? All the times you didn't check how he was doing, if he was even still alive? Hey, how about those goddamn years you *didn't* come back to Little Horton–like it was just a blind spot on the map? Wanna talk about that?"

Asher shook his head. A glint pricked into his gaze. "We'll talk tomorrow. Okay?"

She managed a nod.

"You don't need a tour of the house, Sis? Remember where the bathroom is and everything?"

Dolores ignored the bite in his tone. "Yeah."

"Good. I guess I'll leave you to your sweet dreams." He caught himself on the doorframe. "One more thing. Don't go into Dad's office. That's where it happened." His jaw clenched. "Where they took him."

Five

FAMILY PORTRAIT

Dolores woke with the sun beaming outside her bedroom window. The clock on her phone read seven thirty. Two hours of sleep wasn't ideal, but it would have to do.

A smell of grilled toast and fried eggs hit her as she went down the stairs.

The kitchen door was cracked open, enough for her to pick up distinct voices. Knives screeched against plates, cupboards opened and closed, but Charlotte's Louisiana drawl cut clean through. However much she worked to fit into the Little Horton community, she could never do more than soften that nasal twang.

"We're not debating this, Josie. You're going to school. That's the end of it."

A scoff. "That's cheap, Mom. You can put that at the end of any sentence, because it doesn't mean anything. 'We'll eat waffles every day until we die. That's the end of it.'"

"That's very clever, darling. You're still going."

"Dad is *missing*."

"The FBI said we should go on with our lives as usual."

"To Josie's credit," Asher said, "the FBI sounded as helpful as a couple of umbrellas in a hailstorm. Probably can't tell their elbows from their asses."

"Asher, mind your language with your sister around."

A floorboard squealed, and Dolores pushed open the door before anyone could accuse her of eavesdropping.

Three pairs of blue eyes stared at Dolores.

Asher stood by the window. Earlier, his face looked smooth as butterscotch, but daylight brought out a few wrinkles on his forehead.

Charlotte wore a white robe knotted at the waist over a cashmere pullover. Her hair hung shoulder-length, whitish-blond, and Dolores couldn't tell if the years had turned it whiter. She looked every bit as much the Southern belle as when she married Alexander Hawthorne in her twenties.

It was Josie who knocked the breath out of her. Unconsciously, she'd clung to the first picture she had seen of her baby sister, fifteen years ago: a healthy one-month-old with pink lips and yellow hair. Part of her knew Josie would be in her teens now, as she had known Asher would be a grown man.

Yet at the sight of the elfin-faced girl who sat before a pile of blackened toast, Dolores's jaw slackened.

Josie had her mother's blond hair and the Hawthornes' high cheekbones. A triangular chin, and a tiny bud of a nose that gives girls such an obviously cute air, they have to act twice as mean to get their point across.

Charlotte broke the silence. "Hello, Dolores."

She looked so tired that for a moment Dolores thought they would simply do without the drama, tacitly ignore all the circumstances that cried out for it.

Charlotte cut the heat under the eggs. "Asher told me you got here early this morning. Was your flight okay?"

Dolores had no time to answer before Josie's chair screeched against the floor. She got up, and Dolores's chest constricted because they were the same height. *Fifteen, Josie is fifteen now.*

"Wow," Josie said. "Dolores, *the* Dolores. Sorry. I thought you'd look more like Mom—but of course you wouldn't."

"Don't be rude," Charlotte said.

Asher watched, arms crossed over his chest. For all Dolores knew, he was enjoying this.

"Sorry," Josie said, with the kind of delight known only to teenage girls and evil geniuses.

She bit into the piece of toast she'd carried from the table. "It's not personal or anything. I'm rude all the time—just ask Mom. Like, I had to take a peek while you were sleeping. Not a polite thing to do."

"Josie," Charlotte said, tone laden with warning.

"What? I got curious. Don't I get a pass?" She turned back toward her half sister. "You'd be curious, too, if you grew up with a huge shadow in the house called *Dolores.*"

Charlotte put the pan on the counter. "Time to get to school." Her eyes flicked to Asher.

"I'll drive her," he said. "Come on, Josie."

"Can I get a hug from my big sister first?"

Blood pumped to Dolores's brain. She should rush to her. Josie was her flesh and blood. Hadn't she showered Asher with love when he was a child, before—

Before.

Dolores felt how wrong this was, in her bone marrow. This missing gap between her and her sister, where affection should be. Her feet dug roots into the floor as Josie wrapped her arms around her. Dolores breathed in the smell of coconut shampoo. *Move, goddamn it.* With effort, she managed to wrap one arm around her sister's back. The bones of Josie's shoulder blades bit into her wrist.

Josie drew back, as if to kiss Dolores's cheek. Instead she whispered into her ear, "You are *so* bad at this, they should put you on TV."

Josie grabbed a backpack at the foot of the chair, and Asher locked a hand around her shoulders.

Only when the door clicked shut behind them did it hit Dolores that she was now alone with her stepmother.

As far back as Dolores could remember, she and Charlotte had navigated their relationship awkwardly, inexpert sailors tossed into stormy seas. When Alexander married Charlotte, she was barely fifteen years older than Dolores. The blooming bouquets that adorned the gravestone of his first wife had barely had time to wither. The question was not whether Dolores would hate Charlotte, but how much.

Dolores could remember, as a child, putting sugar in the salt shaker, trying to prank Charlotte into a reaction—into anger. With hindsight, those had been shitty things to do. But back then, Dolores did not think of Charlotte as an actual person. She was just this blond, model-pretty girl who'd invaded her life.

Who's the invader now?

Dolores cleared her throat. "I'm sorry to barge in like this."

"Please, Dolores. You're my husband's daughter. You're family." Charlotte turned to face the counter and scraped the abandoned eggs into the trash. "If you'll sit down and have some breakfast."

Dolores stared at the carnage left by her siblings. Knives dripping with strawberry jam, gutted oranges, and toast so hard she could see the full imprint of her sister's teeth. Like the food at a wake, a pointless protest against death.

Though her legs felt like cotton candy, she couldn't bring herself to sit down.

"I know you want to ask about your father—I appreciate your patience. The only thing I'll ask is that you don't interrupt me, and pay attention. Let's only go over this once. Shall we?" Charlotte turned on the tap and started scrubbing the pan. "I last saw Alexander yesterday at lunchtime. Josie was at school, and Asher only drove in from Madison last night when he heard the news. We finished lunch at one thirty. After that, your father went to his study and I spent the afternoon downtown. I didn't come home until five. Josie was in the kitchen—you know how teenagers are always hungry. We talked about her day, and she told me she hadn't run into her father. We assumed he was working and didn't go near his office. He hates being disturbed."

"I remember," Dolores let out.

The memory squeezed in: late evenings whiled away inside her father's study. Alexander could never stand anyone interrupting his work—that is, anyone other than her. When she knocked at his office door after dinner, he always had a smile and a cookie for her.

Charlotte wiped her hands on a kitchen towel. "I went to get him around dinnertime. I knocked on his door. No answer. I entered. The room—"

Charlotte stopped, but didn't choke out a sob.

Appearances.

Whatever turmoil was breaking loose inside that birdlike frame, Charlotte curbed it before Dolores could hear even a tremor.

The Hawthornes were not the kind to condone vulnerability, to think showing signs of weakness was really a strength. In this house, strength was strength, and weakness was weakness.

Charlotte resumed, calm as Dolores tried to appear when she presented evidence in court. Maybe she and her stepmother could never see eye to eye, but for the first time, at least the professional in Dolores could admire the professional in Charlotte.

"His desk was upside down. A decanter was emptied on the rug. Papers scattered all about and–blood. There was blood."

"I need to see it."

"The office?" Charlotte looked up. "You can't. The FBI was very clear we shouldn't touch anything."

Dolores gripped the top rail of her chair. Even without a body, the scene could teach her a lot. Depending on what they left behind–hairs, shoeprints, DNA–she could learn so much about the people who had taken her father.

It made her blood boil to stand here, a heartbeat away from this well of knowledge, without being able to do anything about it.

"Are the FBI on their way?"

"Yes." A flash of gold glinted as Charlotte checked her watch. "Shouldn't be long now."

Silence dropped between them. Dolores could hear blood pumping into her brain. "Do you–" she began. "Do you have any idea what happened?"

Charlotte paused. "I don't think he woke up one morning and decided to walk out on his family. Other than that, your guess is as good as mine."

"I wasn't suggesting–"

Dolores stopped. Thought Charlotte would bare teeth, finally, pick up their old battle where they'd left it. She had it coming.

Disappearing is your specialty, Dolores. Not his.

But she didn't say anything. The weapons sat safe in their sheaths, which was unsettling. They didn't used to miss an occasion to hurt each other.

Charlotte let out a sigh, as if reading Dolores's mind.

"Things haven't always been easy between us," she said. An offer of a truce? A ceasefire in a time of crisis? "When I married your father, you were the apple of his eye." Her laughter chimed through the room. "That's probably not how you remember it. Little girls take these things for granted—all children do. But God, he loved you. You were not an easy person to rival with."

"Neither were you."

Charlotte smiled. "Despite all that, I'm glad you're here, Dolores. It's what your father would want. However cliché this might sound, he was never the same after you left."

"Stop." Dolores didn't think of catching the word before it was out.

Charlotte's face stretched with disapproval, like it was foolish of Dolores to beg. And why not? After everything—why should Charlotte show her any mercy?

"You deserve to know," Charlotte said, her tone scalpel-clean. "We never talked about you. When you went away, Alexander had all your pictures taken off the walls, and all your things sent to charities. He stopped seeing people who didn't know better than to pretend you didn't exist. You broke his heart, Dolores. You're the only woman who ever did."

Six

APPEARANCES

It never took Wyatt a long time to decide whether or not he liked someone. With Special Agent Paul Turner, thirty seconds had done the trick: long enough for Paul to flash him a grin and call him Big Guy. A bigger man never calls you Big Guy except to draw attention to the fact that they're bigger. True, he probably would have disliked any agent his boss sent to make sure he didn't botch the job, but Paul made the task strikingly easy.

When Wyatt sat through his job interview with the FBI a year and a half ago, he only told one lie: to the question, "Do you feel comfortable working with other people?" Wyatt had answered: "Extremely."

The bells on the church downtown had rung a quarter to eight when Paul joined Wyatt outside the motel. Yes, they could actually hear the bells in Little Horton from the motel parking lot. In fact, they could practically see the town: a steeple and rooftops that peeked through the wood at the city border.

Paul slammed Wyatt on the shoulder on his way to the car, and Wyatt grimaced. What had happened to greeting colleagues with a respectful nod?

"Sorry I kept you waiting," Paul said.

"Sorry you kept the Hawthornes waiting. My time's not great for wasting, but I don't like to play with the feelings of a distraught family."

Paul scoffed at "distraught," like Wyatt was trying to impress him with big words. Then he cut for the driver's seat without asking Wyatt if he wanted to drive. Wyatt let it slide, but opened his mouth when Paul plucked a cigarette from his coat pocket.

"I wish you wouldn't light that."

"Oh, would you?"

Wyatt squared his jaw. He wasn't about to let Paul intimidate him just because the man was a few years older, and acted like everything he peed on would turn to gold.

"I wouldn't mind if it was your car," Wyatt said. "But you don't want to mess with GOVs." He tried to sound comfortable, as if he hadn't spent his first few weeks on the job googling so many acronyms his head spun.

The vehicle they currently sat in looked nothing like Wyatt would have expected before he joined the bureau. A Chrysler 300, silver, with brown leather interior.

"I know how to handle government cars," Paul said. "And I'm *smoking,* not running the damned thing into a wall."

"Devaluing government property–"

A soft purr as Paul flicked his lighter ablaze.

Ten minutes later, they were parking in the driveway of the Hawthorne house. Even if he'd seen the house just yesterday, it was hard not to give in to its majestic aura. The steep roofs and turrets gave it a neo-Gothic air that should have looked gaudy, but bristled the hairs on the back of his neck instead.

"So," Paul said as they got out of the car, "how about the wife?"

"Sorry?"

Paul smiled. "What is she, thirty years younger than him? If the old man was done in, my money's on the wife."

"So," Wyatt tried to follow, "Charlotte marries Hawthorne for his wealth, then sticks with him for thirty years before she kills him? Slow planner."

Paul shrugged. "Maybe she was waiting for her kids to be older. Maybe the guy just took his sweet time to die. Besides, that's *if* he was done in. I'm open to other possibilities. What's your best bet?"

"I'm not betting on anything."

Paul grabbed the lion-head knocker and thumped it against the door.

Charlotte Hawthorne came to greet them. If Wyatt looked at her through Paul's eyes, it made sense that this petite, beautiful woman would only marry an older man for his money. Paul watched too much television, though. This much was obvious just from the way he held a cigarette. His slick black hair, tweezed eyebrows, and Colgate-white smile all told Wyatt the same thing. Looks mattered to Paul. But looks could be deceiving.

"Agent Holt. Agent Turner." Her Louisiana accent was jarring in a town as bland as Little Horton. "Please, come in."

She led them into the living room, where another woman sat waiting for them. She made to stand, but Paul raised a hand. "Please, don't trouble yourself."

The woman sat back and smoothed her dress over her lap. Her long black hair hung loose around her shoulders, and she had very dark eyes, tipping her beauty from casual to intimidating.

Though she could not have looked less like the rest of the Hawthorne family, with their blue eyes and blond hair, she could only be the exiled daughter. Dolores.

Wyatt wiped his palms inside his pockets. It was a testimony to his acting skills that people always assumed he was more comfortable than he felt. Yesterday, Charlotte had received them in the kitchen, and this new room opened the gap in Wyatt's chest a little deeper. That gap of being an impostor, of not belonging. He struggled not to take in the marble mantelpiece, the fireplace, the Rockwells.

What really surprised him, though, was the sword that loomed over the art pieces on the wall. The blade shimmered as it caught the light from the chandelier, the handle golden–*gold?*–and massive enough to knock a boxer out cold. Carved letters drew Wyatt's eye, but he didn't want to approach it and look like a kid at a museum.

FOR CHARLOTTE, WITH LOVE.

Wyatt pivoted toward the mistress of the house. She had followed his gaze to the sword.

"Alexander gave this to me as a wedding present. He said it was a tribute to my extraordinary strength." Her lips curled above her teeth. Wyatt couldn't tell if she was mocking the idea or savoring it. "The first thing about me he fell in love with."

Before he could reply, Paul said, "That's a really moving story." His hand moved to Charlotte's arm. Wyatt made a mental note to always keep a yard of distance between himself and his new partner.

"Ma'am," Paul said, "you told us everything you could last night. There's no reason you should go through this ordeal again." He actually flashed a look at Wyatt, as if to say, *I can use big words, too.* "Unless you remembered something you'd like to tell us, you don't have to stay while we talk with your stepdaughter."

Charlotte opened her mouth, closed it, and looked at Dolores.

It was immediately clear there was as much trust between these women as between two inmates from different gangs.

"Of course," Charlotte said, her smile smoothing over the cracks. "I'll be down the hall if you need anything."

Paul took a seat in a wine-colored armchair and looked detestably at home.

Wyatt turned to Dolores. "Miss Hawthorne, I'm Special Agent Wyatt Holt, we spoke on the phone yesterday. This is my partner, Paul Turner."

Dolores nodded. "It's Diaz."

"I beg your pardon?"

"I took my mother's name after high school."

"Right," Paul cut in, "Miss Diaz."

"If you don't mind," Wyatt said, "we have a few questions for you. Do you have any objections to us recording this? It's standard procedure."

She nodded. "I haven't seen my father since I moved to Los Angeles after high school. Charlotte must have told you that."

"Did you call each other often?" Paul asked. He'd taken a pen out of his pocket—not to write anything down. From what Wyatt had seen of the man, he just liked to hold things in his hand. Lighter, pen, keys. With anyone else, Wyatt would have deduced "shy speaker in high school," but not with Paul. Clearly not.

"Never," Dolores said.

Paul raised his eyebrows in mock surprise and smiled. *Jesus, he must think that smile looked pleasant.* "Never? Not on holidays, special occasions?"

"Never. I got a card and a picture when Josie was born, and I sent them one after I got married. Other than that, we sent each other cards for our birthdays and Christmas. That's all."

"Cards," Paul repeated. "Not letters?"

She shook her head.

"You're sure your father didn't write you?" Paul prodded—and was he *trying* to make her feel like a suspect?

She held eye contact with Paul, and repeated with emphasis, but no anger, "Yes, I'm sure. You're free to fly to Los Angeles and check my mailbox if you think it'd be a good use of federal funds."

Well, Wyatt thought, this was as good a moment as any to butt in. "I'm sorry if the question feels personal, but was there a reason for this falling-out?"

"I didn't say there was a falling-out."

"That's true," Wyatt said. "I assumed, because why else would you not talk to your family for so many years?"

Silence filled the living room. Paul twisted the pen in his palm. "Did you get along with your father? Before you moved out."

Dolores looked at the wall. Among the paintings by more famous artists hung a portrait of a man: tall, gaunt, blond hair cropped short. Late forties. Blue eyes stared out at you, true to life and glistening. Alexander Hawthorne. Wyatt would expect any man painted lifelike and framed in gold to look chilling, and yet, the artist had caught the amused slant of Alexander's mouth, the aloofness in his gaze. He had a childlike air about him, like he was impatient to get the sitting over with so he could go birdwatching or something.

"I'm sorry." Dolores turned her attention back at them. "I just don't see how that's relevant to your investigation."

"We're trying to get a full picture," Paul said.

"My father loves me, and I love my father. There was no falling-out."

"Can you tell us when you last heard from him?" Wyatt said.

"Two months ago, for my birthday."

"Was the card unusual?" Paul asked.

"No. Cream paper, cursive font. He always sends the same kind."

"Did he write anything inside?"

"Beside his signature, no."

Wyatt didn't want to make it look like he and his partner were trading silent information, but couldn't stop himself from meeting Paul's eyes.

He looked back at Dolores, half expecting her to get angry now. Instead, she said, "I'd like to see my father's office."

Before Paul could answer—*Sorry, we can't let anyone who's not investigating the case see the crime scene. Protocol, you understand*—Wyatt said, "Lead the way."

Surprise snatched the smirk off Paul's face.

In the hall, Charlotte was at the door and gave a violent start at their exit, black liquid leaping from cups on a silver tray. "Jesus, you scared me. I was just about to bring you coffee—where are you going?"

"Dad's office," Dolores answered.

Paul gave Wyatt a look that said, *For some reason.* But Wyatt knew what he was doing. You wanted someone to trust you, you started by making them feel like you trusted them.

Dolores navigated through the first floor with confidence, but paused when she reached the door of the study. Polished pinewood, tall enough that not even Paul needed to bow his head before he entered.

Nothing had changed since yesterday. The desk was overturned, feet facing the ceiling. A pungent smell of whiskey and ammonia had soaked through the carpet. Though no yellow tape barred the entry, Dolores remained at the threshold as she took in the scene. Her eyes scanned from the shelves of books to the liquor cabinet, and finally to the place where the commotion happened.

"Can I ask about the evidence?"

Paul's eyes dug into his face like lasers. Wyatt opted for vagueness. "The local police collected the evidence. We ran a double check, of course."

Dolores bent toward the ground. The fact that she managed to do this with some semblance of grace, and wearing heels, told Wyatt a lot.

"Did you find the bullet shell?"

Wyatt was too startled to answer.

Paul feigned naivete. "Sorry?"

"There's gunpowder on the carpet. Dried urine, and a lot of blood for a gunshot wound. About what you'd expect from a large caliber. Then a body was dragged out like this"—she indicated the movement with her fingers, where the fibers of the carpet had darkened under friction. "When will you get the test results back to see if the blood type matches my father's?"

Paul cleared his throat. "You've worked crime scenes before?"

"It's not exactly in my wheelhouse. I'm a forensic pathologist, but I've worked a few, yes."

"Wait." Paul's face brightened. "You're not the Dr. Diaz from that L.A. Strangler case? The one who turned the jury against that rich kid because fiber from the curtains placed him at the victim's house?"

"Carpet fiber," she corrected.

"Carpet fiber," Paul repeated. "Our forensic team uses that case to teach trainees. Brilliant."

Dolores paused. Having graduated first in his class, Wyatt could always tell when a person was both uncomfortable with praise and used to it.

"I'm glad it's of use to the FBI," she said.

Wyatt lowered his eyes, a silent apology. "If you're used to crime scenes, Miss Diaz, then you know how this looks."

"Someone died here."

Paul shrugged. "Or went to a great deal of effort to make it look like they did."

Dolores's breath hitched as his meaning hit home. "Are you trying to say my father faked his death? That's ridiculous. He would have never done a thing like that."

Paul cocked his head to the side. "Like you said, Dr. Diaz. You haven't seen him in eighteen years. People change."

She shook her head. "My father was a public figure. Becoming a senator was his dream. All he could think about was his legacy, what he'd leave of himself in the world. He would never do anything to tarnish what he's worked for his entire life."

"Not even if–" Wyatt stopped himself. There were only so many ways to say this without coming off as insensitive. "If he thought his reputation was at risk?"

This was it. He watched Dolores carefully, waiting for a reaction. Her eyes gave nothing away as she turned back to face the crime scene. "From the footprints, it looks like two people were in the room with my father. The police got that, right?"

While she had her back to them, Paul sneaked a look at Wyatt. Clearly, he was used to handling interrogations very differently. "Yes," Wyatt said. "But the evidence only tells us so much. We don't know when the prints date back to."

"The mud looks fresh."

"There's no telling who left the prints, either," Paul said. "No offense to the Little H PD, but we don't know how they handled the scene. It's possible one of their guys left them."

Wyatt repressed a groan. People like Paul were the reason FBI agents had a bad rep with local law enforcement.

"Back when I lived here," Dolores said, "lots of people came in and out of my father's office. He liked to see colleagues at home. Did you ask Charlotte if he had visitors yesterday?"

"None that she knew of."

Maybe more to annoy Wyatt than to throw off Dolores, Paul said, "Would you describe your father as a paranoid man?"

She swiveled toward them. "No, of course not."

"Why not?" Paul prodded.

"He just–he's a very down-to-earth person."

"He trusts the people he works with? The people he lives with?"

Her jaw squared. "Whatever you're trying to ask me, Agent Turner, I'd appreciate if you would just say it."

Paul held her gaze as he slid his hand into the pocket of his jacket. Wyatt should have known he couldn't resist the theatrics. He pulled out a single sheet of paper, protected by a plastic film.

"Your father wrote you a letter before he disappeared," Paul said. "At least, he started one. It looks like he was interrupted."

Dolores's hands balled into fists.

"So," Paul went on, "you see how it's strange that you say he never wrote you before."

"Can I see it?"

Paul handed the paper to Dolores.

Dolores, my angel.

I know that I have failed you as a father. There are things I've done for which I can never forgive myself—so how can I expect you to forgive me? All I can hope for is you remember me as you once did and know that everything I've done, I've done for you and for this family.

IN DAYS TO COME, YOU MAY LEARN THINGS THAT WILL CHANGE ME IN YOUR EYES FOREVER. I ASK ONLY THAT YOU HOLD ON TO THE IMAGE OF THE FATHER YOU REMEMBER. OF EVERYTHING I'VE DONE, THERE IS NO GREATER REGRET THAN WHAT

Wyatt watched her eyes run frantic over her father's final words. As she reached the last three, Dolores turned white.

At the bottom of the page, in a hand shaky with haste, Alexander Hawthorne had written:

TRUST NO ONE

Seven

TELL-TALE HEARTS

"You behaved like a jerk in there," Wyatt said as they made their way back to the Chrysler.

"Oh, did I?"

Paul tossed the car keys in the air, caught them, tossed them again. Wyatt's arm lurched forward so he could snatch the keys before Paul did. "I'll drive."

"Wow. Is this the moment when we have the conversation, set the ground rules so we don't step on each other's toes?"

Wyatt slid inside the vehicle and adjusted the distance between the driver's seat and the pedals.

"Okay." Paul sighed. "I'll start. How long have you been with the bureau?"

Wyatt started the engine. He wasn't about to let Paul interrogate him.

"Oh, a guessing game. Let's see, you're what? Thirty, thirty-one? Thirty-one. You could have been working a law enforcement job before you joined the FBI, but if I had to guess–and apparently I do–I'd say you worked a desk job. No offense. But I saw you typing your notes in the car yesterday, and that was some professional shit. You type faster than I drive. By the way, how about hitting the gas? Speed limit's not ten."

Wyatt held back so hard from pushing the accelerator, his foot started to cramp.

"So what did you do? Accounting? Informatics?"

"I don't see what that has to do with anything," Wyatt ground out.

"My point is, I've been doing this a lot longer than you. I'm not trying to sound like a jackass. Maybe there's no way *not* to sound like a jackass when I say I know what I'm doing and you don't. You ever worked kidnappings before?"

Wyatt didn't reply.

"I take it that's a no. So maybe you want to watch and learn. The bureau wouldn't have sent me if they thought you could handle this on your own."

Wyatt's knuckles turned white around the wheel. Hawthorne was his case. He'd built it from the ground up. Who would have cared about a retired senator from Wisconsin if he hadn't looked into it? Thank God he *had* worked desk jobs before, because any FBI agents expecting to chase bad guys around the clock got a wake-up call when it hit them how much paperwork came with the badge.

But Wyatt liked paperwork.

Most people joined the bureau for the TV show glam. Fraud got Wyatt into it. Fishy finances, corruption. Nothing as sexy as murder or terrorism, but that's what made him tick.

Still, when he came to his supervisor with a case so tight all it needed was gift wrap, she'd given him a skeptical look. "You want to go to Little H, and prove former Senator Hawthorne got some dubious payments to fund his campaign two decades ago?"

To Wyatt's credit, his supervisor had a way of giving a suspicious edge to every sentence. He might have been handing her a sandwich from the cafeteria, and she would have said *You bought me a tuna sandwich with pickles and mayonnaise?* in the exact same tone.

"Hawthorne served two terms at the U.S. Senate. Even now, he's active in public life. A couple months ago, he was on CNN, and when the anchor asked him about that campaign in 2003, he just looked–" Wyatt shook his head. "Jesus, I don't know. Ever read 'The Tell-Tale Heart'?"

"Did you just ask me if I read 'The Tell-Tale Heart'?"

"Hawthorne looked like the man in Poe's story. Cut to the bone, you know? Guilty. He evaded the question–"

"Are you telling me politicians evading questions is the concern of the bureau?"

"I'm telling you I got suspicious. If someone was greasing his paw, don't we want to know why, and who, and if they're still doing it? Fraud's right in my wheelhouse, and Hawthorne is one of ours. He spent most of his life right here in Wisconsin. Better search your own backyard for skeletons before you dig up anyone else's, right?"

Two days later, Wyatt was checking into a motel outside Little Horton. Twenty-four hours after that, Alexander Hawthorne vanished from the face of the earth.

On *his* watch, or so everyone would say. Wyatt's corruption case had mutated into a kidnapping, or a murder, and it had happened right under his nose.

To add insult to injury, his supervisor had called to say she was sending backup, aka Paul. With ten years of experience as a special agent, he was just the man for the job, and, she'd promised, "You'll get along."

The words rolled through Wyatt's brain as Paul lit another cigarette. He took a deep breath. They weren't five-year-olds in the sandbox, and Paul wasn't the kindergarten bully hogging all the toys. They were federal agents, and one of them had to start acting like an adult.

"You're right," Wyatt said. "I've never worked a kidnapping before." The cigarette smoke clogged his throat and he resisted the urge to cough. "But this isn't a regular kidnapping. No ransom. No call from the kidnappers."

Silence settled. After a while, Paul said, "The wife–she was eavesdropping on us earlier. Did you catch that?"

Wyatt thought of Charlotte's agitation when they ran into her in the hall. Bringing them coffee–an obvious pretext to excuse her presence outside the door.

"Yeah," Wyatt said.

"What'd you make of it?"

"She's the protective kind."

Paul chuckled. "Protective of her children, maybe. But her stepdaughter?"

"You're saying she eavesdropped because she doesn't trust us?"

"Or doesn't trust her."

Wyatt pondered this. It was clear enough the two women didn't trust each other. Clear to Wyatt, at least, for whom trust came as easy as breathing underwater. "Maybe it's not that dramatic. Her husband is missing, she's dying for information. Could be, listening outside the door was better than biting her nails."

"Yeah, well, you can't tell me she and her stepdaughter are peas in a pod. There's a story there."

"There is." Wyatt pulled his spiral notebook out of the glove box. "Hawthorne remarried soon after his first wife died. Dolores was the only child from his first marriage."

"You dug that up when you were looking into the old man's finances, did you?"

"I like to be thorough. Did you even read my report?"

"Yes," Paul answered, too quickly. "Okay, I read some of it. It's like a hundred pages long."

Wyatt decided to give him a pass. "The Hawthornes are an old family. They came into money in the 1860s."

"Dairy?"

"Railroads. Silas Hawthorne, Alexander's grandfather, sold his stocks in the 1930s. Made some investments, hit the wrong mark. The family never lost its money, but by the early 2000s, most of it had run out."

"So, they were broke?"

"No way to say how much. In this town, pride keeps a house standing even when all the bricks and mortar are gone."

"Don't think Little H is the only town that goes by that MO."

Wyatt gauged him. Paul basically had "big city'" tattooed on his forehead, but the way he'd said this gave him pause.

"Yeah," Wyatt said finally. "They were broke. Ran late on payments, took out a lot of loans. They definitely didn't have the kind of money that went into Hawthorne's campaign in 2003, when he ran for Senate."

"So what happened?"

"For a while, things looked tight. Then in a matter of weeks, the Hawthornes were swimming in cash again. Billboards of Alexander Hawthorne flooded the highways. Suddenly, he was touring, donating to charities, the whole charade. Hawthorne crushed his opponent in the race. And that was the end of their money problems."

Paul rolled his lips together. "Doesn't necessarily spell trouble."

"Except the funds didn't go through any of the proper channels. Whether he got it in cash, checks to settle his debts, or all of the above–it just flowed below the surface. All we can trace is what it bought Hawthorne. Not where he got the money from."

"So who's Mr. Benefactor?" Paul waited for a reply. "Come on, a hundred pages and you haven't covered that?"

"I've got my list of suspects. You know what really interests me?"

"I'm dying to find out."

"Hawthorne was never one to put out for lobbies. Still a Republican, don't get me wrong. Deregulation, big on firearms."

Paul snorted. "Apparently, he prefers swords."

"But he never gave corporations cause to tip their hat at him. Didn't push for pro-business legislation or cozy up to companies. Nothing that'd warrant such big donations."

"All right," Paul said. "I'll bite. What's your take, Big Guy?"

Wyatt thought of mentioning the look on Hawthorne's face during that CNN interview. His "Tell-Tale Heart" look. But Paul would laugh him off. Gut feelings didn't hold much sway among FBI agents.

"The way I see it, Hawthorne must have known something. Something big enough that it could ruin very powerful people–people who must have bought his silence, all those years ago."

Paul picked up the thread exactly where Wyatt wanted him to. "The man's over eighty now. And from what he wrote his daughter, he's full of remorse." He tossed his cigarette butt out the window. "You think he disappeared because he decided it was time to talk?"

Eight

TREASURE HUNTS

Dolores trudged to her bedroom like she was passing through a wall of molten wax.

Trust no one. The blood. The marks on the carpet. Her thoughts spun from one to the other, until one landed, irrefutable.

My father is dead.

She felt the pain, an arrow stabbing below her breastbone, but it would not break through.

She refused to believe it. Maybe someone had died in that room, but it could not have been him.

The Hawthorne house without her father would be like a body without a soul. If he had died, the house would crumble in on itself, the bricks would bleed with his murder. Yet the cherrywood walls, the antiques with their museum smell, all whispered to Dolores that her father was just around the corner, that she could meet him any second going up the stairs.

She opened the door of her bedroom, bathed in powdery sunlight.

How strange, after so many years trying not to think of the past, to have it within her grasp. A whiff of her childhood came back to her–of grandiose birthday celebrations. Her father was never content to hand her a gift and cut her a slice of cake. "I'm the grand-gesturing kind," he used to say.

Instead of birthday parties, he would organize treasure hunts, which were as exciting as the gifts themselves. When the FBI asked her about the letters earlier, all she could think about were the handwritten clues her father would sprinkle throughout the house.

His last gift to her had been the opportunity to witness an open-heart surgery. Dolores had stared from the observation room, transfixed for the whole four hours.

The cluster of scrubs around the operating table had made her think of insects scrounging for the flesh of an overripe fruit. When their fingers began to work faster, the monitor beeping to indicate a plummeting heart rate, Dolores had felt so removed from the scene, it was a moment before she realized the patient was dead.

I can take this, she told herself. But she cried for half an hour in the bathroom before she called her father and asked him to pick her up.

"I'm so sorry it happened that way," he said as he drove her home. "Was it thoughtless of me to take you?"

"No."

"If you go to med school, you'll see a lot of people die."

"I know. I wasn't afraid."

She sensed from the way his eyes held hers in the rearview mirror that there was no use in lying. He knew her inside and out. Still he said, "Of course you weren't, my angel."

Dolores closed her eyes.

She needed to face reality. Every trace of evidence hinted that her father had been killed. Yet in her gut, in her bones—she knew this couldn't be true.

If he were dead, I would feel it. The way twins did when their sibling died, or partners who had lived together for decades.

Her mind kept going back to the letter.

Trust no one.

Why did she feel like he had catapulted her back to the old days of the treasure hunts—like this was the beginning of some new game?

Three knocks rapped on the door before it flew open.

Dolores sat up. She'd forgotten how, in this house, privacy was almost an abstract concept.

Charlotte entered, holding a steaming mug. "I thought you could use coffee."

"Thanks," Dolores managed.

Charlotte put a coaster on the bedside table, then set down the mug.

Spikes of discomfort shot at Dolores's legs, but she pretended Charlotte's intrusion didn't bother her.

"So," Charlotte said. "Did the FBI want to show you something in the office?"

Dolores twirled the spoon inside the coffee mug. Grains of sugar stirred at the bottom. "They only did it to humor me. I've seen a handful of crime scenes before–I wanted to know if I could make something out of it."

"And did you?"

Dolores was never a good liar. "Nothing the FBI doesn't already know."

She expected Charlotte to dig her nails into that, but instead, she drew closer to the bed. Dolores stiffened. The urge to get up tugged at her so bad she had to grip the sheets.

Before Dolores could think to protest, Charlotte's fingers sliced the air between them and closed around a strand of her hair.

"You've gotten so beautiful. You've always been beautiful," she amended. "You know, when I married your father, I had this idea our life together would be a fairy tale. Age doesn't matter when you're twenty, does it?" She chuckled, as if to mock her own childishness. "I was Cinderella, swept off my feet by this fascinating older man–granted, too old to be a prince." Her lips pinched tight together. "But he treated me like a queen."

Dolores tried not to flinch when Charlotte made eye contact.

"Then I met you, and you were so desperate for me to be the evil stepmother."

Dolores swallowed back the apology on her tongue. *It makes you look weak,* Charlotte used to say.

"I always hated these stories–stupid rivals' tales. We should teach girls to be allies, shouldn't we?" She sighed. "I know you don't like me, Dolores."

That glossed over the fact that Charlotte had never liked her, either.

"I know we've had our issues. But I'll tell you what–I don't have the energy for enemies right now. So maybe we can set aside our differences until your father comes back. Be allies?"

Dolores nodded. All that mattered was for Charlotte to stop touching her, prickling every nerve in her body to life.

It wasn't fair to Charlotte, but "fair" had nothing to do with it. Her stepmother was woven into her darkest memories, a golden twine braided with spider legs. Already, the foundations of Dolores's life in Los Angeles were turning into sheets of glass. It shouldn't unhinge her like that. Charlotte touching her hair.

It shouldn't feel like a ghost knocking at the door . . . knocking a very faint bell.

Yet she worried that if Charlotte did not take her hand off in the next few seconds, she'd slap it away.

"Yeah," Dolores forced out a reply. "I think that's a good idea."

Charlotte smiled. A close-lipped smile, because a tooth on her lower jaw looked just a tiny bit crooked. "Well, you're welcome to stay here as long as you want. You've been a stranger too long. When will your husband join you?"

"He–" Dolores stammered. "There's no need for Max to come. I'll fly home tomorrow."

"All right."

Finally, Charlotte got up, and Dolores compressed a sigh of relief.

"Let me know if you need anything. I'll be downstairs."

"Wait."

Charlotte swiveled back toward her.

"Lately, was Dad acting . . . unusual?"

"Well, your father is an eccentric man. He's always unusual."

Dolores thought of the letter again. *There are things I've done for which I can never forgive myself.* What could he have been talking about? In her relationship with her father, there was nothing to regret.

Nothing–

She faltered. Nothing he could have known about.

"I mean, do you know if he was talking to anyone unusual?"

"Talking," Charlotte repeated. It was crystal clear she didn't like where this was going. "About what?"

Dolores wanted to say it. *About me.* But her cheek still burned where Charlotte had touched her. She wasn't sure she could take what lurked behind the surface of pretense.

If her father had found out the truth about what happened in her senior year of high school, Charlotte couldn't have been the one to tell him. It was Charlotte who had insisted on keeping it a secret.

"The Winslows are powerful people, Dolores," she had said, as she drove Dolores back from one of her checkup exams, after the surgery. *The surgery.* That was how Charlotte referred to it. Never, *the pregnancy.*

Dolores had hated every appointment, every time the doctor's hands had touched her. "This isn't a good time for your father to make enemies. That old snake, Gregory, will keep his son away from you, as long as we stay discreet on our end."

Charlotte's hand had shot away from the wheel to squeeze Dolores's wrist. She remembered how forced it felt. How much it cost Charlotte to touch her, how much it cost her to let herself be touched. "Of course, you don't want your father to find out. It would break his heart, you see that, right? I told him you had appendicitis. That you and Jacob broke up, and you didn't want to see the Winslows ever again." Charlotte smiled. "What your father doesn't know won't hurt him."

Dolores had nodded. What else was she supposed to do? Her relationship with Charlotte was no bed of roses—more of a bed of thorns, really. But she had been the grown-up, her only ally in all of this.

There was only one other source the truth could have come from, unlikely though it was.

"Did he talk to the Winslows?" Dolores asked.

The triangle of Charlotte's jaw flattened. The air between them grew thick, until Dolores felt she was breathing steam instead of oxygen. "Why would he do that?"

"I just thought—"

She stopped. What *was* she thinking?

Her father might not have known about what Jacob Winslow had done to her, but he knew that Dolores did not want anything to do with them. That had been enough for him.

What Jacob had done.

Dolores cursed the turn of phrase.

She blamed Charlotte for it. Charlotte, who only ever talked about the assault in euphemisms—and then, only when talking about it was strictly necessary.

It was always, What That Boy Did.

Like the specific word starting in R did not exist in Charlotte's dictionary.

Maybe it's for the best.

Better to have vague turns of phrases to match the blanks in her memory–Dolores did not remember the assault, or even waking up in a drugged state. She barely remembered anything that happened that year. The doctor's appointments rolled in a mist of dread. Avoiding conversation, burning off all the corridors in her mind that led to the Night She Didn't Remember. To Jacob Winslow.

The memory of her own body at seventeen faded somewhere below consciousness.

Sometimes, Dolores doubted she had ever been a teenage girl at all, a girl who had not been raped, whose stomach showed immaculate skin instead of a scar like a Halloween smile, crooked and red.

"Dolores," Charlotte cut in. "Now isn't the time to chase ghosts. We've got enough to worry about. I don't want you going anywhere near the Winslows while you're in town."

It took Dolores a second to register it was an order. She stared at her stepmother. "Trust me," she said, honestly, "they're the last people I want to see."

Charlotte's shoulders relaxed. "All right. You should rest now. You've had a long night."

The door clicked shut behind her and Dolores sat still, her heart rate refusing to relax. Replaying the conversation in her mind, she couldn't shake the thought Charlotte had been deflecting, when she asked about Alexander's recent behavior. Of course he was eccentric. But that was a bullshit answer, and Charlotte knew it. If he hadn't been acting strange, why would he have written to her about his regrets, after eighteen years of sending empty cards on her birthdays? What could have been the trigger?

In the days that follow you may learn things that will change me in your eyes forever.

"What are you up to, Dad?" she whispered. She could picture the slant of his smile when she turned the house upside down, scrounging for clues.

If Charlotte wouldn't talk to her, she'd have to look for answers elsewhere. And she had a good idea where to begin.

Dolores checked the time on her phone. Half past eight. She could make it in time if she hurried.

Nine

BETTER THAN WAFFLES

Kate Butcher figured that moving in with your partner was like throwing your relationship under a microscope. Everything about the other person just got *bigger*.

For instance, it never hit Kate before just how often Leo volunteered to do things for her. "Let me get that for you." "Do you need help looking for your keys?" "I'm going to the kitchen, you want something to drink?"

She didn't hate that about him. She just noticed it. Granted, when she thought about most guys she'd dated, who would slam a door in her face instead of holding it—maybe she should count her blessings.

But it did nothing to stop the shiver of annoyance that crawled down her spine when they walked to her car, and he stopped her hand on its way to the knob. "I'll drive."

Leo took speed bumps at six miles an hour, and actually moved his foot off the gas at a green light, just in case it was about to turn yellow. "I'd rather drive safe with a cop in the car," he winked.

To calm down, as the pumpkin-clad streets flashed them by, Kate made a mental list of everything she liked about Leo. *Freakishly handsome. Knows how to listen. Loves oral sex.*

His eyes darted from the road. "You okay?"

"Yep."

Kate tried to blunt the edge in her voice.

If you didn't make yourself so difficult to like, her mother said, *you'd find life a hell of a lot easier.*

But Kate preferred to look at it from the other end. If her life were a hell of a lot easier, then she wouldn't be so difficult to like.

"Just this damned case," she told him.

"Cripes, I hope the old bugger is all right."

Kate sighed. She'd been patrolling the area last night when the call came in from Charlotte Hawthorne, so she was the first person to discover *the crime scene.*

Most days, Kate's job boiled down to chasing street cats, doling out parking tickets, and the occasional sweating through presentations about drunk driving at Horton High.

When it came to thrill, Little Horton was a kiddie pool.

Well. Except on Halloween.

But then their one celebrity went missing, and by sheer luck, Kate was the officer on call.

At least, until the FBI barged in, and Chief Franklin pushed her off the case to give it to his drinking buddies.

Kate forced her attention back onto Leo. His perennial tan still took her by surprise. With his blond hair and chiseled body, he belonged on a surfboard in some paradise beach. His family lived in Australia until he was ten–not that Kate could contemplate meeting them without breathing into a paper bag. Leo had been around the States–New York, Chicago–before settling in Little Horton a year ago.

You would think he would hate it here. Kate hated it, and she had nothing to compare it to. But Leo sweated optimism.

Some people tended to see the glass half full. Leo saw it filled to the brim.

Why he'd taken an interest in Kate when he moved in was a conundrum she would have loved to submit to Nobel Prize laureates.

"I wouldn't worry too much," she said. "Something like this happens, it's gotta be about money. His kidnappers have a gazillion reasons to keep Hawthorne alive."

Kate gazed out the car window, not paying attention to the streets until a woman came into view–Leo's driving gave her ample time to recognize her. "Holy shit."

"What?" Leo said.

"That's Dolores Hawthorne."

"The senator's daughter?"

Kate cursed the fact that even a newcomer like Leo knew Dolores by name.

"Are you sure?"

Kate wished she wasn't. But there was no mistaking that statuesque pose, raven hair, and legs for days.

"Well, do you wanna go say hi?"

Kate shot him a look, like he had beans for brains.

"No," she said, tearing the word into two syllables.

Leo parallel-parked across from the diner. Everything about Ruby's screamed "1980s," from the bubble-gum vinyl seats to the Madonna posters. The smell of fried eggs and fried mushrooms hit them as they squeezed through the customers.

They shouted their orders over the music and the braying four-year-old in the next booth who had dropped his chocolate ice cream. Kate massaged her skull with her fingers. A plate brimming with waffles slammed onto the table.

"There you go, babe," Ruby said–the Ruby from Ruby's. Stout as a rugby player, in the neighborhood of sixty, with hair dyed a much prettier red than Kate's, she called everybody "babe," and the look on her face dared you to take her up on it.

"Cheers, Ruby," Leo smiled, taking care of niceties. Before breakfast, Kate was as feral as the cats crawling the streets.

"I take it you heard?" Ruby said. "About Senator Hawthorne." A lot of people still called Alexander that, although his term had ended years ago.

"Yeah." Leo winced. "We were just talking about it."

"And his oldest is back in town."

"Dolores." He nodded. "We bumped into her on our way here."

Ruby's eyes gleamed. "So it's true."

"Well–"

Kate elbowed Leo under the table.

"By God, if I ever ran into a sweeter child than Dolores Hawthorne. D'you know her mommy used to come here with her? Every Sunday. A nice woman, Celia was. You gotta love Charlotte, of course."

"You gotta," Leo said, to be polite.

"But I just felt bad for that little girl, with her daddy remarrying so fast. Hear she's grown into a splendid young woman."

"I wouldn't call her young." Kate clenched her fist around her fork, to send a message.

Ruby pushed out a smile, and finally popped back into the kitchen area. Leo was mercifully silent as Kate speared her fork through a piece of waffle. It glistened with syrup and melted into her mouth. *Heaven.*

She looked back at Leo. "Thanks for not talking to me until I had my first bite."

"I know better than to stand between a junkie and her high."

Leo sipped his coffee while she ate. It had done little good to get rid of Ruby. From nearby booths, chatter bubbled with Dolores this, Senator Hawthorne that.

Kate groaned. "What is this, the Second Coming?"

She was about to shovel another forkful into her mouth when her police radio came to life.

"Butcher, you there?"

Kate pressed the button, hoping Nathan could hear her over the mush of music and chatter. "What is it?"

"I know it's your day off, but the chief wants you over at the station."

Kate's eyes darted toward her plate of waffles. "Like, in half an hour?"

"Like, now."

"Son of a bitch," Kate dropped the radio into her purse. "I need the car," she told Leo.

"Sure. I'll walk. I can use the exercise."

Kate tried to smile.

How was it that when they'd started dating, she had marveled at how Leo was such a nice guy, and now the exact same thing made her want to run for her life?

Nathan walked out of the station to meet Kate as she slid from the car. Roughly the size of a young grizzly bear, Nathan was difficult to miss, even if he hadn't been the only cop in the parking lot. Some people can't help drawing attention. Kate could do little to avoid it aside from shaving off her carroty hair. But Nathan *worked* for it. If he earned a dollar for every push-up he did in a day, he could take retirement within a month. Add in a large auburn beard, and you got Nathan Gunn: virile American, or oversized leprechaun.

"Hey," he said, heading for the police car beside Kate's Honda. "Hop in, Butcher. I'll brief you on the way."

"What, I can't take a second to hit the lockers?"

Jeans and a hoodie had seemed fine for breakfast at Ruby's, but for work? Kate still struggled for some of her colleagues to call her "Officer" and not "sweet pea."

"Nah, you're fine. You got your badge, right?"

"Right, but–"

"Then let's go."

Kate got in and slammed the car door. "Let's get one thing clear, Gunn. You don't snatch me away from breakfast, then drive me around without explaining what's going on."

He chuckled. "Bottom line, Muller's on his bathroom floor puking his guts out."

"Shit."

"That's exactly how he described it. Obviously, he can't work the Hawthorne case. Not today, maybe not tomorrow, and it's not like we can put a pin on a kidnapping. So you're with me."

A flutter spread through Kate's chest. "I'm with you."

"Yeah. The chief thought it made sense, since you were at the scene yesterday."

Kate stared out the windshield. To think she got up expecting to spend the week chasing street cats. A kidnapping case. Possibly a murder. There weren't enough waffles in the world to compete with this.

THEIR FIRST STOP WAS Michael Burke's private practice. In his seventies, Burke was the town's only doctor and medical examiner, so all the evidence they'd collected at the crime scene yesterday had gone to his lab before the feds could claim it.

"I hope he's working his ass off," Kate said. "If he dawdles, it's gonna look bad for all of us."

Nathan's hands tensed around the wheel. In their dislike for the FBI agents who'd barged into town, they had landed on their first common ground ever.

"Can't we just ring him up?" she asked.

"You know Burke's not a phone person."

Kate pressed her palms against her thighs to stop them from fidgeting. She didn't like Dr. Burke. He used to be her pediatrician at the Cauldron County Clinic, before he got his private practice in Little Horton. It wasn't that he was a *bad* doctor, per se. But when he stuck a needle in her arm to give her a vaccine, he always left a bruise. Never warned about the sting before he poured peroxide onto a wound.

Some patients had got it a lot worse. Horror stories, botched sutures that left scars twice as large as they should have been–they still stiffened when they passed him in the streets. "The Ripper," they called him.

Kate could only cross her fingers that he was better with evidence than he was with kids.

Nathan parked beside Burke's BMW, so shiny that Kate's fingers twitched to drag her keys down its flank.

"Damn," Nathan whistled as they got out. "Shoulda become a doctor instead of a cop."

A cold wind snuck through the collar of her hoodie. Kate thumped on the door.

"Come on," Nathan said. "Maybe he's with a patient."

She looked at the near-empty parking lot.

Nathan shrugged. "They could have walked."

Kate turned back and tried the knob. The door was unlocked. "Dr. Burke?" she called.

The moment she entered the building, her brain went numb and every hair on her body hardened. The smell of fear, adrenaline, and human waste hit her like a rolling train.

"God," Nathan said, knuckles pressed to his mouth.

Before she could think, Kate had drawn her gun.

The entryway stretched into a corridor, fitted out as a waiting room. Magazines were piled upon a plastic table. The door of Dr. Burke's office was ajar.

Kate made herself take one step after another, hands moist around her Glock. She pressed the muzzle against the door.

It slid open and a boulder dropped down her stomach.

Dr. Burke lay facing the ceiling, his skin a grayish yellow, tongue lolling out of his mouth. Ragged shapes like jelly beans lay scattered on the ground where his brains had been blown out.

Ten

THE GHOST OF LEMON PIES

One of the things her mother taught Dolores before she died was that to pick up on the latest gossip in town, you shouldn't go to a café or a bar. What you wanted were the school gates: before the mothers picked up their kids, or right after they dropped them off.

Dolores could have walked the distance to the primary school instead of driving. As the saying went, if the place was in Little Horton, and you were in Little Horton, you could walk it. But she wanted discretion, declined driving Charlotte's very identifiable red Volvo and opted for her father's car.

"It's downtown," Charlotte said.

"What is Dad's car doing downtown?"

"You know your father, Dolores. He starts driving somewhere, then gets taken by the urge to stretch his legs."

On the way to her father's car, Dolores could not stop herself from taking in the familiar streets. The town was dressed for Halloween. In that respect, at least, Little Horton was the prettiest girl at the ball. Hating Halloween in L.A. was one thing, but here? The town mocked you with its barrels of apples, its carved pumpkins that sat at the foot of every house, every store. Garlands hugged bars and restaurants, trees dangled with string lights, plastic spiders, and cardboard witches riding broomsticks.

Dolores could almost taste her childhood in their plastic gleam, the many hours spent carrying buckets of corn syrup so Charlotte could write messages on the mirrors, decorating the house for the fabulous Hawthorne Halloween party.

Conversations braked to a halt at her approach. Probably, she would not have drawn more attention if she had strolled the streets naked.

"Is that Dolores Hawthorne?"

"Got to be, looks just like her."

"Little Horton's runaway child returns."

"Did you hear her father–"

"Horrible, just horrible."

She released a sigh when she spotted her father's car and slipped inside, locking herself in a bubble of silence. Her throat jammed at the thought that her father had been in this car the day before. Undertones of peppermint aftershave teased her nostrils. Eighteen years since she had last breathed it in.

Dolores started the car. If she didn't keep moving, she'd break down– and what use would that be to anyone?

The primary school in Little Horton was tucked at the end of a steep, narrow road. Dolores's palms moistened against the wheel as she squeezed through.

She parked by the garish-green gates, from which there rose shrill children's laughter, cracked open the window, and checked her phone. Nine o'clock. She was just in time to hear the bell.

Flocked at the gates was the usual cluster of women. Dolores kept her head down, phone pressed against her right cheek for cover. She didn't need to wait long before the Hawthorne name came up.

"Gosh, I *cannot* believe this is happening. Senator Hawthorne, of all people! Who'd want to harm the man?"

"I don't buy into the whole kidnapping thing. I mean–when you hear of someone being taken, it's always a young woman, isn't it?"

"Could be a ransom thing."

"If it *were* ransom, why not take Josie and blackmail Alexander? It's so *weird* to do it the other way around–to leave the women to deal with the crisis, and take the seasoned politician as a hostage."

A beat of silence. "I mean," a woman said. "There's another explanation. Some are saying–you know. That Hawthorne made himself disappear."

A chorus of outraged gasps greeted the theory. "That's absurd."

"Like Hawthorne is just another white-collar crook! He did more for this town in fourteen years at City Hall than anyone else did in a hundred."

"Well, you gotta admit the old man was acting up lately."

Dolores's pulse quickened.

"He was! You know what I heard from the baker last week? That every day, Hawthorne orders himself two slices of lemon pie."

"So?"

Dolores's stomach turned, as if she'd swallowed a handful of glass.

"So, the old man hates lemon. It's what he used to order for *her*. On her birthdays."

The women fell silent. Beyond the gates, the children had cleared the schoolyard, and for a moment Dolores could hear nothing but her own heartbeat. She could see herself, sitting across from her father in the kitchen, flushed from her treasure hunt, digging into a mountain of lemon curd as Alexander shook his head. "How can you stand this, Dolores? It tastes like dish soap."

She closed her eyes, focused on the bones of her head. A dam against the tide of memories. But she was in free fall, floating outside her body as the past grew hands and drew her into its depths.

For eighteen years, her father's absence had left a gaping wound inside her, which only time had managed to sew back shut. Now, the stitches were starting to pop, one after the other.

If I let it out, where will I stop?

Love was not the only thing bleeding out of that wound.

Spiders waited their turn to crawl through the cracks, for their venom to spread from her buried traumas to her entire organism.

"Well," a woman offered, "so what? We all know he worshipped Dolores."

"For all these years, he couldn't stand to hear the sound of her name."

"We all grow nostalgic with age."

"You know what I heard? That the feds have been in town for weeks, looking into Hawthorne's finances."

"Ridiculous! You couldn't corrupt Alexander Hawthorne if you were Mephistopheles. If you think he staged this to cover up some dirty secrets, you're out of your mind."

A hum of agreement passed among the women. "No, no. It's got to be nostalgia. Apparently, Dolores isn't the only person from his past he was thinking about. I got it from Lou Laurie last week that Hawthorne was at the Winslow house."

Dolores froze. She willed herself to take one breath after another, but the air bounced back against the walls of her mouth.

The thought of her father in the same room as Jacob sent scorpions down her throat.

Charlotte could ignore it all—smile politely and make small talk when she ran into Jacob or Mr. Winslow.

But it was wrong to imagine Alexander, cheated into casual interactions. Maybe because if he had known What Jacob Had Done—

Let's call a spade a spade, Dolores.

If he had known about the assault, he would have chased the Winslows from town, like Brutus did with those old Roman tyrants.

Laughter among the mothers. "I'd sooner believe the president was shaking hands with Russia. We all remember the Feud."

She said it as if referring to a well-known historical battle.

"Lou Laurie must have got it wrong. The Winslows and the Hawthornes haven't spoken since—"

Dolores startled as her phone rang against her cheek. "Single Ladies" filled the car. She had changed the ringtone after she left Max—with ten ounces of tequila in her, it had seemed more clever than it was.

The mothers all turned around. Dolores dropped the phone on the passenger seat, hurried to put the car into motion. But by the time she maneuvered the vehicle out of the tiny slot, she could feel the women's stares dripping like honey.

Great. Now everyone would be talking about what a sneaky little eavesdropper Dolores Hawthorne had grown into. She parked the first chance she got, and grabbed her cell to check the ID. Her thoughts funneled toward the worst. There'd be a voicemail from Agent Holt. *We found your father—I mean, his body.* Or Charlotte, in a cold distant tone, telling her not to panic but that she'd received something in the mail. An ear, a toe, a finger?

A sigh blew out of her as she read the screen. One missed call. Amy.

She pressed call, and a minute later, her friend's chirpy voice boomed, "Hey! Is this a bad time?"

"A bad time for you to call me, or as a philosophical outlook on my life?"

"You know you use humor as a defense mechanism, right?" Amy sighed. "Tell me. Or I can drop by, if you like."

Dolores winced. "That's going to be a tad difficult, seeing as I'm in Wisconsin."

A beat of silence. "You're *what*?"

"I–it's hard to explain. I'm having a family emergency."

"Okay. Okay," Amy repeated, in a fake calmness that cried out how uncalm she felt. "You wanna explain?

"I don't know where to start."

"I'll give it a shot. You're having a family emergency. How about starting with 'Holy shit, you have a family?' No offense. But you never talk about them–I just assumed your parents had died or something."

Dolores sighed. She'd told herself she wasn't being cruel, never mentioning her family to anyone in L.A. Just–careful. Like they were antique pieces of furniture she'd take out of the basement when she had found *just the right spot.*

Then she never had.

What about now? Asher's burning hatred. Josie's tiny frame against her. Was she really going to sit here and deny their existence?

"I have a half brother and a half sister," she blurted.

"What?" A rustle as Amy settled into her couch. "Are you serious? How come you never mentioned them?"

"I never–I'd never even met Josie before this morning. Asher was just a little boy when I left. We don't talk. We *haven't* talked since I moved to Los Angeles."

"How do you not see your family for that long? Are they awful?"

Dolores tried to think of her last year in Little Horton. The way the ground opened up beneath her, every time Charlotte walked into a room. In the streets, the eyes that lingered. The rumors spread by Jacob's father. *The girl's a slut. Just like her mother.*

"It's just so fogged up."

"Fucked up how?"

"No, I mean, a literal fog. My whole childhood–" She shook her head.

"I've spent the past eighteen years trying to forget it. I left Wisconsin in a bad place. Then life got crazy with work and Max and I couldn't sit down for a minute and think about my siblings, or my father. It's as if, as long as I didn't think about them, they were–safe."

"And if you didn't talk to them, you didn't have to rip the scab off that old wound, is that it?"

Dolores fought the urge to cover her stomach with one hand.

The words Amy used–"scab" . . . "wound." Ridiculous. Dolores cut open bodies routinely, and it didn't make the vertical scar on her abdomen ignite.

Max had mentioned it the first time they slept together. He traced his fingers along the scar, from the hem of her pubic bone to her navel. "Kind of a big scar to have your appendix taken out."

She'd fought the urge to wriggle away. "It was an open appendectomy."

"A what now?"

"It leaves a bigger scar."

The pain had lasted for years, after the surgery–much longer than biology could explain. But it had been over a decade since she'd felt it so vividly.

Appendicitis, she thought. *And you manage to keep a straight face when you call Max a lying bastard?*

"Dolls," Amy said, "are you okay?"

"I'm sorry. I must sound crazy."

"When are you coming home? Please say tonight. I'll come get you at the airport and we'll watch a whole season of *Desperate Housewives.*"

Dolores grabbed her forehead with her palm. That sounded nice. She'd kill for a hug right now, for Amy's sun-bleached hair to tickle her face.

What in the devil's name was she still doing here? What good did it do anyone to have her in Little Horton? She could go back to L.A. and her father would still be missing; her family would still hate her. Maybe she had better leave now, before the chasm that had opened up inside her had time to widen.

Her phone vibrated as a second call came through.

"I have to go, Amy."

"What is it?"

The air in her mouth turned sour as expired cream. Wyatt Holt's number lit up her screen.

Eleven

WOLVES

Some people turned dead still with anger, but Paul was obviously the jittery kind. When they tried the M.E.'s number and no one picked up, the muscles in his jaw twitched.

"We'll call again," Wyatt said.

Paul allowed the phone to ring once, twice, then shot to his feet. "Why don't we pay the good doctor a visit."

Wyatt didn't protest. He was learning that most of the time, it was less energy-consuming to let Paul have his way.

As they got in the car, Wyatt said, "You're in a hurry."

"Well, there's a theory I'd like to play out. Better to rule it out from the get-go."

Wyatt refused to bite. Paul should volunteer his theories, not tease them. This wasn't a salesman's pitch. Paul would give in first, anyway. There was clearly a limit to how long the agent could stand not hearing himself talk.

Paul's eyes darted toward Wyatt as he drove. "Before we're neck-deep into this case, wouldn't you like to make sure there's an actual life at stake, and that the old man isn't playing us for fools?"

"You mean–did Hawthorne hear I was poking around his financial records, and take to the hills?"

Paul shrugged. "If he did, I bet the evidence will show it."

Wyatt considered this. "Depends on whether the man knew what he was doing. There wasn't a lot of blood. He could have used his own, without disabling himself."

"I'll buy that." Paul tilted his head. "But the urine? A man as proud as Hawthorne, peeing on the floor of his own office?"

"How'd you know he's proud?"

"He's a politician."

The Chrysler rolled through the streets of Little Horton, squelching through soggy leaves.

"If he staged the whole thing," Paul said, "he didn't do it alone."

"Charlotte?"

"Charlotte. She would have pushed for that little detail. The urine, I mean. Hell, I can picture her collecting samples of her kids' pee to make sure they're not on drugs."

Of course Paul would be the speculating type.

"Come on," he prodded. "That letter Hawthorne left Dolores? It's so—theatrical."

Wyatt made a fist, and watched the knuckles roll as he rubbed his fingers together. "The letter's the one thing bothering me, actually. Say he did stage his death. Make himself disappear. Why write his daughter, when he knows it's going to draw her into this?"

Paul thought for a second. "Because he wants her here. Wants to make sure she's got a front-row seat for whatever he's got planned?"

Wyatt fought a shiver. "Maybe," he said.

Paul glided the car into the parking lot of Burke's private practice, but they were not the first to arrive. Cruisers shimmered in the mangled rays of sunbeams coming in through the clouds.

Paul said, "They gotta be kidding."

"Stay cool."

Paul slammed his door so hard birds broke away from the trees paving the street.

"Wait!" Wyatt said. "If we barge in here and go alpha wolves on them, we'll lose them for good. We *can't* afford to lose local police, Paul. They'll make our job impossible."

"Aren't they doing that already? You think they're all in there having coffee, maybe, and it has nothing to do with the case? Goddamn it. A man's life is on the line, and they don't have better things to do than nurse their egos?"

Wyatt refrained from sharing his observation that Paul looked like he knew a thing or two about ego himself. "We stay calm. Show them we aren't the enemy. Trust's a two-way street."

Paul opened the door.

Cops everywhere: in the waiting room, inside the office. Wyatt scanned for faces and landed on the officer who'd been first on the Hawthorne crime scene. Her bushy red hair made her hard to miss. Next to her stood a man, the lower half of his face hidden under a reddish beard. He'd look very convincing on a Viking helmet or advertising Guinness.

"Officer Butcher," Wyatt said. "Please, would you mind filling us in?"

Air hissed through her teeth. "Dr. Burke is dead."

Wyatt opened his mouth, and closed it.

Paul was silent for five full seconds. "And you were going to tell us when?"

Though Officer Butcher had to crane her neck to meet Paul's eyes, she didn't cower. "We got this under control. Didn't think to call you."

"Didn't 'think' to call us?"

"That's what I said."

Wyatt pondered how to ease the situation without physically getting between the two. "When was the last time you had a murder in town?" he asked.

Viking answered first: "A long time." His badge read "Nathan Gunn."

"Seventy-plus years," Kate cut in. "In 1950 a guy called Jeremy Krone took a shotgun to a party downtown and fired at the crowd."

"Something like that must leave a scar on the community," Wyatt said.

Kate shrugged. "I don't know about scars. It made it into one of the Halloween songs."

"People don't kill each other here," Nathan said. "They just leave. Some kids split when they blow their eighteen candles, don't look back."

Kate looked at her partner. Wyatt wondered if they had the same kid in mind.

"But the ones who stay don't lose their shit like that," Nathan said. "This is an outsider. It's got to be an outsider."

Wyatt sucked at the inner flesh of his bottom lip. Hawthorne had disappeared less than twenty-four hours ago. Now, the town's doctor was found dead in his practice. You didn't need Quantico training to connect the dots.

"An outsider," Paul said. "Right. Just driving by, decided to knock on a couple doors at random." He didn't give the officers time to reply before he waved his chin at the office. "I want your people out. Now."

Nathan chuckled. "Excuse me?"

"I said get your team *out*. This is the second crime scene you're compromising."

Kate clenched her jaw. "We're law enforcement agents. Just like you."

"And what do you enforce on a daily basis?" Paul said. "Make sure people aren't giving blow jobs while driving?"

"Look," Wyatt interjected, "we all have the same goal here. We don't want to tell you how to do your job—we just want to help."

Kate snorted. Wyatt couldn't blame her. "Help" was something you could wave off politely. It didn't come with federal badges.

"If I understand right," Wyatt said, "your medical examiner is dead. Who else can you rely on to do crime scenes? Autopsies?"

Kate went on glaring at Paul a while before she answered. "Melissa Dylan assisted Burke on autopsies, I think. She just started out as a mortician."

"Graduated how long ago?"

"Last July."

Paul laughed. "Terrific."

Wyatt rubbed his fingers together, resisting the urge to grip the bridge of his nose. They could call someone from Milwaukee, but that would be tantamount to insulting the local PD, not to mention that it'd take hours. Despite the odds pointing to the contrary, the case might still be a kidnapping, and kidnappings didn't sit too well with waiting.

Paul grabbed Wyatt's arm.

His back muscles stiffened like puppet strings. Every instinct told Wyatt to push Paul off him, punch him, whatever it took. He dragged in a breath, forced his body to realize his partner wasn't about to attack him.

You hear all the time that people get used to violence, Wyatt thought. Yet no one talks about the fact that your body never reacclimatizes to the absence of violence.

Paul grinned, like the idea of the century had just occurred to him. "Let's use the daughter."

"Sorry?"

"Dolores Diaz. She's worked crime scenes before. She said so."

Wyatt shook his head to make sure he was getting this straight. "You wouldn't have let her near the crime scene this morning, and now you want to involve her in the investigation? It's against protocol."

Paul leaned into Wyatt, his breath tickling his ear. "What do you prefer? The first rube these guys are gonna pin us with? Or a hotshot L.A. doctor with a list of certifications as long as my dick?"

From the fact that Kate and Nathan looked merely annoyed, Wyatt assumed they hadn't caught that.

Paul looked back at the officers. "We'll go with the daughter," he said.

And was he trying to show he was the boss of them, or the boss of him?

Twelve

THE RIPPER OF LITTLE HORTON

Dolores promised the FBI to get there as soon as possible, hung up, and started the car. It was a while before the news sank in.

Dr. Burke, dead. Her old pediatrician. As he was known to some–

A shudder broke at the tip of her spine.

The Ripper of Little Horton.

Flashes of his rotund face came back to her. Pig cheeks, swollen and sleek. Eyes that smiled wetly, the way you imagined a toad would. The jar of red lollipops that twinkled on his desk.

She tried to focus on the road. The streets she had roamed, holding Asher's hand. The familiar haunts where she'd gone with friends. With Jacob.

Her hands clenched around the wheel.

The thought that he could spring up anywhere at any time–

God, what had her father been doing at the Winslow house?

Dolores bit her tongue. Maybe there was some irony to the fact. If there was a list of people in Little Horton she had hoped never to see again in her life, Dr. Burke would have been close to the top. Right below Jacob Winslow and his father.

Having gone to med school, understanding the intricacies of the surgery Burke had performed on her, might have softened her to the man a little.

Yet it hadn't.

She hated him absurdly. Childishly.

For putting his hands on her, if only as a medical expert, at the moments when she least wanted to be touched. For the sight of his gloved fingers, his ogre smiles, his stale breath. For the scar forever twisted into her flesh.

It took Dolores ten minutes to get to the practice. The parking lot was packed with cruisers. Officers clustered around the entrance, near the two FBI agents. Paul Turner spotted her first. "Dr. Diaz. I'm glad you could make it."

Paul's face was all smiles, but Dolores could read a room as well as anyone. The FBI asked her to come for lack of a better option—meaning, no one from the local PD would do. She doubted they would make it easy for the FBI to get a spit-free sandwich anywhere after this.

Wyatt gave her a nod of acknowledgment. "Miss Diaz. Thank you for coming on such short notice."

Dolores eyed the building. "Is he—"

"It happened in the office," Wyatt confirmed, with a look of contrition. Dolores sensed that whoever had come up with the brilliant idea of calling in the missing person's daughter as a forensic expert, it had not been Wyatt. "We're sorry to have to rely on you like this."

"Please. Whatever I can do."

An oak smell rose from the wall panels in the lobby as they entered, and Dolores's fists clenched of their own accord. The sight of these plastic chairs, the pastel-colored tables, cut a path clean through the fog of her memory, like clamps yanking a chest cavity open.

The last time she had been in this room spider-crawled down her neck.

Paul squinted at her. "You all right, Dr. Diaz?"

"Fine." She slipped inside the scene suit, overshoes, and gloves, robing herself with professionalism. Dolores Hawthorne wouldn't be of use to find her missing father. But Dr. Diaz, the forensic expert, might.

She finished putting on the protective gear while the cops glared, casting a hostile chill into the air. This wasn't right, for Dolores and the FBI to go in without anyone from local law enforcement. Though the Little Horton PD had likely never seen a crime scene outside television, their cooperation could mean the difference between a tough case and a cold one.

Wyatt was clearly of the same mind as her. He cleared his throat as he slapped on his gloves. "Anyone here good with cameras?"

A dense silence followed.

Somehow, Wyatt managed to sound casual. "I'm *really* bad at pictures—one look at my Facebook profile will tell you that. We're going to need someone to photograph the crime scene. It'd be great if one of you could help, if it's not too much to ask."

The officers shifted on their feet. No one likes to jump on a pity offer.

Finally, a woman stepped forward. Aside from Dolores, she was the only person not in uniform. Hair that red was hard to forget. Though her cheeks had slimmed a bit and the bags beneath her eyes had deepened, that orangey tangle had not changed at all. Nor had her *Come near me and I'll shove you* look. Yet Dolores couldn't place her for a moment.

"I'll do it," the woman said. "I worked for the *Little Horton Herald* after high school." She added, in a saccharine tone, "If those credentials suit you."

Wyatt ignored the jab. "Thank you, Officer Butcher. I appreciate that."

Officer Butcher, Dolores thought. Of course. Kate Butcher.

Even as the puzzle pieces came together, a chill ran down her frame. She had gone to school with Kate, had seen her every day for years. And if Wyatt hadn't spoken her name just now, Dolores wouldn't have remembered she existed.

Someone handed Kate a set of PPE and they walked into the office.

Dolores's attention went to the body first, as it always did. Dr. Burke lay on his back, eyes open and glazed. A streak of saliva had dried down his cheek. The entry wound, where the bullet penetrated his forehead, was no bigger than a dime, but from the splatter on the wall, Dolores expected an exit wound as large as her fist.

Clicks filled the room as Kate photographed the body. Dolores bent toward the ground, looking for shoeprints. The indentations patterned across the carpet hinted at a rather large size.

"Think they're the same we found in your father's office?" Paul asked.

"There were three sets of shoeprints at the first crime scene," Dolores said. "Here, I can only make out two. I'll need to compare them to say for sure."

"What can you tell us?" Paul prodded.

"Can I get a light?"

A flashlight slid into her hand. She flicked on the button, and dark red gleamed under the beam.

"That's weird," she said.

Paul crouched beside her. "What is?"

"Blood. He left us a perfect bloody shoeprint."

"Well," he said, "that's a good thing, isn't it?"

"Too good." She looked back toward Kate, and Wyatt, who stood by the door. "Did you notice how drenched the road is? In the fall, this town turns into a swamp, but the killer didn't drag mud into the office. So he's careful. Then he leaves this neat shoeprint for us to find. To step into the blood, he would have needed to walk around the victim's head. Why would he do that?"

"To pick up the bullet?" Wyatt offered.

Dolores lifted Dr. Burke's head a few inches. It peeled off the ground with a wet *squish*. The bullet had torn through the occipital bone, so it would have continued its trajectory.

She got to her feet and looked at the wall, so covered in blood and gray matter, she might as well have been searching for a dot in a Pollock painting.

"Well, that's something," she finally said.

"What?" Paul was breathing down her neck again.

Dolores pointed to the projectile lodged into the wall. "He didn't just leave us the shoeprint. He left the bullet."

"So," Paul said, "he's not gonna get an award for killer of the year."

Dolores stepped back to view the entire scene. "It doesn't explain how he got blood on his shoes. Why didn't he just leave? From the size of the entry wound, he would have been standing here when he shot him." She retreated so her back was almost flush against the door. Wyatt stepped aside to make space for her. "He fires, kills Burke with a single shot, and doesn't think to retrieve the bullet. Yet instead of slipping out, he waits for a pool of blood to form around Burke's head and steps inside it to leave us a pretty shoeprint."

"Maybe he was confused," Paul said.

"Maybe he wanted us to find it."

Wyatt had been standing silently by the door. Though almost as tall as his partner, he didn't take nearly as much space.

"You keep saying 'he.'"

"From the size of the shoeprint, the killer's almost certainly male. The trajectory of the bullet backs it up." She mimed a gun with her fingers. "Dr. Burke is almost six feet tall. If I shot him, I would angle the gun upward–like this. The killer did the opposite. You can tell from how the bullet hit the wall. Anyway, I can get an estimate when I measure the footprint. Your foot's usually fifteen percent of your height. My guess would be six two."

Paul opened his mouth again, but Dolores was faster. "I'm assuming Burke was working on the evidence you collected at my father's office. Does he have a lab here?"

Kate lowered her camera, revealing a blanched face. "Y-yes. Mostly he uses it for personal studies. He said he'd work on the evidence all night."

"And did you check it?"

"What?"

"Did you check his lab?" Dolores said. "It doesn't look like a coincidence that the medical examiner was murdered, when he was part of a missing person investigation. Maybe the killer wanted to cover his tracks." She pressed her lips together. "Did anyone think to check whether the evidence was still in Dr. Burke's lab?"

Thirteen

MURKY WATERS

Dolores had done this job long enough to know there was no such thing as a typical crime scene. Some came with blood, vomit, urine, or fecal matter. Some came with all of the above.

Dr. Burke was different, somehow.

The sight of him sent a jolt of disgust through her fingers. It had nothing to do with the fact that his brain splattered the floor. Dead bodies had about the same effect on her as a cup of coffee by now. She would have been just as sick touching the man if he were alive.

A coppery taste hit her tongue.

Dr. Burke was not the evil caricature her seventeen-year-old mind had made him out to be. He had a family, relatives who would miss him, and he had been gruesomely murdered.

But it did not loosen the grind in Dolores's teeth.

He could have died a thousand deaths, and still, she would not have found it in her to be sorry.

The officer with the beard had gone to check the lab while they were collecting evidence in Dr. Burke's office. When he returned, Wyatt stepped into the hall to talk to him.

Kate let her finger hover above the shutter button, and Paul leaned closer to the door.

"The lab's been trashed," she heard the officer say. "No trace of the samples we gave him yesterday."

"You're sure?"

"Yeah. I helped bag the evidence and label it. It's gone."

Wyatt returned to the room. No one pretended they hadn't been listening.

"Maybe we'll get it back when we find the killer," Kate said.

Dolores shook her head. "If the chain of evidence's been broken, it doesn't matter. Everything found in my father's office is compromised. We can't use it in court." She looked down at the floor. "We'll examine the lab before we do the autopsy. Maybe the killer left something there that'll help us make an ID."

By the time they'd finished examining both the office and the lab, the muscles in her neck were taut as bow strings.

Paul and Wyatt headed out first, leaving her alone in the lobby with Kate. The officer's face was white, a few red locks pasted to her forehead.

"First dead body?" Dolores asked.

"Yes."

The edge in her voice took Dolores aback, and she figured it must be nerves. Kate probably had little control over what came out of her mouth right now. Most likely, she was counting her blessings that she hadn't thrown up in front of two FBI agents at her first crime scene ever.

Dolores glanced above her shoulder, to make sure the lobby was clear. "Look," she said. "You don't have to come to the morgue. Obviously, this is your case," she added when a scowl burrowed into the officer's forehead. "I promise to call you personally if we find anything. You can even listen to the autopsy record if you want." She pursed her lips. "But it's going to get a lot uglier at the morgue. There's no reason for you to go through that."

Kate glared at her with such open hostility, Dolores had to dig her feet into the carpet to stop herself from running. She wasn't used to open confrontation. Passive-aggressive was the Hawthornes' MO.

"If I said something to offend you, I'm sorry. I was just trying to be nice."

"Yeah," Kate said. "That's your go-to, isn't it?"

"What?"

"Playing nice. Someone could toss you in a dumpster and tie you up, and you'd just help them with the knots, right?"

Dolores stared, mouth dry. What had she ever done to Kate Butcher that the woman would hate her this much?

"Not that people ever tossed *you* in a dumpster, Miss Popular. Did the town throw you a homecoming party yet? If so, do me a favor. Don't invite me this time."

Dolores was too shocked to conjure an answer for a while. "Kate, I have no idea what you're talking about."

A sliver of steel crept into the officer's eyes. "You think I couldn't tell when you first saw me? For a second, you had no idea who I was."

Dolores couldn't deny that.

Kate snorted. "That's what I thought. You come back here after two decades, and the whole town knows you at a glance. But you? Nah. You made it big in Los Angeles. Forgot all about the small-town rubes you grew up with. You and those FBI agents make a great team." Her shoulders squared. "I *will* come to the morgue. Thanks for worrying."

Kate pushed past her, and Dolores's legs turned to marmalade. A vase clattered to the ground as she caught herself on the reception counter.

She needed to leave this building. Right now.

The murky waters of her past in Little Horton swam up her throat in a black, bitter tide.

Fourteen

DEATH ANATOMY

Wyatt would have never pegged Melissa Dylan for a mortician. A twenty-two-year-old with curtain-straight hair, UV-tanned skin, and lashes so thick with mascara that he figured every blink must be a chore.

After she and Dolores finished the preliminary examination–weighing Burke, measuring him, and recording any external marks like scars and tattoos–Dolores asked, "You've done autopsies before?"

Melissa shook her head.

"Most people here die from natural causes," Kate volunteered from her spot by the door. "Autopsies are the exception, not the rule."

Dolores looked reassuringly at Melissa. "That's okay. I'll talk you through it. First, we use the scalpel to make the incision. Then we saw through the rib cage and detach the organs from the spine. You can weigh them for me."

Melissa looked less shaky than Wyatt felt. Still, he didn't want to sit this one out. Not when Kate stood there planted like a flag in the doorway, and Paul had asked him in the car, "You got a strong stomach, Big Guy?"

Dolores looked up at them. Wyatt got the feeling her explanation had been meant to scare them off.

"This is going to take anywhere from two to four hours. I only need one law enforcement agent present to conduct the autopsy. We can call you when we're done."

Paul smirked. He smelled like the cigarettes he'd chain-smoked in the car, which was actually a small improvement on the formaldehyde. "That's very thoughtful, Dr. Diaz."

Dolores's lips pinched together. "Don't take this the wrong way, but I'd prefer you to be out there investigating my father's disappearance. Not to mention"–she glanced at Melissa–"a first autopsy is stressful enough without three law enforcement agents as an audience."

"Think you might find something you won't want us to see?"

Wyatt snapped to attention. His eyes shot toward Paul. Had he really just said that?

Dolores held Paul's gaze. "Suit yourselves."

And the massacre began.

On TV, autopsies never look like they need much muscle power, but sawing through bones and flesh was clearly as much exercise as Wyatt's morning jog. He'd imagined pathologists removed the organs one by one, but instead Dolores pulled out the whole block of heart, lungs, liver, and kidneys and dissected them on the table.

By that point, Kate had turned positively pallid. Wyatt still felt on the safe side of queasy, and Paul–Wyatt did a double take. Paul's eyes were actually roaming up and down Dolores's body. Wyatt's throat closed up. He couldn't think of a less appropriate place to check out a woman.

"So," Paul said, "what can you tell us about the man?"

Dolores lifted an organ covered in blisters. "See his liver? It's in an advanced stage of cirrhosis, which would indicate chronic alcoholism."

Kate let out, "Dr. Burke?" Then covered her lips.

"Aside from that," Dolores said, "the man was healthy. The cause of death was a shot to the head with a fifty-caliber revolver. Based on rigor mortis and the fixedness of lividity, he's been dead between six and eight hours." She turned to Melissa. "Do you agree?"

Melissa nodded. "Lividity is fixed," she said, indicating the spots where the blood had pooled in the body, "but those haven't turned purple-blue yet."

Dolores looked back at Wyatt and Paul. "We're going to put the organs back in and sew him up."

Clearly, there was nothing more for them to see here. Paul conceded, "Well, we've been in your hair long enough. Thank you for your assistance, Dr. Diaz. Naturally, the bureau will compensate you for your work today."

Dolores looked coldly at him. It didn't look like she appreciated having her autopsy turn into a battleground for law enforcement agents to prove their nerve.

"I don't need compensation. I need you to find my father."

It could have come out pleading, which Wyatt would have expected from a family member. But if anything, her voice had a commanding quality.

RAIN BLEW INTO THEIR faces when they stepped out. The door of the morgue hadn't yet slammed before Paul fished a cigarette out of his pocket.

Wyatt unlocked the Chrysler and sat behind the wheel.

"You're awful quiet," Paul said.

"I don't get it."

"What?"

"How you operate. You keep making it sound like we don't trust her. Dolores."

"I don't," Paul said.

"And you really need her to know that? Can't you act like a professional? We're FBI agents. To a lot of people, that's intimidating. It's our job to make them trust us. When you go to the doctor, they don't just prod and poke you without explaining what's going on."

"As a matter of fact, I could think of worse things than playing doctor with Dolores Diaz."

Wyatt's hands clenched around the wheel. Why would Paul even say that?

They weren't old buddies at some bar "talking women."

There was more to it than that, though.

Dolores seemed to Wyatt the kind of woman you went on a first date with wearing the suit you saved for job interviews, the sort you took to fancy restaurants, not fast-food joints. *Not* the kind you checked out while she was elbow-deep into a man's organs.

He kept his eyes on the road. It was raining so goddamn much, he could barely see ten yards ahead of him.

Paul continued, more seriously, "I know what I'm doing."

"Then you're good at hiding it."

"Jesus, Big Guy," he laughed, "haven't you noticed? I push people's buttons. See what makes them tick."

Wyatt's jaw unscrewed as he realized, "You're doing it with me."

It didn't look like Paul minded having been found out. "I do it with everyone. Don't take it personally. I'll tell you what, though. It doesn't make me a bad agent."

"No," Wyatt conceded. "It just makes you an asshole."

He jumped in his seat as something slammed against the car. His foot dug into the brake pedal, his heart somersaulting. Wyatt checked the rearview mirror, but there was no car following them. The Little Horton streets were deserted.

"Shit," Paul said.

"I–" Wyatt couldn't drain the horror from his voice. "I hit something."

"I *know*."

He stumbled out of the car. The headlights beamed like yellow eyes into the drizzle. A car door opened and slammed, but Wyatt couldn't see Paul, couldn't see anything but the trickle of blood that rain slowly washed down the tarmac.

Oh God.

A kid? A kid who'd been playing in the rain—where were the damned parents?—you really couldn't see anything in this weather and, Jesus, had he just killed a kid?

In his mind's eye, he saw him: dark eyes, chestnut hair, scrawny cheeks.

He followed the blood. The enormity of his crime pressed against his teeth like a scream. When he found the dark mass bleeding on the ground, there wasn't even room for relief.

Wyatt brushed the blood-matted fur with his knuckles.

Paul walked up to where Wyatt was kneeling. "It's just a cat. Whole town's full of them. Didn't you notice? Like rats in some cities. Little H could probably open a pet store."

Wyatt closed his eyes. His fingers curled into the cat's fur, stroking between his ears.

"Well, come on," Paul said. "Before one of us gets hit."

"I'm sorry," Wyatt whispered. He rubbed his hands against the wet road, washing the feel of the dead cat off his fingers.

When he stood up, Paul was looking at him like Wyatt had just taken part in some strange ritual.

They got back in the car. Wyatt sat there for a moment without starting the ignition.

He felt Paul's eyes on him. "It's just a damn cat."

Wyatt put the car in drive and wheeled into the rain.

Fifteen

REMEMBER, REMEMBER

The evening air hit Dolores as she and Melissa stepped out of the morgue. Sunset came fast here, a black curtain dropping over Little Horton. The whole day had gone by in a blink.

Melissa glanced at the parking lot. A Honda sat catching the rain. "That's my car. You want me to drop you somewhere?"

"No thanks," Dolores said. Her father's car was in the street across from the morgue. Still she added, "I'll walk."

"In this weather?" Melissa cocked a penciled-in brow at the sky. "I promise, I'm not going to murder you and bury you in the woods."

"It's not that," Dolores said. "I just–I could use the exercise."

In truth, she had no idea where to go from here. After a crime scene and an autopsy, she craved a shower, but the thought of returning home to Charlotte, Asher, and Josie knotted her stomach.

"Okay then," Melissa said. "Thanks for not making me feel like a fool in there. Happy Halloween."

Dolores managed, "Happy Halloween."

She started toward downtown, weighing her options. Check into a motel? Now that she was assisting the FBI in a murder investigation, she couldn't very well leave town. She didn't see herself spending another night at her father's house, but what choice did she have?

Dolores sighed. Her family had every right to burn her off the family tree. Two decades she'd been away. Not a visit. Not a phone call. She wasn't a Hawthorne anymore. Couldn't even remember what being part of this family felt like.

Cramps clenched her insides, and Dolores covered her abdomen–but this time, it wasn't the scar that hurt. As the adrenaline of the autopsy wore off, she remembered that the last thing she'd eaten was a handful of peanuts during her flight.

The diners she walked past all struck a familiar chord. Better to go somewhere she'd never stepped foot in before, so she opted for a bar. The smell of beer, French fries, and sweat hit her as she slid through the door.

The place was so packed Dolores had to squeeze her way to the bar area. Chip crumbs splattered the counter, which somehow smelled sticky. Scribbled in chalk on the slate walls was a small food section, smeared with corn syrup handprints. "Grilled Cheese & Fries. Cheese Curd Burger. Mozzarella Sticks."

Why did everything in Wisconsin come with so much cheese?

A waiter arrived, sleeves rolled up to reveal tattooed forearms. "What can I getcha?"

"I'll have a martini," Dolores said, and realized at that moment that she had walked into this bar to get blind drunk.

THE FIRST DRINK HIT her like liquid fire, leaving her so sore, Dolores could only croak out the next orders. The evening whistled by. She texted Amy to get started on the *Desperate Housewives* marathon without her. The phone felt warm in her hand as she eyed it, itching to text Max. Not something needy and sad, which was precisely how she felt right now. But a witty text. A sexy text. An *Aren't you sorry you fucked your yoga teacher* text.

Chatter billowed from nearby tables. Was this Dolores Hawthorne? Did she look drunk, was she crying, why wasn't she crying?

With each drink, Dolores cared less about what town talk would say tomorrow.

Her father's voice in her head–

You're a Hawthorne, Dolores. Our family has been in Little Horton for as long as there has been a Little Horton. So have the Winslows. He'd sigh. *People in town will always talk about us, just as people everywhere talk about the weather. It's the way of the world.*

Dolores stared at her drink. As far as she knew, her father hadn't spoken to the Winslows in two decades. Why visit Gregory now? Nostalgia? Rekindling their old friendship, as they got older—was it really that simple? Then why had Charlotte lied about it?

Before she could give it more thought, a man pulled out the stool next to hers. "This seat taken?"

Dolores looked up. It was her brother.

"How did you find me?" she asked, then cursed herself. She'd basically invited Asher to treat her like a runaway teen.

"Mrs. Green called. Asked if you had a doppelganger or if my sister was back in town."

"Who's Mrs. Green?"

Asher rolled his eyes. "History teacher? Terrible breath, smoked like a chimney?" Dolores's face must have looked as blank as she felt. "Well." His jaw tightened. "You sure did put Little Horton behind."

Dolores didn't answer. There was no point in explaining how precious little she remembered from her childhood. After the surgery—

Jacob.

Everything got swept up into the tide of dark waters that rolled around the first eighteen years of her life.

During her internship, a man training to become a psychiatrist had told her trauma turned your mind into a sponge. "You can soak it up as much as you like with what you know happened. But every time it comes down to it, you're gonna panic, and you're gonna squeeze all the juice out again."

Dolores remembered nodding, trying to look polite. Forcing out the word, "Fascinating," while the scar on her abdomen blistered to life.

"Ash—" she started.

"Is it true Dr. Burke was murdered?"

Dolores hesitated. It wasn't wise to discuss the case with her brother, let alone when she was drunk. Yet his eagerness pierced through the polish in his tone. Of course he was dying for information. She would be, too, in his place.

"Yes."

A spark lit up his gaze. "Was it the same guy who took Dad?"

"I don't know. It looks like it." She drained what was left of her glass.

"I can't talk about the investigation. If I knew anything about Dad, I'd tell you."

Asher hailed the waiter. "I'll have a gin and tonic." He raised an index finger—nothing like the chubby hands she used to kiss after reading him bedtime stories. "One drink. Then I'm taking you home."

"Don't talk like that, Ash."

"Like what?"

"Like you're my father."

He spoke in a low tone. "Then don't go out to bars getting drunk and making a scene."

"Wow. Charlotte really drilled that into you. The great Hawthorne appearances paradigm. What does it matter that everything collapses so long as we look the part?"

"You're talking nonsense. Think about Josie. What kind of example are you setting?"

Dolores laughed. "Josie has known me for five minutes. If I'm a role model to her, Charlotte's doing something wrong."

She immediately tried to swallow the words back. Whatever she might think of Charlotte, she was still Asher's mother.

Her eyes darted to her brother, who looked like he was about to spit out spiders. He'd probably been waiting for this since she got here—for a reason to explode.

"You really don't give a shit about this family, do you? Mom overheard you talking to the FBI. Said you told them to call you Diaz."

The sharpness of his voice cut deeper than she expected. Maybe it would be easier if she could think the man sitting before her right now was a stranger. But he wasn't. He wasn't.

"It's my name," she said, keeping the cracks from her voice.

He snorted. "That says it all, right? You hated Mom. You never thought of me as your brother. You just fucked out of town as soon as you got the chance. Let Dad pay for your education. Never called. Never wrote. You are as much part of our family as a fucking roach."

The waiter swooshed a gin and tonic in front of Asher. His cheeks grew red. Had he been preparing this speech since he was five?

"Dolores—"

"You're allowed to hate me," she said. Willed herself to look up from her glass. The least she could do was take his anger full force. She finally pried her neck up, and her lips parted in surprise as she saw the tears in his eyes. "Asher–"

"What I said. God, that was awful."

"It's all right. I deserve it."

Now that the poison was out, she could see her brother again. The little boy who had loved her, that she had loved. And that she had left.

"Why did you do it?" he said.

His tears felt worse to her than his anger had. She wished she could cry with him, for him. For them both. But since she had left Little Horton, an ice lake had settled inside her, freezing everything in its wake. That's what trauma was like to her, she supposed–not water that the sponge of her mind kept squeezing out, but ice. Ice that made everything smooth and hazy, a shiny surface through which she could not make out the waters below.

But it's quiet here. Oh-so-quiet, Ash.

"I couldn't take it," she said.

"Couldn't take what?"

This town. My skin. My life.

She couldn't take the secrets, keeping the truth from Asher and from her father. Living around an abyss only she and Charlotte could see–Charlotte, of all the people in the world. Dolores bit back a sigh. Some irony, that overnight, the person who had been her enemy since her father remarried became her only ally.

"I just had to leave," she said. "I know you can't understand that. I know it was awful, and there's no excuse for what I did. But I want you to know I'm sorry, and that it wasn't because I didn't love you."

The word prickled like salt on her tongue. She said again, "I never stopped loving you, Asher."

His jaw squared as he fought more tears. He gulped down his drink so fast, he half choked on a slice of lime. "Shit," he winced, before his eyes grew serious again. "Don't go, okay?"

"Okay."

He frowned. Maybe he'd sensed all along she was dying to jump on the next flight, to disappear again.

Shame rushed to her cheeks. Since she'd gotten here, she had thought of no one but herself. If the FBI hadn't called her to do an autopsy, she would have flown back to Los Angeles tonight. And how fair was that to Ash?

It fully hit her for the first time. How cruel this must have felt to him. For her to vanish from his life without asking for permission or forgiveness, so all his love had no choice but to stay bottled inside him and rot.

"Okay?" he repeated.

"Yeah, okay."

"I meant–"

"I know what you meant. I'm not leaving, Asher."

His hand lay flat on the bar, and she grabbed it. He shuddered. The back of his hand felt huge beneath hers. "Okay," he said.

DOLORES LAUGHED SO HARD, a geyser of gin ran up her nose. "Oh, no. She caught you in bed?"

"Yep. Well, manner of speaking," Asher said. "We weren't so much 'in bed' as doing what you'd expect consenting seventeen-year-olds to do there. That's how I came out to my mother. Mom, meet my boyfriend's ass."

Dolores wiped the tears that ran down her nose. "God. Did Dad know?"

He shrugged. "I never told him, and I know Mom didn't. As to whether he wondered why I never brought a girl home–well, you know Dad. Until something is slapping him in the face, it's not real. And even then. Someone could point a gun to his head and he'd have the gall to squint at it and decide it's a carrot."

Dolores carried her glass to her lips. Better they didn't talk about their father. "What did Charlotte do when she found you?"

"Washed her eyes with bleach, I think. Nah, she didn't do anything. My naked boyfriend just became one more thing we didn't talk about."

She let a few seconds slide past. "If it makes you feel better, I can think of something even more embarrassing."

"More embarrassing than Mom catching me naked with a boy?"

"How about catching my husband screwing another woman?"

Asher gaped. "No. When did it happen?"

"Last month."

"Well, shit." He was silent a moment. "Speaking of love interests . . . did you tell Jacob you're back in town?"

Dolores said nothing. Pictured the bones of her head, white, precise, and clean. *Lacrimal. Orbital. Parietal.* Pictured them so hard they seemed to ignite, until her flesh began to feel radioactive.

"I mean," Asher continued, "you probably heard he's been voted into office."

This was too much. "Dad's old office?"

"Yeah. He's our new mayor. Well, not new-new. It's been a few years, but—I mean, you didn't look him up? Not even once? You guys were crazy for each other."

She brought her glass to her lips, to hide her face from him. This was precisely why she had left Little Horton. Not just because she could run into Jacob, picture him springing from every street corner like a jack-in-the-box. But because his name might drop at any time, in the safety of her own house. They'd be sitting at the kitchen table, having breakfast, and Asher would ask, *Why don't we have Jake over anymore?*

The word Charlotte never spoke would blast through her mind, shatter the ice. And she would have to pick herself off rock bottom all over again.

Asher went on, "I think he's going for the same strategy as Dad. Mayor of a small town, so he can look more human when he goes for the Senate."

"You make it sound like that was Dad's strategy, not Charlotte's."

Dolores heard the prick in her voice. The Jacob she knew would stick to small-town politics. Jacob was the kind of guy who could swim in the lake all summer but freaked out at the sight of the ocean.

She sipped her drink, pretended her throat wasn't clamping up.

Not that he was *the Jacob she knew* anymore.

"I mean," Asher said as he scratched his chin, "he's married now. I should have probably started with that. Jesus, I'm a bad drinker. Anyway, I don't see much of him anymore. I do hang out with Teddy from time to time."

"Teddy."

Dolores closed her eyes. As he'd called himself, "the fun and more handsome Winslow brother." Growing up, she had been almost as close to him as to Jacob, but he left town right around the time she entered high school. They hadn't talked since she and Jacob broke up. Even if she'd wanted to, even if it hadn't been for the Feud—she couldn't have suffered the reminder.

"Well," Asher amended, "not 'hang out.' But we both live in Madison, and when we run into each other—you remember Teddy. Before you have time to say you've got something cooking, he's filled you with a pint of beer and forty minutes' worth of *long time no see*."

"How is he?"

"Pretty good. Took over his father's company. Unless Wisconsin falls out of love with cheese, I wouldn't worry about him." Asher reached for his glass and raised it to eye level. Empty. "Should we order another round?"

Dolores sighed. "We should probably go home."

They tried to put up a strong front, staring at the bell by the exit to help themselves walk straight. When the night air hit them, Asher collapsed against her shoulder. "It's freezing."

"You should come to L.A. Summer all year round."

"Sounds worth dumping your family over."

His jabs didn't sting anymore. Cracking jokes instead of showing vulnerability was carved so deep into the Hawthorne mold, Dolores wouldn't have been surprised to hear a great-grandparent had come up with the concept.

"You bet. No constant drizzle. No dairy mania." She tripped against a pumpkin by the entrance of a store, and orange goo exploded against the wall. "No goddamn Halloween stuff all over town."

"I'd forgotten about Halloween," Asher said. "I guess with everything going on, we'll have to cancel."

Dolores grunted. "At least we're safe from Charlotte's fanaticism. That's one thing I'd love to never go through again in my life."

Asher's hand slipped through her fingers as he came to a stop.

Really, she needed to learn to shut up sometimes.

"Sorry, I didn't mean *she's* a fanatic, just—you know how she goes crazy with Halloween."

Asher's eyes narrowed, like he was looking at her through tinted glass. "What are you talking about?"

Dolores chuckled. "I'm talking about slaving for a whole week to decorate the house, baking enough food to feed an army. I'm talking about Charlotte using us as child labor to fuel her Halloween frenzy."

But Asher went on staring, as if she had turned into a question mark.

"What?" she asked him.

"Are you being serious?"

She tried to ignore the icy finger curling down her spine. "Yeah. Sorry if that sounds cynical. I could never buy into this whole Halloween thing."

Asher shook his head.

"What is it?"

"Nothing. It's just–" He took a breath. "I mean, you used to take me trick-or-treating for hours on end. We hogged the bathroom all afternoon, painting each other's faces. Don't you remember how excited we got shopping for our costumes? How happy?"

Shivers broke down Dolores's neck.

She didn't remember.

Even as her brother went on, all she could see was that black tide rising to the surface. Impenetrable.

Her past. *That night.*

Nothing–nothing?

The taste of caramel apples. Charlotte's fingers through her hair.

Hands dripping with blood.

The essence that squeezed out of the sponge, every time she soaked it up.

"You made it fun for me," Asher said. "*You* decorated the house, Dee. Not Mom. You hung fake cobwebs on the chandeliers, smeared corn syrup over the mirrors. *You* planned the annual Hawthorne party. Dolores–you used to love Halloween."

2003

October 28

Sixteen

ONCE UPON AN OCTOBER

"Dee!"

Her brother's voice wrenched her from sleep. "Dee-Dee, *Deeeee-Deeeeeee!*"

Dolores started from the couch so hard she dropped to the floor. The rug burped out a whiff that smelled like the inside of a jewelry box.

"What, what?"

Asher stood before her, perfectly calm. "Someone's on the phone for you."

Dolores sighed. *I should scold him. He can't go running around screaming at people.*

But the rebuke melted like hot butter on her tongue.

The kid couldn't touch her chin on his tiptoes, yet from the moment he was born, he'd begun a reign of tyranny over Dolores, with his rosy cheeks and angel eyes.

"Yeah." She ran her palm over her face. "I'll be right there."

She ambled toward the telephone, which Asher had left face down on the counter. Stifling a yawn into her hand, she picked up. "Hello?"

"Hello," Jacob said.

Her pulse went through the roof. "Jake," she said, immediately echoed by Asher's maudlin, high-pitched imitation: *Jaaaaake.*

"Is this a bad time?"

"Not at all."

Asher tugged at the hem of her shirt. "Dee-Dee, can I have cereal?"

Charlotte had strict rules as to how late in the afternoon Asher could have a snack. But Charlotte wouldn't be home until six, and a few minutes of privacy with Jacob sounded like heaven.

"Go pick which ones you want. I'll be there in a sec."

Jacob chuckled into the phone. "Asher's one lucky kid."

"Oh, you know," she said, aiming for casual, like she didn't feel guilty for spoiling him. "It's hard not to have a sibling his own age."

"Are you kidding?" he said. "I would have killed to have a sister like you."

"That would have made it hard for you to date me."

He stayed silent. Her pulse throbbed at her temples.

"Is this the moment when I tell you why I called?"

"I mean, if you want."

"Do I have to make something up? I just really had to hear your voice."

Dolores sighed. If she wasn't stuck babysitting Asher all afternoon–

"Deeeee-Deeeee!" her brother screamed from the kitchen.

"I'll be right there!"

"I love the Ash-Man," Jacob said, "but he's a handful. I *could* come over and help you watch him."

"I'd love that." Reluctantly, she added, "But you know you can't come over when there's no one else in the house."

"There is someone else," he protested. "Asher."

"Mmm." She feigned pondering. "For some reason, my five-year-old brother doesn't meet Dad's standards for a chaperone."

Jacob let out a breath. "How come before we started dating, I could spend all the time I wanted in your house, and now it's all chaperones and curfews?"

"Come on, Dad loves you. He's just old-fashioned."

In truth, Dolores half expected her father to leap for joy when she started dating his best friend's son. All their lives, the Hawthornes and the Winslows had been close as only small-towners can be. The Winslows lived at the other end of Little Horton, half an hour's walk if you dragged your feet. They were perennial guests at the Hawthorne dinner table: Jacob, his father, Gregory, and his older brother, Teddy. In the early days, Evelyn Winslow also made it to the gatherings, but she had died before Dolores could remember much about her.

That Dolores and Jacob both lost their mothers at a young age carved a bone-deep understanding between them. Part of them would always be unfinished, their bodies filled with an abyss of grief that never needed explaining. There was more to it, of course, or she might as well have dated Teddy.

What drew her to Jacob? It wasn't just his bookworminess, the fact he could quote Jane Austen verbatim.

It was that perfect way her face fit in the crook of his neck. The crunchy thickness of his hair, the raw Jacob-smell of his body that broke through his cedarwood shower gel.

Before last summer, Dolores had been the anti-teenage-girl stereotype. Though, caving in to peer pressure, she'd gone on a few dates, a book on human anatomy was more likely to keep her attention than a boy.

She couldn't say how it happened—she'd always thought of the Winslow brothers as family. One afternoon, she and Jacob were sitting on her bedroom floor, doing homework, between them a textbook open on drawings of plants, animals, bacteria.

She was explaining the difference between unicellular and multicellular organisms, when he said, "Dolores?"

"What?"

"I think—never mind."

"Okay, now, you have to tell me."

He shook his head. "You'll laugh in my face."

"Will not."

"I think I want to kiss you."

She laughed in his face. Could not help herself. It felt like yesterday she, Jacob, and Teddy were running around in the garden, shooting each other with imaginary guns. When she looked at Jacob's lips, the only thing she could think of was the time he'd tried to teach her to whistle in one messy half hour of frustration and spittle.

"Like," she said, "as some sort of experiment?"

"Yes." He sighed, and admitted, "No. I just—can't stop thinking about it for some reason."

"Right now, or the whole afternoon?"

He tilted his head. "It's been a few weeks."

"A few weeks!"

He never even started a book without telling her about it.

Something warm fluttered down her stomach as she looked into his eyes. He had beautiful eyes, a green the color of glass that washed up onto the beach.

"Okay," she heard herself say. "So, you have to do it."

His face crumbled. "What?"

"To get it out of your system."

"Oh. You think that's gonna work?"

"If you don't, you'll just keep thinking about it."

"Okay then." A beat of silence. "Like, now?"

She grabbed hold of his turtleneck sweater. Paper rustled as his knee skidded against the textbook. When his lips met hers, she remembered thinking how soft he felt, how familiar. The smell of his gel and the caramels he'd been popping into his mouth all afternoon. She closed her eyes, and pictured the blood in her veins flowing, the atria pumping away as her ventricles contracted, her brain releasing oxytocin. It was beautiful, like the symmetry of stars aligning.

They pulled away, breathless, shell-shocked. That was the moment Dolores started daydreaming about things other than anatomy.

She sighed into the phone. "Actually, I think my dad and yours might have cast a spell to get us to fall in love."

"That'd explain a lot. So, you think I should call my dad, ask him to have the spell lifted?"

"I mean, it's worth a try."

"You think so?"

"Don't you?"

"Oh, I do," he hurried. "Matter of fact, I'd love being able to sleep again without thinking about your body–"

"Deeeee-Deeeee!"

Dolores groaned. "I better go before he strains his vocal cords."

"Can I drive you to school tomorrow?"

"That'd be great."

Jacob released a deep exhale. "Goddamn spell you put on me," he said.

Asher stood perched on a kitchen chair, arms stretched dramatically toward a box of Waffle Crisps. Dolores picked him up–God, he was getting heavy. Before she knew it, he'd be a grown man, slicking his hair back like Teddy.

She grabbed his cereal, poured it in a bowl, and went to the fridge. On the milk carton, a chestnut-haired girl stared back at her, a Julia Roberts smile splitting her cheeks. Dolores's throat tightened.

Did they have to print her face on milk cartons, on top of the posters taped to every lamppost in town? All the other cities in America had stopped doing it years ago. Dolores found it disturbing. The missing children, gazing out from inside your fridge.

Dolores poured a trickle over Asher's cereal, and he grabbed the carton. A couple of weeks ago, he asked his mother why they put girls on milk cartons, and in a moment of weakness, Charlotte answered they were the girls who milked the cows. If you asked Dolores, that was worse than the Santa lie. Now Asher only wanted milk that came from milk-girl cartons. "She looks like *you*."

Dolores didn't need to look to know it was true. Charlotte had mixed the two of them up all summer at work.

"Come on." She ruffled her brother's curls. "If you finish your bowl we can go for a walk."

She wrapped him in his fleece-lined jacket, threw on a hooded coat, and headed out. Orange leaves squished under their boots as Asher made her talk about the feast they would have on Saturday. He couldn't get enough of Halloween. His mother, who still called Louisiana home, didn't get what the fuss was about. She tolerated it because of how much it mattered to everyone in town. But teenage girls, more than anyone else, know when they're being talked down to. To Charlotte, the Little Horton Halloween spirit was pagan, verging on blasphemous. And of course, since Dolores cared about it so much, it had to be stupid.

"Popcorn?" Asher asked.

"Sure, popcorn. Locust-shaped chocolates, pumpkin cookies–"

"And you'll take me trick-or-treating?"

"I'll take you trick-or-treating."

"I'll help make the punch?"

"You'll help make the punch."

"I can stay up past bedtime?"

Dolores stopped mid-stride. Children were malicious little creatures. "Come on, Ash. You know Charlotte gets to decide how late you stay up."

She stiffened her resolve against his robin's-egg eyes.

"I wish *you'd* decide. You're so much cooler than Mom."

Dolores couldn't believe the petty flood of pleasure that rushed to her collar.

They walked past a streetlight, and there it was again: that smiling face from all the milk cartons.

MISSING

Please help find KRISTEN HOROWITZ, last seen on the evening of August 29. Kristen is seventeen, five feet and six inches, with chestnut hair and brown eyes. If you have any information about Kristen please contact the police.

Dolores's eyes lingered on the photograph. She hadn't known Kristen well before this summer, when Alexander hired her and Dolores as "assistants" at City Hall. Charlotte still worked there as city manager, and he must have thought this would amount to quality time. So, Dolores spent July and August making coffee, vacuuming floors, and answering the phone. The one upside was she got to hang out with Kristen, who beamed even when she and Dolores were on their knees scrubbing the floor.

"As far as summer jobs go," she'd said, "this beats McDonald's."

That may have been true. Still, Dolores couldn't have mustered one drop of enthusiasm about it, if not for Kristen.

It used to make Dolores laugh, the idea of "vibrant young women." As opposed to what? Porcelain dolls? Automatons?

But when she got to know Kristen, she realized there might be a kernel of truth in it.

Kristen didn't bubble like champagne—she swept you up in a cut-no-corners wave of tequila. She had a way of moving, when she darted to her feet to get coffee or leapt for the phone, that made it look like the steps to a dance only she could hear the music to.

They traded thoughts about friends, books, college. Kristen wanted to study engineering. "I don't care how I'll get the money. I'll whore out if I have to."

Dolores laughed, because a gasp behind the door indicated Charlotte had heard.

"You want it that bad?" Dolores asked.

Kristen sighed. "You know what it feels like, when something always made sense to you, when it *couldn't be* anything else? I used to build things out of junk, even as a kid. Okay, it helped that there was a lot of junk around the house. Junior's room is *crammed* with plastic-bottle toy trucks and UFOs made out of cheese boxes."

A smile cut into Kristen's cheeks when she mentioned her younger brother. She was clearly as smitten with Junior as Dolores was with Asher.

"I swear," Kristen said, "I keep waiting for him to get tired of it. When he turned ten, I saved money for *months* to buy him a real toy truck, and when he tore open the wrapping, he looked at me like I'd handed him a math equation. It's like he can't see the point in playing with something I didn't make myself."

"Sounds like he's lucky to have you."

"What about you?" Kristen asked. "What d'you want to do after graduation?"

Once, Dolores would have answered in a heartbeat. She had known she wanted to save lives since she was five, when her mother berated her for throwing herself in front of a car because "it was gonna shoot into the birds!"

But lately, money had been tighter around the house. Paintings had disappeared from the living room, as well as a few lamps and chandeliers. Alexander claimed he'd given them to charity, and Charlotte went on about how she'd always hated them, but Dolores hadn't been born yesterday.

"I don't know," she said. "I guess it depends."

"On what?"

Money, she thought. But she didn't want Charlotte to overhear. "I wanna go to college," she said. "But I'd hate to be away from my family. And Jacob."

Dolores could relate to the sigh Kristen let out. Jacob's name came to her mouth as easily as breath now, and she had hated boy-talk, too, before Jacob Winslow had colonized her brain.

"I swear to God, if you don't shut up about that boy, I will hurl you out the window."

Dolores laughed, and Kristen did, too, revealing the small gap of a missing molar. You would never have known it was gone if she didn't smile so damn wide.

"And don't think I'm the single girl who can't stand hearing about love. I have a boyfriend, too. But we're keeping things hush-hush."

"Why? Is he older?"

Kristen smiled. It looked like some kind of private joke. "Sure. He's older."

Dolores tried to shake off the remembrance. She shouldn't worry so much. Even Kristen's parents had vowed she'd run off. Teenage girls did it all the time. Maybe her secret boyfriend lived in Madison. Maybe he dumped her and Kristen decided to dump Little Horton.

But after all that talk about college, how could she not even finish high school?

Dolores's chest pinched.

Ahead of her, Asher leapt from pool to pool that the morning rain had washed into the path.

Maybe Kristen hated Little Horton, and maybe she didn't care much for her parents. But how could she leave her brother without saying goodbye?

Downtown, the church bell rang six and wrenched Dolores out of her thoughts. "Asher, come on! We'll be late for dinner!"

Seventeen

THE BOY WITH THE YELLOW RAINCOAT

It was a good thing Dolores lived for science while Jacob was more partial to literature. If they'd shared any classes, everything the teachers said would have flown into one ear and straight out the other. Instead, they had to endure the whole morning apart until lunch.

9:05.
10:10.
11:45.

Her heart throbbed for him, hungrier even than her growling stomach.

A smell of boiled rice wafted to her as she entered the cafeteria. Her eyes scanned for Jacob, when the *BLING* of clattering metal snatched her attention. A tray lay upside down, its contents splattered across a three-yard radius. Above the mess stood a plump girl with carroty hair, which at the moment looked a lot less red than her face.

Kate Butcher.

Dolores had sat a couple of seats from her during study periods.

Hoots broke out.

"Way to go, Butch!" a guy cried out.

Soon the whole cafeteria was chanting, "*Butch, Butch, Butch.*"

Dolores put her tray down and crouched, looking for salvageable items. The girl was on her knees, trying to clean up the mess. Her cheeks glowed red behind her pigtails, and her eyes steered clear from Dolores.

Amidst a pile of overcooked greens and French fries, Dolores retrieved a plastic-wrapped brownie and handed it over. "Here."

Kate's eyes shot venom at her. "Fuck off."

It surprised Dolores so much she knocked her head into a table.

Kate sprang to her feet, shoulders hunched, like she was trying to hide her face.

"You okay?" Jacob appeared beside Dolores, putting a hand on her shoulder.

"Yeah," Dolores managed, a little shaken.

They made their way to the two tables where their friends sat in the back of the cafeteria.

"What's her beef with you? Wouldn't let her copy off you in a test?"

Dolores shook her head. "I don't know."

"Don't mind her," Nathan said, sporting a Leonardo DiCaprio haircut and a Che Guevara tee. "Butcher's got a beef with everyone. You ain't special or anything."

"Gee, thanks."

Fortunately, everyone was quick to move on from the tray incident to the Hawthorne Halloween party. What they would bring, what they would do, what they would eat. Everything except what they would dress as.

Nathan prodded Jacob on the shoulder. "Haven't seen Teddy in ages. Is he coming back for Halloween?"

As a rich and handsome twenty-one-year-old who had been the first crush of most of the female youth of Little Horton, Teddy Winslow was a fascinating specimen to high school boys.

Jacob swallowed his mouthful of congealed pasta. "Can't say. He has a lot of work."

Nathan rolled his eyes. "Bosses, right?"

"It's even worse when the boss is your dad."

Dolores snorted. "Tell me about it."

"At least working for your dad is interesting," Jacob told her.

"Sorry, playing maid for Charlotte is interesting?"

"Well, no. But I mean, he's Mr. Mayor, running for the U.S. Senate. Not to talk shit about my dad, but who wants to work for Big Dairy?"

"Yeah," Dolores teased. "Who *wants* to make shitloads of cash and flood Wisconsin with cheese?"

He sighed, but there was a gleam in his eyes as he held her gaze. "Well, maybe I don't wanna keep wading in dairy money. Call me crazy, but I think there's better things in life than making farmers miserable and America fat."

"Like politics?"

"Not Washington politics," Jacob admitted. "But look at your dad. You think he ever wakes up wondering what's the point of it all? No. He goes to work, does what he can for his neighbors. Everyone in town knows him."

"Everyone in town knows *you*."

He shook his head. She knew what he meant. Everyone knew him because he was a Winslow, not because he'd ever done anything worth knowing.

"I don't know. Teddy keeps saying life in Madison makes Little Horton look stale as a train station sandwich, but"–he licked his lips–"I can't see myself going to the supermarket without running into a familiar face. What's the point of having a great career if you don't belong, if you're not part of a community?"

"Jesus, will you stop," Nathan said. "I'm getting all teary."

Dolores touched the tip of her sneaker to Jacob's shoe under the table. "I think it's lovely," she said.

Nathan snorted. "You'd think he was lovely if he was wearing a tutu."

"You'd look *great* in a tutu. Food for thought, if you haven't found your costume."

Jacob popped open the wrapper of his Sundae Crunch Popsicle and poked her on the nose with it.

Nathan sighed. "Get a room."

Whenever they hung out with their friends now, everything Jacob and Dolores did that didn't include the group became *get-a-room* material. And it wasn't like either of them could say what they both thought– that, as a matter of fact, they damn well wished they could.

"God, look at that." Dolores swiveled as Jacob opened the door of his Cadillac. Nathan pointed at the school gates. A little boy sat with his back to the metal, a sketchbook in his lap. A mop of light brown hair hung above his shoulders, and although it wasn't raining, he wore the most detestable yellow raincoat Dolores had ever seen.

"Isn't he a little young to go to high school?" she asked.

"He's not a freshman," Nathan said. "He's Kristen's brother."

Dolores's mouth turned sour. "You sure?"

"Sure, I'm sure. One of my exes used to babysit him–I think he's kind of autistic. All he does is sit in his room and draw all the time."

"What's he doing here?"

"Waiting for his sister, I think."

Jacob sighed. "That's awful."

Nathan shrugged. "Apparently, he took it real hard. Kris was the only person who took care of him around the house."

"What about his parents?" Dolores asked.

Nathan mimed a bottle with his thumb.

Dolores's grip tightened around the strap of her backpack. Before she could stop herself, she started toward the gate. Up close, Kristen's brother looked a little older than she had first pegged him for. A rash of acne blossomed on his forehead.

"Hey." She crouched down to his level. "I'm Dolores."

He looked up at her, ink-blue fingertips clutched around his notebook. "The mayor's daughter. I know who you are."

"Okay. And you're–"

His upper lip jutted out, almost defiantly. "I'm Junior."

"Pleased to meet you, Junior." She glanced back toward the car. "My friends and I were about to head home. Think we could give you a ride?"

Silence. The kid's dark eyes bore into her like diamonds.

"Do your parents know where you are?"

"I'm twelve. I can walk home by myself."

Dolores nodded. Well, that was a little better than *Fuck off.* "Okay. I'm sorry I bothered you."

She got to her feet.

"You have to help me."

Dolores pivoted back toward him. "Help you? How?"

"Find Kristen. It's not true, what the police are saying. She didn't run away. They say she packed a suitcase but that's not true. She didn't pack it. I was there."

Dolores shook her head. "Um–did you tell the police that?"

"They won't listen to me. Maybe they'll listen to *you*."

"Why would they listen to me instead of you?"

He was silent awhile. "Do you promise?"

She chuckled. "Do I what?"

"Promise. To help me," he went on, more solemn than any twelve-year-old had any right to be.

"Sure. If I can."

Dolores resisted the urge to rake her shoe against the ground. The kid was making her uncomfortable, with his too-tight jaw, his too-serious eyes.

He nodded, as if she had passed some sort of test. "Then ask your father, Dolores."

The hairs on her body bristled. "What?"

"Ask your father to tell you where she is."

"What–" she managed. "What does my father have to do with this?"

His eyes poured out an avalanche of seriousness. "Just tell him to bring her back. I want her to come home."

PRESENT DAY

Eighteen

DESPERATE TIMES

Dolores helped Asher stay steady as they teetered toward the house.

"Watch out!" He pulled her to the left as something brushed past her ankle.

"Was that a rat?"

"A cat," Asher said. "Little Horton's got a bit of a feline problem."

"I noticed."

"It started a couple years ago. You know when they put all the kittens in those Valentine's Day commercials?" He paused, thinking. "No, you wouldn't. Local TV. Anyway, cat-mania hit us full throttle. People gave kittens away for first dates, birthday presents. Didn't last long–didn't have to. You know how fast cats reproduce? The cops are losing their minds over it."

"Oh, well. Let the cats have it."

"What?"

"The town. Little Hortoners had their chance. Might as well close everything up and declare the First Feline Republic of America."

Asher's laughter echoed into the night.

The air smelled of damp leaves and chimney fire. You just didn't get smells like that in Los Angeles. Dolores filled her lungs with ice-cold, smoky air. Yes, this was what autumn smelled like. Funny how she'd lived all these years away from Little Horton and somehow had never stopped to think that seasons didn't have a smell in California.

As they reached the house, Asher put a finger over his lips, using his spare key to unlock the door. "Oh, shit."

Light flooded the entry hall. Charlotte stood by the kitchen door, robe-clad, livid. "Just what is the matter with you?" She snapped her fingers in Asher's face. "Your father is missing, and you go out and drink yourself blind?"

His shoulders squared, his spine snapped straight. The metamorphosis sobered Dolores. He could have been a private getting told off by his sergeant. "I'm sorry. I didn't think–"

"No. Clearly, you didn't. You're a Hawthorne, Asher. You can't just go about making a show of yourself for the whole town to see. Think about your sister."

Sister. Dolores felt a gap inside of her, like a door slamming shut. Already, she was a spectator, an outsider to a family scene.

"We need to be smart about this," Charlotte said. "Stick together."

Dolores's palm slapped against the wall for balance.

Something her father said once, about Charlotte–about desperate times and desperate measures.

If the apocalypse ever happens, Dolores, I want you to go to your stepmother. She is the strongest person in the universe. I wouldn't make it out of the house. He'd chuckled self-deprecatingly. *But Charlotte? Hellfire could pour from the sky, the devil's minions could crawl the earth, and she would be the last person standing.*

She shook off the thought and looked at her brother. Humbled, cheeks burning. Heat broke loose in her chest. She spoke without thinking. "It's my fault. I started it."

Her stepmother did not even glance her way. "Dolores, stop apologizing all the time. It makes you look weak."

"I didn't apologize. I said I started it."

Finally, Charlotte sized her up. "Really? Is Asher still a little boy you can trick into making mistakes?"

"Mom–"

Charlotte put a hand up. "Stop it. The both of you. I know you're afraid. I know you miss your father. But there is a man out there killing us."

The words spread a chill through Dolores. Beneath the haze of alcohol, something ticked. Why would Charlotte put it like that? A man killing *us*.

A floorboard squeaked upstairs. Charlotte turned toward the staircase as footsteps padded away. "Wonderful. We woke Josie." Her eyes settled on Asher. "Get some rest. We'll talk in the morning."

Asher didn't put up a fight before starting up the stairs, but Dolores stood planted in front of her stepmother.

To her blurred mind, Charlotte looked like a Botticelli. Far more beautiful as a woman of fifty than she had been as a girl of twenty.

"Something you want to say, Dolores?"

There was. But she couldn't string it into a coherent sentence just now. A sense of something not right, something missing. Her father's note. *Trust no one.*

"Well?" Charlotte prodded.

Dolores rolled the words in her mouth. "You know something. About Dad. About why this is happening."

"Why would you think that?"

Dolores watched her for a moment. "Because you're afraid," she said finally.

Charlotte's lips pursed tight as a line of sutured skin.

"You're not angry Asher made a fool of himself tonight. You're not worried about what people will say. You're afraid," she repeated.

"You've been back less than twenty-four hours, Dolores, and already you're neck-deep in other people's business."

Dolores tasted a rare kind of anger in her ground teeth. "This is my business, Charlotte. He's my father."

It sounded wrong. Cheap.

He was everything, she could have said. *We were the whole world to each other before you ever met him.*

"Is that what you were doing at the primary school this morning? Minding your own business?"

There was no point in denying. "Dad went to the Winslows' last week."

Charlotte didn't look surprised Dolores had found out.

"Why?"

"You can ask him when we find him."

"What *aren't you* telling me?"

Charlotte kept quiet. Dolores remembered that anger had no effect on her—that it just burst against her like soap bubbles.

"If you knew what was good for you, Dolores, you'd stop poking around. Keep out of trouble."

She shook her head. "Why are you doing this? Why are you shutting me out?"

"You little fool." Charlotte laughed. "I'm not trying to hurt you. I'm trying to protect you."

Nineteen

A BITE FROM THE ABYSS

Dolores dreamt she was floating down a river bordered by walls the color of maple leaves. Goo sank beneath her fingernails when she clawed at them, and it smelled sweet, like ripe pumpkins.

"You gotta stop fighting it," a girl said.

Dolores rolled over. Cats howled on each side of the shore. Floating next to her, arms drifting through the water, was Kristen Horowitz.

Her heart-shaped face, so much like Dolores's at that age, her black hair melting into the murky river.

"Fighting what?" Dolores asked.

Kristen gave her a *cut the crap* look. It was so familiar to Dolores that she shuddered. How had she forgotten the way those almond eyes scrunched up whenever Kristen was about to tell off boys who thought they could explain shit to her?

"Come on. Acting dumb is only good for getting boys to do what you want."

The current grew stronger. Chunks of pumpkin tore out of the riverbank and dropped underwater like nuggets of gold.

A whirlpool of black hair swamped her field of vision and suddenly, Kristen was on her, her thighs squeezing Dolores's hips. She had no time to drag in a breath before they started to sink. A scream bellowed from her throat. They went down, and the world faded above.

Sand billowed as they hit the bottom. Dolores opened her mouth, and choked.

Kristen's face was so close, her nose brushed against Dolores's cheek. "I said, stop. Fighting. You wanna find your father? Then listen to me. You've got to stop fighting and *remember*, Dolores."

The word rippled through her.

"You think I haven't *tried*?" she said.

For a long time, not remembering had felt like the worst of it. Being left only with the aftermath, her life ripped out of its axis. Any memory would have been preferable to the black void, the absence of explanation, waking up to find an amputated stump where her seventeen-year-old self had been.

Above, Dolores could see the black gleam of a rising tide. The cats on each side of the shore stretched crooked backs toward the sky.

It's okay–Jacob's voice in her head. *They don't bite, Dolores. They just howl and howl.*

Kristen said, "Bull. Shit. You don't want to remember. Since you got here, you've done everything you could not to remember. You have to stop fighting it, Dolores. Remember the night you went to your father's office. Remember your promise."

Dolores's eyes prickled with water. "I don't–I can't."

"Damn it. It's like you're not even trying."

"I *am*!"

"You're not, or you would ask yourself the right questions. But you're afraid of the answers." Kristen's eyes softened. "*Why* would I leave my brother, Dolores? Like you left yours?"

Dolores woke with a gasp. The sky outside the window was pitch-black–the clock on her phone read three in the morning.

She pressed a hand to her chest and felt her racing heartbeat.

All that was left of her dream was the sweat that had soaked through the sheets, and a taste in her mouth like rotten pumpkins.

Twenty

THE EMPEROR OF CHEESE

Wyatt never got the whole cheese thing. Melted, sliced, smeared. After California released its "Happy Cows" campaign, Wisconsin had fired back. Billboards boasted round-bellied cows who stared benignly while you drove by–"Happy Cows *Really* Come From Wisconsin!" The girl in the ad had dark hair, dark eyes, and a smile that reeked of dental veneer. They printed it on milk cartons, too, and apparently, on go-cups, even if you'd ordered your coffee black.

Wyatt sighed. He doubted cows were happy either in Wisconsin or California. One in four suffered from mastitis, which infected their udders so bad the cheese made from their milk basically qualified as solid pus.

"You want a bite or what?"

Wyatt looked away as Paul tore a chunk out of his sandwich. It was seven thirty in the morning. They'd stopped at a bakery in town where Wyatt got a coffee and Paul got some monstrosity dripping with melted cheddar.

Waiting in line, they were treated to an earful of town gossip. The murder and the kidnapping got their share of the spotlight, but Dolores's return made up a surprising slice of it. Paul squeezed into the conversation expertly. It should have been difficult for him to blend in. Wearing a suit, dripping with so much confidence that if he stepped onto a podium and grabbed a mic, no one would stop him.

Yet the locals seemed flattered by his attention.

"Dolores Diaz, yes," Paul said, like he and the balding man with tortoiseshell glasses drained pints together every Friday. "She's quite a woman."

"Yeah, you could say that."

"Hell"–Paul smiled–"from what I gather the whole town knows her. What did she do? Sing in the choir? Perform in school plays?"

The man tilted his head. "All that, sure. But mostly–well, people my age, we watched her grow up. Her father was mayor for most of her childhood. Not that I'm complaining–I would have voted him in for fourteen more years. They still take care of the preparations for the party each Halloween, d'you know that?"

Paul managed to look like that was information he could use somehow.

"Anyway, you had Mayor Hawthorne, doing a better job than most clowns do in Washington, and this little girl following him around. He adored her–so, you know, everyone kinda adored her."

"Tragic he disappeared, right before she came back," Paul said.

The old man's face lengthened. "Yeah."

Paul prodded, "You wouldn't happen to know why she did that? Moving to L.A., and not coming back?"

The man shook his head. There was a stiffness to his voice now. "Can't expect girls like her to stay holed up in Little Horton. She's got a big career now."

"Did she have to get it in California?"

After that, the man didn't look available for conversation. Wyatt had no idea how Paul did it–how his social skills were always *on*. Wyatt's were like a suit he put on for interviews and eagerly stepped out of as soon as he could.

He drained his cup in under a minute, and waited until they walked past a recycling bin before he tossed it. Paul cleared his throat. "Sure you don't want a second dose? No offense, Big Guy, but you look–well, you look like insomnia and drug addiction fucked one sweet night and spat you out nine months later."

From the glimpse Wyatt had got of his reflection that morning, Paul wasn't wrong. Wyatt's face just didn't handle pressure well. He hadn't shaved since he'd got to Little Horton, and stubble gave his cheeks a gaunt look. He could blink away the tiredness that crept under his eyes, but he couldn't do anything about the shadows eating up his cheekbones.

"I was up late last night. Working."

"So was I," Paul said. "Did all my homework on our eight o'clock appointment, just to impress you. Your report was airtight. Ever considered writing novels? The boring kind?"

"Dazzle me with what you learned, then."

"Gregory Winslow. Seventy-nine, Caucasian, filthy rich, and–this actually wasn't in your report–last year *The Times* dubbed his business 'an Empire of Cheese.' He's the CEO of one of the four companies that hog three quarters of American dairy money." Paul grinned. "Do I get a gold star?"

He bit into his sandwich. The cheese that dribbled down Paul's baguette probably belonged to Gregory.

"So." Paul wiped drizzle off his forehead. "Winslow was a good friend of the Hawthornes, back when Alexander needed money for his campaign."

"Yes."

"And Winslow is the only person in town whose pockets are so full of cash, he could throw five hundred K out the window and his bank accounts would barely know the difference."

"Yes."

"You know you're annoying when you do that?"

Wyatt cocked an eyebrow.

"*That.* FBI Interviews 101. The less you talk, the more the person in front of you will feel compelled to. What's up with that, Big Guy? You getting back at me for pushing your buttons? Treating me to your interrogation tactics?"

"Maybe you just like to talk, Paul–and I like silence."

Paul chuckled. "So, aside from the likely coincidental fact that Hawthorne needed money for his campaign, and Winslow had enough to sneeze banknotes, why's he worth our time?"

Wyatt shoved his hands into his pockets. His fingers were freezing in the crisp morning air. "Alexander went to see Gregory Winslow, a week before he disappeared."

"Two locals hanging out?" Paul mimed surprise. "Call CNN."

"As Little Horton gossip goes, Winslow and Hawthorne stopped talking to each other the year Alexander was elected to the Senate."

"Two decades ago." Paul weighed this. "Supposing Winslow's responsible for those money inflows that spiked your corruption radar. Why would their friendship come to an end after the loan–bribe. Whatever you wanna call it."

"What, you're surprised buying a man's silence can put a strain on a relationship?"

"If someone gave me enough money to win the U.S. Senate, I'd butter up to him."

"I bet you would." Wyatt shook his head. "Guilt was eating at Hawthorne as he got older. You've read his letter."

"Then, if our cheese emperor *is* behind the bribe, he had a shitload of reasons to get rid of the old fellow." Paul exhaled. "There's only one thing I can't make sense of."

"What?"

Their shoes squished on the mantle of autumn leaves paving the sidewalk. "If you lived on an island of cash the size of Great Britain, why the fuck would you settle in Little H?"

Wyatt shrugged. "It's his hometown. Where else would he go?"

He pulled the car door open, and Paul tossed the rest of his sandwich into a trash can. A pang stabbed Wyatt's chest as he watched the half-eaten baguette drop down the heap of garbage.

"Well," Paul said, "let's go."

Wyatt's hand tightened around the car door handle. As a teenager, scavenging trash cans for food, if he had seen Paul drop such a gold nugget, he would have hugged the man. Now, he wanted to punch him in the face.

The Winslow house was more sober than the Hawthornes'. Ochre bricks, steep roofs, Victorian architecture. None of that baroque wink that dared you to have a look inside and see if you could believe your eyes.

A man came to meet them at the door. About six-one, slim, with hair cropped short and more pepper than salt. Lines streaked his forehead, clouding a green gaze that could have been handsome. Tired. The kind of face that should be printed on a poster and shown to anyone who aspired to become a politician.

"You must be the FBI."

"I'm Special Agent Wyatt Holt. This is my partner, Paul Turner."

The man greeted them with a handshake dry as a desert. "Good to meet you. I'm Jacob Winslow."

"Mr. Mayor," Paul said. He *had* done his homework.

Jacob's face darkened, as if embarrassed. "Please, come in."

The interior was conservative, nothing to gawk over, until they entered the living room. Wyatt did a double take.

A gutted bearskin rolled over the floor, fully furnished with a head, snout, and toothy mouth. Four massive canines forced open the dead creature's jaws. The bear's eyes stared vacantly ahead, and Wyatt found himself staring back.

"If you'll wait here," Jacob said. He halted before he reached the door. "Listen, my father doesn't go out in public anymore. Since I moved back in, he hasn't had many visitors. He's an ill man, is what I'm trying to say."

Wyatt willed his eyes to stay on Jacob. Naturally, all they wanted to do was go back to the bear, because who *the hell* would have a dead bear for a rug and was this shit even legal?

Jacob cleared his throat. "We value our privacy a lot. I'd appreciate it if you could take that into consideration."

"Of course," Paul said.

Jacob eyed them uncertainly.

Paul flashed his detestable grin. "Look, Mr. Mayor, we aren't looking to take part in town talk. Our priority is to find Alexander Hawthorne, bring him back to his family. You know the Hawthornes well, don't you?"

Jacob's mouth hardened. "I used to. When I was a boy, we spent a lot of time together. With the years, we just–stopped making time for it, I suppose."

Paul glanced at Wyatt, and Wyatt avoided his gaze. The mayor was not a good liar. But there was no need to make him realize that they knew that.

"Right, right," Paul said. "Things like that happen. It was just around the time Alexander's daughter left town, wasn't it? That you stopped making time to see each other."

From Paul's tone, it was clear his homework had included a detour on Jacob Winslow's love affairs.

"Dolores Diaz. Were you in contact with her those past two decades?" Paul said. "Before she came back to town yesterday."

Jacob stared at them for a moment. "It's true then. Dolores is back in town?"

Wyatt watched him closely.

That tilt in Jacob's voice. What was it? An old boyfriend, whose first love still felt raw when he brushed over the scar tissue where his broken heart had bled? As they say, the first cut is the deepest.

Or was it something else?

"I, uh–" Jacob blushed. "I'll get my father."

He went out the door, and his footsteps retreated down the corridor.

Paul turned back to Wyatt. "Holy hell." He crouched to examine the rug, head inches from the bear's maw. "I mean, I know people here like to hunt, but fuck me."

"You'd better look for a 'Made in China' tag," Wyatt said. He sat on the couch, hard as a slab of metal. The Winslows could get bear rugs, but they couldn't get comfortable sofas?

"So." Paul heaved himself back to a standing position. "There's residual feelings there, huh? Between him and Dolores. Crazy. After two decades, I couldn't remember the people I went out with if they bit me in the ass."

A groan escaped Wyatt. Was it so hard to keep one's ass out of a conversation?

"And what was that about his father? Doesn't want us to spread the word that he's–what? Dying? Senile?"

"We'll know soon enough."

"What does he think we are? Idiots?"

Wyatt refrained from observing that Paul had nearly put his head into a dead bear's mouth.

Embers crackled in the fireplace. The air smelled of cigars, conquest, and whiskey. Paul moved over to the mantelpiece and grabbed a framed photograph, holding it up for Wyatt to see. Three men smiled beside the body of a dead deer. Camo jackets bulged over their puffed chests. Wyatt recognized Jacob, in his late teens, standing next to a tall graying man. Gregory. At his right, a boy around Jacob's age, who looked so much like him he could only be his brother.

The door opened and Jacob wheeled his father into the room.

Somehow, Gregory Winslow was a more horrifying vision alive than Dr. Burke had been as a corpse. Seventy-nine? Wyatt would have placed him over ninety without blinking. His eyes, the same jade-green as his sons', looked like they had been pushed into his skin. Jowls hung almost down to his collar, and his cheeks were the special kind of gaunt that only spells one thing: cancer, and the kind that kills you slowly.

Paul put the picture back on the mantelpiece. "I was just admiring your family." He motioned to the third man in the picture. "Is this your other son, Mr. Winslow?"

"My eldest. Teddy."

The old man's voice sounded like grinding gravel.

"Well." Jacob remained standing behind Gregory. "You had questions for my father. Whatever you want to know—"

"You may leave us, Jacob."

Jacob's face crumbled. "Father, the doctor said you're not supposed to strain your voice."

"The doctor's dead. You wanna save my voice, you'll spare me the trouble of repeating myself."

Jacob met his father's eyes, gave the two agents a meek smile, and left.

Gregory wheeled closer to the fireplace, where he fed the fire tidbits of lint from his pockets. "So, you want to talk about Alexander."

Wyatt considered this. One man in town was missing, another one dead. Why did Gregory assume they had come about the former?

"We understand you used to be a close friend of the Hawthornes," Wyatt said.

Gregory hunched his shoulders a millimeter, in a way that faintly resembled a shrug. "We got along. Our children got along, and Little Horton is a small town. After a while, both Alexander and I were widowers. Misery loves company."

"When was the last time you talked to him?" Wyatt asked.

A smile twisted the edges of Gregory's lips. "Town talk will say we had a falling-out, decades ago. *The Feud,* they call it," he scoffed. "That's absurd. Alexander is still a good friend. But we were busy men, and after our children graduated, we simply couldn't find time for the old gatherings."

"Couldn't find the time," Paul repeated. "Yes, that's exactly what your son told us. I imagine, in a town like this—what is it, two thousand inhabitants? You were seeing far too many people to make room for your oldest friend."

The undertone in Paul's voice was hard to miss. Still, Gregory pretended to miss it.

"When was the last time you saw Alexander?" Wyatt repeated. The old man looked keen to avoid the question, and Wyatt wanted to see if he'd lie.

"He came to my house last week."

"What did you talk about?"

"Nothing in particular."

"Aside from that visit," Wyatt asked, "when was the last time you'd seen him?"

"I can't remember exactly."

Wyatt didn't lose patience. They could be at this all day. "Less than six months ago?"

"More."

"And he didn't give a reason for his visit?" Paul asked.

"Social calls are legal in this country, aren't they?"

Paul smiled amiably.

Gregory was like a snake playing dead at the bottom of a hole while Wyatt and Paul poked him with a stick. If they didn't draw blood, he wouldn't give them an inch.

"Did you ever lend money to the Hawthornes, Mr. Winslow?" Paul asked.

Wyatt focused wholly on Gregory's reaction. Movies liked to make you think a good agent just *knew* when someone was lying to them, but in truth, you could never tell for sure. A guy could swear on his life he had been at home watching TV, cool as a cucumber, when a security camera had caught him raping a woman in a hotel elevator.

"No."

Paul made an exaggerated frown. "You're aware they ran into trouble, during Alexander's first Senate campaign."

"Alexander is far too proud to tolerate a loan. It would have signed the end of our friendship."

Silence settled. The fact that the supposed Feud had followed the Hawthornes' money problems sat in the room like the proverbial elephant.

"Speaking of ending relationships," Paul said. He reached into his pocket for the note Alexander had written Dolores. "You mentioned Alexander's children. Surely, you remember his eldest."

"Dolores. Of course. Alexander worshipped her. It damn near broke his heart when she flew out to the other end of the country."

"Do you have any idea why she did that?" Paul asked.

A crooked grin fought its way to the man's lips. "That's what children do, Agent Turner. They leave."

"So," Paul prodded, "he didn't fight with his daughter, that you knew of? There was nothing–emotional?"

"Alexander wasn't the type."

"What about when you saw him last week? Did he seem unhinged?"

Gregory heaved out a sigh. "He seemed like a man visiting an old friend."

"So, you can't think of a reason why he would write this?" Paul handed the letter to Gregory.

For a few minutes, there was no sound but the sputter of the fire. Gregory's eyes skimmed over the letter, and he met Paul's gaze dead-on when he handed it back. "No reason whatsoever. Maybe the old fellow did go off his rocker. Last time I saw him, he was perfectly fine."

Wyatt and Paul stayed silent, until Gregory cleared his throat. "Don't misunderstand. Alexander wasn't the kind to jump at shadows, but he did serve two terms in Washington. The fish tank is so full of sharks, you learn to outswim the other fish or you become lunch. He made enemies, is what I'm saying."

"What kind of enemies?" Paul asked.

"Oh, you'd have to dig through his records. For every piece of legislation you give your vote to, you're making half the country angry."

Wyatt glanced at Paul, whose lips formed a taut line. They both knew a wild-goose chase when they saw one. Wyatt had just opened his mouth to speak when the pen Paul had been capping and uncapping dropped to the floor, bouncing back against the head of the bear. Paul bent to retrieve it, and Wyatt repressed a sigh.

He hoped Gregory didn't find the move as transparent as he did.

Half hoping to distract him, Wyatt said, "Michael Burke's murder suggests something a little closer to home. Did you know him well? Burke?"

"As well as a patient gets to know his doctor. That's to say, not much.

And before you ask, I can't think of anyone who'd want him dead. He just didn't stir anything profound enough for that."

"He's got quite a reputation in town," Paul countered. "What do they call him?" He paused, in mock reflection. "The Ripper of Little Horton?"

"Wild exaggerations. Drama queens love to rave, and Little Horton has its fair share of them. The doc could have been a little gentler when he gave shots, but that's nothing to kill someone over. Is that all you wanted to ask me, gentlemen?"

"Yes, thank you." Paul went to collect the recorder on the table.

Wyatt waited until they had left the house to say, "When you dropped your pen, earlier."

"Uh-huh."

"You better not have done the thing where you check to see if Gregory's shoes are clean."

"I sure did."

Wyatt shook his head. "You watch too much TV. The man probably gets up from his wheelchair every once in a while."

"Yeah, well. Until we get the lab results back, all we know about our killer is his shoe size."

"And it didn't occur to you to just ask Gregory that?"

"That's your problem, Big Guy. You make everything so straightforward."

Wyatt's eyes narrowed. The grin on Paul's face was larger than the interview warranted. "What? Don't tell me you found mud on his shoes. Blood?"

"No, nothing like that. But I don't think the old man is as confident as he looks. If you ask me, Hawthorne wasn't the only one who got a little paranoid."

Wyatt sighed. "Why don't you just spit it out?"

"Not much into foreplay, are you? The guy keeps a gun taped beneath his wheelchair."

Twenty-One

OPERATION CATS

Kate arrived at the station first thing in the morning. It felt good to wear her uniform again. The memory of the autopsy had loomed over every bite of breakfast, but she soldiered on. Today, her body wasn't allowed to quit. She might help her team catch a killer. For once in her life, she was–

"You're on Cats Duty," Chief Franklin said.

Kate took a step back, like he had sucker-punched her.

Chief Franklin was a bulky man who sported a nineteenth-century mustache. As town talk had it, the mustache had already existed, thin as a rat's tail, when Chief Franklin was in high school. Over the years, a man with less willpower would have succumbed to public opinion and shaved the damned thing off, but not the chief. Today, it drooped over his mouth, flamboyant, huge. It did more to prove Chief Franklin's courage than a Medal of Valor would have.

"What?" Kate said. "But I'm on the Hawthorne case."

When the chief asked her inside his office, she was sure he'd want to give her a pep talk, reinforce the importance of not letting the FBI treat them like rubes.

Calling the room an "office" was generous, but up till that moment, Kate had been in a generous mood.

"We won't get the preliminary results from the lab before noon," he said. "What are you gonna do until then, sit on your ass?"

"But Chief, there's so much more I could be doing. We have to interview Burke's patients–"

"Muller and Gunn are on that."

"Muller?"

"Yeah, didn't you hear? His stomach made a full recovery. He got back to work this morning."

Kate's hands balled into fists. Her brain fumed and she fed it images of peanuts being ground into dust, a whisk thrashing through a bowl of whipped cream. Most people who coped with anger issues would hit the gym when they felt that particular spark ignite. But when Kate was in such a mood, nothing but baking would take her mind out of it. It had all the sweetness of comfort, and all the violence of a run.

Calm down. Life was hard enough as the only female police officer in Little Horton. If she lashed out against her chief, it would get a lot harder. *So calm the fuck down.*

"Sir," she said, "no disrespect to Muller, but I was on the case before he even got that stomach bug."

"Are you saying Operation Cats isn't important?"

Kate swallowed back the retort *It's called Operation Cats,* which sounded like an answer of its own. "I'm saying, this is my case."

Under his mustache, it was difficult to tell if he was serious. "You'll get a call as soon as we have work for you. That'll be all."

Kate slammed her fist against the desk. Papers wafted into the air and the chief sat back. The air between them loaded with shock. Kate's gut turned liquid and she battled against the heat rushing up her collar.

The chief's office door was ajar, her coworkers clustering outside.

A torrent of apologies pressed against her teeth. If she apologized now, this whole department would brand her a hysterical woman.

"Sir, if you can give me one reason why you're not putting Muller on Cats Duty–one that doesn't have to do with the fact that he has a dick–I'll get out of your office and we can both do our jobs."

Chief Franklin eyed her a moment before he resumed, in the tone zookeepers use to handle wild animals. "Like I said, Butcher. We'll let you know if anything turns up. You're on Cats Duty till further notice."

OPERATION CATS, WHICH HARDLY got mentioned at the station without someone breaking into an Andrew Lloyd Webber song, was actually no picnic. They'd brought in an animal control officer when the craze was in its early days, hoping they could nip this in the bud. "A'course," he'd told them, "to pick the cats off the street doesn't get at the root of the problem. It's like putting a Band-Aid on a hemorrhage. What you want is to get your hands on the colony."

"Colony?" Kate had asked. She'd been on Cats Duty that day, too.

"That's what we call the strays who come together. Like a wolf pack."

"I thought cats were territorial."

"Common misconception. They like to stay in groups. Eat together, sleep together. You find the colony, then you can really sew up that wound, keep it from bleedin'."

Kate found the image a bit extreme. Though she would never let her colleagues know it, she didn't hate Operation Cats as much as she should have. The cats mewling in the backseat, the zoo smell that filled the station until someone drove them to the Humane Society.

For two hours, she patrolled around town, cat crates cramming the backseat of her police vehicle. Her wipers could hardly keep up with the rain.

Her phone vibrated and she picked up, handling the wheel one-handed. "Hello?"

"Hi," Leo said. "I thought you'd let this go to voicemail. Aren't you busy with your big case?"

Kate chewed on the inside of her cheek. It wasn't Leo's fault. He wasn't rubbing salt in her wound on purpose. "Change of plans. I'm on Cats Duty this morning."

She willed him not to say anything along the lines of *That sucks,* or *Wow, I'm sorry.* The more considerate he sounded, the more she'd want to rip his head off.

Bob Marley said something about just wanting to love someone and treat them right–but he didn't say how unsettling it was to be on the other end of that love, when you'd never been treated right in your life.

"Well, if it helps," Leo said, "when I walked home from Ruby's yesterday, I saw a bunch of cats around City Hall."

"That's weird," she said. "There's no place near City Hall where cats would want to hang out."

"Where *do* cats hang out?"

"Junkyards. Dumpsters. Anywhere they might get food."

"So, maybe it was a coincidence."

"I'll check it out. Not like I have better things to do. Thanks, Leo."

WITH ITS RED BRICKS and white pillars, City Hall would have looked haughty in its own right, even without the Latin proverb carved above the entrance: *"Unitas per servitiam."* Kids loved tagging over it after a few drinks, but Kate didn't get sent to patrol the area often. In her teens, she'd notoriously been part of the tagging brigade.

"No cats," she said under her breath.

With this weather, though, it was no wonder they weren't roaming about. She drove around the block, eyes low as she scanned the streets. She was about to make a wholly illegal U-turn when her foot hit the brake. A tabby darted out from under a car and disappeared behind City Hall.

Rain whipped against her face as she stepped out of the vehicle and bolted after the cat. The space behind City Hall divided into two streets: one led to the local school, the other to a small train station that was more of a quaint habit than a functional business. Aside from that, there was nothing but a stone wall that glistened with rain and slime. Kate looked around, but the cat had vanished, as cats do.

She was making a mental coin toss to decide which street to take, when her foot kicked into something. A metallic clatter sounded as a bowl spilled on the ground. She stepped back, and her jaw fell slack.

Someone had been feeding the cats.

Since the stray cats pandemic hit, the police had drilled the same message into the head of every Little Hortoner. *Don't feed the cats. No matter how hungry they look, it'll only make things worse. Call the police. Take them to the station. Don't. Feed. The cats.*

Kate crouched. The kibble was gorged with rain. Impossible to say how long it'd been here. A shadow on the wall caught her eye and she flicked on the flashlight on her phone, cupping her hand to shield it from the rain.

And–

"Well, shit," she said.

A hole in the wall.

The entry was large enough that Kate could squeeze her head and shoulder through. She raised the flashlight, and half a dozen pairs of eyes twinkled at her.

Bingo.

Kate crawled back out as unthreateningly as she could. She'd raised her phone only an instant, to turn off the flashlight, when it caught something shiny sparkling under the beam. It was a bag. Maybe nothing more than forgotten trash–that'd explain the cats. But the texture didn't ring right. Rich and thick, it glistened under her light like melted charcoals.

Not a trash bag, or even a backpack. She studied the shape more closely. A sailor bag. Raindrops beaded down its waterproof surface. This wasn't the sort of thing you'd leave lying around.

Something in Kate twitched.

A gut feeling, the kind of thing cops made fun of each other for. This whole scene felt wrong–it felt *staged.*

The bag. The cat food.

Someone had fed the cats so she would find this hole, *so she would find this bag.*

Her heart throbbed all the way to her throat.

As if the hole would snap shut and eat her hand, she proceeded millimeter by millimeter, propped on one elbow so she didn't have to lie belly-flat on the ground. She hauled the bag out of the hole and fell back on her ass as it pulled free. It was lighter than she expected.

The bag was tied shut. Should she open it now, under all that rain? If there was evidence in there, she might as well be spray-hosing a crime scene. But protocol said not to move evidence. Then what? Call for backup? What if there was nothing in the bag but dirty gym clothes? Hadn't she done enough damage to her reputation today?

Grunting, Kate clutched the bag to her chest and ran for her car. It gave a rustle when it dropped on the passenger seat. Anticipation balled inside her. She grazed the rope, tied into an elegant loop. *Too elegant.* Like a birthday gift–or a Halloween trick wrapped into a treat.

Kate tugged at the rope until the bag bloomed open, and jumped back so hard her head knocked against the car window. Her lips parted, but no air entered.

Her hands gripped the edge of her seat and she choked, "Oh God. *Oh God.*"

Twenty-Two

THE FIND

"What? Louder," Paul said into his phone. "I can't hear you, it's pouring out here."

Wyatt and Paul hurried from the parking lot to the police station, trying not to get soaked. Wyatt's breath hitched as he watched Paul's face for clues. A call from the bureau could only mean one thing. The lab had forwarded their preliminary report.

By the time they reached the lobby, Wyatt's hair was already dripping. Officers glanced up at them, laughter in their eyes.

"Would you like a towel, Agent Holt?" Chief Franklin asked.

Since his mustache might be covering a smirk, Wyatt thought it wiser to decline.

"Okay," Paul said. "Thanks." He hung up, and his eyes settled on Chief Franklin. "Is there somewhere we can talk?"

He took them to a break room that smelled of sweat and instant coffee. No windows. A plate of jam-filled crescent rolls on the counter.

"Why don't you have some coffee, Agent Holt," Chief Franklin offered. "You look like you could use it."

"It's true, man," Paul said, grabbing a croissant. "You look like shit."

Wyatt poured himself a cup. "They got the test results back?"

"Yeah. It's not good news."

"No fingerprints, I assume?"

"Only Burke's. For a killer who leaves neat bloody shoeprints, he's really mindful of where he puts his hands."

"Well, he probably wore gloves," Chief Franklin said. "Anyone who's watched *NCIS* would know to do that."

"The print at Burke's office matches the ones from Hawthorne's study," Paul added. "One set, at least. They identified three sets of shoeprints at the first crime scene. One of them was Hawthorne's."

"So, we're looking at two killers?" Wyatt shook his head. "I don't buy it. Burke was clearly a one-man job. The third set of prints could belong to anyone. Friends, family."

"So," Chief Franklin cut in, "we have no DNA, no fingerprints–nothing to go on but the guy's height and his shoe size?"

Paul gobbled the rest of his crescent roll. "Don't forget his gun."

Wyatt looked up. "What about the gun?"

"Like Dr. Diaz said, a fifty-caliber. They're thinking a Smith & Wesson Model 500."

"A lot of people here have guns," Chief Franklin said. "For hunting, shooting cans in the yard."

Paul cocked an eyebrow. "A fifty-caliber is a bit much to shoot cans."

"You can check out the gun shop on 143 West Avenue." Chief Franklin grabbed his police radio. "I'll tell Gunn and Muller to meet you there."

The radio exploded into static before the chief could carry it to his mouth. Wyatt couldn't make out the words, only a frantic female voice.

Chief Franklin groaned. "Butcher, I don't want to hear it–" But he cupped his hand around the radio, cradling it to his ear. "Can you repeat? I'm not getting this right."

The features on his face crumpled and for one magical moment, his mustache lifted from his upper lip. "You found *what*?"

Twenty-Three

DESPERATE MEASURES

Dolores woke to what felt like ten thousand bells exploding against her temples. The sun blazed through her bedroom window, sharpening into an arrow that stabbed through her left eye. One thing she hadn't missed about Little Horton? Never being able to sleep in because the church bellowed its morning song every day at eight.

She went down the stairs and found her siblings in the living room.

Her heart plummeted all the way to her stomach.

A dead body lay on the coffee table, atop a picnic blanket. Blood had pooled on the cloth and dripped down the paper towels that littered the ground.

Charlotte presided over the scene behind an armchair, a perfect, pretty despot. Asher knelt over the body, smearing blood down his face.

A pair of scissors winked at the chandelier as Josie raised it above the dead man.

"No!" Dolores cried.

Too late. Her sister's hand came down in a perfect arc and she plunged the scissors into the man's chest.

Dolores blinked. Clouds of cotton poured out as her sister dragged the blades down to his waist. The fabric tore open in a loud *riiiip*. Josie met her eyes over the mannequin–the body *was* a mannequin.

"Why don't you gimme a hand, Sis? You're the autopsy expert."

Dolores waited for the adrenaline shooting through her veins to wear itself out.

Eyes fixed on the ground, Asher looked as bad as she felt. A gurgling sound rose from his stomach as he poured his hand into a dish of udon noodles, soaked in beet juice, and shoved them into the dummy's stomach.

Jeremy Krone. Dolores remembered now. During the Halloween Tour, his body would float over a flock of terrified tourists, fake guts dripping from his ripped-open chest.

"Good. You're awake. I wanted us to have a *family* chat before taking Josie to school." Charlotte spoke the word magnanimously, including Dolores. "I understand this is a difficult time for all of you. But until the FBI finds your father, we can't afford to fall apart. He might not be mayor anymore, but the town looks up to us. To flaunt your pain would be an act of surrender."

Asher stared down at the dish of udon noodles.

"So, that's the priority then," Josie snorted. "*Looking* under control."

Charlotte's tone sharpened. "The priority is for us to stick together. When someone came after your father, they came after us." Her hands gripped the headrest of the chair. "An act of war against him is an act of war against this entire family."

"'An act of war'?"

"Shut up, Josephine."

The room dropped into silence. From the slack in Josie's jaw, it was clear she was unused to such language.

Dolores was surprised, too.

All the years she had known Charlotte, the one thing that could be relied upon was that she would keep her temper in times of crisis.

Charlotte closed her eyes. "I don't know what I need to do to make you understand how serious this is."

"Mom," Asher started, timidly. Wanting to come to Josie's rescue, no doubt, yet not daring to draw attention to himself after what he'd pulled last night. "Look, we're all worried. But the fact that Dad's missing–it doesn't mean we're all under attack."

Charlotte held eye contact. "Until things go back to normal, we're going to act like we are." She released a breath. "I think it's best we stay in pairs at all times. Stick to public places, if we have to go out. Of course, it'd be better if we didn't leave the house after dinnertime."

A lump of dough went down Dolores's stomach. So, after not seeing her family for eighteen years, she was supposed to see them every second of the day?

"I know it's not comfortable," Charlotte went on. "But comfort is a luxury we can't afford right now." She glanced at her watch, blond hair bobbing atop her shoulders as she looked up. "Go wash your hands, Josie. I'll drive you to school."

Josie hoisted herself to her feet, hands held up so the beet juice wouldn't drip all over the furniture.

Dolores shuddered. A flash of herself, at seventeen, holding her wrists like this–hands dripping with blood.

She heard herself say, "How about I drive you, Josie?"

Charlotte's eyes shot contempt, like Dolores had taken an unforgivable liberty. And hadn't she? For all Josie's life, she'd been a signature on a postcard. What gave her the right to spend time with her now?

Josie looked astonishingly malice-free as she said, "I'd love that."

"Are you even sober enough to drive?" Josie asked.

Dolores strapped her seat belt. Sober, yes, but a mug of coffee would have been a good idea.

The car purred into gear and they took off. Dolores stole glances at her sister. Blond hair tied into a ponytail, blue eyes emphasized by eyeliner. She was very skinny, which didn't surprise Dolores. Charlotte valued thinness in women.

It took a few minutes before it hit her that she was driving to her old school from memory.

"You don't wear your wedding ring," Josie said.

Dolores wrapped her left hand tighter around the wheel. "No."

"What's your husband like?"

She hesitated. There was nothing to build upon with her sister. No shared memories–only a crater, whose frayed edges sent ripples of pain through her system. *We might as well have honesty.*

"We're getting divorced," she said.

A beat of silence. "Maybe we can throw you a divorce party," Josie offered, "since we didn't come to your wedding. Did you tell Mom?"

"No."

"If you want, I won't tell her either. Do you really cut dead bodies open for a living?"

"Among other things. What else do you want to know?"

She tried not to shift under Josie's eyes, a tiny lamp crisscrossing over her minutely.

"Why did you never come and visit?"

Dolores pictured the headache, beating at her temple. *Sphenoid, ethmoid, orbital.*

"You said I could ask."

"I know." Dolores waited, scrounging for words that would make sense of the situation.

But how could she explain?

Why hadn't she come back, in eighteen years? Why hadn't she ever picked up the phone and talked to her brother and sister?

Because if she talked to them, the possibility of talking to her father would have swelled inside her, unbearable.

Because I loved him too much. Because his love wasn't enough.

Because she couldn't think of Little Horton without resurrecting the old Dolores Hawthorne and murdering her in one same breath.

"I'm sorry, Josie," she said. "I don't have a good answer."

"It can't be worse than Mom and Dad's version."

"What did they tell you?"

Josie smiled. "Nothing. They never talked about you. I was five by the time I learned you existed."

A rolling train all made of frost smashed into her sternum. Dolores saw herself, reacting to this crisp piece of news. *I feel nothing,* she thought, at the same time warmth prickled her eyelids.

She bit down on her bottom lip, hard, to keep the tears from falling.

"I know, right?" Josie said. "I think they did it for my sake. How could I miss you if you didn't exist? But all the avoiding and lying only made you *bigger.* At first, I thought you were an imaginary friend Asher used to have. When I learned the truth, everything clicked. Your absence was there, in every sentence Dad spoke. It's like–like corn."

A car honked behind Dolores. When had that light turned green?

"Corn?"

"I learned about that on YouTube. Corn is like, the Napoleon of crops. Took over the country. We never *think* we're eating corn, but it's in all our food. Sodas, bread, meat. You were like that for me. Suddenly, I had a sister, and you were scattered in all the air I breathed."

Silence settled in, broken only by the rain drumming against the windshield. Dolores couldn't speak.

Josie chuckled. "Funny, right? I bet you don't think about me in a year as much as I think of you in a day."

Dolores's hands clenched so tight around the wheel, she could make out the ivory bones bulging through her skin. "Josie–" She stopped.

How cheap would an apology sound to this fifteen-year-old stranger, this fifteen-year-old sister, to whom she had been nothing but a dark cloud that loomed over their father's gloomiest hours?

"I'm sorry," she said.

Wished she could give her something more substantial. Josie let out a sigh. "Yeah."

Dolores parked opposite the school. There was a sense of timelessness to the gates. Same navy-blue paint, same cluster of kids and chaos of ambient chatter.

She had been there so many times with Jacob, she half expected his shape would emerge. His gelled black hair, his sunshiny smile. The place between his neck and shoulder made for her face.

Charlotte's voice in her head. *You can't trust That Boy, Dolores. He's playing you. He's been playing you for years.*

Instead of Jacob, the memory of a little boy came back to her. A boy in a yellow raincoat, with eyes like black diamonds, slouching against the school gates. There one moment and gone the next.

Josie grabbed her backpack and opened the door.

"Josie," Dolores called.

Maybe it was the thought of Jacob, quickening her heart rate. Her mouth ran dry, her brain out of things to say. It didn't matter. Nothing could be worse than letting her sister leave like this.

She ran through the possibilities–

I really am. Sorry.

I wish things had been different.

All falling short of what she owed this teenage girl she should have learned to know inside and out. Yet she could not name Josie's favorite color or a single thing she liked.

Finally, she asked, "Is there anything I can do?"

Josie didn't shake the question with easy disdain. She considered her for a long time. "No. It's enough that when you go back to Los Angeles, you know I exist, too."

Twenty-Four

THE OTHER WINSLOW

"Holy hell. Dolores?"

Dolores's hands tightened around her go-cup. Of course it had only been a matter of time before she ran into someone she knew. She should have driven straight home after dropping Josie off, but the idea of listening to any more of Charlotte's martial nonsense rammed a migraine into her head. What harm could it do to grab one cup of coffee?

So she'd stopped at Rise and Shine, a coffee shop where the tile floor conjured images of checkerboards, and the smell of margarine belied the card plastered to the display case: "REAL butter."

Her stomach sank as she turned around.

Jacob.

Dolores opened her mouth on a solid scream of terror.

His hair was thinning but still dark, and his green eyes were unblemished by the years.

It was what she had dreaded since she'd boarded that plane to Milwaukee. For the past twenty-four hours, she had jumped at shadows, imagined Jacob in the face of every man who was roughly the right age. Part of her had known this would happen.

That she would not be lucky enough to leave town before she ran into the man who had been her best friend for the first eighteen years of her life, and who had haunted the eighteen years that followed.

Then a grin ate up the bottom half of his face.

Dolores's mother used to say men came in a hundred different shapes, but they only had two different kinds of smiles. Dog smiles, and fox smiles.

Jacob's had been like a golden retriever's. Unqualified joy. A dog smile, if there ever was one.

And sure as the earth was round, the one that stared Dolores in the face right now was a fox smile.

The man before her was Jacob's older brother.

"Teddy," she said.

"Well I'll be damned." He looked her up and down, then down and up. Like she had exploded into a million pixels and he was trying to glue her back together.

He wrapped her into such a tight hug she blushed, the smell of sandalwood and almonds filling her nostrils. Teddy believed in dressing down, standing out through accessories. If he wore the right cologne, shoes, and rings, he swore he could pull off a job interview in a plain shirt and jeans. Of course, it couldn't hurt that he was so full of cash, he probably bled money.

Dolores closed her eyes. Ten minutes ago, she couldn't have named one memory she had of Teddy. Now, with her lungs full of his smell, she saw him sitting at the dinner table, regaling Asher with magic tricks.

Before Dolores had time to say a word, Teddy sat her down at a table where a slice of blueberry pie sat half-eaten. "I can't believe this," he said, "you. You look fantastic! Not that you didn't always." He hailed a waitress. "Minnie! Get us another slice of pie. My treat. Sweet lord, if I had to make a list of the people I never expected to see again in this sorry excuse for a town."

A plate slammed in front of Dolores, oozing with pie filling that looked objectively like clotted blood. The napkins were printed with spidery characters. She caught a few words–"Circus"; "Knife"; "1902." So customers could read about the macabre Halloween incidents baked into Little Horton folklore as they gobbled their scrambled eggs.

God, Dolores thought, *I hate this place.*

"Well, you could knock me down with a feather. How long are you back in town? Have you seen Jacob yet?"

Dolores opened her mouth. She'd forgotten how many words Teddy could cram into twenty seconds. "No. I mean–I just got here."

"So did I. Had to travel up north to meet a supplier so I thought, what the hell. Let's pay the family a visit."

The thought of explaining what she was doing in Little Horton turned Dolores's stomach. Fortunately, Teddy didn't give her the chance.

"You know what? We should have dinner together. The Hawthornes and the Winslows, like the good old days." He laughed. "Well, now that we're grown-ups I suppose we can lose the chaperones."

Dolores pictured it despite herself. The old Hawthorne-Winslow gatherings, Teddy sweeping them all into his tango of words, turning every anecdote into stand-up comedy. Jacob, laughing without restraint. She remembered wondering if it cost him—not to be the funny, handsome brother, the one who made everything look easy. It never looked like it did.

But then, he always knew how to fool me.

Teddy studied her more closely, maybe sensing her discomfort. "You heard Jacob is—well, married? I didn't want to be the one to tell you." He leaned into the table, so close she could smell blueberry pie on his breath. "Between you and me, I just don't think he and the wife really *click*. I mean, there's nothing wrong with Annette. We're not exactly friends, and I don't like to speak ill of my brother's wife—"

"I'm married too," she blurted out. Technically, it wasn't a lie, and she had to stop him from talking about Jacob, somehow.

Teddy's eyes glanced at her left hand, ring-less. Dolores resisted the urge to hide it in her lap.

"Oh. I guess you would be. A knockout like you. It's kind of a shame, though. I always rooted for you guys, even after you broke up after that Halloween party."

Dolores's breath hitched. The diner had turned into a sauna. It was too much. Teddy. *Jacob.* An ache speared through her abdomen, and her hand went to the scar before she could think.

Flashes of her last interaction with Jacob bubbled to the surface.

"Help me understand, Dolores." The genuine agony in his voice, like she had pressed a hot iron to his chest.

After Halloween, 2003—her last Halloween in Little Horton—Dolores had been homeschooled and barely ventured outside. Jacob had showed up at her house every day for weeks, but Charlotte had stood guard better than a bloodhound.

When that didn't work, he started calling the house. But again, Charlotte blocked him from getting through to her. Dolores would know it was Jacob on the phone from the look in her stepmother's eyes, before she hashed out the razor-sharp reply, "Don't call here again."

That day, though, Dolores had been the only one home. She wouldn't have picked up, but the call came from an unknown number. She pictured Jacob at the pay phone outside the gas station, where the cashier could watch him talking to her through the window.

"I just want to know what I did wrong," he said. There were tears in his voice. "You're my best friend, Dolores. I can't lose you. Please, I just want to understand–"

That was as far as he got before Dolores had the good sense to hang up the phone.

"You okay, Doll?"

Dolores looked down at her hands, latched around the edge of the table. "I'm sorry, Teddy. Will you excuse me a minute?"

She squeezed out of the booth and headed for the restroom. Sweat pasted her hair to her forehead as she rushed for the sink. The water ran so cold that she gasped at the first splash of water. But it didn't stop her from cupping her palms under the faucet and splashing herself again, and again.

The scar on her stomach seethed through her clothes. Rationally, Dolores knew it didn't make sense. *It's just in my head.* Like phantom pain where a severed limb should be. It wasn't real. It couldn't be. Still, she snaked a hand beneath her dress and touched the scar to make sure it wasn't bleeding.

Someone knocked at the door. "Dolores?" Teddy called. "Sorry to bother you, but you left your phone on the table. I didn't want to pick up, but it kept ringing–"

Dolores came out of the bathroom. Teddy watched her dubiously as he handed her the phone. "They said they were FBI agents, and they wanted to talk to you. It sounded like an emergency."

THE MORGUE'S PARKING LOT was packed. Wyatt hadn't told her what this was about, but given the location, he clearly hadn't asked Dolores here for a game of tic-tac-toe.

They must have found a body. But whose?

Her stomach clenched as she parked the car alongside a police cruiser.

My father's?

What if this was about identifying a body? What if–

No, she reasoned. Serial killers tended to use the same MO. If her father was dead, why wouldn't the killer have left his body in the office, like Dr. Burke's?

She pressed her knees together, so hard the skin would look bruised when she removed her thermal tights.

He isn't dead, he can't be dead.

Gone. Taken. Spirited away.

Like the beginning of a fairy tale, where the patriarch fades from the pages because with him there, there'd be no danger–no adventure. But he always returns at the end, to welcome his heirs back into his realm.

She waited until she was sure she would not hyperventilate before she got out of the car.

Dolores stepped inside the mortuary, where three people stood waiting for her. Paul Turner offered a smile of greeting. Kate looked like she'd seen a ghost, her red hair frizzy from the rain and wind.

Wyatt fixed serious eyes on her. "Miss Diaz"–he sounded cool–"I apologize for calling you on such short notice."

Paul cut in, "What my partner is trying to say is, we really appreciate your coming here."

Dolores studied him for a moment. "I hope you don't take this the wrong way, but I don't usually perform autopsies with an audience this size. I wasn't aware the last one would set a precedent." She kept her tone even, so he wouldn't mistake this for lack of confidence. To cut a dead body open was not a circus show.

"As a matter of fact, we didn't ask you here for an autopsy."

Paul stepped aside, and her eyes settled on the metal slab around which everyone had gathered.

A black bag sat on the table, splayed open on a cluster of human bones. The years had licked them clean–Dolores had never seen bones so perfectly white. "This was inside the bag." Paul produced a photograph, tucked between two sheets of plastic. It was faded but legible.

Something ticked inside Dolores—like the lyrics of a lullaby, forgotten until the tune starts and the words swim back to the surface.

A Julia Roberts smile. Eyes that sparkled with youth, a face framed by a tangle of chestnut curls.

"You recognize that girl?"

Dolores shook her head but heard herself say, "Yes."

A chill bristled the room. Paul tilted his head and stared at her, unabashedly. Though more discreet, she could feel Wyatt's eyes on her as well.

She blinked, and in the brief lapse of darkness, she was sinking down a murky river, bordered by pumpkin flesh. Phantom words tickled the hairs on the nape of her neck.

Remember, Dolores.

Kate cleared her throat. "That's Kristen Horowitz. We went to high school together. She went missing almost twenty years ago."

2003

October 29

Twenty-Five

THE FATHER YOU REMEMBER

"You're awful quiet," Jacob said.

Dolores stared at the road, a lump the size of Texas in her throat. Everywhere she looked, she saw Kristen's brother, his unwashed hair, his eyes boring into hers.

Ask your father. Tell him to bring her back.

What was that supposed to mean?

Nothing, she told herself. Of course it meant nothing. Twelve-year-olds made things up all the time, didn't they?

Jacob's eyes darted from the road to check on her. "That kid freak you out or something?"

"I don't know. Maybe."

He reached for her leg and the car veered slightly. He wasn't very good at driving one-handed. "Father won't be back from work for a few hours. Wanna stop by my place? We can have a beer before I take you home."

Dolores checked Jacob's watch, pressed against the wheel. Half past three. Charlotte had her book club at four thirty, and she would want Dolores home to look after Asher.

"Just one," she said.

When they got to the house, he went to slide his key into the lock and frowned.

"What?"

"It's unlocked."

"I thought your dad was at work."

"Me too."

Footsteps sounded down the staircase, and Teddy stepped into the hall, in jeans and a shirt the color of cranberries. Dolores couldn't get used to his new haircut. His dark mane cropped short, all the rebel-youth vibes smoothed out of him.

"What are you doing here?" Jacob asked.

"Is that a way to greet your big brother?"

Teddy drew Jacob into a hug. He was a hugger: friends, family, boys as well as girls. He hugged Dolores, too, crunching the air from her lungs.

"I was gonna surprise you tonight at dinner, but I take it you lovebirds want to sneak a little time alone before that. You want me to, like, drive around the block so you can screw around?"

Dolores slammed him in the shoulder with her backpack.

"We were just going to get a beer," Jacob said.

"Sure."

The three of them settled in the kitchen. Jacob didn't like to hang out in the living room–Dolores wouldn't either if hers had a dead bear on the floor.

Teddy pulled three beers out of the fridge and popped them open. Dolores felt her body relax as she took the first sip, ice-cool, bitter bliss.

"Wait a second." Teddy narrowed his eyes. "You kids legal?"

"Think I'll take flak from a guy who drank before he was old enough to drive?"

Teddy sighed. "I liked you better before you had a girlfriend, Jake. What happened to the four-eyed kid who respected his elders?"

"He got happy."

Teddy pointed at Dolores. "You're a terrible influence."

Jacob licked beer foam off his lip. "So, what are you doing in town?"

"Father asked me. A meeting with retailers, boring boring boring."

"You're staying in town for Halloween, right?"

"No can do."

"Oh, come on," Jacob said. "I don't like to flatter you, but the guys all ask after you."

"I'm sure they do. Who doesn't like their friend's cooler older brother? Honestly, I wish I could, but Dad's working me to the bone." He turned to Dolores. "You're quiet."

Dolores buried her face behind her beer.

"Junior creeped her out," Jacob explained.

"Which Junior?"

"Junior Horowitz," Jacob said.

Teddy shrugged, like the name didn't ring a bell.

"Come on, you know the Horowitzes," Dolores said. "Kristen worked at City Hall with me this summer."

"Oh, Kristen's brother. I went out with a few of his babysitters. What about him?"

Dolores shook her head. "I don't know. I just wish Kris would come back, or at least call her brother. It's downright cruel, what she's doing to him."

"When a teenage girl runs off," Teddy said, "it's usually not to phone home every weekend."

"Not every weekend. But come on. Her parents reported her missing."

"They both know she left to get some breathing space," Jacob said. "I hear Junior was the one who asked them to go to the police."

"Yeah, well, it just goes to show how hard he's taking this. I can't believe Kris would just take off without–" Dolores stopped mid-sentence and sat back in her chair, looking at Jacob. "Hey, how come *you* know his name, anyway?"

Jacob shrugged. "Junior? I don't think that's his actual name."

"That's not what I meant."

Jacob stared at his beer.

A glint snaked into Teddy's eyes. He smiled his fox smile. "Well, Jacob was–shall we say, 'cozy,' with Kristen a while back. Don't look surprised, Doll. You girls kinda look alike, don't you? Dark eyes, dark hair. A man's gotta have a type."

Dolores stared at Jacob, waiting for confirmation. It'd be just like Teddy to bullshit her. But the look on Jacob's face could mean only one thing.

"For real?" she laughed.

"It lasted like ten seconds."

Teddy snickered. "Don't sell yourself short, man."

"I mean"–Jacob rolled his eyes–"it wasn't serious."

It occurred to Dolores that this was the sort of thing girls got jealous over. She and Jacob had been friends for so many years, though, the girlfriend reflexes were long in coming. It'd be different if he were seeing Kristen *now*. But she'd been on dates, too, which she'd told Jacob about while splayed on the grass at the square, tossing M&M's into her mouth.

"You're a jerk," she said.

Jacob blushed. "What?"

"Please, get into an argument." Teddy cracked open a pack of cookies. "I haven't had my dose of lovey drama this week."

Dolores shot him a *you started this* look.

Jacob tried to follow. "Because I dated Kris, I'm a jerk?"

"Because you didn't tell me. I thought you told me everything."

"Trust me," Teddy winked, "he doesn't."

"I wasn't gonna tell you about girls, Dolores."

"I told you about boys."

"Because you're a girl," he said.

Dolores shook her head. "I can't believe Kris never mentioned it."

She had spent a big chunk of the summer pining after Jacob to Kristen, and Kristen had never thought to bring up their history?

"That's just–weird. Why wouldn't she let me know?"

Teddy shrugged. "Maybe she thought you'd draw your claws out."

Dolores rolled her lips together dubiously. "We went to the same school for three years. If I had claws, Kris would have seen them."

Teddy went back to the fridge and held out another three beers. "One more?"

Dolores eyed the cans, dewy with cold water. "No. I really have to go."

She stood to kiss Jacob, and Teddy drew her into another hug. "See you at dinner," he said.

The thought of the family meal didn't usually make Dolores nervous. But the minute she pictured her father, she saw Junior again, waiting for Kristen outside Horton High.

I want her to come home.

THE DINNER TABLE WAS big enough to be split into two areas: the grown-up side and the kid side. It felt mildly ridiculous for Asher and Teddy, five and twenty-one, to be sitting in the same corner. Teddy once pointed out it made as much sense as sitting Alexander with Charlotte, but Dolores had sneaked him a look so icy, he had not dared speak to her for a full hour.

Dolores pushed tidbits of saltine crackers onto the side of her plate. Charlotte always cooked traditional Southern meals when the Winslows came over. Admittedly, she wouldn't have had an appetite even if they'd been having something more appetizing than oyster casserole. What Junior had said earlier still looped about in her mind.

Thank God for Teddy, who talked more than Dolores could have if she'd multiplied herself by three. "So get this, I've tried it four times now. Beats all my old pickup lines. You drop next to a girl in a bar and go, 'Sorry, you look like a smart gal, would you mind clearing something up for me?' Sure–she usually says sure." He looked at Asher, and Dolores clenched her fork. Her brother was a bit young to be educated in the fine art of picking up girls. "And you say, 'I'll give you a hundred dollars if you can tell me what a supply chain coordinator's job is.' She laughs. Effect of surprise. Of course, she wants to know why *you* want to know. You say, 'Simple enough. It's my job. I've been doing it for six months now–high time I find out what it consists of, ain't it?'"

Asher roared with laughter and spluttered all over the table. He was a good audience.

Teddy shoveled a forkful of grayish glob into his mouth. "Can't believe I wasted my breath asking if that seat was taken for so many years."

Dolores sighed. "Can I burst your bubble?"

"I've been told I can't say no to a pretty girl."

"You don't need to work that hard, Teddy. Pickup lines are overrated. You can just say 'Hi.'"

"Spoken like a true buzzkill."

Jacob winked at Asher. "Don't listen to Teddy, Ash-Man. Jobs are *not* only good for hitting on girls."

Dolores caught movement in her peripheral vision, as Gregory scooped the last of the casserole off his plate. "Dolores," he said, "Alexander was telling me how well you did at the science fair last year."

Dolores shifted on her chair. It was always a challenge to convince her body that Gregory Winslow was talking to her, not trying to bark her out of existence.

"Are you still thinking of applying to med school after college?"

She looked at her plate. "I haven't decided yet."

Jacob frowned. "Are you kidding? You keep acing your biology tests. I'm not sure the teacher bothers to correct them anymore."

Now, she really wished she'd told him about all the furniture that had been sold over the summer. But there were things even a best friend couldn't know.

She shrugged. Jacob got the message and filled his mouth with casserole.

Gregory let out a sigh. "I wish you'd take an interest in science, my boy. It does no good to anyone, filling your head with *books*." Spoken with the same disdain he saved for the word "immigrants." Dolores bit her tongue. Her eyes glided to her father, but she could make out only the contour of his face. He was in his own world. A whole dinner was too much for him not to get lost thinking about music, or politics, or what was for dessert.

Jacob licked his lips, trying to come up with an answer. Fortunately, he didn't have to provide it, because Asher cried out, "Mom," with a finger pointed at Dolores. "Dee-Dee didn't finish her plate."

Dolores glared at her brother. He was at that age when he didn't question ratting on her.

Charlotte glanced down. "You hardly ate anything. You're not on one of those fad diets, are you? These things are dangerous, Dolores. A girl died last summer in England, and when they examined her, they found she had eaten nothing but pineapple."

"What's a fad diet?" Asher asked.

"I'm not on any diet," Dolores said.

Charlotte gazed at Alexander expectantly, and he smiled. He always looked like this when Charlotte turned to him for backup–like he couldn't understand what there was to back up in the first place. "I've been thinking of going on a diet myself," he said. "Pineapples are a recipe for failure, but scientists are making quite a case for grapefruits."

Charlotte exhaled, and Dolores wiped her mouth with a napkin to stifle a laugh.

She waited until Charlotte had gone to bed before she knocked at the door of her father's study.

"Come in."

At sixty-one, Alexander Hawthorne couldn't look a day younger than his age. He was one of those people you imagined had always looked old. Spectrally tall, with no hair left to speak of, gaunt cheeks but enough pink in them that he didn't scare children in the street. His sprightliness took most people by surprise–he still beat Asher when he raced him at the square.

Dolores closed the door behind her and sat atop a large coffer, where her father stored books of every kind. A radio played in the background, Louis Armstrong refusing to dance with Ella Fitzgerald.

"Dolores," he said, round glasses perched on his nose as he looked up. "Your timing is brilliant. I was hoping we could talk. Cookie?"

He opened the apple-shaped box on his desk, brimming with cookies–chocolate chip, gingerbread, oatmeal. As a kid, she'd planned and plotted ways to break into her dad's office, all so she could raid that box. Never mind that they kept the same cookies in the kitchen cupboards. They just didn't taste as good as they did coming from the apple box.

Dolores grabbed one even though she wasn't hungry for it.

"Now," Alexander said, "why would you evade Gregory's question like that about med school?"

"What do you mean?"

His gaze sharpened. Despite his apparent aloofness, he saw more than he let on. "Darling, when girls your age played with Barbie dolls, you cut open your stuffed animals to see what they were made of."

Dolores bit her lower lip, but his eyes didn't relent. "Med school is expensive," she said.

Alexander pointed at the wooden coffer she sat on. "So is this. Seventeenth-century oak. It belongs in a museum."

Dolores glided off the coffer and sat on the floor. "You don't have to protect me from the truth or anything. I'm not a kid. I know we have money problems."

Alexander exhaled, plucked a pecan sandie from the apple box. "Cards on the table?"

"Yeah, sure."

"We *had* problems. Especially with the campaign going on. Trust me, med school is a drop in the ocean compared to running for the Senate."

He shoved the cookie in his mouth and chewed thoughtfully. "It's all better now, though," he said, after licking his teeth clean. "Scout's honor."

Dolores stared, not knowing what to think. When a family like theirs ran into debt, it took more than selling a couple of paintings to haul it back to the surface.

"We're good?"

"We're good. All you need to worry about is schoolwork and reading tons of books."

Dolores opened her mouth, then closed it.

Alexander plucked a second cookie from the box. "Don't tell Charlotte, okay? She watches my plate more closely than yours."

"Right. It's actually not money I wanted to talk about."

"I'm all ears."

Dolores looked at her hands, and ran an invisible finger along the length of each bone. "Did the police ever talk to you about Kristen Horowitz?"

Two seconds of silence. When Dolores looked up, her father was perfectly composed. "Yes, of course. Smart girl. Worth ten times those parents of hers, if you ask me." His right cheek hollowed as he sucked it in. It made him look comically wraithlike. "If I weren't the mayor, I'd give them a piece of my mind."

She weighed this a while. "Doesn't being the mayor make it even more your job?"

"You would think so." He sighed. "Politics is complicated. As long as there's no evidence of abuse, I can't just go about berating my neighbors. Appearances."

She licked her lips. "Appearances. It's just, Kristen's brother said something weird this afternoon."

Alexander's brows didn't knot like a caricature. But somehow, he seemed to frown with his eyes. "I didn't realize you talked with that boy."

"He was waiting for his sister at school."

"I see. Well, what did he say–Junior, isn't it?"

Dolores's gut twisted. For no reason she could explain, she felt like he knew damn well what to call the kid.

"He wanted my help, to find Kristen."

He chuckled. It sounded almost real. "Are you Inspector Gadget now?"

She held his gaze even as the urge to blink burned her eyes. "He said to ask you to find her, Dad. That you'd know where she was."

A silence thick as maple syrup dropped between them. Dolores's pulse quickened.

Alexander locked his fingers together above the desk. "What a strange thing for a young boy to say. I imagine he's very disturbed. Maybe he saw me on television and imagined I'm this all-knowing person. Or found me spooky. All those ad campaigns, they do me a world of good, but there's a downside to becoming a public figure. Do you know, a woman wrote me last week to say her daughter saw me on a billboard, and there's no placating her out of the thought that I'm the bogeyman? The bane of not being handsome. You count your blessings you took after your mother, Dolores." Alexander stroked his chin. "Maybe I should grow a beard, like Abraham Lincoln."

Dolores waited for him to go on. "You *don't* know where Kristen is, then, or why Junior thinks you do?"

"Of course not."

Finally, the words she had been waiting to hear all afternoon. But the lump in her throat did not melt completely.

"Why would he say something like that?"

Alexander shrugged. "Why is the ocean blue?"

"It's not," she said. "It filters the red in the light because red has longer wavelengths. We only see the surface as blue, anyway. No light can get to the depths past a few thousand feet, so it's actually pure dark."

Alexander chuckled. "I should shelve you with the rest of my encyclopedias."

"Then the police didn't mention this to you?"

"Darling"–he looked shocked–"do you think Junior said anything like this to the police? Twelve-year-olds know the difference between what's real and what isn't. What he tells a teenage girl to scare her, or get her attention, and what he tells the authorities are probably two different things." He laughed. "My dear girl, is that what had you so upset?"

He got up from his desk and sat next to her on the floor. After he folded his extraordinarily long legs, he planted a kiss at the top of her head. "If I get elected to the Senate, you'll hear plenty of strange things about me. We all love to bad-mouth politicians. You just remember the father you know, Dolores. Can you promise that?"

She nodded, and his smile warmed.

"Good. Now eat your cookie. Before Charlotte gets on about your weird pineapple diets."

The chocolate chips had started to melt between her fingers. The cookie crumbled in her mouth when she brought it to her lips, the richness almost too sweet.

Her father got to his feet and turned up the volume on the radio. Frank Sinatra's "Fly Me to the Moon" crackled to life. "Ah." Alexander sighed. "You know the cure to old age, don't you, sweetie?"

"Uh–cookies?"

"Dancing."

"*Dad.*"

His hand wrapped around hers as he helped her up. "Come on. Don't break your old man's heart."

Dolores let herself be carried by Sinatra's light baritone. Her father led the dance, as skillful on his feet as he had been in his youth. One of the things Dolores remembered best about her mother was how happy she'd looked when Alexander danced with her. How she threw her head back when he spun her around the room, bursting with laughter.

He still danced with Dolores, every once in a while. Never with Charlotte.

Dolores shouldn't treasure that, and yet, she did. That her father's handsome swing moves were all for her.

Alexander sang over Sinatra, his voice deep and surprisingly in tune.

He spun her around, and a giggle tore out of her as he caught her by the waist, dipping her toward the floor.

By the time the song ended, Dolores had forgotten the lump in her throat, and the black diamonds of Junior Horowitz's eyes piercing through hers.

PRESENT DAY

Twenty-Six

TO THE BONE

Dolores had always loved jigsaw puzzles, a thrill vibrating in her fingertips when she put the last piece where it belonged.

"Can you tell us anything?" Paul asked.

Dolores had forgotten about the small crowd clustered inside the morgue. Once she'd started arranging the bones into a human skeleton, her brain had cast a haze over her surroundings.

She didn't answer Paul's question. From what she'd observed in the past couple of days, Agent Turner had the patience of a four-year-old. He could use the practice.

The light, dry feel of the bones tingled through her gloves. Someone stepped closer to the table, and Dolores caught a mop of red hair in her peripheral vision.

"Do you think it's her?" Kate asked. "Kristen."

"I don't specialize in forensic anthropology," she said, cautiously. "This is just an estimate. You'll want these bones examined by an expert–"

"For God's sake, her picture was *in the bag*. Do you need a special diploma to make the connection?"

Kate's voice cracked as she spoke. Dolores could imagine how trying the day had been for her. "Where did you find the bones?" she asked.

Kate drew back, forehead aimed at the floor. "In the wall behind City Hall."

"Local police are examining the scene," Paul added.

"With all that rain," Dolores said, "I doubt you'll find anything." She took a FOCUS LED and ran the light down the length of a radial bone.

"Where are you going?" Paul asked.

Dolores looked up to see Wyatt near the door. "The bones didn't get there by accident," he said. "Right behind City Hall? Whoever put them there wanted to send a message. Maybe it's time we had a chat with the mayor."

"Now?" Paul asked.

Wyatt stared at him for a moment. "There's enough of us watching. Wouldn't you say?"

Wyatt strode toward the Chrysler in the parking lot. When he was done at the morgue, Paul could ride with the cops, take a lesson in humility, and stink up their car with his damned cigarettes. Or he could walk. This was Little Horton, for heaven's sake.

Before this investigation started, Wyatt had never seen a dead body. When his parents died, he opted for closed caskets. It had been a nasty car accident, and there was no money to put into postmortem reconstruction. The caskets themselves cost three thousand apiece, three thousand more than what Wyatt's parents had left him.

He dropped in the driver's seat and wiped rainwater from his eyes. The face he glimpsed in the rearview mirror could have been that of a heroin addict who'd broken into his car.

Earlier, he'd told Paul he'd been up late working, which was true. But when he had finally gotten into bed, dead bodies had crammed his vision and dangled sleep out of reach. The Little Horton PD weren't the only murder-case virgins. Bribes, fraud, illegal donations–that was Wyatt's bread and butter. He'd never seen one drop of crime-related blood until this week.

God, that girl's bones. Such a tiny pile of bones.

His gut twisted and he opened the car door, afraid he'd throw up.

Once he'd recovered enough, he started the vehicle and drove slowly, eyes peering for cats.

When it was him roaming the streets with no place to call home, he would have wanted people to care whether or not they ran him over and left him to die.

PAUL DROPPED HIS PHONE in his pocket as Dolores stepped back from the autopsy table. Whether he'd been doing something useful or playing Animal Crossing, there was no way to tell.

"So?" he asked.

"She was five feet and six inches tall. I put her between sixteen and nineteen."

"Her?" Kate said.

"The pelvis is the best indicator for gender. Girls' are wider and circular. If she were male, we'd get more of a heart shape." Dolores moved on to the collarbone. "The clavicle completes growth around twenty-five. She was definitely younger than that, but yearly growth varies so I can't get much more precise."

"How long ago did she die?" Paul asked.

"The bones are weathered. How they got in that state depends on where she was buried. Did you dig up Kristen's medical record?"

Kate shook her head.

Dolores indicated her forearm. "The radial bone was broken–from how well it mended, probably during childhood. If you find something like that in Kristen's file, it could help us confirm the bones are hers."

"If she could afford a hospital," Kate muttered. "Not sure we should count on that."

Paul said, "Would have been easier to identify her if you'd had teeth to work with, right?"

Shudders crept down Dolores's spine. The absence of teeth could mean only one thing. Someone had pulled each tooth out of this girl's mouth. *After she died. Let it have been after she died.*

An image flashed in her mind: a Julia Roberts smile and the tiny gap of a missing molar. She approached the black sailor bag that had been put aside as evidence.

Paul's gaze followed her. "She wasn't buried in the bag, was she?"

"No. It's brand-new." The material was solid, water-resistant. Dolores eyed it for a moment. Why a sailor bag? Little Horton was landlocked.

There was no sailors' shop around, no reason for anyone to have such a bag lying around.

"Why didn't he just use a trash bag?"

"What?" Paul said.

Dolores turned back to Kate. "Kate, what did the knot look like when you found the bag?"

"I don't know. A loop."

"Was it a sailing knot?" When Kate didn't answer, Dolores tried again. "Did it come undone easily?"

"Yes."

"Did it look pretty?"

"What?"

Dolores repeated, "Was it a pretty loop? Even, symmetrical?"

"I don't know."

Paul was watching her intently. "Does it matter?"

Dolores chewed on her tongue. "Doesn't it strike you that whoever did this put themselves through a whole lot of trouble? They dug up the bones. Bought this bag. Slipped an old picture of Kristen inside, and they didn't just tug on the rope to close it. They tied a knot. Nowadays, knots on a bag like this are almost decorative. Why did they bother?"

Now both Kate and Paul were staring at her.

"They placed her body inside a wall, but they didn't treat her like yesterday's trash. They wanted to do better than that," Dolores said. "They wanted to show her some respect."

Twenty-Seven

MR. MAYOR

The alleyway behind City Hall was shrouded as if in a fog when Wyatt arrived. It wasn't pouring, but the constant drizzle made it difficult to see clearly. Jacob Winslow stood at a distance from the scene where the bones had been found. The local PD was about to wrap up. Yellow police tape surrounded the area. Two crates stood side by side next to the wall and yellow eyes glinted in the darkness. A cop with acne scars turned to Wyatt. "Nothing here. Well, nothing but cats. You can call someone from Milwaukee, but they won't find anything but soggy pet food and cat hair."

Wyatt nodded.

The policemen headed back to their vehicle, and Wyatt swiveled in time to catch Jacob turning away. "Mr. Mayor. If there's somewhere dry we can go to, I'd like to have a word with you."

THE MAYOR'S OFFICE WAS smaller than Wyatt expected. On the desk, a framed photograph of Jacob and a brunette, angled to face visitors. Wyatt took note of that. But what really surprised him was the portrait of Alexander Hawthorne, looming over the rest of the decorations. The slant of his hooked nose and his impish blue eyes sent ice running through Wyatt's veins.

Jacob shifted in his leather chair. "He was the mayor for a long time.

People looked up to him. He's the only man from Little Horton who made it to the Senate."

Wyatt pointed out, "For now."

Jacob Winslow had looked embarrassed enough at being called "Mr. Mayor" earlier. Wyatt wanted to shine a beam on him and watch him react.

Jacob cleared his throat. "Can I offer you a drink, Agent Holt?"

Wyatt shook his head. Few people could tolerate silence under pressure–and Jacob was under pressure. He scratched the insides of his palms. Sweat glistened at his temples. This was not the same man Wyatt had met this morning at the Winslow house.

"I, uh–I'm not sure how I can help you."

"Would you say you have secrets, Mr. Winslow?"

Jacob blanched. "Beg pardon?"

Wyatt might not have experience in interrogating violent criminals, but he did know a thing or two about grilling politicians who'd committed tax evasion.

"Secrets," he repeated.

"I don't–I don't understand."

Wyatt let him simmer for a few seconds. Jacob Winslow had no future in politics, unless he taught his face how to lie.

"Do you know why the police were investigating the area behind City Hall?" he asked.

"They found a bag, hidden inside the wall."

"What was inside the bag?"

"Bones. Human–human bones."

"That's right. Someone placed human remains behind City Hall. Placed them there so the police would find them. They left food to draw stray cats, knowing full well one of the police's priorities right now is animal control."

"I don't see where you're going with this."

"Really?"

Wyatt looked into Jacob's eyes. Most green eyes were brown-green or blue-green, but the Winslows' were green-green. Those eyes were the last handsome thing about him.

Finally, Wyatt shrugged. "It looks to me like someone is accusing you of having skeletons in your closet."

Jacob was dumbstruck for a second, opening his mouth, and closing it, before he managed, "Is that how you see it?"

Wyatt held up his phone and zoomed in on the picture he'd taken of Kristen's photograph. "You recognize her?"

Jacob didn't tense or knot his brows in overdone puzzlement. If the sight of Kristen made him anxious, he hid it well. "Yes. That's Kristen Horowitz. She left town decades ago."

"How do you know she left town?"

He raised one shoulder. "That's what everybody said."

"She was reported missing, though. Wasn't she?"

"Yes, but–wait. You're not saying the bones are hers?"

Wyatt didn't answer. He was more interested in what Jacob assumed he was saying.

The mayor ran a hand over his face. "Jesus. Jesus Christ."

His surprise looked genuine. Had he been acting the part of the bad liar this whole time so he could pull this off? If so, he deserved an award.

"You know, I've seen pictures of you in high school, Mr. Winslow. With your ex-girlfriend. Dolores." Wyatt paused a second. "Looking at this girl, now, the resemblance strikes me. Doesn't it strike you?"

"What–what resemblance?"

Wyatt pushed out a breath. "Kristen Horowitz. She looked a lot like Dolores did, in high school. Didn't she?"

"Some people thought so."

"Did you think so?"

A spike of bravery in Jacob's tone. "What are you getting at, Agent Holt?"

Wyatt wasn't moved. "For a friend of mine, only blondes do it. Bleached hair, flaxen hair, golden hair. Doesn't matter. But they have to be blond. Funny how some people have a type–a comfort zone of attraction. Were you ever involved with Kristen Horowitz?"

Jacob was silent. The room filled with the sound of rain battering the roof. "I know my rights. I don't have to answer your questions."

"You don't," Wyatt allowed. "But then–can you blame me for thinking anyone would accuse you of keeping secrets?"

Jacob licked his lips. "Respectfully, I don't think what happened has anything to do with me. Lots of people work at City Hall. Any one of them could have been targeted by this–this cruel joke. Or it could have been some kind of statement. An attack on authority. It could have been any number of things." His nostrils flared. "I won't let you frame it as some sort of accusation. No one's accused me of anything, have they?"

"Then you have nothing to hide?"

Jacob spoke his next words like they were meteors whose trajectory required careful handling. "I have no idea why anyone would plant bones behind City Hall to suggest, as you put it, that I have skeletons in my closet. Frankly, I find it in bad taste you'd even think of it like that."

Wyatt really *was* on familiar ground now. All politicians treated accusations like insults, as if you dirtied yourself by throwing them in the air.

Wyatt got to his feet. Jacob was obviously keeping things to himself, but he doubted he'd make a dent in that façade. The man was either a bad liar or an excellent one. But bad liars didn't confess with more gusto than good ones.

"Well," he said. "Thank you for your cooperation."

Jacob blinked at the sudden dismissal.

"One more thing. I'm going to ask the police to set up security measures–people need to feel safe. Seeing as you're the mayor, it's better they learn it from you."

"What do you have in mind?"

"Increasing police presence and patrols around the neighborhood would be a start. One man is missing, another is dead, and someone is planting bones behind City Hall. Trust me, I hope we catch them before something worse happens, but if we don't–"

"Exactly how could this get any worse?"

Wyatt held Jacob's gaze. "Tomorrow is Halloween, Mr. Winslow. I'm not one to be superstitious, but if what I keep hearing about this town is true–that's not the luckiest night of the year for you."

Twenty-Eight

CURIOSITY KILLED THE CAT

Kate felt better leaving the morgue than she had yesterday. Better because she hadn't needed to swallow her own vomit every five minutes. Better because, despite how horrifying today had been, part of her felt thrilled. *She* had found the bones. Alone. Chief Franklin couldn't very well kick her off the case now.

Her mother's voice pierced through her bubble of guilty bliss. *Kathleen Butcher, you should be* ASHAMED *of yourself. If those bones belong to Kristen Horowitz—and only detectives with meatballs for brains would doubt that—it means your schoolmate was* MURDERED. *You do not take joy in a girl's* MURDER.

"Smoke?"

Kate turned to find Paul cupping his palm over his lighter. A small flame caught the end of his Marlboro.

What had put it into this guy's head that he could strike up a conversation with her?

She couldn't decide which made her take a bigger dislike to him: that he had spent the past two hours breathing down Dolores's neck, or that when he wasn't doing that, he had the gall to check her out, like a woman studying human remains was a turn-on or something.

Kate glanced at the cars in the parking lot. "Looks like your ride took off."

"Looks like it."

"Why don't you jog. Don't FBI agents get paid to work out?"

Paul sighed. "You know, we could be at this all day. You call me a city prick. I treat you like a dumb rube."

"As in, you haven't been doing that?"

"Fair enough. You don't have to like me. I sure as hell don't like you."

"You're used to being the most annoying person in the room, aren't you."

"People never seem to realize it's hard work."

His eyes shimmered with amusement, but no malice. "Rivalry aside," he said, "can I ask you something? What is it with Halloween and this town?"

She let out a laugh. "Just a tourist trap."

"So, there's nothing out of the ordinary I should look out for? No one's gonna go bananas and shoot at the crowd, turn into a werewolf at the stroke of midnight?"

"What are you, a moron?" Kate scowled. "Is that what 'FBI' stands for? Freaking Brainless Idiots?"

Paul stared for a moment, then burst into peals of laughter so loud, Kate took a step back. His cigarette dropped to the ground. Kate resented the rush of pride that prickled her stomach.

"Holy hell, Butcher. It's the first time I heard that one."

"Don't have a heart attack or anything."

He shook his head. "Didn't mean any disrespect—it's just, you know. Some folks 'round here seem pretty superstitious."

"Yeah, well. All you gotta look out for is a party in town with drunk tourists, and locals trying to look like they aren't sick of this."

She didn't mention that no one in Little Horton flicked the pages on the calendar in October without a sprinkle of anticipation. You looked forward to it, you dreaded it, or a bit of both. When you considered the long list of killings, accidents, and natural disasters that had struck on Halloween in the nearly two centuries the town had existed–the Jenkins massacre in 1874, the blizzard of 1906–you figured another incident was bound to pile on top of that list, at some point. Maybe next year. Maybe this one.

The agent lit another cigarette. "By the way . . ."

Kate's shoulders squared. She sensed, in the casualness of his tone, that this bit of light fun was meant to soften her as he circled around the one question he'd been meaning to ask.

"I was just thinking, you're about Dolores's age, right?"

Kate waited until he made eye contact, refusing to look like he'd fooled her. "What kind of a question is that?"

"What I meant is, you would have gone to school with her."

"So?"

"So, you ever found out why she left town?"

Her jaw hardened. "I wasn't her goddamned therapist."

She heard the bite in her tone. Paul must have heard it, too, because he prodded. "Come on. A rich daddy's girl takes off one day and never comes back? The town must have crawled with rumors."

"What does town gossip matter to the FBI?"

"Just curious."

She held his eyes. "You wanna talk about superstitions? How about 'Curiosity killed the cat'?"

He pretended not to pick up on her hostility. "That's an idea."

"Yeah." She wished she could sound glacial. But her anger was always the sort that bubbled over like volcano lava. "I'd watch out if I were you, Mr. FBI. In case you haven't noticed, one thing this town's got plenty of is cats."

Paul grabbed hold of her wrist when she started to head toward her vehicle. "Kate."

She bristled. "Keep your hands off me."

"You don't like Dolores."

"Oh, you've noticed, have you? Was it tattooed on her ass or something? You sure as hell checked that out plenty."

"I want to understand."

Kate's throat closed up. The air in her lungs thickened into concrete.

"Because I've asked around," Paul said, "and it seems to me everybody in this damned town loved Dolores. Sweet girl. Well-mannered. So what's your problem with her? She did something to you?"

"I just don't like her! That's my right, isn't it?" Kate ground her teeth. Hated the shrillness of her voice, the warmth brimming her eyelids. "Like you said, she's a rich daddy's girl. Does that sound like my kind of person? Now back off!"

Paul let go of her arm and Kate whipped back toward the parking lot. The rain on her face was cold—so why did her cheeks prickle with heat and salt?

She started the car before her vision had cleared.

She'd sooner drive into a pole than let that FBI agent see her in tears.

Twenty-Nine

THE HAWTHORNE CHILDREN

When Dolores got back from the morgue, Asher was the only one home. Josie was still at school, and Charlotte had gone to a committee meeting.

Dolores collapsed onto her bed, not minding when she heard Asher come in. After she helped him not throw up on his shoes yesterday, she figured they had officially stopped being strangers.

"You were at the morgue, then?" He sat next to her.

"News travels fast. You heard about the bones behind City Hall?"

"Yeah. Any idea whose they are? Or, you're probably not allowed to say, right?"

Her cheek sank into the pillow. She wondered if Asher remembered Kristen Horowitz–or, as he'd once called her, the milk-carton girl.

The memory slipped in before she could brace herself. Pouring milk on Asher's cereal. Kristen's face, smiling at them from the carton.

Had she been dreaming of her lately? Dreaming of a dark river where memories floated like stray pieces of furniture and a ripe pumpkin smell prodded against the bounds of her sanity?

How long before I remember more? Before I remember everything?

Downstairs, the entry door opened and closed.

"That'll be Mom," Asher said. Dolores groaned. Light footsteps trotted up the stairs. "And Josie."

A moment later, the door flung open.

"Look at *us*." Josie crawled onto the bed next to her siblings. Dolores caught a whiff of cherry deodorant. "The Hawthorne children, all in the same room." She reached for her phone.

"You better not take a selfie," Asher said.

"Too late. Say hi, Sis. It's about time you started taking fresh pics. Your Facebook profile is awful, you know?"

Dolores's eyelids drooped from exhaustion. She wanted to tell them to stay, to keep filling the room with their reality.

Josie's words looped around in her head. *The Hawthorne children.*

How long since Dolores had been either of those things.

Thirty

THE BEAR

Gregory Winslow pulled a whiskey glass from the cabinet and wheeled himself back to the coffee table. He checked the roman numbers on his Rolex. Ten to six. Teddy was late.

Gregory muttered under his breath, "As always."

His eyes strayed to the picture the FBI agent had disturbed this morning: Teddy, resplendent, ready to eat up the world. Parents weren't supposed to have favorites, but who could blame him? Jacob was such a complicated kid. Life gave him lemons and instead of making lemonade, he cut the damned fruit open, dissected its entrails, weighed it with and without its skin. Overthought everything. Not to mention, drawn to misery. Gregory should have known he'd turn into a Dem.

Teenage Jacob smiled at Gregory from the picture, and the old man wrenched his eyes away. Well, Jacob hadn't always been like this. Weird? A little, but in a cocky, endearing sort of way. Politics had done it to him—and that girl, of course. Dolores.

Gregory poured himself a drink. For all he knew, Teddy had followed some miniskirt out of a bar and wouldn't be here until tomorrow. Still, Gregory wished he could talk to the boy, if only to slip in a word about those FBI agents. He hadn't dared mention it over the phone.

Teddy would take it like a man. At least one of his sons would. Lord knew, Gregory hadn't expected Jacob would go berserk when he told him—

The living room door squeaked open.

Gregory drained his glass and wheeled himself to face the door. He hadn't heard Teddy come in. "Fashionably late, heh?"

He stopped short as the muzzle of a Smith & Wesson met his gaze. Time flattened into a palpable, two-dimensional cage. Gregory felt it squeeze him until his organs were ready to shoot out of his eyes.

The gun fired.

A tornado of shrapnel exploded into his head, and Gregory raised a hand to catch his jaw as it dropped to the floor in a mess of blood and teeth.

Except his hand didn't move. Lead smashed through his extremities. He was conscious of a loud *thud* as his body plummeted to the ground.

He blinked. A scream wanted to tear out of his throat, not because his tongue lay inches from his eye on the ground–but because of the bear. For the first time, the grizzly bear that adorned his living room floor was looking at him straight in the eye. And Gregory would swear the bastard was about to eat him alive.

Footsteps drew near. Gregory caught a glimpse of black leather derbies.

The shoe rose until it filled his horizon and, in an eruption of agony, came crashing down on what was left of Gregory.

Thirty-One

SMOKE

When people asked Dolores what her favorite thing about Max was, she always made up something. *His strength. How safe he makes me feel.* The one time she'd heard someone ask him the same thing, he'd cocked an eyebrow and said, "Do you have *eyes*?" She'd punched him in the shoulder, asked him to quit being a prick. But what he'd said was crude honesty. She and Max fucked all the time. Every decision they made as a couple was rooted in that fact. Moving in together? So they didn't waste time driving to each other's places and they could fuck more. Getting married? Who doesn't want an excuse for a vacation where everyone will expect you to do nothing but fuck.

They didn't get bored of each other the way envious friends predicted. The day Dolores walked in on Max screwing his yoga coach, he'd been inside her that very morning.

Yet no matter how often they did it, no matter that she stopped taking the pill and Max never wore a condom in his life, her period came regular as clockwork.

"We have to go to a doctor," Max told her once. The way he looked at her stomach when he said this–looked at the scar–she knew he meant "you."

"Yeah," Dolores had said. "Okay." But always, she made excuses not to go. Too much work. Cases came in just when her day was wrapping up, and she rescheduled, rescheduled, until Max must have figured out she'd never made the appointment to begin with.

Having a kid mattered to him. The older he got, the more it mattered. Childless couples made him say things like, *Can you imagine never leaving something of yourself in the world?*

Dolores wouldn't reply. She knew he was narcissistic when she married him.

It got to the point that he actually yelled at her one night, something he didn't do lightly. *How hard can it be? You work in a hospital. Take a break, have them look at you.*

She'd laughed, like it was silly. *It doesn't work like that.*

Sure it does. Have them take an X-ray. I mean, look at it. He'd grabbed a fistful of her shirt, to expose the scar. *It's not right. Maybe they messed up something with your—*

Dolores slapped him across the face.

The thought of what she was doing had never entered her brain. Instinct had shot through her hand and before she could stop herself, her palm was burning with pins and needles. Max had stared at her in silence, stunned.

At that moment, Dolores knew it was over. The cheating was just an easy way out.

It wasn't that she hit him, really, but the cold look in her eyes as she did it—the fact that he saw the truth for the first time. That there was a gaping chasm inside her that he could never know, because she had spent her whole adult life making sure she would never know it herself.

Something tugged at Dolores's hand. Her eyes blinked open, took in the burgundy drapes, through which a triangle of moonlight fell on her sister's face. So young. Dolores couldn't remember ever being that young.

"Sorry," Josie said. "Mom asked to wake you up for dinner. And yes, you have to come. She'll make it worse for you if you don't."

THEY ATE IN THE kitchen, which was a good thing. The dining room would have been too full of the old Winslow-Hawthorne gatherings. Charlotte talked in excruciating detail about tomorrow's activities. Over the years, she had obviously warmed up to Halloween—had no choice if she wanted to blend in. You can move to Paris and persist in hating baguettes, wine, and cheese, but you'll find it a pretty lonely life. And lonely was the last thing Charlotte knew how to be.

"Committee members will go as Puritans." She looked at Dolores. "I don't have a costume for you, of course, but I'm sure I can dig up something."

"Seriously," Asher said, "we're not canceling the party?"

"Of course not. Hundreds of tourists have booked their tickets for the tour. You know how crucial they are to the town's economy."

Dolores wanted to say that maybe, the fact someone had been murdered would slow the tourists down. But a town known as "Little H"–short for "Little Halloween" as much as "Little Horton"–probably couldn't get macabre enough.

"You mean," Josie said, "it'd *look* bad if we didn't show up."

Dolores watched Charlotte closely. This couldn't all be about the Hawthornes acting like Little Horton's city upon a hill.

Charlotte straightened in her chair. "Really, it's simple, darling. I'll be downtown, at the party–I can't afford not to be. And I would sooner have you where I can keep an eye on you, around hundreds of witnesses."

"That's ridiculous," Josie said.

Asher sat back, pushing his half-eaten plate away. "Mom, no offense? I'm really not in a pumpkin-carving mood." She shrugged, like his remark didn't warrant a reply. "You want us to put on smiles, dress up, tell tales to give some asshole tourists a scare? With Dad gone–"

"Your father would want you out there, Asher. He understands the importance of leadership–understands determination keeps a house together when everything else collapses. In all these years, no matter what he was going through, the town came first. Always. If he were here this wouldn't be up for debate."

She got to her feet and started washing the dishes.

Dolores drew in a breath. She could picture this house the way Josie had painted it earlier–never speaking of the missing sister, a tacit agreement between reality and all family members.

Go through the motions, look and act the part.

Like living in a house on fire and thinking that as long as you pretend not to smell smoke, the flames won't melt your flesh and char your bones.

Asher's chair raked against the tile as he got to his feet. Josie cast a sheepish look at her mother, tense shoulders hunched beneath her dress.

"You can go," Dolores mouthed.

Josie disappeared after her brother, and soft footsteps padded up the stairs.

"Can I help you?" Dolores asked.

A wry laugh from her stepmother. "Like the good old times, Dolores?"

She joined Charlotte by the sink. Charlotte washed the plates fast, like a factory worker at an assembly line. Dolores rubbed the plates dry, dishes, forks, knives, and realized she knew exactly where to put them.

"Thank you," Charlotte said, without looking up from the sink. "I know it's a lot to ask, but I want you downtown tomorrow for the festivities as well. You used to care about this so much. I wish I'd understood then. This town needs rituals and traditions. Especially in times like this. Besides . . ." She paused. Dolores could tell this was the real reason. "Your brother and sister will come if you do."

Charlotte chuckled as she rinsed her hands. "Strange, isn't it? How quickly resentment gives way to love. I expected them to hate you. They did hate you, all those years. Especially Asher."

Dolores rubbed her fingers inside her palm. It unsettled her to be with Charlotte, alone. Stirred the dark waters she had been wading in since she got back to Little Horton.

Just say it, she thought. *No. I won't come to the Halloween party.*

She didn't owe Charlotte anything. Maybe her brother and sister. But not Charlotte.

Instead, she said, "Did you hear about Burke?"

Even after she heard it out loud, Dolores couldn't make sense of why she asked. She'd had eighteen years to talk about Dr. Burke with Charlotte if she wanted–and why would she? It was much safer to live around those uncomfortable truths, pretend everything was fine.

Smell the smoke?

What smoke?

Charlotte didn't turn from the sink. "Don't ask questions you know the answer to, Dolores. It's beneath you." She dried her hands with a dish towel hanging from the oven door. "I know you performed the autopsy."

She said this as if Dolores had tried to keep it a secret. "Burke was the medical examiner around here," Dolores pointed out. "He wasn't going to autopsy himself."

"The FBI could have called one of their own."

"I don't care who I have to cut open if it helps them find Dad."

Charlotte bristled at the mention.

"That's all that matters, right?" Dolores said. "You'd do everything you could, tell us everything you knew, if it helped bring him home. Wouldn't you?"

Charlotte ran the dish towel through her fingers. "I wish you hadn't been the only doctor they could rely on. It disgusts me, to imagine you touching that man."

Dolores reeled back. Her stepmother's words hit her like a bee sting, wrapped in sugar. "Does it?" she managed.

Charlotte kept quiet for a moment. "It's funny you should bring him up," she finally said.

But the silence that dropped over the room didn't sound funny to Dolores.

She resisted the urge to clutch the scar across her abdomen. Remembered the pain tearing through her, hot, blaring white, so dazzling she saw stars.

"I suppose you find it easy to judge me now," Charlotte said. "At the time, you of all people were grateful I handled the matter privately."

Dolores gritted her teeth, hard enough that jolts of pain shot down her back molars. "Grateful" was not the word for what she had been.

As if reading her mind, Charlotte let out an exhale. "How could I have known, Dolores? You think I could predict the complications? Burke swore to me he could handle the surgery."

"And you took his word for it."

The clock ticked. The faucet dripped, and Dolores wanted to push Charlotte aside and turn off the damned thing. Oxygen pressed for release against the roof of her mouth.

The words blurted out, beyond her control. "You didn't think to question it—why would you? You knew he was a ripper when you sent me to him."

Charlotte didn't have time to answer before a succession of knocks hammered at the front door.

When Dolores looked back at Charlotte, she gasped, because her stepmother had grabbed a kitchen knife from the drawer.

"What—"

"Don't move, Dolores."

Charlotte made her way toward the hall, and the door opened. Dolores clutched the edge of the table.

She heard Charlotte say, "Get out." With as much venom as had ever come out of her mouth. "You have no business here."

"I have to see her. Please, Charlotte."

Dolores's breath hitched. It was a man's voice.

"Get *out of my sight* this instant."

A rush of footsteps sounded upstairs, and Charlotte cried, "Josie, don't come down!"

There was the sound of jostling in the hall—the man must have brushed past Charlotte—and in a moment, he stood before Dolores.

She stepped back and bumped into the table.

His face was all panic. Pasty skin, black hair dripping from the rain. His eyes called to her with an urgency that filled her entire capacity for thought.

Help.

Help me.

Her hands brushed against his chest to push him off, and it was only when she touched him that recognition hit her.

Maybe his smell did it. Maybe the echo of his voice from the corridor, or some inexplicable fragment salvaged from a boy she had once known absolutely.

"Jacob."

This haggard man looked nothing like the boy she remembered. His cheeks were gaunt, his face harsh. The image of Teddy from the diner this morning swam before her eyes—he looked more like the Jacob she'd known than the real Jacob did now.

Time stretched on. It could have been ten seconds, or ten thousand.

Ever since she'd returned to Little Horton, she had watched street corners carefully, pulse racing with every step. Dreading to run into him.

Yet now he was here, in her father's kitchen, a whisper away from her. . . .

And there was no fear.

Instead, a blanket of quietness engulfed her. The way she used to feel, seeing him for the first time after pining for him all morning.

An urge to hold him seized her, absurd. Almost irrepressible.

The kitchen door flung open, and someone entered. Josie? Charlotte?

Jacob said, "My father is dead. Murdered. I found his body."

A glint caught Dolores's eye as Charlotte's knife hissed through the air. "If you don't leave my house this instant, Jacob Winslow, I will gut you like an animal."

Thirty-Two

APOCALYPSE

Dolores's heart ran frantic as she registered what was happening. Charlotte's knife whooshed past Jacob's ear and blood broke in ruby droplets along his cheekbone. "*Now,*" she said.

Dazed, he stumbled back until Dolores's hand fell from his chest. His eyes dropped and he scurried out like a bad dream. It was only when he brushed past Josie and Asher in the doorway that Dolores noticed them, their jaws hanging open.

"Holy shit," Josie said.

Charlotte headed to the hallway, maybe to satisfy herself that Jacob was gone.

"Mom," Asher said. "Was she holding a knife at Jacob? That is what just happened? Mom just *cut* Jacob with a knife?"

Dolores didn't know how to answer. Charlotte stepped back into the kitchen, slipping past Asher, and walked to the sink. She turned on the tap, rinsed the knife, and put it back inside the drawer.

"Mom," Josie said, "what the fuck?"

"Language."

"*Language?*" Josie repeated. "How about knives? Aggravated assault?"

Charlotte turned to them, looking composed. "Josie, when I tell you to stay in your room, I intend for you to do exactly that."

"But–"

"No buts, darling. Asher, why didn't you make sure she stayed upstairs?"

Asher shut his mouth.

Charlotte's eyes slid between her son and Josie. Dolores was invisible again.

"What the hell just happened?" Asher asked.

Charlotte smiled, her *Little-Horton-town-committee* smile. "When your father was taken, darling, I stopped being your mother."

Asher's eyes grew the size of marbles. "But–"

"We're at war, and I'm your commanding general. My priority is getting all of you through this alive, and as long as this family is under threat, you will do as I say."

Dolores shuddered. Her father's words, from another lifetime ago. *If the apocalypse ever happens, Dolores, I want you to go to your stepmother. She is the strongest person in the universe.*

Asher shook his head. "You're out of your mind."

"You *assaulted* the mayor!" Josie said.

"Oh, believe me, he won't press charges. No one outside this room saw it, and as far as we're concerned, it didn't happen. Am I making myself clear?"

Josie and Asher went on staring.

Dolores tore herself out of her paralysis. One hand found the wall for balance as she stumbled out of the kitchen.

"Where are you going?" Charlotte called after her.

The corridor turned to molasses under her feet. Without bothering to put on her coat, she reached for the knob of the front door–and found it locked.

Dolores turned around.

Charlotte stood in the hall, arms crossed over her chest. Asher and Josie had followed her. She repeated, "Where are you going?"

Dolores tasted bile in her throat. "To find Jacob."

The words sounded absurd, and yet she knew, immediately, that it was the right thing to do.

All this time. All this *fear*. Senior year, homeschooling, barely getting out of the house to avoid Jacob. Her stepmother, telling her over and over about the assault. Of the two of them, Charlotte was the only one who remembered that Halloween night. Yet she and Jacob had never talked about it. How had they never talked about it?

The need gripped her, urgent, fresh with the feel of his chest against her fingertips. To talk to him, now. She was no longer a teenager. Not only was she ready for the confrontation that would have sent her spiraling before—she needed it.

What had just happened in the kitchen came back to her. The absence of horror in her heart as she touched him.

Charlotte's lips pressed into a near-invisible line. "Unless the FBI asks, this family is no longer on speaking terms with the Winslows."

"Come on," Asher said. "Dee can't see Jacob because you and Gregory had a fight decades ago?"

"Jacob knows he isn't welcome in this house. As do his brother and father." Her eyes drilled into Dolores. "As do *you*."

"His father was murdered," she said.

A sliver of doubt flashed in Charlotte's eyes. "If he told you that, he's lying."

"Why?" Dolores asked. "Do you think they're behind what happened to Dad? What aren't you telling us?"

"If Gregory is dead," Charlotte said, "his sons can go to the police. It isn't our business." Her voice hardened. "And I don't want you touching that man's body, Dolores. Let the FBI do their dirty work. It's time we started looking after ourselves."

Dolores said, "Give me the key."

A look washed over her stepmother's face that Dolores had never seen. Only parents looked at their children like this. Disappointment. Bone-deep, as if your body had started rejecting one of your own limbs. Dolores's mother had died before she had a chance to be disappointed in her, and Alexander—

Alexander's love had been too blind for disappointment.

Charlotte nodded. "I see."

Dolores steeled herself so she wouldn't break eye contact. This shouldn't hurt. After all, Charlotte wasn't her mother.

Yet a ball of thorns sank into her chest. Shredding flesh, cutting into organs.

Charlotte's hand bridged the distance between them in a swift thrust. A *click* as the lock came undone. "Why do you push me like this, Dolores? You know how I hate clichés—how I hate this part." Their eyes met. "If you leave right now, you'll find somewhere else to sleep tonight. And every other night that you're in town."

Dolores said nothing. She could spend a whole month in this house, with her past swimming back to the surface, and still not get any closer to unraveling its secrets. There was no point here, looking for the truth. This whole family had been built on lies.

Yet it didn't stop the ball of thorns, or slow its agonizing descent.

"Mom!" Josie objected.

"You can't," Asher said. "It's her house, too. Dad wouldn't want this."

Charlotte's eyes didn't leave Dolores. "Dad's not here to protest, is he?"

Dolores grabbed her purse, her coat, and didn't cast one last look at her sister and brother as she pushed open the door and left home, just as she had done eighteen years ago.

Thirty-Three

THE BLUE NOTEBOOK

The reality of what she'd done didn't hit Dolores until after she'd walked a few blocks. She had no car, no place to spend the night, and her shoes squished out water with every step.

Her eyes swept the streets for Jacob.

Part of her couldn't believe she had gone after him like a stubborn teenager in love. *Like the teenager I once was.*

Dolores clenched her fist around the collar of her coat. It had been a long time since she had buried all feelings of affection for Jacob Winslow. Eighteen years was long enough to forget even a first love.

And how could she have gone on loving him, after What He'd Done?

Seeing him tonight–it shattered the image of the monster she'd created. That *Charlotte* had created.

Her fingers prickled with the warmth of his chest. *I have to talk to him. I have to know.*

The merest movement sent her heart somersaulting, but it was only cats, or a gutted beer can rattling along the road. Though her tongue itched for it, she held back from crying Jacob's name like a lunatic. If anything, it might push him deeper into hiding.

She had known Jacob long enough to know he suffered in silence. An evening came back to her, when Gregory Winslow had berated his son at their dinner table–it was not the first time, or the last, but it *was* the most memorable.

They couldn't have been older than sixteen. Gregory's voice came back to her, grinding. "If you wanted to make your old man proud, you'd pull your head out of your sissy-books and learn about the family business. Like your brother." Teddy had the decency to stare at his plate. "There's nothing there real life can't teach you, and nothing they'll teach you that you can use in real life! Aren't I right, Al?"

Dolores's father emerged from his thoughts, like he'd been caught eating the last slice of chocolate cake. "Uh–yes, yes, quite right."

A malicious smile spread to Mr. Winslow's eyes as he produced a blue notebook–Jacob's notebook. How could Dolores have forgotten? He was writing a story in there–nowadays, people would probably call it fan fiction. It had started when they read *Pride and Prejudice* for school. Dolores had to will her brain into focus every few lines, but Jacob ate it up like a McDonald's special. The notebook arrived shortly after.

"It's just," Jacob explained, "she stops at the most interesting part."

"Darcy and Elizabeth's happily ever after is the interesting part?"

"Yeah." Jacob looked at her like she was crazy. "I don't get why all the books stop there. Anyone can fall in love. I want to see how they stay in love. How they handle it when money runs short, or Elizabeth loses her mom. What about how they react to the issues of years to come? Would Elizabeth travel to New York for the Seneca Falls Convention? Would Darcy support her? Would he crack under pressure if his friends criticized his wife's strong character, or would he damn it all and take the trip with her?"

Dolores chuckled. "Okay, I'm sold. I want to read *that* book. Think we can get Mrs. Jennings to change the program?"

Jacob gave her his golden retriever's smile. But he didn't let her read his story. She only heard it that horrible evening, when Mr. Winslow read from his son's notebook. Dolores had felt the full length of each second. Tears of rage had welled in her eyes as she dug her fists into her thighs below the table.

Incredibly, Jacob didn't break down or ask his father to stop. His lips puckered as he clenched his jaw, so hard Dolores thought his teeth would crack. What she remembered most was how transparent his feelings were. She couldn't have learned more if he had run her through a point-by-point exposition.

Eventually, when the air had gotten toxic enough to eat through steel, Gregory stopped. He made a noise between a sigh and a snort. "*Pride and Prejudice*, of all books. Like one of those isn't enough."

"Thank you, Father," Jacob managed. "I think you gave a decent delivery."

"You being smart with me?"

Although his face looked like he had spent half an hour on the torture rack, Jacob resumed eating.

According to Teddy, Gregory's problem with Jacob was that he just didn't get him. But Dolores called bullshit on that. Mr. Winslow's problem with his younger son was that he didn't know *how* to bully him.

Dolores sank her fists into her coat pockets, her fingers numb. That memory upset her now–why did it upset her so much?

She grabbed her phone and scrolled through her list of contacts until she landed on Teddy's name–he'd made her take his number before she left the diner this morning. The phone rang, and rang, and finally Teddy said, "Hello?"

"Teddy–"

"Just kidding! Be sure not to leave me a message–I won't listen to it. If I want to talk to you I'll call you back. Bye!"

Dolores groaned and scanned the streets, the alley of trees and their coat of leaves paving the ground. *He can't have gone far.* At the same time, he might have gone anywhere.

Out of ideas, she searched for Wyatt's number in her list of recent calls.

He picked up on the first ring. "Hello?"

"Agent Holt, this is Dolores Diaz. I think there's been a murder at the Winslows."

"Where are you?"

Concern broke through his voice. She figured he must hear the wind around her, know she was outside–and that if a murder *had* just taken place tonight, a killer must be nearby. It hadn't struck Dolores to see it that way until Wyatt's voice mirrored it back at her.

"I–" She looked around for a street name. She'd been too rattled to check where she was going. "Look, you have to send someone to the Winslows'."

"All right," Wyatt said. Even over the phone, his confidence was like a balm. "Do I have your permission to locate you?"

"What?"

"Cruisers are patrolling the town. I'd like to send the nearest one, to make sure you're safe."

"I'm–"

"Fine. I know."

She heard the smile in his voice. She wanted to let it soothe her, let him take the whole situation out of her hands. But her heart went on punching against her rib cage. Part of her wished she hadn't called him, so she didn't have to hear the turmoil in her own voice.

"Yes. You have my permission."

"All right. Miss Diaz, I'd rather we stay on the phone until the police find you. Does that sound okay?"

"Yes."

"Good. Now, what makes you think anyone's been murdered tonight?"

"Not anyone. Gregory Winslow."

Professionalism kicked in. She pictured herself sitting in a courtroom, any evidence from the autopsies dependent on whether she was held as a credible authority.

"Jacob Winslow came to my house, unhinged, to tell me his father had been murdered."

"Unhinged," Wyatt repeated. "Did he hurt you?"

The words almost came tumbling out. *No, of course not, Jacob would never lay a finger on me.*

She blinked back the images that swam to her eyes. Jacob's face as his father humiliated him.

Sphenoid. Temporal. Lacrimal.

Dolores pictured the bones of her head, hardening against unwanted thoughts. She wasn't a schoolgirl, wrapped around Jacob's finger. But how her resolve had softened at the sight of him, how she had put her guard down. Wanting to trust him.

What does that tell you, Dolores?

She willed out a rational answer.

He has power over me. He can still fool me like he did back then.

Jacob had lied to her. Manipulated her. Assaulted her.

Dolores had believed it so long that it sounded true, the way trite expressions do when you never question the grounds they're built on.

But that logic had one deep flaw, which Dolores had overlooked until she saw Jacob tonight. Until she remembered the notebook, the look on Jacob's face that night.

He had always been a terrible liar.

"Miss Diaz?"

"He didn't hurt me. He was in the state you'd expect someone to be after finding their father dead."

"Then you both went outside?"

"No. I followed him out. I mean—he went out, and I went after him a few minutes later."

"Why did you wait?"

The longer Dolores stayed silent, the more it would seem to Wyatt like she was hiding something. Yet what could she say? That her stepmother came at him with a knife? Charlotte might not be Dolores's blood, but she was family. You didn't tell on your family.

"I don't know. It all happened so fast," she said, annoyed by how cliché she sounded.

She picked up on Wyatt's sigh at the other end of the line. "I see. Can you think of why Jacob went to you tonight? Are you close to him?"

Dolores's breath hitched. "No."

Memories burrowed through her mind, so foreign they might have belonged to someone else. Of the Night She Didn't Remember. The night she would never remember. And could never forget.

Halloween night, 2003.

Herself, on the bathroom floor, at seventeen. A mug of cocoa smoldering between her hands, yet she couldn't feel the heat—could only feel a great, ice-lake cold inside her soul. Charlotte's mouth moving, making noises that didn't connect into logical sentences.

I don't ever want you to see That Boy again—
If he touches one hair on your head I'll—
Gut you like an animal.

"Miss Diaz?" Wyatt said.

Dolores tried to will out a word, to prove she was all right. But she couldn't, because standing on the sidewalk across the street was a seventeen-year-old girl with dark hair and eyes.

A barbed-wire necklace latched around her throat.

For a moment, it was like looking into a mirror—those magical mirrors in fairy tales that sell you deceptive dreams, that make your wishes come true and eat out your sanity.

Then the girl smiled, revealing the gap of a missing molar, and Dolores knew it was Kristen. The girl she had been dreaming about since she came back to Little Horton.

She closed her eyes, and in a flash, the girl was gone.

Don't you dare collapse, she thought.

Her father might still be alive, *must* be alive, and she needed—needed—

"Miss Diaz," Wyatt repeated. "Can you confirm to me you're not in danger?"

Her father's face, with his smiling eyes, splintered into her like a wound.

A cruiser pulled up beside her, and the door of the passenger seat flew open.

Kate Butcher sat behind the wheel, lips drawn tight. "You just spell trouble, Dolores Hawthorne. Don't you."

Thirty-Four

RIPPLES

Wyatt waited until Kate confirmed she was with Dolores before he hung up and let out a ragged breath. In the past few days, he'd seen Dolores in her father's office turned crime scene, had seen her cut into the body of her old pediatrician, and she had given not the slightest sign of faltering. It was oddly unsettling to hear her upset now. Was it the news of Gregory's murder? Her ex-boyfriend's visit?

Paul took a left turn, fifteen miles above the speed limit. Wyatt jerked back against his seat. "You know, I'd like us to get to the Winslows' alive."

Paul ignored the jab. "Dolores Diaz. You're worried about her?"

Wyatt fidgeted with a shirt button, then forced his hand back in his lap. "Did I say that?"

"Nah, you sounded cool, man. Some people have a poker face—but damn, you have a poker *voice*. I'm starting to get to know you, though." He missed a red light, and Wyatt caught himself on the car door. "I'll bet you're not surprised that, of all the people the mayor could have gone to after finding his father, dead, he went to Dolores. She knows more than she's letting on. You agree?"

Wyatt opened his mouth, and closed it. Hawthorne's letter. The look on Dolores's face when she saw Kristen's photograph. How she had shaken her head when asked if she knew her, at the same time that she answered, *Yes.*

"I think she's at the heart of this. Whether she knows it is another matter."

"Yeah," Paul said, like that was obvious. "Why'd you think I put her on the case to begin with? If we hadn't asked for her help, she would have hopped back on a plane to Los Angeles."

Wyatt stared, a little surprised by his partner's pragmatism. Finally, he said, "She's too close to the case."

"I know. We'll call someone in from Milwaukee. It's not like we can rely on her to perform autopsies for–for more people she knows."

Wyatt followed Paul's thread of thought. "You think her father is dead."

"Hell, I don't know. It's been over forty-eight hours. We haven't gotten a ransom note. If we were going to find the old man alive, odds say we would have. Someone sure as hell died in that office."

Wyatt gave this some thought. "If the killer did shoot Hawthorne, why take his body? If that were his MO, he would have taken Burke's and Winslow's."

"So, maybe we got two assailants, and one of them died while Hawthorne was getting kidnapped. I've seen the man's medical records. Over eighty, maybe, but in great shape. Tough as old boots, as they say. Could be he gave his kidnappers more of a fight than they expected. Besides, he knew this was coming. Wrote the note. Acted paranoid. Maybe he got his hands on a gun, shot one of his attackers before he was taken."

"Serial killers tend to act alone."

"Serial killers tend not to target rich old men."

Wyatt couldn't argue with that.

"Speaking of Alexander," Paul said. "He's a rather tall man."

Wyatt looked back at Paul. "What?"

"Maybe he lost half an inch with age, but based on his medical info, still over six feet."

Wyatt knew where this was going. One of the only things they knew about the killer was his height. "So is the man dead, or is he just playing dead and settling scores? You can't have it both ways."

"I know that. But it's the only two theories that make sense. You said it when we first got here. The bureau was on his tail. Secrets were about to resurface."

It was one thing to assume Hawthorne had faked his death to escape facing legal repercussions for financial misconduct. But the killings were a game changer.

"You think Hawthorne went on a killing spree, at the ripe old age of eighty?"

"Correct me if I'm wrong, but your corruption case hinges on Hawthorne getting paid off to keep his mouth shut about something that happened two decades ago. Paid by the Winslows, most likely–yes?"

Wyatt considered.

"Come on," Paul said. "It's enough of a coincidence that Gregory Winslow was the only man in town with enough money to get Hawthorne out of debt. His death is the cherry on top. No way is he not tied to this whole mess."

"Yeah, okay. But why did Gregory need to bribe Hawthorne?"

Paul shrugged. "A lot of incidents triggered by one common denominator–we find what caused the ripples, and it'll lead us to who's doing this. Dolores left town, Winslow and Hawthorne stopped talking to each other. Kristen Horowitz went missing. And good old Dr. Burke bought his private practice."

Wyatt's eyes shot up in surprise, and Paul grinned. "Did you think I just sit on my ass when we're not together? Hawthorne isn't the only one who won the jackpot in 2003. Our good doctor hadn't been doing so great prior to that. Student loans to pay off, and he wasn't the sharpest person with a needle. But suddenly, Burke has the money to buy himself a practice in Little Horton. How did that happen?"

Wyatt shook his head. "What are you saying?"

"Of course, the fact that his lab was trashed would make us think the killer was after the evidence. But what if that's a trick? What if Burke was one of the intended victims all along? What if he's connected to whatever happened all those years ago?"

Wyatt thought for a second. "Suppose he is. You think Alexander decided to kill these men now, after keeping silent for years?"

"You know damn well what I think, Big Guy, because you're thinking the same thing. This is revenge killing."

Wyatt's arms broke out in goose bumps.

"So, Hawthorne is old. Maybe that makes him more dangerous.

What has he got to lose? You were there with me this morning. You can't tell me there isn't a shitload of unfinished business between Hawthorne and old Winslow."

"Jacob Winslow's no doctor. Maybe his father isn't dead."

"Maybe," Paul said.

But when they entered the Winslows' living room, they both knew they wouldn't need a doctor to confirm it. A lumpy mixture of blood, teeth, and brains splattered the carpet.

"Hell," Paul said.

Wyatt's vision blurred, and the next thing he knew he was bent in half, palms moist against his pants. *God.* He could be sorting through CEOs' fiscal records right now.

The air that came into his lungs tasted like carbon dioxide. His rattled nerves begged for release–to laugh, scream. Do anything but stand here in front of a body that had a splash of red where his head should be.

Paul's hand touched his shoulder, and Wyatt jumped. "You okay, Big Guy?"

"Yeah." He staggered back to a standing position.

Paul reached for his phone. "Chief Franklin, this is Agent Turner. We're going to need an APB on Jacob Winslow."

The words snapped Wyatt back to attention. "You think his son did this?"

Paul shrugged. "Maybe not. But he fled the crime scene–gotta be involved, one way or another."

"There could be another explanation."

"Then he better come forward and give it to us. In my experience, people run when they're guilty."

Thirty-Five

TOXIC

"Dolores?" Kate repeated.

If she had known Chief Franklin would reward her for all her trouble with street patrol, she would have thought twice about jumping for joy over that bag of bones. She'd been driving back to the station, strays mewling from their crates in the backseat, when she got the call about Dolores.

Graduating from cat-sitter to babysitter.

The past few days had been trying–too much thrill and horror and letdown. By now, Kate's anger was like a tide of toxic waste. She was dying to lash out at someone, and God knew, the release would be twice as good if that person was Dolores.

But something wasn't right. Kate stole glances at her passenger. Her hands sat tucked in her lap, but they were shaking. She didn't hear three out of five words Kate said.

Her tires screamed on the asphalt as she parked in front of the police station. She opened the car door and glanced at Dolores. "I, uh–I'll just be a sec." She debated adding, *Don't go anywhere,* or something soothing. But before she could will out the words, she was flinging the car door open.

Kate grabbed the two crates from the backseat, and one of the cats erupted into a riot of meows. As she stepped into the police station, he sneaked a paw through the bars and clawed at her palm. "Ouch! Stop that!"

Nathan laughed on his way out of the break room. "You yell at cats, now?" He grabbed one of the crates from her hands.

"Don't start. I need to talk to the chief."

"Chief Franklin's on the phone with the FBI. Doubt he has time to talk to you."

"Yeah, well, I have our forensic expert in my car and she's not in a state to cut anyone open, so what do I do?"

"Take it easy, Butch." Nathan maneuvered his way to the locker room, refurbished as an improvised cat shelter. "Don't trust her with a scalpel, eh? Bitch didn't even recognize me. Think she's gone a bit loony?"

Kate pushed out a deep exhale. Why did men assume she was in a chatty mood today? "Maybe she didn't want you to get friendly. If I were in her shoes, I would have forgotten you, too."

"That goes straight to my heart, Butch." He sucked his teeth. "Maybe I shouldn't be surprised, given what she did to Jake back in the day."

Kate raked the carpet with her boot. "You gonna tell me what's going on, or are we gonna gossip?"

"Right. Bottom line, Jacob's MIA."

"What?"

"Yeah. Just took off–I don't know why. Clearly, he didn't do anything wrong."

Kate snorted. Old friends were notoriously great judges of character.

"Look," Nathan said, proving her point. "I've known Jake forever. He wouldn't hurt a fly. He must have–I don't know, snapped. What would you do if you walked in on your father, dead?"

Kate caught her tongue between her teeth.

"Oh," Nathan said.

Of course, he knew Kate didn't have a father, and *she* knew that he knew. Because if he hadn't been the first to call her "Butch" in high school, he had been the one to theorize that the lack of male figures in her life had "swung her for the other team."

Kate felt the torrent of anger finally release. "I don't give a shit what your high school pal thought when he found his daddy's body, okay? This isn't the Bros Over Hos PD. Mayor or not, Jacob has to answer to us, and you can bet your ass he will."

She put the crate down, tucking it in a corner so the cat wouldn't topple it over. "Son of a bitch. Wouldn't like to be the one who has to find that one a home."

"What are you talking about?"

"Volunteers at the Humane Society," she said. "They're gonna get a handful with him."

Nathan chuckled, and the hairs on Kate's arms bristled. For a second, he looked exactly like the high school bully he had been. "Holy hell, Kate. You believe that?"

"What?"

"What we tell the town, so they don't form a pet protection committee or something. Didn't think anyone at the station was stupid enough to buy it. Kids, pet-loving families–sure. But not cops."

"Who are you calling stupid, you big ape?"

"Butcher," he said, "there is no Humane Society."

Blood pumped to her brain in a wave of acid heat.

"We take them to the pound and they kill the little freaks."

Thirty-Six

STRAYS

Air whizzed in her ears as Kate shot out of the station. *Calm down. Pretend you're baking. Raw peanut butter, hardening with flour, chocolate chips and pecans—*

Kate threw herself back into her car and banged the door shut. Dolores glanced at her, doe-eyed, and Kate raised up a palm. "Don't talk to me. Sorry, just—please shut the fuck up for a minute."

Kate started the car and hit the gas. She'd become a cop because she wanted to do good in the community. That it sounded cliché didn't make it any less true. She didn't do it to be a bully, but because she was *tired* of bullies.

And what good had that done? In the eight years she'd worked for the Little Horton PD, what had she achieved aside from getting disrespected ten thousand ways and killing cats?

Kate sighed and looked at Dolores. "I shouldn't have yelled."

"That's all right."

"Am I driving you home?"

Dolores answered in a deadpan tone, "Charlotte kicked me out."

"What?"

A car honked and a driver yelled at Kate to watch the fucking road. She'd missed a stop sign.

But damn. Charlotte Hawthorne, with her smile like melted butter?

"I never know if I like the woman," Kate's mother once said. "She acts warm enough, but I get a feeling if I stuck a thermometer in her she'd be cold as the Arctic."

"Jesus. You wanna talk about it?"

"I really don't."

So Kate kept driving, and somehow, it never occurred to her to drive Dolores to the motel.

The wheels purred against gravel as she parked in her driveway. "I have a couch," she said. "You can sleep there. That way I can keep an eye on you."

"Did your boss ask you to do that?"

Kate was silent for a second. "Yeah."

If Dolores knew she was lying, she didn't call her out on it.

Kate twisted the doorknob all the way to stop it from squeaking–it was way past Leo's bedtime. She and Dolores padded into the kitchen, the tile so clean it gleamed back at them. *Jesus, I'm dating a neat freak.* Kate poured a spoonful of instant coffee into a donut-shaped mug, which she'd bought as a private joke when she became a cop. "You take sugar?"

"Oh. No, thank you."

Kate repressed an eye roll. Dolores was probably the kind of person who scraped the butter off a slice of toast.

Kate put the mug in the microwave, snatched a mix of dried fruit out of the cupboard, and placed it on the countertop. "So she kicked you out. Charlotte." Dolores didn't reply. "It's really getting to her head, isn't it?"

"What is?"

"Power. Popularity. I've got to hand it to her, your stepmother knows a thing or two about getting her way. If your family hasn't been in Little Horton for three generations, you're a newcomer. But Charlotte?" The microwave beeped. Kate grabbed the mug and slid it to Dolores's side of the counter. "Everyone acts like her opinion is divine law. 'Is this pie good?' 'Should we push this book into the school program?'"

Kate chuckled. She'd never liked Charlotte Hawthorne. Or, really, any Hawthorne, and anyone else who acted like people should buy a ticket if they wanted to breathe the same air as them.

"Let me tell you, if that woman had kicked me out of my own house, I would–"

Kathleen, you're being INSENSITIVE.

Kate shoved a handful of cashews in her mouth and chewed.

"It's not my house anymore," Dolores said simply.

"Like hell it isn't! You grew up there, didn't you?" Kate scowled at her silence. "Typical."

"Typical?"

"She kicks you to the curb, and you just roll over so she can get your other side? I don't like you, but I'll drive you there right now if you'll stand up to that woman."

Dolores stared down at the donut mug. "Why aren't you with your team?" she asked. "A body's been found. The mayor's missing. You shouldn't be stuck here with me."

To her surprise, Kate blurted out an honest answer. "They don't want me there. In case you haven't noticed, I'm not exactly Miss Congeniality."

Dolores ran her thumb over the brim of the mug. A strange look came over her face. "Do you know if they've found Jacob yet?"

"Nope."

Kate didn't hold the bite back in her voice. The last thing she wanted to think about was Jacob and Dolores, together.

But the woman looked so shaken she let out a sigh, and added, "He can't have gone far. We'll find him. I mean, we better. Can you imagine what we'll tell the tourists? Two dead bodies, one missing person, and our own mayor AWOL?"

"You forgot Kristen."

A block of ice went down Kate's throat.

"I didn't remember her," Dolores said. "Until today."

"So it wasn't just me you forgot then," Kate said, then bit her tongue. *Kathleen Butcher, why are you cracking jokes at this* DISTRAUGHT *person?*

Dolores shook her head. "But I think–I think I've dreamt about her. Now, it keeps coming back to me. Did you know she had a boyfriend? A secret boyfriend."

Kate shrugged. "How much of a secret could he be if she told you?"

"She didn't tell me his name."

Kate put down the bowl of dried fruit. "Didn't the police find him? Back when they thought Kristen had run away?"

"I don't know. I don't think they cared all that much, to be honest."

"Yeah. I guess not."

The Horowitz family hadn't been the sort to make the front page. Kate grew up a stone's throw away from them. Circumstances could have pushed her and Kristen to be friends, or at least, friendly. But Kristen was so untouchable, with her pretty hair, her glossy lips, her mile-long legs beneath tweed miniskirts. Beautiful girls scared Kate back then worse than a pack of alligators. Although the Horowitzes, too, must have scraped money from under the couch at the end of each month, Kristen had that confidence about her. It radiated from her pores, came off in waves in her sweet bubble-gum smell.

Power.

Pretty girls had power in a way Kate felt in her bones that she never would. The power to make people like them, want to protect them. To make them think they *mattered*.

Kate shook off the thought. What a load of horseshit. It hadn't stopped Kristen from disappearing into a hole, had it? Maybe she had been better at surviving high school than Kate. Dated rich kids who bent over backward for her. But in the end, as far as Little Horton was concerned, Kristen was forgettable. Just like her. If Kate had disappeared, who but her mother would have given a flying fuck about it?

Kate licked her lips. "For a long time, I thought Kris was an asshole for dumping her little brother like that. Junior. You remember him?"

Dolores's eyes dropped toward the floor.

"I mean," Kate continued. "Her parents might have deserved it, treated her like garbage. But not Junior, right?"

Kate's mom took pity on the kid once when she saw him playing outside in his yellow raincoat, which he wore all year round whether it rained or not. "Why don't you go ask that boy if he wants to come in for a snack?" her mother said once, nudging Kate in the ribs.

"Because," Kate had groaned, "he'll think we like him, and we won't get rid of him for a million years."

A few months later, Kate and her mother had watched as the Horowitzes packed their belongings into a 1980 Chevy pickup. Kate's gut had twisted and she had known, even before the mailman confirmed it, that the Horowitz family had been evicted.

Kate's mother sounded appalled. "But winter's just a few weeks away!"

"Yeah," the mailman said. "I mean, they were never regular with rent, but they always scraped by in the end. Must have run out of friends."

With hindsight, that sounded odd to Kate. That they ran out of "friends." Like it was more than money they lacked. Like someone had wanted them out of the way.

"You have no idea who he could have been?" Kate said. "The secret boyfriend. Sounds like a plausible suspect, but then"–she shrugged– "Kristen was dating a lot of boys. Finn Jameson, from the football team. You remember him? He would have hung the moon for her. I think even Nathan had a thing going with her at some point," Kate mused. A wave of queasiness, as she pictured the adult, Viking-bearded Nathan leaving flowers in Kristen's locker. "God, they were pathetic, pining after her like dogs in heat."

"She went out with Jacob, too."

Kate's jaw as good as dropped to the floor. "*What?*"

Dolores was still staring at the donut mug. Kate could tell the words had come out before she'd weighed them, that she would like to drop the subject now.

She studied her for a while. There was something about the way Dolores had spoken Jacob's name just now–something that drained humor out of Kate's mind.

An undertone of *fear*. Hairy and raw; the sort that has sat in your chest, catching the dust for years.

Though she knew she was making her uncomfortable, Kate prodded. "Kristen and Jacob dated?"

"Yeah. Way before we–" She stopped.

Two days ago, Kate had seen Dolores coolly cut open Dr. Burke's chest and drain his intestines, but *now,* she looked like she might be getting nauseous.

"I'm sorry," she said, "I'm really tired."

It took a second for Kate to realize she'd been dismissed. Classic Hawthorne, dismissing someone in their own home. Still she couldn't resent it just now–was too unsettled by that flash of vulnerability. "Sure," Kate said. "I'll show you where you can sleep."

The living room couch was faux leather, sprinkled with cushions. Kate fished out two plaid blankets from the closet under the stairs, plushy against her palm. It made her think about the strays at the station.

Her throat jammed and she remembered all the times she'd been on Cats Duty, cat crates in her backseat, bitching about the feral smell of her vehicle–but she always smiled when all those yellow eyes met hers in the rearview mirror. Dark balls of matted fur inside the cages. Those cats wouldn't be winning any beauty contests. But then, Kate always liked people who didn't win better.

"Here," she said, handing the blankets to Dolores.

"Thank you."

"Don't mention it." Kate hoped she would take that literally.

"I meant, for everything. You didn't have to be nice to me."

Kate tilted her chin. "You think you're the only one who can be nice?"

"No. I just–" Dolores shook her head. "Like you said. You don't like me."

Discomfort crept up Kate's collarbone.

I've asked around, Paul Turner had said to her, *and it seems to me everybody in this damned town loved Dolores. So what's your problem with her?*

It wasn't just that Dolores was a Hawthorne, beautiful, smart, popular. In high school, Kate didn't have anything in particular against her–until that Halloween party.

She stared at Dolores for a long time, trying to determine if the woman was playing her. The utter lack of self-consciousness in that statement–*You don't like me.*

Halloween night 2003 had been one of the most humiliating moments of Kate's life. Could Dolores really not remember?

She shrugged, trying to chase away the thought. "I don't like anybody," she said.

Thirty-Seven

MASKS

Dolores dreamt she was home, but home was her bedroom at her father's house. She sank into the mattress as though it were ice cream.

"Jacob," she said.

The room spun, shadows contorted along the burgundy drapes of the canopy. A low whistle came out when she breathed.

Her lips parted and she tried to push the word out–"Jacob"–when the knuckles of a fist pressed against her teeth.

It pushed for entry, cracking open her mouth until the skin tore at the edges of her lips.

Dolores thought, *OPEN YOUR EYES,* but everything was midnight-black. *Sphenoid, frontal, lacrimal.*

She could taste the saltiness of the fist down her throat.

By the pricking of my thumbs–

Even with her eyes closed, she saw Jacob, on top of her, older, ugly, terrified.

Laughter trickled into the room. It rained down on Dolores, made even more horrible because she couldn't tell where it was coming from.

Then Jacob gripped the bottom of his chin and ripped his face off. It peeled like a mask and behind it he was young, and handsome, and smiling.

That smile.

Dolores screamed, and screamed, but there was no sound, nothing but the fist, the grin, her body sinking into the bed of ice cream.

"Hey!"

Dolores sat up, her jaw snapping shut so hard she chipped a tooth.

"You okay?" Kate asked. Her hair was a cloud of uncombed red, and she wore a Lion King T-shirt atop boxer shorts. She stood at some distance from the couch, palms up.

Dolores hugged the blanket to her chest, heart pumping against her fist. Dawn broke through the window, the world outside an ocean of orange leaves.

A chill crept down her back at the realization. Today was Halloween.

Thirty-Eight

THE HAWTHORNE-DIAZ CAMARADERIE

WhatsApp Group conversation: "The Hawthorne-Diaz Camaraderie."

Asher:

> Fuck, Dee, are you OK?

Josie:

> (Mom-voice) Watch your language around your sister, Asher.

Asher:

> Josie, can you give the conversation a normal name?

Dolores:

> I like it. Sounds very 1789 France.

Asher:

> Yesterday was bullshit. You don't have to leave.

Josie:

> What he means is, please don't turn this into a pride thing?
> Also, come back, pretty please. Two's company, three's a mutiny.

Asher:

> It's your home as much as Mom's.
> Dad would kill her if he knew about this.

Josie:

> So, are we going to talk about Mom's little guillotine moment?

Dolores:

> Have work today. Maybe squeeze lunch?

Josie:

> Some of us go to school. See you downtown at the party???

Leo was the last person Dolores would have pegged as Kate's type. Hollywood-handsome, and the kind of nice that overflowed, like foam bubbling out of a champagne bottle. Dolores declined his offers of breakfast, coffee, and a shower.

"If you're going to check into a motel," Leo offered, "I can drive you. You don't have to call a cab."

Dolores ran her tongue over her left incisor, where a tiny speck of enamel was missing. She needed space to think. "I'm fine."

"But–"

"She's *fine*, Leo," Kate cut in.

A taxi honked outside Kate and Leo's house three minutes after Dolores called for one. On a normal day, it would have taken half an hour.

But Halloween was no normal day. Tourists. They poured out of buses before Dolores even reached the city center: families, couples, friends ready for the authentic Halloween Town experience.

Dolores closed her eyes. She shouldn't be here for this.

"So, you a townie?" the driver asked, with such a wide smile he couldn't know how condescending he sounded. He went on about how lovely "Little H" was, praising the decorations as if Dolores had taken an active part in creating them. He talked so much, Dolores couldn't have squeezed in the sentence that lay thick on her tongue, even if she'd wanted to—*I've changed my mind, forget the motel, please drive me to the airport.*

The desire to run throbbed through her. To get out of here, before it was too late. Before past and present collapsed in on themselves.

Before the avalanche.

If I leave, now, if I choose flight again, will I be able to live with myself?

Oh, yes. The answer didn't take long to come. Dolores was very good at living around things.

Her phone warm in her hand, vibrating with her siblings' texts. The Hawthorne-Diaz Camaraderie. After eighteen years, she might not know how to be a Hawthorne anymore—but maybe she didn't have to. Maybe she didn't have to *be* a Hawthorne, to have her family.

I leave, and then what?

She could go back to Los Angeles, find happiness again. But what about Asher and Josie? She couldn't leave them now, any more than she could leave behind her pulsing heartbeat.

She wasn't a teenager anymore. It was about time she stopped running.

"Here we are." The driver parked in front of the motel. He cleared his throat when Dolores didn't move. "You change your mind?"

"No."

Dolores paid him and got out of the taxi. It had been many years since she had made up her mind so absolutely.

Thirty-Nine

SPIDER

"You okay?"

Kate startled as Leo handed her a cup of coffee. She'd been sitting on the sofa, playing with one of Leo's cushions. "Yeah."

Her lips puckered at the first sip. When they'd moved in together last month, Leo had asked how many sugars she took in her coffee and she said two, not wanting to admit the real answer was six.

"You look a little off."

"Not used to waking up to a woman screaming in the house," she said. Couldn't tell Leo about the cats. If he knew that all the strays he'd led her to discover had not, in fact, been sent to the Humane Society, she would be dealing with another screaming person.

Leo exhaled. She looked up from her coffee. "Look, Kate, I know you got a lot on your plate. But since you spotted Dolores in the streets the other day, you've been–"

"What?"

"You've been acting strange." He tilted his head left, then right. "I guess I'm trying to ask, did it upset you to have her here?" He hesitated. "I just thought since she clearly isn't your favorite person, and you had it so rough in high school . . ."

"You think Dolores bullied me?"

She laughed. Wondered if what Dolores had done to her counted as bullying.

"Well, didn't she? You never said what your problem with her was."

Kate stiffened. That same uncomfortable nerve Paul had disturbed outside the morgue. "I'm fine. Just not looking to invite her for another sleepover."

"It's just–"

"I bet you thought she was nice. You'd be the type of person to get along with her."

Leo looked at her without a drop of anger. The bomb rising up her throat defused.

"Why are you getting defensive? I'm not interested in Dolores, Kate. I'm interested in you. I just wanna know what she did to you–why it put you in such a state to have her spend the night."

Kate's eyes dropped toward her shoes. Leo wasn't some FBI agent snooping into her past. He was the first man she'd dated who treated her right–so right, she didn't know how to treat him *back*.

She pushed out a sour breath. It was time she met him halfway. "Okay," she said. "But this is not a sob story. You are forbidden to feel sorry for me."

To her surprise, he nodded, as earnest as if she had been about to knight him.

She gathered her thoughts before she began, "We didn't know each other well. Didn't hang with the same crowd. Okay, more like, I didn't hang with any crowd. But in our last year in high school, she–she tried to make friends with me."

Leo shrugged. "Crucify her."

She elbowed him. "She invited me to her Halloween party."

"Okay. Did it not go well?"

Kate pried her jaws apart. "You don't get it. She invited me to make fun of me."

"Cripes."

Kate kept silent. The whole memory tasted rancid. Goose bumps broke out at the base of her neck, like she was shaking a spiders' nest perched right above her head.

She could still backpedal, leave the memory undisturbed.

"What makes you think she did it to make fun of you?"

"I don't remember," she lied.

He looked at her, not fooled. "Don't you think you'll feel better if you tell me?"

Her fist dug a crater into the faux-leather couch. "*Everyone* was laughing at me, Leo. They sent me up to her bedroom. The door was open. And–"

Kate's mouth opened on chalky silence.

"What? What happened?"

She snapped. "Jesus, you really want to know? Dolores was there, okay, naked, and Jacob was fucking her."

Oxygen sucked out of her lungs. Her body went numb.

Why had these particular words occurred to her? Kate wouldn't usually have framed it like this—wouldn't have painted a woman as passive during sex. This wasn't the 1950s, for heaven's sake. Yet as the images streamed back into her brain, she knew she couldn't put it any other way.

Dolores and Jacob hadn't been "making love," or even "screwing." *They* hadn't been fucking, either. Dolores hadn't gasped and said, "Oh, shit, Kate," or pushed Jacob off her. She hadn't met Kate's eyes and drilled into her the knowledge that this was all one big joke, and that Kate was the butt of it, as usual.

Dolores hadn't done anything.

A breath of ice blew down Kate's back.

She had spent her whole adult life trying not to think of that Halloween party, and now it flooded back, so vivid she could smell the special shampoo she'd used to flatten her hair. The gorgeous Hawthorne house, fake spiders dangling from the ceiling and corn syrup dribbling down the mirrors and windows. Kate had felt so out of place, the armpits of her dress soaking with sweat. What if she knocked a vase off a shelf that wound up costing more than her parents' house?

She'd arrived after ten, to make sure she could slip in and out unnoticed if necessary. Wild horses wouldn't have dragged the confession out of her–but this one party could be the magical wand that changed Kate's pumpkin of a life into a beautiful carriage. Give Kate one popular friend, and everything weird about her could become "quirky." No one would think to bully her anymore, because the cool kids never bullied one of their own. Maybe. Just maybe.

Kate had scanned the living room, half dazzled by the chandelier, as she searched for Dolores among the drunk teenagers. Finally, someone spotted her. Nathan.

"Butch!" He opened his arms in mock excitement, like she was his sister home from boarding school.

His greeting shone a beacon of light onto her crimson face. She felt stupid in the dress she'd bought for the occasion, so insanely stupid she could have slapped herself.

"Butch!" the other boys started to cry out. "Butch, Butch, Butch!"

Her back bumped against the buffet draped in crepe paper, where black cauldrons spilled caramel apples.

"You know," Nathan said, a gleam in his eye, "Dolls was just looking for you. She's in her room."

Laughter seeped from the crowd. Nathan's words reeked with mischief, but Kate had gone too far to stop. Part of her was starting to suspect this would turn into a *Carrie* thing, and yet, it didn't occur to her to think Dolores could be involved. More likely she would put an end to the hoax.

That had been her gut feeling. Never mind the narrative she would end up believing for years.

Kate climbed the stairs, her hand smearing sweat up the polished banister.

Her breath hitched as she held her fist over Dolores's door. It was ajar, and there was movement, *noises,* inside. Kate pushed open the door, and her bowels turned liquid. Heat had rushed to her face, not in humiliation so much as shock–

She became aware of Leo now, crouching next to her. "Jacob–" he started. "Jacob did what?"

Kate couldn't answer, or make sense of what had felt so weird and *wrong* about the tableau she walked in on. Why didn't she just apologize and close the door? No one had noticed her. For that matter, why had it felt so humiliating, why was she convinced that Dolores had lured her there on purpose?

Dolores hadn't made eye contact.

Of that, Kate was sure.

Something sticky as sugar wax rained down on her as she stood there, feet growing roots inside the floor. Shame more primal than she'd ever felt before.

Back then, it'd made sense to think it had all been staged. That it had all been about Kate.

But now that she looked back on it, as an adult?

If Dolores meant to humiliate her, what kind of a method was this?

Getting fucked by your boyfriend while someone else watched—wouldn't Dolores have felt her own share of humiliation?

"Getting fucked," Kate repeated to herself. Why did she keep thinking about it like that?

For the first time, she tried to remember exactly what she had seen in that bedroom. Jacob, on top of Dolores—he was still wearing his clothes. Kate searched for Dolores, and it was like cutting a path into a nest of cobwebs. Everything sticky and dark and because of the webs, Kate knew *there must be* a spider somewhere, but it was always tucked in her blind angles, creeping above her on the ceiling, just outside her field of vision.

Jacob hadn't seen her—at any rate, he didn't stop when Kate opened the door, didn't mind her, and why didn't Dolores have a face?

Kate gasped.

Leo's thumb brushed her cheek.

Why didn't Dolores have a face?

Kate had seen Dolores in that bedroom. She hadn't just *assumed* it was her because she was in her room. For all she knew, she could have knocked on the wrong door, but she hadn't, because Dolores was lying on that bed, hair tangled, eyes shut—

Eyes shut?

"Kate?" Leo shook her shoulders gently. "Kate, are you all right?"

From the look in his eyes, she could tell how white she'd gone.

She had forgotten Dolores's face because it had looked WRONG. So wrong that Kate had stumbled back and floated down the stairs, not hearing a word of her classmates' laughter. Suddenly she was in the streets, the night air making her whole body numb. She'd agonized over the thought of seeing Dolores on Monday, but Dolores didn't come back to school. Even a friendless girl like Kate picked up on gossip. She only had to pull her legs up on the bathroom seat when girls *click-clacked* into the room.

"Dolls is *sick*."

"Again?"

"I can't believe her. My parents won't let me stay in bed unless they can fry an egg on my face."

"I think it's mono."

"Nah, she's just bawling her eyes out over Jacob."

"Girl's gotta move on. Didn't he fuck that freshman at her party?"

"I hear Dolly was the one who two-timed *him*."

"Like, to his face?"

"I didn't get the graphic details."

Another girl cut through the giggles. "You have no idea what you're talking about. My sister was at the party. Dolly and Jacob hooked up with each other. Everyone saw them go upstairs together–it was awkward. People *cheered*."

"Ew."

"Then I think they broke up because Jacob was a bad lay or shit."

Vanilla deodorant wafted through the room before the doors swung open and closed.

Weeks turned into months, and eventually the rumor mill reported the Hawthornes had hired private tutors. Whenever Kate caught a glimpse of Dolores, walking down the street, she scrambled for the nearest exit. So much for her Cinderella story. She didn't want to see Dolores's face again. Ever.

"Kate," Leo said now, "you're freaking me out."

"I think–" Kate's mouth was so dry, she could barely get the words out. "I think Jacob raped Dolores at her Halloween party."

"What?"

Kate wrenched free from Leo. Before she realized she was pacing, she kicked against the coffee table. The mug Leo had brought her spilled onto the carpet.

"I don't know. I'm probably making this up."

"Why would you make up something like that?"

Kate laughed, and the notes of madness in it chilled her. "I don't know."

How could she explain? The spider perched on the ceiling, trickling down its web, above her, *on* her, everywhere except where she could see it.

It was this same spider whose legs she had felt creeping down her spine, ever since she had seen Dolores again. When Dolores had spoken Jacob's name in that strange voice, last night—when they were talking about Kristen's secret boyfriend.

Kate clenched her teeth. "Why did she keep it a secret?" she muttered. "Who did she keep it a secret *from*?"

"What?"

She ignored Leo. Had no room in her head for him right now.

Kristen's parents couldn't have cared less that she had a boyfriend, or twenty. Why bother with the secrecy? Maybe the guy was older, or married. Or maybe he already had a girlfriend.

Kate gnawed at the skin stretched taut over her knuckles.

Yesterday, Dolores said Jacob and Kristen had been an item before they started dating. But maybe—

Maybe Jacob had kept dating Kristen, even after he started seeing Dolores. That would be a good reason for Kristen not to tell Dolores who her boyfriend was, if he also happened to be dating Dolores.

Kate munched on this for a second. If what she remembered from that Halloween night was right, if Jacob was capable of rape—was it a stretch to think he might also be capable of murder? Could he have killed Kristen and made her disappear? His family had enough money to cover his tracks and get the rest of the Horowitzes out of the way.

Must have run out of friends, the mailman had said.

But why did the whole family have to go unless they knew something? Unless the killer saw them as a threat?

"Honey," Leo said. "Is there anything I can do? Do you need more coffee?"

Kate lowered her eyes to the brown stain soaking into the carpet. "Shit. I'm sorry, Leo."

"Hey." He kissed her temple. "I asked you to move in, and you said yes. You can take a sledgehammer to the walls for all I care."

Kate let out a choked noise. Nobody was this fucking perfect.

"I'll go clean it up," he said, and trotted to the bathroom upstairs. Kate made her way to the kitchen. A half-full pot of coffee sat on the counter, and she opened the fridge to get some milk. She grabbed the carton, only to jump back with a cry.

A photograph stared back at her, printed below the slogan, "Happy Milk, Happy Drink!"

A girl with a pearly-white smile glowed for the camera. With her dark hair and clean-cut cheekbones, she looked so much like Kristen that Kate felt she had cut her hand on a fragment of the past.

"Son of a bitch," she said.

It was just that damned commercial. "Happy Wisconsin Milk." She'd even seen it before a couple of times—they printed it on billboards, milk cartons, coffees to go.

But it hadn't struck her how much the actress looked like Kristen Horowitz until now.

Or, for that matter, like Dolores Diaz.

Forty

BLACK TIDE RISING

Dolores remembered the first time she'd heard the words. She knew them, yes. Charlotte knew, and of course, Dr. Burke knew. But no one had *said* them until her third year of med school.

Abdominal pregnancy.

"You're not likely to come across one," their teacher said, face splattered with freckles. "The odds are one in ten thousand." He pointed at the corpse, tucked beneath a green sheet.

Nausea snaked up Dolores's body.

She pictured the wound. Flesh open and pink, exposed to their lights, their scalpels, their hungry eyes.

Her scar started to burn.

"What can you tell me about it?"

Hands soared. Dolores tried to breathe. The bones of her head. *Lacrimal. Orbital–*

"It's the least common of ectopics," a student recited. "The fetus grows outside the womb, but not in one of the Fallopian tubes. Symptoms are mild until the baby grows, so it's fairly easy to miss. The longer it goes undiagnosed, the more dangerous it is. Risks of mortality are higher than for other ectopics."

"Very good."

Dolores's breath came out heavy, wheezing.

It calmed most people–meditation. To focus on the air coming in and out of their lungs. But nothing was surer to launch her into a panic attack.

There was little she remembered about the assault. Her lids drooping shut, like they'd been dipped in tar. But the way each breath clawed out of her? That, she remembered. The beauty of its uncompromising mechanics. *Draw oxygen through your nose and mouth. You have two minutes. Or die.* It tattooed itself to the flesh of her heart, as deep as the soul should be.

A vague memory, of telling Charlotte, "I felt like I was being murdered."

Her stepmother's perennial coolness as she pinched her cheek. "You look alive to me."

Dolores paced the room for the hundredth time. The motel outside Little Horton fell under "musty but cozy," without crossing the "seedy" line. The water was tepid, but not cold, the carpet puke-colored but not smelly, and the closest thing to a roach was the polka-dot print on the wallpaper. Dolores paced, and paced.

For the first time in eighteen years, she did not push back against the tide of memories.

She welcomed it.

Tried to zoom in on that Halloween night. Words rose to the surface, but after a while, she realized they were Charlotte's.

That sick, twisted swine.

After we welcomed him into our house. If he so much as shows his face again I'll–

–gut you like an animal.

Dolores shook her head. Couldn't cut past the tangle of Charlotte's threads, twined around her memory. It was pointless to ask anybody else what they remembered. There was no one to ask.

What your father doesn't know won't hurt him.

Dolores halted. The memories stirred about her, a glittering black sea. Charlotte had told her so many times, that it was Jacob–

The twisted swine.

But Charlotte hadn't been there, in that room. And other than what she *felt*–being chain-sawed open, fighting for each breath–Dolores didn't remember a wink of it.

There'd been no reason to doubt her stepmother. Why would she have lied?

But now that she'd seen Jacob again–

His chest bumping against her fingertips. The pulsing need to go after him, the feeling that entered her bone marrow. *This man would never hurt me.*

After a few more minutes, tasting the rankness of her own thoughts, Dolores peeled off her clothes and headed for the shower. She stood under the hot spray, enjoyed the prickle of pain numbing her skin.

If this were a movie, she would cry, pretty, silent tears.

She got out, and tried to get the hair dryer to work for five minutes. Damn it. This was all she needed, to go out with her hair wet and catch her death.

If the coffee machine is out of order, I'm going to scream. She headed out of her room and down the hall, then stopped in her tracks as she reached the breakfast area.

Though the man bending to pick up his coffee had his back to her, Dolores couldn't mistake the tailored suit, the long limbs, the light brown hair that hung below his ears.

Wyatt swiveled and stepped back in surprise, but managed to redirect the plastic cup before he splashed coffee all over his shirt.

"Miss Diaz."

She bit her tongue to stop herself from apologizing. Charlotte was right–it did make her look weak.

Luckily, Wyatt was too polite to ask what she was doing there. "I mean, good morning. I–I was waiting for an appropriate time to call you." He stepped aside to free the space before the coffee machine, looking suddenly too tall for the ceiling.

A smile tugged at her lips as he shifted on his feet. She'd hate for the agent to think she was laughing at his expense. But the sight of him in this place was genuinely, sweetly funny. On the phone last night, he'd sounded so at ease, but this morning, he was like a wild bird out of his habitat.

She had never been alone with Wyatt before, and in this one off-script glimpse, she sensed for the first time the man beneath the armor. The underlying awkwardness in his long limbs, his struggle to think of the right thing to say when he wasn't reacting to a crisis or conducting an interview.

Dolores poured herself a coffee and landed them back on familiar ground. "I assume you need me at the morgue to examine Gregory Winslow."

"If you could spare the time, yes." They started down the corridor. "We called in someone from our forensic team in Milwaukee, but I'm sure he could use your assistance."

"Of course."

He didn't need to explain why. When building a case against a serial killer, it was better to have the same pathologist examine all the bodies.

"If you need a ride, my partner and I can drop you off on our way to the police station."

"Thank you. I could actually use one."

In the parking lot, Paul was standing by the Chrysler, lighting a cigarette. He took it out of his mouth to flash Dolores a smile. "Dr. Diaz. Aren't you staying at your father's house?"

"And good morning to you, Agent Turner."

"Is that Dolores Diaz for 'Mind your own business'?"

They didn't know each other well enough for Paul to act like he knew the Dolores Diaz for anything. He unlocked the car and slipped into the driver's seat, then looked at Wyatt. "You won't let a woman sit in the backseat, will you, Big Guy?"

Dolores protested, "Oh, I don't mind."

The backseat would rhyme with hell for a man as tall as Wyatt. But even as she said it, she knew she was too late. Wyatt clearly thought of himself as a gentleman—and gentlemen would respond to Paul's comment exactly as Paul expected them to.

Wyatt opened the backseat door and somehow made his legs fit in the small space behind her seat.

Dolores sat next to Paul, who couldn't have looked more gleeful if he'd been whistling.

Wait. He didn't . . . he *couldn't* think that just because she'd come out of the motel with Wyatt—

"I suppose my partner told you about Dr. Marley?" Paul said. "Never worked with him, but I hear he's something. You don't get to work with the bureau if you're *not* something, right?"

Dolores refused to treat the comment like it warranted a reply. "Did you find Jacob yet?"

The cockiness on Paul's face went down a notch. "No."

"I thought you had cruisers patrolling the neighborhood."

"Jacob Winslow is the mayor. He can rely on people. If he left town before the police caught him, obviously, he had help." Paul sighed. "That's the problem with tight-knit communities. Everyone helps everyone, except us."

"What about Jacob's brother?" she asked, as Paul stopped at a red light–relieved he *did* stop. Given how he seemed to think yellow meant green, she worried he'd be color-blind to red as well.

"Teddy Winslow?" Paul said. "The police notified him. He doesn't live in town."

"No," Dolores said, "but he was in town yesterday. I called him last night, and he didn't pick up."

Paul's eyes met Wyatt's in the rearview mirror. How such completely different men could exchange silent messages was beyond Dolores.

"We'll be sure to check on that," Paul said.

Outside the window, kids dressed as mini-witches and dinosaurs raced down pumpkin-lined streets on their way to school. Dolores chewed on her tongue.

Dr. Burke, dead, and now, Gregory Winslow. He may not have taken a scalpel to her, as Dr. Burke had, but he had been happy to butcher her reputation. Calling her "a Jezebel," "a loose woman," as soon as she and Jacob broke up. It hadn't taken Gregory long to turn on her, to forget all those times he sat at her father's dinner table.

Her mouth dried as she pictured Alexander.

In days to come, you may learn things that will change me in your eyes forever. I ask only that you hold on to the image of the father you remember.

Could he have found out about the deal Charlotte and Winslow had made, the surgery that almost killed her? Had he gone to the Winslow house last week to confront Gregory?

Her hands were fists in her lap. Paul's eyes glanced down, and she forced them to relax.

Dr. Burke and Gregory Winslow had both played a part in driving her away from Little Horton. They were both reminders of the assault.

What are you up to, Dad? What game are you playing?

In her mind, she could see her father, smiling, as he did at the beginning of a treasure hunt. *I won't help you, my angel,* he'd say, no matter how many times she begged him. *Why?* His lips would twist around a gleeful laugh. *Because you're smart enough to find the answer all on your own.*

Dolores stared at the road. A taste like unsweetened lime coated her tongue, and her face prickled as if–

Ridiculous.

As if someone were watching her.

Whoever was out there, killing these men–what sick sort of justice was he enacting?

Goose bumps broke down her skin.

And just *who* was he avenging?

Forty-One

WIVES

Wyatt left Dolores at the morgue with the FBI's expert, after Paul got her to agree to call them when she was finished. "My partner and I would love to give you a ride back." He winked at Wyatt when he said this, and unease trickled down Wyatt's stomach.

As they walked to the car, he fought the urge to blab. Guilty people talk more than the innocent. Still the words blurted out, beyond his control. "About earlier," he said. Paul gave him a look. "I don't know what it looked like, but I ran into Miss Diaz in the breakfast room before we came out."

"Is that a fact?"

"Yes."

Silence. Wyatt cleared his throat.

"What I'm saying is, nothing happened between us."

"Jesus, man." Paul slid into the driver's seat again. "What are you doing?"

"Excuse me?"

"Why are you defending that woman's honor? What's there to defend? I'm not some dirty old man about to call her a slut. You think I give a shit if she was in there to fuck you or another man or twenty? Good for her if she was."

Wyatt's jaw tensed. He didn't know if Paul was being serious or trying to push his buttons again.

"Don't talk about her like that."

Paul laughed. "Look at you. Seven years younger than me and acting like you were born in the fifties."

"I said—"

"Oh, fuck off, partner. I believe you, all right? If Dolores wanted to get some fun out of an FBI agent, I like to think she would have knocked on my door, not yours. But I've seen the way you look at her."

"She—" Wyatt swallowed. "She's obviously competent."

Paul laughed. "Competent? Come on, Big Guy. You act like she's the prettiest cheerleader in school and you're the pimply nerd."

Wyatt blew air through his teeth.

"You know what, though?" Paul said. "You don't have pimples, man. With a haircut, a little workout, and ten hours of sleep in you, you wouldn't look half bad. I don't see why Dolores Diaz would kick you out of bed. I wouldn't."

Wyatt looked up at Paul, taken aback. He couldn't think of anything to say for a while. "Seriously?"

Paul shrugged. "Like I said. You act the part of the ugly duckling, but you don't look it, man."

Wyatt sighed. He wasn't about to have a heart-to-heart with Paul Turner. Was he? *The guy's an asshole.* But he was also his partner. Besides, seeing as how they specialized in such different kinds of cases, what were the odds they'd ever talk to each other again after this?

"I'm not good with people," Wyatt admitted.

"Are you kidding? You think I'd act like such a pain in the ass if you didn't balance it out? You're slick as a whistle."

Wyatt shook his head. "I mean, outside my job."

"I know." Paul put the cigarette between his lips. "Don't look so surprised—it shows, all right? You can work with people, but not *with* people. When you do interviews, you're in control. You know what part to play. But when someone's on your side, with no façade to keep up, it's a different story. Hey," he said when Wyatt's gaze dropped, "I'm not going to head-shrink you. You should just play it cool, man. Easy does it."

Paul let go of the wheel to slap Wyatt's shoulder, and Wyatt winced. He'd been an idiot for thinking the guy understood the first thing about him.

"I gotta say, it hurts my feelings you didn't even ask what *I've* been up to all night."

Wyatt kept a straight face. "Did it cross your mind I don't wanna know?"

Paul laughed. "I was listening to the records of Charlotte Hawthorne's phone conversations."

In the event of a kidnapping, it was standard procedure to have the family phones tapped, but Paul had preferred to get a warrant, and not give the Hawthornes a heads-up. Not the move Wyatt would have gone for–but then, Paul was the one with experience.

"The body count doesn't change a thing, then," Wyatt said. "If Hawthorne's alive, you still think his wife is helping him."

"That's one important if, but yes."

Wyatt let the thought brew. "You don't think he would be the old-fashioned kind? To protect his woman from the truth?"

"The woman he gave a sword to on their wedding day? She needs protecting?"

That was a fair point. Wyatt asked, already knowing the answer, "Did you catch her red-handed? A conversation between her and the missing husband?"

"No," Paul admitted.

"Of course not. She's too smart not to know we're tapping her phone."

"Maybe so. But you know who she did talk to, yesterday, a little after five?"

Wyatt met Paul's eyes, hazarded a guess. "Gregory Winslow?"

"Gregory Winslow. He called her, to express his sympathies."

"And?"

"Oh, it was all surface. Both of them talking like a troop of law enforcement agents were beaming flashlights at them."

Wyatt cocked his head to the side. "Told you."

"She did say *one* interesting thing."

Paul made him wait for it. Wyatt sighed in annoyance. "What?"

"That she appreciated his concern, and hoped they could find time to see more of each other in the future. She said, 'I know you and Alexander miss the old gatherings. I know you talked about this when you saw each other last week–and I want to tell you *I understand the message.* Loud and clear.'"

Wyatt eyed Paul dubiously. "You're just–quoting that, verbatim?"

"I can play it for you if you like."

Wyatt shook his head. "She understands the message."

"Yep."

"That could mean anything. What else did she say?"

"Thanked him for calling," Paul said, shrugging, "and said she was sure Alexander would come home, unharmed, and everything would go back to the way it was."

A beat of silence. Wyatt tried to picture those words leaving Charlotte's mouth. "What did she sound like to you?"

"Like this was more than empty chitchat."

The words hung in the car for a while. Ultimately, Paul asked, "Where are we on the other wife? Annette Winslow."

Wyatt shook his head. "Jacob made no attempt to contact her."

Last night, after they'd secured the crime scene at Gregory's house, Jacob's wife had been their first stop. As it turned out, she had kept living in the conjugal house, even when her husband moved back into his childhood home to care for his father.

"What about Teddy Winslow?" Paul said. "Think the police got hold of him?"

"I think his little brother got to him first."

"Yeah. No kidding."

Wyatt weighed his next words. "Look, seeing as the whole town would bet their right hand that Jacob's innocent–"

"A town that watched him grow up. Hardly reliable."

Wyatt ignored him. "Let's play into it. Jacob kills his father, then smashes his face in a fit of anger. Why does he go to an ex-girlfriend he hasn't seen in eighteen years? Wouldn't he leave town as fast as possible?"

Paul shrugged. "You get in the state to do *that* to your father, you're crazy enough to do anything."

"Okay, then let's look at the other incidents. It's safe to assume whoever killed Winslow also killed Dr. Burke, and dug up that dead girl's bones?"

"Right."

"Jacob kills the doctor—let's say he has his reasons. But why put that girl's bones right behind City Hall? He knows it'll look like a finger pointing right in his direction."

Paul considered this. "Fine. If he's *not* guilty, why does he run?"

Wyatt let out a breath. "Same reason Hawthorne wrote that note to his daughter. Same reason Gregory taped a gun to his wheelchair. Because he thinks he's next."

Forty-Two

ALL-INNERS

Anyone who owned a television knew doctors had an arrogance issue. From a certain angle, it made sense. How else did you get yourself through ten-plus years of studies before you saw the color of a paycheck? You became your own boss. *You* told your body when it could take a break–and once you were your own boss, you became everybody else's. *Scalpel. Clamps.* Dolores guarded herself against it constantly.

"What do we have here–Christ. Did you ever see so many tumors in your life? Those lungs are like pieces of French cheese."

Before she met Dr. Marley, she would have expected the arrogance factor to metastasize in the combination of "doctor" and "FBI." But he came off as astonishingly ordinary. Five-four on tiptoe, with a smile that recalled Peter Falk as Lieutenant Columbo.

Seeing as he was here to take over forensic work in the investigation, Dolores expected to assist him, but he let her take the lead, and insisted she talk for the record because "I can't stand to hear myself on tape."

When they were finished, Dolores followed Dr. Marley into the reception area, toward the vending machine. "How do you take yours?"

"Black."

He winced. "You black-coffee people fascinate me. I suppose you also take cold showers in the morning, fat-free mayonnaise inside your sandwiches?"

Dolores melted as her lips touched the foam, blissfully bitter. Good coffee, like good lovers, made her forget the bad ones.

"You have children, Dr. Diaz?"

The question hit her like a slap.

"No."

"Me either. With the kind of work we do, it's for the best if you ask me. Married?"

Dolores studied the man through her eyelashes. She got a feeling Dr. Marley was a lot sharper than he looked. "Not for much longer."

"Sorry to hear that. I don't mean to pry–I asked because I could tell watching you work how much you love what you do. Must say you know your way with a scalpel. Some in our line of work choose the dead over the living out of fear–mistakes are hard to live with in a hospital. But not you, clearly. You could save lives with these hands. Makes you wonder."

"What?"

He shrugged. "Who makes that kind of choice? Dead bodies over living ones."

Dolores brushed her thumb against the brim of her cup. "I used to dream about being a doctor. Saving people."

She paused, but he waited her out. "And then?"

"When I was an intern this girl came in. Nineteen years old. Twenty-three stab wounds."

"Sweet lord."

Dolores could see her again with pinpoint precision. The port-wine stain on her cheek. Dyed-pink hair that gave off whiffs of gingerbread shampoo through the cloud of antiseptic, trash, and urine.

"She was still alive, somehow," Dolores said. "A passerby found her in a dumpster; she'd been there–four, five hours. It was mid-July. The heat alone could have killed her. The pancreas was hit, and her liver. Perforated bowels spilling into her abdomen. We rushed her into surgery, but there was so much damage. I've never *seen* a live body with that much damage."

Dr. Marley eyed her intently. "Did you save her?"

The resident's face came back to Dolores, red with exhaustion, as he stopped her gloved hand. *There's nothing we can do.* Dolores had hardened against the idea. A girl didn't survive hours cooking in a pile of garbage all so she could be found and die on an operating table.

"No. I followed her to the morgue. Watched them weigh every organ, collect hairs from her clothes. It was so quiet. In the OR, every second is life or death, but this was all–death. And I just thought"–she licked her lips–"there has to be someone who does something for these bodies, broken beyond saving. Who bears witness to that violence."

"Ah," Dr. Marley said. "I understand. You and me, the lot of us who deal in death, we follow crime behind closed doors, into dark alleys, places even God turns a blind eye to. Because someone has to. We don't save the dead–but we see them. We don't right the ways they've been wronged, but we do right by them."

He drained his cup. Cocoa-sprinkled cream smeared his upper lip. "Just as well we don't have a family. The dead take up too much space. When you love your job that much, when you're *all in,* anyone who shares your life becomes like a mistress. You can't give them weekends or romantic holidays. You can't give them more than what the dead leave you." Dr. Marley pointed a finger at her. "And you, ma'am, you're an all-inner. Takes one to know one."

Dolores stayed silent, the paper cup in her hand turning lukewarm. "It was Agent Turner, right?"

"Sorry?"

"The bureau sent you to take over for the autopsies. But Paul gave you an extra task."

Dolores didn't break eye contact. Dr. Marley was not as clueless as he looked, and this was not coffee-break chitchat. It was a job interview. The personal questions, and the fact he had let her perform the autopsy, all told her as much.

Dolores said, "He wanted you to give an expert's opinion, to find out how good I am."

A smile spread like strawberry jam over Dr. Marley's features. "Well, I don't want to insult your intelligence. You're not gonna ask if you passed?"

She sipped her coffee. Couldn't think of an answer that wouldn't sound arrogant.

"They could use you in Milwaukee, Doctor."

"They use me plenty in Los Angeles."

He chuckled. "Well. If I were you, I'd give it some thought. It's not every day the FBI makes you an offer. It could change your life."

"What makes you think I want that?"

He gave her his Columbo smile. "Like I said, Doctor. It takes one to know one."

Forty-Three

KISS AND TELL

Outside the morgue, Dolores started to text Asher about where to meet for lunch. Tires purred against gravel, and she looked up from her phone in time to see the Chrysler drawing into the parking lot. The door flung open and Paul stepped out. She had completely forgotten about riding back to town with the FBI.

Paul seemed to read as much off her face. "Didn't we have a date?"

"Must have slipped my mind," she said. Four-hour autopsies did that to you.

His gaze was serious. "You'll have to tell me how that happened. I don't usually have that effect on women."

"Where's Agent Holt?"

"Am I my partner's keeper?" Dolores gave him a look, and he relented. "I left him at the police station."

He snapped open the car door for her. She clutched the crisp sheets of paper fresh out of the printer. "Here." She handed them over to Paul. "I was going to give this to you this afternoon. It's a summary of our autopsy findings."

He shoved the key in the ignition and arched his brows. "Why don't you give me the audiobook version."

Dolores repressed an eye roll. "The cause of death was likely a shot to the head."

"Let me guess. Smith & Wesson, fifty-caliber."

"Yes. Given the insubstantial tangible remains, it's difficult to say whether Winslow was still alive when his head was smashed."

"We didn't find any heavy object with blood on it at the scene," Paul said.

"You wouldn't have. He used his foot." That much was plain from the mud residue.

"Hell. Does that suggest a lot of strength?"

"Not necessarily. The cranial structure must have been weakened from the shot."

"So, a woman could have done this?"

She looked up from the pages. "Do you have a suspect?"

"Just crossing Ts, Dr. Diaz."

She slipped her tongue through her lips. Curiosity battled against professionalism.

"Photographs from the crime scene indicated the same shoeprints as at Michael Burke's and my father's office. As I told you before, they point to a male killer."

"Couldn't it be a woman wearing men's shoes?"

"It's possible."

Before she could prod him about this new thread, he said, "Any other footstep patterns at Winslow's?"

"One. Probably Jacob's."

"Speaking of the younger Winslows. Jacob's brother isn't answering our calls."

Dolores thought this over. When they'd run into each other at the diner, Teddy had been his regular, three-hundred-mile-a-minute self. Why would he evade the police?

"Well," she said. "He must have a lot to deal with."

"Really? With his brother missing and his father gruesomely murdered, you don't think it's strange he has *other* priorities?"

Dolores sighed. "Unless their father squandered his fortune somehow, Teddy and Jacob are sitting on millions of dollars."

"Your point?"

"They don't need to run from the law."

Paul glanced at her in genuine surprise before he chuckled. "I appreciate your faith in the justice system."

"Look, I realize personal opinion carries precious little weight here. True," she conceded, "I don't believe Jacob would kill his father. But even if I'm wrong, he could do better than take off and make himself look like the prime suspect. He's well-liked in the community, and he has money–a lot of money. Even if you had a picture of him shooting a hole through his father's head, don't you think his lawyer could convince the jury the gun was really a phone, and he was calling an ambulance?"

She'd been so focused on making sure no emotions were on display as she mentioned Jacob, she didn't notice the grave look in the agent's eyes. His jaw squared. "You think everyone can be bought?"

"Most people can."

Paul looked at her as if she had just poured a milkshake in his lap.

"You're telling me you trust the system that much, Agent Turner?"

"You're telling me you *don't*?"

Dolores shook her head. She wasn't about to debate public corruption with an FBI agent.

"So," he said, "the fact Teddy probably abetted his brother in escaping law enforcement, that doesn't strike you as suspicious?"

"I don't think he killed his father, if that's what you're driving at. Trust me, you could not find a bigger daddy's boy than Teddy Winslow. If he's running, then he thinks it's his only option. He wouldn't be afraid of talking to the police–he's good-looking, good with people. Could sweet-talk you into just about anything."

"Any reason *he* didn't become mayor?"

She let out a sour chuckle. "Teddy could do a lot better than Little Horton."

"And Jacob couldn't?"

Her stomach tightened. Despite his openness and easygoing charm, Paul was no open book. He veered off topic without a prelude. "What did you think of Dr. Marley, then? He any good?"

Well, that was something. Paul wasn't content to just have Dr. Marley check her out. He had the gall to make it sound like he wanted her take on him as well?

"I should hope so," she said. "He's a federal employee."

Paul cocked his head to the side. The vertebrae in his neck cracked. "No kiss-and-tell. I see." Silence settled. His eyes steered from the road to gauge her. "Did he tell you?"

"Tell me what?"

"Don't play dumb, Dr. Diaz."

"You want a plain answer, then say what you mean."

He exhaled. "Look, I don't need that Marley guy to know you're good at your job. Yes, I asked for an expert's opinion—you look to me like you know your stuff, but I don't know the first thing about dead bodies. I specialize in living ones." He gave her a wink.

The disappointment in his eyes hinted he'd been hoping for a reaction—a laugh, even an eye roll. The past few days with Paul Turner had taught her he'd take anything over silence. Would take being hated over being ignored.

Probably the kind of kid who drank two cans of soda at the beginning of a road trip, then nagged his parents every half hour because he had to pee. An only child, most likely. This man had grown up with parents who worshipped his every diaper, without a sister or brother to force him to share the spotlight.

Dolores had met more than one surgeon like him.

His tone sobered. "I get it. I should have told you instead of going behind your back. But it's nothing personal. If anything, it goes to show how much I trust your abilities, that I think you'd be a good fit for the bureau. I'm a hard man to please. You're not mad, are you?"

Dolores sighed. "You know what, Agent Turner? I think you would have made a great doctor."

He said, proving her point, "That's a compliment, right?"

Forty-Four

ALCHEMY

Dolores squinted at the bundle of fabric Asher tossed her. "You're kidding."

"You know what it's like, Sis. You'll stand out if you don't dress up."

She couldn't deny he had a point. Since she'd left Kate and Leo's house this morning, Little Horton had gone from Halloween-hungry to Halloween-crazy. Painted faces filled the streets, cats eyed jack-o'-lanterns that hadn't waited for sunset to shine their bright, toothless grins. The Halloween spirit crackled all over town like the seeds of witchcraft and mutiny.

Asher sat back in the mermaid-blue seat. Ruby's hadn't changed much in the two decades she'd been away. Same posters, same 1980s tunes bellowing from the speakers. But it was the smell that grabbed a fistful of the threads in her memory and made them sing. Stir-fried eggs, pancakes, maple syrup. Virtually *all* diners smelled like this, and yet there was something about this one—cheap perfume, real Italian coffee.

Dolores's mother used to take her here. How old could she have been? Five? Six? Celia would bring books—one for her, one for Dolores—and order two plates of waffles drowned in vanilla ice cream.

Dolores didn't remember much about Celia. Only that she had a heart-shaped face, dark hair, and dark eyes. That she was willing to take her to Catalonia on holiday, but not teach her a word of the language.

That she only saw two kinds of men: dog smiles, and fox smiles—"And your dad's a dog smile, Dolores. One of the good ones."

Dolores ran her thumb over the dress. Plain emerald green. If her mother had died when she was older, or if Alexander hadn't remarried so soon, would things have been different? If she'd had time to figure out what it meant to be half Hawthorne, half Diaz—to mourn her mother properly?

"Thanks," she told Asher.

He shrugged. "You'll need a costume for tonight. I mean, if you've decided to join us downtown, for the party."

She hesitated. Just thinking about the festivities made her stomach squirm.

His face veiled with seriousness. "Hey, no one's making you. Me and Josie, we're part of the committee. At least Mom released you from your obligations."

The words shouldn't sting, yet Dolores lowered her eyes, not wanting to find out what Asher might see there.

"And if you feel bad about Josie's text earlier, don't. You're already getting the Worst Sister of the Year Award."

Dolores chuckled.

"I'm sorry, did I say 'year'? I meant 'decade.' Well, 'decade*s*.'"

"You don't have to go, either. Charlotte can't force you."

"True."

Asher had never been a hard person to read. "But you're going for Josie," she said.

He licked his teeth. "The kid spends enough time without me as it is."

Dolores nodded. Much as she hated to admit it, Charlotte had a point about keeping each other safe. If her little sister was going to spend the afternoon in town, caught up in Charlotte's schemes of Halloween celebrations, then Dolores wanted to have an eye on her.

"Let's go for Josie," she said.

The Halloween celebrations kicked off with tame activities: pumpkin-carving, costume-making, apple-bobbing. Volunteers crowded under orange-and-black umbrellas, but the afternoon unfolded under suspiciously sunny weather.

"I really shouldn't be dressed like a committee member," Dolores said.

"Nonsense," Asher said, his angel curls softening the austere Puritan costume. "You're a Hawthorne."

Dolores blinked at her father's words in his mouth.

"Eighteen years, Ash. That's how long since I've done anything for Halloween but take a Xanax."

"Here." He guided her to a popcorn machine.

Circus-red, propped on black wheels, it looked like it had been stolen out of a circus while no one was looking.

"One spoon of corn, one spoon of oil, one spoon of sugar. Think you can handle it?"

Dolores's eyes scanned their surroundings.

"Mom won't be here till tonight," Asher said. "She's taking care of the activities at City Hall."

"And Josie?"

"Friends are dropping her off after school." He checked the time on his phone. "Right about now."

"Okay." Dolores tried to make the muscles in her neck relax.

"Good luck, soldier."

Asher disappeared, and Dolores went back to sweeping the crowd.

It wasn't Charlotte she was looking for. A nervous beat throbbed against the tight bodice of her green dress. How could she explain it?

This absurd feeling that somewhere, in this avalanche of masks–

She resisted the ways in which her body betrayed her. The goose bumps, the hairs bristling at the back of her neck.

She was being irrational. Probably the Little Hortoner in her, coming back to life.

Yet of their own volition, her eyes searched for a tall, spectral figure among the costumes in the orangey glow of pumpkin fairy lights.

Though her mind knew better, knew that the impossible never happened, even on Halloween–her body could not be cheated out of the thought that *her father was here.*

Somewhere near.

Watching her.

Why not, a voice whispered.

She forced herself to stop. Did she seriously think that he had staged his own disappearance? That he had lured her back to Little Horton, that this was the macabre resurrection of his treasure hunts?

You know me, darling. I'm the grand-gesturing kind.

She caught herself on the chair, behind the popcorn machine.

She hadn't allowed herself to play out the theory, because if he had made himself disappear, it was likely that he was also behind the killings.

Impossible. Every fiber of her being rejected the idea.

Maybe he had fled because he feared for his life.

But her father was not a killer.

And if he had been–

A frosty breath blew down Dolores's neck. She turned around, but there was no one. *Everyone.* All the population of Little Horton, not to mention visitors, pooled in the square in a ballet of plastic masks, dresses, and cloaks. It was so packed you couldn't even feel the cold.

Dizziness forced her to stop staring.

Even if her father had it in him to kill someone–and he didn't, of course he didn't–why would he have targeted Dr. Burke and Gregory Winslow? Why would he have pushed Jacob and Teddy into hiding?

Dolores dug her nails into her palms. He couldn't be avenging her.

Appendicitis.

It would break his heart, Dolores.

What your father doesn't know won't hurt him.

Something rose up within her in protest. A murmur released underwater, that this picture wasn't altogether right.

But she couldn't put her finger on why.

It was madness–madness.

To look for her father among the multitude of monsters and masks.

Dolores fought the chill that ran down her spine.

Then why did that special shine radiate through her–the one she only felt when he was looking at her? Why did her chest brim with that feeling, like alchemy–the spell that burst to life at the crossroads between his eyes and hers?

Forty-Five

THE GIRL WITHOUT A FACE

Kate spent all morning looking into what had happened to the Horowitz family after their eviction. Their leaving town, so soon after Kristen's disappearance—it didn't feel like a coincidence, now that Kristen's bones had turned up. Especially if a powerful family like the Winslows had been involved.

And the bones' being planted behind City Hall, not to mention Gregory Winslow's being murdered, all hinted as much.

It was just a hunch, but still Kate felt more useful than she would have at the station.

She was on the phone when Leo came home for his lunch break.

"Yes," she said, "I understand. Privacy does matter, but—"

The man interrupted to give her a crash course on Big Brother.

Please, don't make me have to drive to Milwaukee and show him my badge. People reacted better when you came to their workplace, because their brain registered you as law enforcement. The uniform, the badge, the boots. But when you called them, it was like part of them thought you were going to sell them vacuum cleaners or Jesus.

"Look," Kate said, "this is part of a criminal investigation. I wouldn't ask if it wasn't important."

The man heaved out a breath. "I'll share your request with my superior. It's the best I can do."

"Thank you," she said, and ended the call.

"Who was that?" Leo asked, hanging his coat in the hall.

"A foster parent agency. I'm trying to find Junior Horowitz. Um–the brother of a girl who was reported missing when I was in high school."

"What does he have to do with the investigation?"

"Probably nothing."

But Leo didn't budge. "It's because of the bones that were found behind City Hall, isn't it? Then they belong to that girl–Kristen? I've been hearing about it at work."

Kate sighed, and he put up his palms.

"I know, you can't talk about your job. But it's not like you breached confidentiality. I can put two and two together."

"We don't have forensic evidence yet. Just strong suspicions. I figured, with the Horowitzes disappearing from town so soon after Kristen–"

"Wait, the whole family disappeared?"

"Not exactly. They were evicted."

Leo gave her the face she tried not to give when he asked if a certain pair of shoes looked right on him.

"Well, it's not nothing. They just–faded from town in the blink of an eye, and no one even thought twice about it. If Kristen's bones *have* resurfaced, I don't think it's a waste of time to look into what her brother's been up to in the past years. Those killings . . ." She thought of what had happened to Dr. Burke. Gregory Winslow. "They look like revenge."

"But," Leo pointed out, "you just said, you don't *know* that the bones are Kristen's."

"Yeah, well. Not like I have anything better to do."

He said nothing for a second. "Okay. Anyway, I was gonna go make some lunch–hungry?"

She followed him to the kitchen, where he started chopping vegetables. Kate looked in the fridge, which boasted little snacking material. Baby carrots, cherry tomatoes, blocks of tofu. The price tag for Leo's Hollywood abs.

"So," he said, "what's foster care gotta do with Kristen's brother? If it all happened when you were in high school, wouldn't he be an adult by now?"

Kate closed the fridge. "Yeah. Turns out, his parents died in a car accident, a few months after the eviction."

"Cripes."

"Junior was still a kid, so he must have landed in foster care."

Leo's veggies sizzled in the pan. "When you're finished working, do you wanna stop by the party downtown? I mean, with everything going on, I'd get it if you didn't."

Kate sighed. She'd never been a big Halloween fan, but today, the prospect made her especially queasy. All the people she might run into. Her colleagues. Nathan. Dolores.

The viciousness of it rushed back to her.

She had *hated* the woman–downright hated her for all these years, because she was wrapped into that sickly sweet cobweb that sent her spiraling into nightmare. None of it had been Dolores's fault. Yet she had been the girl without a face, the face of a dream Kate had spent the past two decades trying to forget.

She cursed herself for the hundredth time that day.

How stupid could she have been to think a teenage girl would set her up to watch her having consensual sex with her boyfriend, that this was Dolores's idea of a prank?

"You're too hard on yourself," Leo had told her this morning. "You were a kid, and you witnessed a crime. Your mind dressed it up into something more tolerable. There's no good reaction to trauma."

It still sounded like an excuse. If Kate had said something, all those years ago, maybe Dolores wouldn't have needed to flee to the other end of the country.

"Kate?"

"Yeah," she said, pushing back against the wave of memories. "I mean–maybe." She flicked the burner under the pan onto high heat. "Are you slow-cooking these vegetables or slow-killing me?"

Forty-Six

TRICK OR TREAT

The smell of popcorn coated Dolores's lungs, so buttery it burned. She dealt each tourist a smile along with the recyclable-paper bucket, said "Happy Halloween," and tried various techniques to fight the olfactory invasion. Breathing through her mouth. Breathing through her nose. Not breathing at all until she absolutely had to. But the harmless movie-theater smell had grown tentacles.

"Can you imagine being that pathetic?" Josie asked, slumped in a garden chair.

Dolores looked up at the flock of tourists. "Pathetic" wasn't as awful a word as the one she'd have used. In the past ten minutes, she'd served popcorn to faux-living dead who might plausibly have risen from her autopsy table. You had to give credit where credit was due.

"I don't know," Dolores said. "Right this minute, I'm feeling pretty pathetic myself."

The line of customers had thinned to a drizzle as the day gave way to dusk.

Her eyes swept the multitude of costumes.

She hadn't gotten rid of the feeling that she was being watched. That a gaunt man would spring from the crowd, unmask—and he'd be there, finally.

Her father.

She was ready to shed tears at the sight of him, to cry so much she would look like a witch melting at the end of a kids' story.

The fantasy had played out a hundred times in the past hour. She would clear everything up with him—the murders, the crime scene in his office—but not before he had buried her in his arms, and mended the broken pieces of who she had been all those years ago. Before Halloween.

A sigh drew her eyes back to Josie. Her sister's fists dug into her cheeks, leaving knuckle-red, fast-fading imprints.

"Are you okay?" Dolores said.

"I know you can't talk about your job with the FBI, but—do you know if they're getting any closer to finding Dad? Some people in school are saying he ran. Like, from debts or whatever. We don't *have* debts. And if Dad had pulled something like that, he'd let us know he was okay."

"I—" Dolores faltered. "I'm sure he would."

Josie studied her behind long lashes. "You don't want to talk about him, do you? Just like Mom. Let's all pretend the elephant in the room doesn't exist. Dad isn't missing, and Mom didn't hold a knife to the mayor's face for no reason." She scoffed. "For someone who calls herself Diaz, you act a helluva lot like a Hawthorne."

"Josie—"

"Asher told me how close you were. You and Dad. That he used to let you stay in his office while he worked. That you spent hours there, and he didn't send you to bed. Drove Mom crazy." Josie paused, her eyes anchored to her shoes in a surprising glimpse of modesty. "It wasn't like that for me and him. We never—he went to my dance recitals, bought me Christmas presents, did all the right things. I know he loves me. But he never let me in. Sometimes I think . . ." She chuckled flatly. "That he never forgave me for not being you. Isn't that crazy?" Her jaw hardened. "If you know something—"

"I would tell you," Dolores said. Yet her stomach knotted as the flow of memories came knocking, and knocking.

Her father's strange smile, that one evening. *My dear girl, is that what had you so upset?*

Dolores cleared her throat. "I'm going to find the bathroom."

Josie gave her a look—*Coward*—then heaved out of the chair to man the popcorn machine. Dolores scanned the vendor stalls until she found Asher, absorbed in the routine of dipping apples into hot caramel. Their gazes locked, and he nodded.

Josie groaned. "You two make the worst bodyguards. We don't *have* to watch each other all the time."

Dolores didn't reply. As a teenager, it was her sister's God-given right to resent supervision.

"I'll just be a sec."

She shuffled through the throng, eyes on the ground. The Halloween masks, the music—it all kicked into the avalanche that was inching closer, and closer. Her father's aloofness as she'd sat in his office. What had he said to her, that evening they danced together? Frank Sinatra on the radio, her father's grip as the room spun around them, everything a blur but his laughing eyes, the warmth of his face. Dolores had gone to him to ask him a serious question. But what? She tried to remember. It was like scratching dirt off a framed photograph, but for every speck she cleaned off, the glass over the picture cracked even more. By the time she had unburied it, all she could see were the cobweb patterns blooming across the glass.

The restroom in the Little Horton city center was shaped like a gazebo, much prettier than a public bathroom had any right to be. She turned on the tap and ran her fingers through the stream to splash her face.

The bathroom door opened, and Dolores looked up at the mirror above the sink.

A gasp tore out of her. Behind her stood a man with a wolf mask over his face.

She pivoted so fast her back hit the porcelain. Her eyes lowered to the man's shoes.

For a second she was sure that they would leak with blood, be the same shoes that had left a bloody print in Dr. Burke's office and crushed Gregory's face.

Her throat closed up as he clutched her arm and pushed her into one of the stalls. Their bodies filled all the space as he pressed her into the wall.

"Don't scream," he said, through a grotesque maw of plastic teeth.

Dolores hadn't thought of screaming. It sounded absurd—*impossible*, like an invisible fist had plunged inside her mouth.

The man whipped off his mask, and the block of clay in Dolores's lungs turned back into oxygen. "Teddy!"

"Sorry I scared you."

"Scared" her? She could barely hear herself think through the blood pulsing to her temples. "What the *hell* are you doing?"

A look of contrition passed over his face. "I'm sorry, all right? I couldn't think of how to get you alone without drawing attention–"

"Not *here*." Dolores pressed her palm to her chest. Sweat had broken out over her entire body. "Why are you and Jacob running from the police?"

He shook his head. "Now isn't the time, okay? I'll explain later. First, you need to come with me."

"I'm not going anywhere until you start making sense."

They stood so close she could taste his breath, sour with anxiety. "You're still stubborn as a mule, you know that?" He sighed. "After my father talked with the FBI, he told Jacob they had important things to discuss. He wanted to talk to me, too. Wouldn't say what about over the phone."

Realization hit her. "That's what you were doing in town. It didn't have anything to do with a client, did it? You came because Gregory asked you."

"Yeah. For all the good it did me. I didn't get to see him before he–" Teddy licked his lips. "But Jacob got the talk. Boy, did he get it."

"What did he tell him?"

Teddy waited a beat. "That if anything happened to him, Jacob shouldn't go to the police."

Dolores tried to blink away the words of her father's note. *Trust no one.*

"That's–"

"Yeah. Crazy, right? Said if anyone came after him, that same someone would come after *us,* and Jake and I should get away from this shitstorm before he–" Teddy halted. She could tell he was quoting his father verbatim. "Before he got every last one of us."

Dolores kept silent. What Charlotte had said, when she and Asher came home drunk the other night.

I know you're afraid. I know you miss your father. But there is a man out there killing us.

Why had her stepmother and Gregory acted as if the incidents were an attack against their family? Charlotte had called it an act of war—all this while, had Gregory Winslow been telling his sons the same thing?

"My father knew what was coming," Teddy said. "And so did yours." He added, with a touch of sympathy, "Shit, Doll. You could have told me what happened to him at the diner instead of letting me ramble. I would have been there for you."

"Knew *what* was coming, Teddy? Why would anyone come after our families? Why are you acting like a fugitive?"

His face closed like a wall. "Isn't it enough that my father thought we should, after what happened to him? Look, I came to you because Jacob's too recognizable. Everyone in this damned town is looking for him. But he wouldn't even talk about leaving until we got to you. He thinks you're in danger. This all started with your father. Right? Come with us, Doll. Those FBI agents can't do shit for us—*we'll* protect you. We'll protect each other."

The mention of Jacob stole her breath for a moment. What had taken over her last night—the desire to confront him, to talk to him—hadn't gone away. Yet the fear that had been missing, strangely absent in the rush of his intrusion, snaked inside her now.

She needed to be careful. Smart.

She couldn't go anywhere alone with Teddy and Jacob. Charlotte would kill her for being so stupid.

Her eyes scanned Teddy's face. A wave of tenderness soared through her. She had known him since before she was old enough to walk. "Teddy, there's things you don't know. Things have changed between me and your brother."

He smiled his fox smile. "So, you won't run away into the sunset with me? That just hurts my feelings. Hey," he added, in a more serious tone. "It's not like we're planning to retire from public life. Just until they catch this bastard. If you don't want to go with us, that's fine. But you *should go*. Hide, while there's still time."

"I'm not leaving my family behind."

"Why not? You've left them before."

Her gut hardened into a knot. "That was different. I was different."

He stood back, as much as he could in the cramped space of the stall. "You are," he said. "It's funny." He wrung the wolf mask between his hands. "It's my first Halloween back, too. Since your last party. Friends kept bugging me to come back but—I don't know. Halloween was yours. It was ours. The spectacular Hawthorne Halloween special." He chuckled. "It didn't feel right, without you."

When he met her eyes again, all thoughts of the past had washed out of his gaze. He slipped her a piece of paper.

"That's the address where you can meet us tonight. We'll wait fifteen minutes."

His hand shot to her cheek before she could protest. "Jacob loves you. I don't know what that's worth after all those years, but I know my brother and *I know* he never stopped loving you. Say you'll come. Please. I don't wanna see him get his heart broken all over again."

Dolores didn't speak. Her mind whirled. *Sphenoid, temporal, lacrimal.*

His fingers curled against her jawline before he took his hand away. He unlocked the door—when had he locked it?—and began putting his mask back on. Cold sweat sprouted at her forehead. She stared as the hideous wolf face slipped over Teddy's, and the mask stared back for a moment.

He pushed open the door and slid out, and Dolores stayed frozen against the wall, heart pounding.

Then an invisible blade sliced through her abdomen, and she dropped to her knees.

Forty-Seven

EYE TO EYE

Dolores threw up every bite of food she'd managed to eat at Ruby's. She knelt there for several minutes, bent over the toilet bowl, waiting for the last of her nausea to subside. When she felt sure she wasn't going to be sick again, she wobbled to her feet and marched toward the cluster of umbrella stands.

The wind shook them into an orange-and-black tide, swelling in and out, like the Halloween spirit had come alive and turned into a giant snake.

"Miss Diaz?"

A hand caught her forearm. Her body swayed and the man reached for her waist to steady her. It was Wyatt. His grave eyes grabbed hold of hers. "Are you all right?"

The line of stalls steadied into umbrellas again. In the distance, she could see Josie behind the popcorn machine, forcing on Charlotte-smiles.

"Yes. Thank you."

Wyatt released his grip and took several steps back. Dark shadows sagged under his eyes. At the moment he probably had more coffee running through his veins than blood.

"I wasn't sure I'd find you here," he said.

"Are you enjoying the festivities?"

Wyatt blushed, and *she* blushed, because she hadn't meant for it to sound accusatory.

"Actually, Agent Turner and I thought we should have someone downtown. As a precaution."

"Given Little Horton's history?"

Wyatt sounded deadpan as he replied, "Given killers' tendency for ostentation." His gaze swept over the ocean of monsters streaming through the streets. "Honestly, I wish the whole thing had been canceled. This feels too much like bait for him."

They started back toward the stands, and the word–"bait"–stuck to Dolores's brain. Come to think of it, what were the odds Wyatt would have found her in such a crowd? Had he followed her because he thought she might lead him to Jacob and Teddy?

Her fist crumpled around the strip of paper Teddy had given her. Wyatt caught the movement. "What's that?"

Lying to an FBI agent was a federal crime when it stood in their way of catching a suspect. And guilty or not, Jacob and Teddy *were* behaving like suspects.

"Nothing," she said. "Just a shopping list."

The safest thing would be to get rid of the note. Yet something stopped her as they walked past a trash can, and she shoved it into the pocket of her dress instead.

They reached the popcorn machine as the last streaks of sunlight melted into the sky. Josie's lips stretched into a grin. "Agent Holt. I'm so glad you could make it." Her eyes roved up and down his three-piece suit. "*Love* your costume."

"Er–"

"You're not gonna miss the tour, are you? Of course, it can't be very thrilling for an FBI agent, but you'll be in good company." She winked at Dolores. "Not that it's *fair* you get to escape committee duties. Agent Holt, don't you have room on that white horse of yours? I'm bored to tears here."

Wyatt scraped the ground as he shifted from foot to foot.

"Josie," Dolores pleaded.

"It's all right. You can take a joke, can't you, Agent Holt? Why don't you take my sister for a drink. She could use a little fun. Couldn't you, Sis."

Wyatt cleared his throat, pasted on a smile. "Sure. Let's get something to drink."

They stopped in front of a stand where a young man was dropping ladles of punch, an orangey mixture lumpy with lemon slices, into recycled cups.

Wyatt stirred his glass. "This won't get us drunk?"

Dolores shook her head. "Even the kids drink it." Wyatt didn't look satisfied. "What do you think we are? Small-town nuts who serve liquor to our children?"

The word "we" burned iron-hot in her mouth.

"Look, Miss Diaz—I don't want to overstep my bounds. But since your sister already made me look like a fool in front of you, I think I'll risk it. Can I make a confession?"

Most people asked that rhetorically, but Wyatt waited for her response. "Of course."

Her pulse picked up. He would tell her he'd followed her to the bathroom, that he'd seen Teddy in the wolf mask, that he knew about the rendezvous tonight.

Instead, he said, "Well, it's more of a favor really. I'd appreciate it if you let me keep you company this evening."

Dolores's lips parted.

"Not because I like your company," he said hurriedly. "I mean, I do like it, but—"

He took a deep breath. Clearly he didn't need Josie's help to feel foolish. "Security reasons. I'd like to keep you company for security reasons."

"Um—of course." They started walking again. Dolores recognized the pathway toward the Halloween Tour. "But what do you mean by 'security reasons'?"

He rubbed his thumb along the edge of his cup. "I don't want to alarm you."

"Please, Agent Holt. I'd really rather you be straight with me."

He nodded. "Well, there's the fact that Jacob went to you after Gregory was murdered. Mostly, though, it's your father's note."

Her hands tightened around the cup. She wondered if there was still time to wriggle out of the agent's offer.

"You told us you didn't talk to him," Wyatt prodded. "Hardly wrote each other. Yet when he thought someone might come after him, you're the person he worried about."

The topic had visibly rid him of his uneasiness. People who were good at their job could always navigate back to confidence–like they carried an invisible platform of solid ground they could land on whenever they needed to.

Or maybe it was some sort of vampire thing, the Little Hortoner in her added wryly. The more uncomfortable she got, the more comfortable he seemed.

"Why you?" he said. "Why didn't he write Asher or Josie? Why the daughter who lives on the other side of the country? Because he wants to make amends, in case something happens to him? Or because he thinks you're connected to this whole thing?"

Dolores kept silent.

If Wyatt sensed her discomfort, he pretended not to. "I'd like to ask you a personal question."

Again, he waited for her answer. "Go ahead."

From the way he said the next words, she could tell he had rolled them over and over in his head.

"Why did you leave Little Horton all those years ago?"

Dolores tasted bile in her throat.

The hot tears that bit into her cheeks as the plane took off, the red-iron blade that speared through her stomach as she dry-heaved over a sickness bag.

After the assault, and the surgery, her life had whizzed into a blur. It wasn't just what happened on Halloween, but the urgency to keep it a secret. Like she was no longer a teenage girl, but a box. The bones of her head, pieces of an armor that must be screwed tight to keep the truth from spilling out.

Sphenoid, ethmoid, lacrimal.

But then, on the plane, she had felt like–like a dome had lifted from over her. She could breathe. Taste her own fears again. And she'd sensed for the first time that there was *life,* that she could be a person again. Away from Little Horton.

Maybe not her father's angel. But more than puzzle pieces struggling to be whole, more than brittle bones licked clean of flesh and soul.

She'd decided on Los Angeles during the year. Studying biology at the University of Wisconsin had been the initial plan. But after Halloween–

Had she known, then? That her desire for sunshine was only a pretext?

She hadn't said goodbye to anyone. Not a proper goodbye. A kiss on Asher's head and a painful hug, because he'd squeezed her with all his might. Then she held Charlotte, dutifully, and saved her father for last.

His arms had been stiff around her and his eyes hadn't met hers when he said, "Have a safe flight."

He had not danced with her since the evening of October 29.

She'd gone out the door, thinking she'd call them later that day, that she'd come back for Christmas and Thanksgiving. And Halloween, of course. This wasn't goodbye.

But then the plane took off and she realized the farther she flew, the more alive she felt. Her guts a havoc of pain and nausea, stabs shooting through the scar on her abdomen.

And the thought made its way in, beyond her control.

I'll never go back.

I'll never go back.

Wyatt stopped walking, forcing her to halt. "When we first talked, you told me you and your father never had a falling-out."

Dolores answered, too fast for thoughts to register. "We didn't. We loved each other. He adored me."

She felt like a spectator, watching an actress speak her lines.

Wyatt pursed his lips. "You know what sounds strange to me?"

It didn't come out suspicious. Something about the calmness in his voice made her feel included—like they were two children on a treasure hunt, unboxing dusty secrets.

"It's how your family accepted it, no questions asked. When I talked to your stepmother, she sounded upset about how you left and never came back. But she didn't sound curious as to *why*."

Dolores's arms broke into gooseflesh.

"Why not?" Wyatt asked. "If I had a daughter who left for college, stopped calling, and never came to visit, I'd go out of my mind. I'd go to L.A. and make sure she was all right."

"What are you getting at?"

The sharpness in her tone surprised her. Wyatt took no notice of it. "You read your father's note."

"So, he had regrets."

"And you can't think of what they were about?"

Dolores didn't answer.

A voice inside her cried, *He didn't know.*

Appendicitis. Appendicitis.

She thought of how her father had treated her after Halloween–but there was nothing to remember, of course. Just a murky river that had swept away all that mattered.

Smell the smoke? What smoke?

She had left her father. Abandoned him.

Because it was too hard to keep the secret from him. Too hard to live in his house, with an abyss between them, to tightrope through bridges all made of eggshells and ice.

"Miss Diaz," Wyatt resumed, his voice the gentle coldness of a midnight tide. "If your father adored you–why didn't he come after you?"

Her hand jolted to a stop. It had moved of its own volition, like the time she'd slapped Max. Heat flushed to her collar. Had she been about to throw her cup at Wyatt?

Horrified, Dolores started walking away from him, but she was no match for his long strides.

"Miss Diaz," Wyatt called after her.

They hurried down the route of the Halloween Tour, past the bridge that had collapsed, past the restaurant that had caught fire, past all the disasters that had woven Little Horton into folklore.

"Please, help me understand. Help me find your father."

She walked faster. He walked faster. There was nothing more she could do short of breaking into a run.

"There's only one explanation that makes sense to me. Your father didn't come after you because he knew why you ran. And he blamed himself for it."

Dolores whipped back toward him. "What do you want me to say? That he hurt me? That he wasn't the most wonderful father in the world? He was. He never laid a finger on me."

"He let you go."

"He let me go because he couldn't stand *to look at me.*"

She closed her mouth, not believing the words had come out.

A flock of tourists shimmered ahead, dangling orangey lanterns. Their guide, some youngster with his face painted into a skull, spoke in a theatrical voice. She couldn't make out his words, but she knew which stage of the tour they were at. The paved ground broadened into a plaza. The streetlights flickered. An audio of howling wolves and laughing maniacs blew out of speakers half concealed behind grinning pumpkins.

This was the place where Jeremy Krone had emptied his gun into a crowd in 1950, killing four, wounding two.

Dolores looked up at the pulley system and the wires stretched taut above their heads. "We should move."

She'd never liked this part of the tour, where a life-size mannequin floated above the plaza. The tourists always screamed so loud, you could hear them at the other end of town.

But Wyatt stood firm in front of her, refusing to veer off topic. "Why couldn't your father bear to look at you?"

"I don't know."

His hand locked around her forearm. "I think you do."

The wires squealed above them. Gasps broke from the group and the guide spoke in a deep baritone, "Some say on Halloween nights, the ghost of Jeremy Krone rises from the dead, so he can gorge himself on the blood of fresh victims!"

Dolores flattened herself on the ground, taking Wyatt along, just as the mannequin glided down from the wire system above their heads. Her knee prickled where her dress tore against the gravel. Their paper cups spilled and the mannequin stopped in its tracks directly above them.

She panted for breath. The ghost didn't usually fly so close to the ground.

The cables groaned under its weight.

A few raindrops hit Dolores's face as she looked up. One caught her in the eye, and her vision turned red. The rain that dripped into her mouth tasted wrong, like copper and salt.

"Are you okay?" Wyatt said.

A scream sliced through the air, so raw Dolores felt in her bones that the horror was real. This was no tourist delighting in a cheap thrill. The scream went on, shrill and gutted, and only when her throat clamped up in pain did she realize *she* was screaming.

The mannequin did not wear a sheet, and bullet holes stared at her instead of eyes, but that was not why Dolores screamed.

She screamed because the mannequin was not a mannequin.

She screamed because the mannequin was her father.

Forty-Eight

DEMONS

Patience was not Kate's strong suit. She tried to sit down with a book while waiting for the Dawsons' call, but her leg twitched so badly under the table she had to get up to pace the room.

She'd spent most of the afternoon on the phone, going through the list of Junior Horowitz's foster homes. A very long list. As it turned out, Junior had changed foster parents more often than Kate's grandmother had changed husbands. All the families she talked to gave the same story.

"Strange kid."

"Not mean, but not easy to love."

"He just didn't connect with us."

In her mind's eye, Kate saw Junior in his yellow raincoat, playing by himself in the park outside her mother's house. *If we invite him, he'll think we like him and we won't get rid of him for a million years.*

A pecan pie cooled on the counter. She'd *had* to bake, in order to make the day tolerable. A couple hours ago, Leo had gone out. "To stretch my legs," he'd claimed, though Kate knew he was going to check out the party in town. He'd taken to Little Horton traditions fast.

Kate was on her knees, scrubbing scorched maple syrup off the oven door, when her phone rang. She scrambled to her feet and picked up. "Hello, Mr. Dawson?"

"Yeah," the man said, dragging out his vowels. "Yeah, that's me. You, uh–the foster service tells me you wanna know about Junior Horowitz? He's not in any trouble, is he?"

"No, no. I just want to ask you a few questions. I'm Officer Kate Butcher, with the Little Horton PD. I can't get into details, but it's possible you could help us with an ongoing investigation."

"A'course," the man said.

"How long did Junior stay with you?" Kate began.

"Three months."

That was the longest he'd stayed with any of his foster families.

"And that was in–"

"2007."

So Junior would have been sixteen. "Can you tell me what he was like?"

The man chuckled. "Well, like most kids who end up in the system, he had his demons." He pronounced it *deeemns*. "Not that he ever acted violent or anything. I wouldn't have had that around my wife."

"What kind of demons?"

"Sorry?"

"You said Junior had demons."

"Oh. Well, yes, a'course he did. What with his parents dying and all. It was his sister he fixated on, though."

Kate's eyebrows perked up. "He told you that?"

"Uh–not exactly. But it showed. Couldn't stand to have a girl her age around the house, or even see one that looked like her on TV. D'you know the agency never told me Junior had a sister? Had to find out one evening when me and the wife was watching TV, and that Wisconsin senator was on the news–"

"What senator?" Kate cut in. Didn't think of blunting the urgency in her voice.

"'Scuse me?"

"What senator was that?"

"Oh. Senator Hawthorne. I voted for him twice."

Kate stood stunned and silent for a while. "What did Junior have to say about him, sir? If you remember."

"As a matter of fact, I remember perfectly. It shook me up. I thought Junior was in his room, me and my wife watching TV, and suddenly Senator Hawthorne's on the screen, and Junior says, 'That's the man who took my sister.'"

Every hair on Kate's body stood up. "What?"

"I know, right? Kid scared the bejesus out of me. He was just standing there, behind us, eyes on the screen. I told him—Jesus, Mary, and Joseph—he couldn't go around spooking people like that. But he stayed so serious—so *calm*. And he said it again. 'That's the man who took my sister.'"

Kate forced herself to sound like she could believe what she was hearing. "Did he ever mention it again?"

"No. It was toward the end. Couple weeks later, Junior ran out on us, and that's the last I ever saw of him."

"Do you—do you know if he got put in a different family?"

"I know he didn't, or he would have been put back with us. I really liked the kid." He chuckled. "For no reason I can think of. We only had the one picture of him, but I had it put up in the paper, in case anyone saw him."

Kate grabbed a pen. "What newspaper was that?"

"The *Walworth Gazette*. It was August, I think."

She wrote the name on the back of her hand, and realized it was shaking. "Thank you, sir."

"Glad I could be of help."

Kate hung up, her fingers sticky with specks of charred syrup. She googled the newspaper and grabbed a fork. All the baking had shot her appetite, but you didn't need an appetite to eat pie. She stabbed her fork into the middle of it and tore off a chunk, scrolling through the *Walworth Gazette* archives. 2010, 2009, 2008 . . . 2007. The notice was on page two of the August 13th edition. A picture of a middle-aged couple—presumably Mr. and Mrs. Dawson—and a sixteen-year-old who stood awkwardly between them, taller than them both.

She took a second bite of pie and zoomed in on Junior's face.

Shoulder-length chestnut hair, his jaw hardened into a man's. He looked nothing like the boy Kate remembered.

And yet—he looked familiar, all the same.

Those hard cheekbones, the long slant of his nose. His features clearly etching toward handsome.

The look on his face. That serious, quiet look—

A gasp broke from Kate's lips, so sudden she choked. Metal rattled against porcelain as she dropped her fork and coughed out a mouthful of pie.

"Son of a bitch," she said. "*Son of a bitch.*"

Forty-Nine

CROOKED

Dolores's brain didn't register what happened after her father's body slid down the cables above the Krone Massacre Plaza.

Someone's hand clutched the sleeve of her dress. "Come on."

She shivered in the night air, her father's blood drying on her face. The landscape around her faded into the night. No Halloween lanterns, no streetlights. Where were they? How long had they been walking?

The vision of her father's crucified body struck her again, like a rock dropping into a pond.

Her legs broke into a run. She had to go back. The bullet hole in his forehead came back to her, but she brushed it aside, paid it no mind.

Hadn't her father's lips been moving? Surely they had. And his eyes had probably blinked.

Those eyes where her father's smiles always began, that set her alight with a special spell only he could cast.

Those eyes that had fled her, ever since Halloween.

After that Halloween party, there had been no late-night talks in his office, no more dancing, no more cookies from the apple box that tasted like shards of magic.

Dolores might have left her father, and Little Horton—but he had left her first. He had left her with his coldness and his silence.

Her dress tore against brambles, her shoes sank into mud. What were they doing in the woods?

"Don't." Wyatt caught her forearm. "You can't go back."

"I can save him."

"No."

"I can still save him."

It took both his arms to restrain her. Flashes entered her mind, a hysterical version of herself, struggling to break free. Yet she couldn't stop. She *knew* if she ran back to her father she could save him. One touch would be enough. Her hand would brush his cheek, and life would stream back into his eyes. She would cry hot tears that would melt the ice around his heart.

He'd say, *I'm so sorry, dear child.*

She'd say, *I've been dead, too.*

Then they would both cry and shatter into pieces and pick them up, together.

"Your father is dead. You can't help him now. It's over."

The words wouldn't sink in. Her father was alive. The dead body with a ruby wedged between his eyes had barely looked like him.

Why had she screamed like that? Surprise. Yes, it must have been surprise. The body was a look-alike, a double of the sort magicians used for their grand tricks.

Yet she had known him on sight. Eighteen years older and dead, as dead as the corpses she autopsied routinely, as dead as she felt now from the core of her being.

"Come on," Wyatt said, gently, and took her hand as he led her deeper into the woods.

Dolores felt weightless, outside her body, and when they reached the cabin she couldn't say how far they were from Little Horton or if they had crossed into a different world.

Wyatt sat her down in a wooden chair, its splintered arms biting into her wrists. He struck one match after another, candles flickering until Dolores could make out the room.

The cabin was barely bigger than the closet under the stairs at her father's house. Drawings hung on walls fallen into disrepair. The wood had rotted, though not enough that she could see through the planks. An odor of wet earth and moldy cedar seeped into her lungs.

Why had he brought her here? Why–

She squinted at the shapes that littered the ground. Toys heaped in a corner—in the dim light, they looked like pieces of junk. Sardine boxes on wheels, monster men made out of beer caps. Dolores's lips parted. Why did these toys look so . . . familiar? Plastic-bottle trucks, cheese boxes turned into spaceships.

And in the midst of these crooked creations, a shimmer caught her eye. A transparent plastic bag, catching the light of the candles.

Dolores gasped—couldn't have seen it right.

Inside the bag were a pair of black leather derbies.

Light danced over the shoes' polished surface and for a moment they seemed to shine, like Halloween pumpkins.

Dolores looked up as Wyatt put down the last candle and turned back to her.

"I'm sorry you had to go through this tonight," he said. "It must have been a terrible shock."

"What is this place?"

Wyatt glanced around the room. "I used to spend hours playing here. Kind of musty now, isn't it? Back in the day, it looked great, though. I wouldn't have been ashamed to say I built it—well, not alone. My sister helped."

Dolores's throat narrowed to the size of a pebble. "You never told me you grew up in Little Horton."

"I know."

Their eyes locked. A wave of recognition rose within her, but Dolores pushed back against it, refusing the familiarity of the dark eyes, the chestnut hair.

She looked down at her hands. The arms of the chair bit into her flesh—and not because the wood was old, as she first thought. It was probably the only thing in this room that was brand-new. Flecks of blood stained the wood where it had splintered. Where it had been *scratched*. Her thumb brushed against the fingernail marks dragging along its flank.

She looked back at Wyatt. "My father sat in this chair. Didn't he?"

His voice was its usual shade of quiet when he answered, "He did."

Fifty

JUNIOR HOROWITZ

Bile swam to Dolores's mouth, but she didn't feel the rage until she was lunging at him. Wyatt's hands closed like vises around her shoulders. She might as well have hit a wall. His strength dazzled her. The look on his face showed no sign of effort, no emotion, as he thrust her back into the chair.

"Please, Dolores. I don't want to hurt you."

She laughed. The sound bled with despair. "You don't kidnap people unless you want to hurt them."

"Maybe that was true with your father. But not with you."

Dolores gripped at the arms of the chair. The claw marks trenched into the wood were like a stab to her chest.

Her father had done this.

Her father with his handsome dance moves, his treasure hunts, his theatrical hatred of lemon pie. She was closer to him now than she had ever been, sitting in his car, living in his house.

She could still see his body, tied to the cables of the Krone Massacre Plaza, like a grotesque Halloween trick.

An urge to claw Wyatt's eyes out boiled inside her. But she knew now how strong he was.

He had said he didn't want to hurt her. Not that he wouldn't.

"What do you want?" she said.

"To talk. I found out most of what I needed from your father." He caught the look on her face. "I understand you're angry, Dolores, and you're not going to want to hear this. But your father got what he deserved."

Dolores dug her nails into the wood to stop herself from lunging at Wyatt again. Feeling the indentations left by her father. *Like walking into his footsteps.*

Was he still alive when she flew back to Little Horton? This whole time, was he within reach? If she had wandered into the woods could she have heard him scream?

Her spit burned thick as hot wax as she said, "My father did nothing wrong."

Wyatt smiled. "Let me ask you something, Dolores–did you keep your promise?"

"I don't know what you're talking about."

"All those years ago, when I asked for your help. Did you tell your father to bring Kristen home? Did you tell him that her little brother missed her?"

Cement poured through Dolores's veins. Her eyes searched inside this grown man for the ghost of the young boy he had been. "Junior," she said.

Wyatt's shoulders relaxed. "I admit, I was nervous you'd recognize me."

Dolores couldn't breathe. He looked nothing like the twelve-year-old who'd sat waiting for his sister outside school. Yet, in an inexplicable way, the way bones resemble a human body, he did.

"Why?" she said. "After all this time, why–"

"Why now?" The words ripped the air, and a shiver ran through her body. "When else was I going to get revenge, Dolores? As a scrawny orphan without a penny to his name? After my parents died, after foster care, I spent the end of my teenage years in the streets. That takes a lot out of you. I had no family, no money. In the winter, I spent my nights at a Salvation Army shelter. We had to register, but I never used my full name." He laughed dryly. "Plenty of Juniors out on the streets. I don't know how your father found me–just that one day a man walked up to me, looking for a Wyatt Horowitz Jr."

Dolores's heart punched against her rib cage. Could she slip past him, reach for the door?

He looked up, gluing her to the seat. "Not that I knew he worked for your father then. All he told me was I had a *secret benefactor.* You can bet I wanted to believe that. It sounded straight out of a Dickens novel. From the streets, I went to an apartment, which I *owned.* I could sign the papers under any name I wanted. I chose Wyatt Holt, and made the change official after college. I joined the FBI, partly so I could trace where that money came from. But that wasn't the only reason."

He paused. "If you had a sister who disappeared, and nobody could be bothered to give a damn—wouldn't it make you even more determined to find out what happened? Here's a thought," he said. "If Kristen had been a Winslow or a Hawthorne, do you think people would have been happy to think she'd run off, let the matter rest?"

It was a moment before she managed to pry words through her ground teeth. "I don't know what happened to Kristen. But I *know* my father didn't have anything to do with it."

He held her gaze. "Your father can do no wrong, can he? You wanna hear something about good old Mayor Hawthorne, community icon, local celebrity?"

Shivers broke down her back as he crouched down to her level. "On the night Kristen disappeared, *I saw* your father inside her bedroom. Packing a suitcase."

Dolores sat absolutely still. *You're lying,* she wanted to say. But why would he?

"That's right. He broke into our home—everyone knows where everyone's spare key is in town, don't they? Then he raided her wardrobe. I remember every detail. You never forget the pain, do you, Dolores? Your brain might—but not your body. In your blood, in your bones. You remember."

Dolores felt her nails biting into her palms. The scar on her abdomen was on fire.

"He moved so fast, he looked like a tornado, spilling clothes out of her closet. He didn't hear me come in. He knew my parents were out of town that weekend. But from the look on his face, I could tell he'd forgotten all about me."

Wyatt pressed his fist against his mouth. Dolores wanted to flee the scene he was calling to life. But she was there with him in the Horowitz house, as her father turned, horrified, to discover the little boy in the doorframe.

"We looked at each other—it felt like a lifetime. His eyes were so wide I thought they'd roll out of his sockets. I didn't ask what he was doing. I was too scared. Now I reckon he must have been as scared as I was."

He fell silent for a moment. "So, I ask you, Dolores. What would you have done? You tell the police that the mayor took your sister, but of course, they make fun of you. You're twelve, your clothes come from a thrift store, and you look a couple food stamps away from starved. What do you do? Well," he said, "I joined the bureau. Thinking no one else might care about getting justice for Kris, but *I* did. Do you know how hard it is to drag yourself through college, to sift through books about economics, when you've scrounged through trash cans for your next meal? But I made it, so I suppose it was worth it. Then when I had access to the resources I needed, I tracked down my secret benefactor."

The line of his lips tightened. "That's when I knew. Before that, I thought—God knew what I thought. Maybe over the years, I convinced myself I hadn't seen what I saw. That I dreamt your father's presence into Kris's bedroom, like everyone told me I had. But I didn't dream the tuition money, the new apartment—the new life he gave me. You understand *what that means*?" His eyes narrowed. "I climbed my way to the top, on a hill made from my sister's bones. All so your father could look himself in the mirror. Ease his guilt about the sister-less, parent-less boy whose family he pushed to eviction. That was him, too. Did you know? He confessed it when he sat in that chair. One phone call to our landlady, and we went from her charity case to a family of drug dealers who might start cooking meth in her kitchen. She kicked us out the first chance she got."

He chuckled. "A good politician, your father. I was the one person who knew what he had done. So, he had to get me away from Little Horton. Stop me from talking to anyone—especially to you. He had his qualms, of course. All that money he gave me—the way he saw it, he was giving me a shot at a better life."

Dolores shuddered under his black gaze.

"Well, when I found out who my secret benefactor was, let me tell you, I didn't feel grateful. In fact, I felt like the man who destroyed my family had been feeding me my sister's murder in a silver spoon, drowned in sugar."

Dolores bit back the avalanche that pressed against her lips. Her father would never have hurt Kristen, or any girl. And yet–

That look in his eyes, that night in his office.

My dear girl, is that what had you so upset?

"So," Wyatt said, "I built a corruption case against him and got myself sent back to Little Horton. You know what's funny? I wasn't even the first to get there. Apparently, the older he got, the harder the old man found it to cope with his guilt. He talked to Gregory Winslow, told him he wanted to come clean. That didn't sit too well with the old bat. Sure, Winslow was old and dying of cancer, but he couldn't let your father ruin his legacy. So he hired a hit man."

A look of mercy passed over Wyatt's face.

She remembered that moment of humanity when they'd talked over the phone, those seconds of hesitation before he told her her father was missing.

"I may have killed your father, Dolores, but the first thing I did when I got to Little Horton was save his life. For hours, I'd been sitting in my car outside his house, trying to decide what to do. Then Gregory's hit man arrived, picked up the spare to your house. Instinct got the better of me. I followed him upstairs to Alexander's office–he had a gun to your father's head. I shot him. Then I buried him here." He motioned toward the woods.

"I don't–I don't understand."

His jaw tightened. "Really? You're a smart woman, Dolores. What's your best guess?"

To take part in this made her skin crawl, and yet, she wanted answers. Maybe as badly as Wyatt did. "You think my father and Gregory killed your sister."

"No. They only covered it up."

He straightened back into a standing position. The excitement dimmed in his eyes and through the cracks, Dolores saw how tired he was. Killing people at night and pretending to investigate their deaths by day couldn't leave much room for sleep.

Acid rose up her stomach. She saw Wyatt this morning at the motel, getting coffee. How fresh was her father's murder on his hands? Had he just scrubbed the residue powder from his fingernails?

"I'm sorry I had to bring you here, Dolores. This isn't what I wanted. I suppose I could keep being careful, get away with what I've done. But I'd have to be patient. And I'd have to kill you."

Dolores said, "What's one more dead body to either of us?"

"No." He shook his head. "No one I killed in the past week was innocent. Burke and your father both took a bribe from Gregory and let my sister's killer walk free. In a way, I took a bribe, too. So maybe I deserve to be caught."

He took a step closer. Dolores had to crane her neck so she could look at him.

"But I won't stop until I've finished this. And you're going to help me."

"Help you?" Disgust cracked in her tone, but he seemed not to hear it.

"You're going to help me find Jacob and Teddy Winslow," he said. "Or neither of us is walking out of here."

Fifty-One

SPECTACLE

Paul let out a curse as his vehicle screeched to a halt. In the past few hours, Little H had broken into chaos. Girls dressed as dragonflies huddled in the crowd with Supermen, Pennywises walked beside Wonder Women, and one member of the living dead was holding hands with–Paul darted his head outside the car window to make sure he was seeing this right–a giant strawberry.

He shot out of the car. "Hey!" He tried to get hold of a man in a lobster suit, but he skittered away like Paul had been about to boil him. Paul pulled out his badge and shouted, "FBI!" which usually parted crowds like Moses through the Red Sea. But he could barely hear himself in all the pandemonium.

"Fucking hell," Paul grunted as he started shouldering his way through the stream of tourists.

His eyes darted from left to right. Where the fuck was Wyatt? He was supposed to be downtown at the party in case something like this happened.

As he approached the Krone Massacre Plaza, it felt like he had stepped into a church. The group huddled in the square wore Puritan costumes, and above them, hanging from a cable system, was a man, arms stretched into a cross. Tall, gaunt, face dry as papyrus. A bullet hole tore open his forehead.

Alexander Hawthorne.

Paul clenched his jaw. Winslow's death had been a show of violence, but this was spectacle. There was no other word for it.

The son of a bitch is making fools of us.

He strode forward, and the first face that greeted him was Charlotte Hawthorne's. "Please, could you take down his body?"

Her blond hair, tied in a braided crown around her head, put all the sharp angles of her face into focus. She stared at him, her eyes pale blue marbles. No turmoil. Paul had seen women react to the death of a loved one like this. Like it was their duty to restore order when everything else had collapsed.

"Agent Turner, please. If you need to take pictures, do it quickly and take his body down. This is obscene. His children shouldn't see him like this."

Paul followed Charlotte's gaze to the sidewalk, where Asher and Josie were sitting on the curb. Josie unburied her face from her brother's shoulder, and two sharp eyes drilled into Paul. She sprang up and shot toward him like an arrow. "Where's my sister?" she demanded.

"Jo, don't–" Asher tugged at her arm, but she yanked free.

Josie raised her chin. "She was with your partner."

"What?" Paul wasn't about to take attitude from a fifteen-year-old, but guilt snuck into his chest as he took in the tears that had dried down Josie's cheeks.

"Dolores left with your partner and now she's just *gone*. And she wouldn't have gone when Dad–"

"Darling," Charlotte said, "you're hyperventilating. Take long, deep breaths."

Paul looked at Asher. "Is this true?"

"Yeah," Asher said, a faraway edge to his tone. "She left with Agent Holt like an hour ago."

Now, that was something else.

Paul took in the tableau of the Hawthorne family: Josie panting for breath, Asher hanging a haggard arm around her, Charlotte looking straight ahead of her–as if the corpse of her crucified husband would disappear eventually, as long as she refused for it to exist.

Paul let out a breath. He had failed them–all three of them. And Dolores, too.

"Look." He aimed for a reassuring tone. "If what you say is true, you don't need to worry. One thing I've learned about your sister is that she can keep her head in times of crisis. Besides"–he forced on a smile–"she can't get much safer than with an FBI agent. Can she?"

Before anyone could reply, Paul heard a woman shuffling through the crowd, screaming, "Police!"

Finally.

He turned back toward a breathless Kate Butcher. This wasn't as good as having his partner, but it would do.

Her eyes were wild as she took in Alexander's body. "Son of a bitch." She stood frozen for a moment, before frantically sweeping the area for backup. Her eyes settled on Paul, and she ran to meet him. "We need to go."

"Take it easy. Someone's got to handle the crime scene. Forensics are on their way–"

She clutched at his sleeve. "You don't get it. We need to *go*. I know who did this."

Fifty-Two

AVALANCHE

"I don't know where Teddy and Jacob are," Dolores said.

Technically, that was true. She'd never even glanced at the address scribbled on the paper Teddy had slipped her.

Wyatt stared her down, and she resisted breaking eye contact. "I know they approached you at the party."

Dolores didn't answer. If he knew that, he would have searched the whole city for the brothers instead of following her around. *But would he have?* Catching a man in a crowd was hard enough, but a man in a mask, in a crowd full of masks?

"Teddy drove here from Madison in a red Mercedes. Neighbors spotted his vehicle last night, around the time Jacob was wandering the streets. He picked up his brother, but they swapped cars before they left town. I've been watching everything from their phone records to their credit card activity. If they'd called a friend, I would know. If they'd booked a flight to go into hiding, I would know. This afternoon, Teddy made a cash withdrawal in Oneida. That's a ten-minute ride from here. They're still around, because they're waiting for someone. And that someone sure as hell isn't Jacob's wife."

She stared at Wyatt for so long, tears sprang at the corners of her eyes.

"This isn't an interview, Dolores. You don't have a right to remain silent."

"You think Kristen would have wanted this?"

He laughed. "As a matter of fact, yes, I think my sister would want justice. That disgusting doctor, who bought his practice with her blood money? Your father, who hired her at City Hall out of charity—he sure liked his charity cases. But he still helped Gregory make it look like Kristen had run away, in exchange for a check. He still buried her body in those woods and ripped out her teeth."

A shudder broke down Dolores's back.

To picture her father laying a finger on Kristen—

Absurd. As absurd as the image hovering on the verge of her mind, of his body hanging in the square.

Wyatt leaned in, clutching the back of her chair. Dolores's cheeks prickled at the warmth of his breath.

"Most of all, though?" he said. "Kristen wouldn't shed one sorry tear for the Winslow brothers."

Dolores's mind clamped shut.

The boys she had known since childhood. Kristen, and those hours spent sorting papers at City Hall, the way she moved like she was dancing to some inaudible song. How she mimicked Charlotte behind her back and Dolores couldn't stop herself from laughing until her abs ached. Teddy bringing life to the dinner table. Kristen's bones. Jacob, and the spot in the crook of his neck made for her face, the crunchiness of his hair under her fingers.

A tremor crossed Wyatt's lips. He didn't like standing this close to her, any more than she did. "Why are you protecting them? After what Jacob did to you."

Shock stabbed into her. She didn't ask, *How do you know?*

If she asked, he would say, *Your father told me,* and her father never knew, could never know.

It would break his heart, Dolores.

But it wasn't just the fact Wyatt knew.

It was how the words jarred against her deeper instincts. The memory of Jacob, yesterday, as he came to her. *Came to her,* after all these years. After they banished him from the house. In the naked truth of his face, she had seen it. Incomprehension. She'd tried to resist, because she should know better. Could not believe what her eyes saw, what her bones told her.

That Jacob had no idea why she had left him, and Little Horton, all those years ago.

"You *do* remember, Dolores?" Wyatt said.

She opened her mouth, to say, *I do.*

Only she never had.

The pain. Charlotte's golden threads braiding into a truth she learned to accept. *Jacob raped me.* Seeing him again had shaken its foundations. Shaken everything.

Dolores steeled herself against the memories, like pressing her palm to a wound to stop a hemorrhage.

A black bullhead mask. Charlotte's hand in her hair.

Teddy's voice. *It's my first Halloween back, too. Since your last party.*

"Dolores?"

She could have laughed, it was so ridiculous. Hadn't she spent the past day trying to remember that Halloween night? And now that she felt it creeping closer, her whole being rose into battle. Stopped the truth from surfacing, pushed back against the tide that blackened her horizon.

The wave towered, and still she fought it, tried to seal her mind against it.

Lacrimal, orbital, temporal.

No crack could be allowed, the dam could not be breached.

An avalanche was coming.

She lunged forward, hardly aware of what she was doing. Wyatt blocked her as she tried to duck under his arm. Her head throbbed at the impact.

"Is that your default mode? You don't want to know your father made a girl disappear, so you forget about it. You don't want to hear me say what your ex-boyfriend is, so you run. Is that it?"

His mouth hardened as he slammed her into the chair. "When Kristen went missing—that upset you for what? A week? Then you went on with your life, and you didn't think much when my family disappeared from town. Good riddance, right? Out of sight, out of mind."

What your father doesn't know won't hurt him.

A lightning-like scar cracked the ice inside Dolores. The urgency of keeping it up throbbed inside her.

"You built your life on *my* past, Dolores," Wyatt said. "On my family's bones. Don't you think it's time you faced yours?"

2003

October 31

Fifty-Three

BY THE PRICKING OF MY THUMBS

Dolores wrung her hands, dripping with fake blood. She was Lady Macbeth, in a red dress that would have dragged dust off the floors if they hadn't been thoroughly vacuumed.

Nathan grabbed her arm and teetered with her toward the sanguine-crepe buffet. His breath reeked of whiskey. He was one of those people who considered it rude to arrive sober to a party.

"C'mon, you can't just stand by the door, waiting for Prince Charming. Aren't you supposed to be a feminazi?"

Dolores exhaled. The person who had her glancing at the entryway every five minutes wasn't Jacob at all.

"If you must know," she said, "I'm waiting for Kate."

Nathan licked his lips, brows furrowed.

"Kate Butcher?"

"Butch!"

"Don't call her that."

"The girl's a freak. Why'd you invite her?"

Dolores shrugged.

"Didn't she try to bite your head off the other day?"

"Maybe if you and everyone else weren't such dicks to her."

Nathan put up his hands. "Jesus, don't go all sisterhood on me."

She didn't bother to explain. It wasn't how everyone chanted that nickname at Kate in the cafeteria. It was the look on her face. That closed, iron-gates look, like a prisoner who just wants to do their time and crosses their fingers there will be a tiny bit of them left by the time they get out.

"I just wanted to be nice," she said.

"That's your problem, Dolls. You're nice to everybody."

She slipped out while Nathan spiked his glass with whiskey. The kitchen was a mess. Towers of dishes in the sink, the table loaded with cakes, juice cartons, and candy. She grabbed a plate of cranberry cookies, not minding the fake blood she left on the porcelain rim. There'd be so much to clean tomorrow anyway.

A cool voice behind her *tsk-tsk*ed.

"By the pricking of my thumbs, something wicked this way comes."

Dolores swiveled to see a boy in the doorway. His face was concealed from the nose upward by a black bullhead mask. She knew him by his short black hair, his way of standing, and the green eyes that gleamed at her behind the mask.

"Jacob?"

The corners of his mouth twitched–the farthest thing from Jacob's golden retriever smile. He lifted his mask above his forehead.

"Shame on you, Dolores," Teddy Winslow said. "I'll be sure to let my brother know you can't tell us apart."

She rolled her eyes. "It's not your looks so much as your brains. I didn't expect you to quote Macbeth."

"Touché." Teddy grabbed a cookie from her plate. "Jacob leaked your costume. Seeing as he didn't think I'd be coming."

"What happened to Madison? Thought your dad had you crawling under paperwork."

"I know, I know. Don't tell anybody I'm here, okay? Father thinks he's teaching me *responsibilities.* His way of punishing me."

"Punishing you for what?"

Teddy bit into his cookie. He glanced around, feigning secrecy. "Is Jacob here yet?"

Dolores paused. The question had a funny ring to it. Like he knew the answer already. "No. Something came up."

"Don't tell me. One of his friend's in a bad place."

"How do you know that?"

"Because you and Jake are the same, Doll."

"Decent people?"

"Mother Teresas."

Dolores sighed. "You remember Austin, from Jacob's book club?"

"No. I repress all information having to do with my brother's nerdiness."

"Well, he just got dumped. Jacob's gonna try to make him come to the party. But when he called, it sounded like they were neck-deep in tissues and beers."

Teddy reached for her plate and scratched the icing off a sugar cookie. "You're saying Jake's missing the party of the year for this? Not to sound mean–"

"Right."

"But nerds get dumped. Just the way of the world." He licked crumbs of sugar off his finger.

Dolores appraised him. That funny feeling in her chest again–that none of this was news to him. That he'd learned it from Jacob or a friend of theirs before he even got here. That he was playing some kind of prank on her.

She shook her head. Teddy and his tricks.

"Well." He tossed the cookie on the table. "What's a man gotta do to get a drink in this house? Kill someone?"

TEDDY PUT HIS MASK back on before they went back into the living room. "Seriously," he said, "not a word to anyone. If my father finds out I was here, he'll fire my ass."

"Right. We'll just call you our mystery guest. That won't make people suspicious at all."

His lips curved half an inch. "Let's say I'm Jacob. See how many of his pals fall for it."

Dolores groaned. "You guys are worse than twins dressing up as each other."

"Worked on you, didn't it?"

She elbowed him as they strode into the living room. And actually, it did work. A lot of their friends were so drunk by then that a masked Teddy looked close enough to Jacob. Dolores repressed eye rolls when Teddy shot her satisfied glances. Meanwhile, she watched for Kate Butcher and crumbled cookies onto her plate.

"Come on." Teddy wrapped a hand around her waist, steered her away from the door. "This is your party, Lady Macbeth. Prick your thumbs, will you?"

"What?"

He shoved a cup into her hands. "Have fun."

It was only half full, and Dolores drained it in one gulp. Heat flushed to her face. The minutes ticked by, each longer than the last. After a quarter of an hour, Dolores was forcing her eyes open.

No way. She'd put so little booze in the punch, Asher could have drunk it. All the baking and party prep must have sucked dry her energy reserves.

She snaked toward the couch, careful to avoid touching anyone with her bloody hands. *I'll just close my eyes,* she thought, and dropped on the couch. Her head buzzed. Everything felt dull. Like the time Charlotte had slipped her codeine during her first period.

Laughter howled into her ears.

"Jesus, what a lightweight. My grandparents are still awake right now."

"All work and no play makes Dolls a dull doll."

"Why don't you tuck her into bed, Jakie-Boy?"

Someone picked her up from the couch, and her arms and legs dropped like they'd been dipped in gold. Teddy? Jacob?

The room broke into applause. She tried to grab around the boy's neck but the air split into tiramisu layers, soft and blubbery. He walked up the stairs, carrying her, a prince and princess out of a Disney movie. A door swung open. Dolores opened her mouth—to speak felt like carving through diamond. "Jacob?"

The mattress squealed under her weight. His weight. He planted his knees on each side of her, like war flags into foreign land.

The warmth of his breath on her face told her how close he was.

Panic dug fingernails into her heart. She forced open her eyes. The face above hers was masked, but those eyes—

Green as his brother's.

Jacob? Teddy?

He took in her horror, and the bottom half of his face broke into a grin.

Dolores's whole body went cold with fear.

It was his fox grin.

PRESENT DAY

Fifty-Four

TRAGEDIES

It came as a relief to Wyatt that he didn't have to rip off Hawthorne's fingernails to get the truth out of him. Pain made him uncomfortable, whether it came from humans or animals. No doubt, he'd make for a very tepid torturer. But sometimes things happen exactly at the right time.

When he'd come to Hawthorne's house a few days ago, the old man greeted him like Wyatt was the sword of justice. If there'd been no hit man from the Winslows, if Wyatt had simply walked up to his door and said, *I'm Junior Horowitz, and I've come to track down the men who killed my sister,* possibly Alexander Hawthorne would have answered, *You've found me.*

The past eighteen years had changed Wyatt beyond recognition, but Hawthorne looked the same in his eighties as he had in his sixties. The same hawk eyes, the gaunt face, the tall elegance that had sailed him through public life.

After Wyatt shot Gregory's man, he told Alexander he worked with the bureau. But when he started to drag the body out of the room, the old man appraised him anew. "Are you supposed to move that?"

"These are special circumstances. Would you help me carry him down the stairs?"

After a short pause, Alexander obliged. He was strong enough to meet Wyatt halfway as they hoisted the body from the floor.

Although Wyatt hadn't entered this house prepared to kill someone, the turn of events didn't make him panic. The conscious thought had never entered his mind—that he would take down all those responsible for what happened to Kris. But that was what it all boiled down to. Going back to the old cabin and drilling a chair to the floor. The fifty-caliber, bought under a different name. The shoes, one size bigger than his own. He was creating a killer before he even acknowledged that he'd come back to Little Horton to avenge his sister.

When they had carried the body to the ground floor, Wyatt said, "I'm going to drive my car into the backyard, so we don't give your neighbors a scare."

Alexander looked at him. "You're not really an FBI agent."

Wyatt pulled his badge out of his pocket and raised it to Alexander's eyes. The old man's face turned absolutely white. The name on the badge was the same as the one on the papers for the apartment that had been purchased by a "secret benefactor" fourteen years ago.

Hawthorne's voice didn't shake as he managed, "So it is time."

After that, he didn't put up any resistance. He went to Wyatt's car willingly, and even volunteered a couple of shovels from his garage for them to bury the body.

But when it came to telling his story, it'd be an understatement to say *Alexander didn't resist.* A Catholic in the confession parlor didn't get that talkative.

The lie Wyatt had told his boss about seeing Hawthorne on CNN had proved to be more than accurate. A tell-tale heart *was* beating in Hawthorne's chest. And tell, it did.

"I don't want to make excuses for myself," he'd said, as he sat in the wooden chair in the cabin. Wyatt hadn't even needed to restrain him. "But I suppose that's what it'll sound like. A man who tells his side of a story always puts himself in a better light." He took a deep breath. "August twenty-ninth, 2003, after dinner, I went back to City Hall for some files. The place was closed and empty—or supposed to be. I found the door unlocked, lights burning in the reception hall. You remember your sister had been working for me that summer?"

Wyatt didn't answer. His teeth clenched so hard, a headache was starting to lodge above his left eye.

"I found her lying on the carpet, and Teddy Winslow pacing the room like a wild animal. He went crazy when he saw me. 'Oh God, Mr. Hawthorne, sir, it's not what it looks like.' His pupils were so dilated, his eyes could have been marbles. I took your sister's pulse and called a doctor while Teddy raved on about what happened. They were fooling around, just having some fun. From what I could see, the kind that came in pills and bottles. Then Kristen OD'd. She took the drugs willingly, he told me. They'd been in a relationship all summer, but Teddy couldn't let it get out because–"

He fell silent. Wyatt didn't prod him. If the old man thought he would make this easy on him, he was kidding himself.

"Soon, Teddy's father, Gregory, arrived, and the doctor, Michael Burke. He confirmed what we all knew. That Kristen was dead, and there was nothing we could do for her. Gregory took center stage then. His son had enough drugs in him to land him in jail. If the police found him with a dead girl, who overdosed on his drugs, he could wave goodbye to his promising future. Besides, they were obviously in an–intimate relationship. Teddy was twenty-one, and for him to be sleeping with a seventeen-year-old–"

Hawthorne hesitated. Clearly didn't want to speak the words "statutory rape" to Wyatt's face.

"Gregory said he wouldn't let a stupid accident ruin his son's life. The only people who knew about this were Teddy, Michael Burke, and I, and Gregory wanted to keep it that way. He offered me and Burke the kind of money you can't refuse." Wyatt's silence lay thick between them. "In any case," he amended, "we didn't refuse it. Gregory decided we had to make it look like Kristen ran off, and sent me to his house to pack her things. Her parents were out of town, so there'd be no one home." His eyes dropped. "We didn't think of you."

People rarely did.

"I never told Gregory you had seen me that night. I guess–I was afraid of what he'd suggest we do. The real price of what I'd done started to sink in, before I even saw the color of that money. Gregory and I were friends, but this was no friendly arrangement." He moistened his lips. "He owned me. I didn't realize how much yet. I drove to the edge of the woods with Kristen's body in the trunk of the car, and I–I pulled out all of her teeth. Then I buried her."

"You better remember exactly where," Wyatt said.

The old man's face drooped with exhaustion. He looked a hundred years old as he answered, "I do."

Then he told Wyatt happened next. How Teddy's "accident" with Kristen looked a little more suspicious after a party full of teenagers saw Teddy's brother carry a drunk Dolores to her bedroom on Halloween.

"Who could say if it was a first, for either of the brothers?" Alexander said. His hands wrapped like talons around the arms of the chair. "Teddy. Then Jacob. I watched these boys grow up. I *cared* about them. I never thought–"

He interrupted himself. "Yes," Wyatt said. "You never think the psycho in the paper is somebody's neighbor. Like you don't think the elderly man who eats two helpings of lemon pie every week has it in him to rip a girl's teeth out." Wyatt's jaw was bracket-straight. To Hawthorne's credit, he didn't break eye contact. "You knew, then," Wyatt said. "The whole time, you knew what happened to Dolores. And you just–let Jacob get away with it."

Fierceness bolted into the old man's eyes. For a second, Wyatt saw the hawk behind the man, the politician who would cut for the jugular when his opponents showed weakness. "Just what was I supposed to do? My hands were tied. Even if I gave back to Gregory every penny of the bribe–by that time, I'd aided and abetted him in covering up a girl's death."

"A death that looked increasingly like manslaughter as the facts rounded up," Wyatt said.

Alexander kept silent, but Wyatt could see the thoughts brewing behind his forehead–thoughts that must have been brewing for nineteen years. What would an autopsy have shown, if Kristen's body had made it to a morgue? What kind of drugs did she OD on? GHB? Rohypnol? *Did* she take them willingly? For that matter, was anything she did with Teddy that night consensual?

Wyatt appraised Hawthorne more closely.

His cheeks were dry, his voice had never cracked. *A Hawthorne to the backbone,* townies would have proclaimed.

And yet, there was something broken about the man. Though he would die–Wyatt didn't see a way around it–he felt at least Alexander had paid for his crimes. He'd paid for it with what he loved most in the world.

Dolores.

"So, legal reprisal was off the table," Wyatt said. Found himself wanting to press his thumb into that wound, now that he'd caught the thinly sutured gap in the old man's chest. "How did Dolores feel about that? You ever explained it to her—why the man who raped her would never go to prison?"

Hawthorne flinched. Like the word might still hurt him, physically, after all those years. "Dolores doesn't even know what happened. I was away for the campaign at that time, but Charlotte took care of it. The poor girl didn't remember a thing the next morning, she said. Better–better that she didn't. How could I be the one to tell her, to shatter her life like that? It would have been selfish. Better to–to stay away from her, no matter what it cost me. To avoid laying all that on her shoulders. She would have seen it all in my eyes, I know she would have. What she didn't know couldn't hurt her."

Wyatt repressed a sigh.

Yes, he thought wryly. Alexander Hawthorne could be painted as a kind of tragic figure, in a Lear sort of way. Tragedy did have a thing for rich white men. "You don't think it *was* on her shoulders? That her life had been shattered already?"

But Hawthorne didn't seem to hear him.

It dawned upon Wyatt with crystal clarity that to the old man, this had never really been Dolores's tragedy. It had been his.

"Eighteen years," he said, to Wyatt, or to himself. "I haven't seen her in *eighteen years.* Or spoken to her," he laughed. As if he found it absurd, or realized he would never speak to her again. "If you'd told me once anything could come between us, I would have laughed you out of the room. It's the old cliché. People say all the time they'd crawl through fields of broken glass, swim through lakes of fire–but I *would.*"

A smile broke down his lips, oddly beautiful.

"If you told me, right now, I could carve a portal in time to go back, to save her, and I had to peel the skin off my flesh to find it, I'd beg for a knife."

Wyatt revealed the holster at his hip. "How about a gun?"

Alexander didn't answer. Wyatt stared at him for a long time. "But you could have seen Dolores, at any time."

Hawthorne's face grew icy. Wyatt had seen that same look on Dolores's face. "She didn't–she doesn't want anything to do with me now."

"*You* don't want anything to do with her, because she's a reminder. Right? You say it was all about protecting her, so she wouldn't find out the truth from you. But that's only part of the reason, isn't it? You can't look at her and not think that you buried a seventeen-year-old girl in the woods. That your daughter's rapist walked free because you were indebted to the boy's father. See, that's the difference between us, Alexander. You chose not to see your daughter. You *chose* to lose her. Because I didn't see my sister those past eighteen years, either, only it wasn't a domestic flight and a bit of emotional baggage keeping me from her."

Alexander's mouth closed. It was the only time Wyatt had betrayed anger.

After scorching the old man with his eyes, he managed, "Keep talking."

In the end, Hawthorne's tale left him with only two people who may or may not have been involved in the cover-up. Jacob Winslow, to start. Maybe he hadn't been at City Hall when Kristen died, but Kris had been his girl before she was Teddy's.

As far as his sister's boyfriends went, Jacob had seemed decent. But what did Wyatt know about the guy? If he could rape Dolores, then he could have done it to Kristen first. Maybe the brothers worked in tandem, as sick as it sounded–sicker things happened all the time.

The second blind spot was Dolores. When Wyatt mentioned her for the first time, he'd actually had to restrain the old man.

"Dolores has nothing to do with this," he said. Wyatt could see himself shape-shift in Hawthorne's eyes, from avenger to persecutor. "She was Kristen's friend. You have no business getting her mixed up in this."

Maybe so. But Dolores had turned a blind eye, all those years ago, when Wyatt set her on her father's trail. True, she had been a kid then.

But so had Kristen.

Had Dolores left Little Horton because she knew what her father had done? Had she kept silent about the cover-up?

I'll have to find out for myself, Wyatt reckoned. Even if Hawthorne had the answer, it was clear he'd carry the secret to his grave.

Wyatt debated telling the old man that his daughter was back in town. That he spoke to her, every day.

It would have been the final torture—not just for Hawthorne to imagine the threat Wyatt posed, so close to his darling child, but to know that Dolores was here, in Little Horton, almost within his grasp. To let the old man die with the tantalizing smell of all those might-have-beens in his lungs, see that portal he spoke of open wide enough that he could make out his daughter's face through that sliver of dream-like shine.

But Wyatt had said nothing, in the end, before he shot him.

Who would have thought his one act of mercy would be for the man who had ripped out his sister's teeth?

Looking at Dolores now, sitting in the chair her father had occupied, a pang of regret tugged at his chest. He wished he could be the drawn-back, pleasant Wyatt who had enjoyed her company over the past few days.

Ever since he'd brought Hawthorne to this cabin, Wyatt had been leading a double life: Daytime Wyatt, and Nighttime Wyatt, whose violence nauseated him when he'd rediscovered it in broad daylight.

If he'd had a choice, to seal his fate inside one of these alter egos—

Kristen's bones flashed into his mind. The toys she gave him, plastic-bottle trucks, stick men made out of matches. How she hugged him, so tightly it hurt, when they sat against his bedroom door, while their parents hurled plates at each other. *It's us against the world, Junior. Us against the world.*

Dolores had disappeared for eighteen years, and the whole town remembered her. Wyatt couldn't take a step anywhere without Dolores-this or Dolores-that slapping him in the face. How long had these same people cared about Kris? And if Dolores had gone missing, would the town have just assumed she'd run off and not bother to conduct a proper investigation? Or would they have canvassed the woods, moved heaven and earth until they found her?

Wyatt shook his head. You didn't choose violence, or vengeance. They chose you. If law enforcement had given Kristen justice, Nighttime Wyatt would never have needed to exist.

He glanced at his watch: 10:45. How much longer until he missed the rendezvous and the Winslow brothers slipped between his fingers?

"Dolores, did you hear what I said? You really want to risk your life to save a killer and a rapist?"

He drew in a cool breath, then gripped her shoulders. He hated the invasiveness of touching her, but she was probably in shock.

Her back stiffened as she roused to life. She sprang from the chair, her body like a bullet as she hit him, teeth bared, nails out. Wyatt took a step back. She could have been one of the feral cats he fed behind City Hall.

He reached out to grab her wrists, but she was faster—a vision flashed through his mind, her careful hands slicing a scalpel into Burke's chest. Then her fingers slashed the air and pain exploded in his left eye.

He grabbed her throat. A volt of disgust shot down his stomach, so strong she had time to claw his face again before he pushed back against her and they both went down. She writhed beneath him as he pinned her wrists above her head, conscious of every way in which his body touched hers. His limbs hardened into concrete, and he turned away.

If he looked at her he would see himself, and he would look too much like Teddy Winslow, and Dolores already looked so much like Kristen.

"I understand," he said. His vision blurred pink, and he knew she'd drawn blood when she scratched him. "I killed your father. You want justice, like I do. If you tell me where they are, Dolores, I'll walk into the police station with my hands in the air. Tonight."

Surely, she'd hear how reasonable he sounded. If he could discharge his gun into Teddy's face until it looked like a spilled pot of blueberry jam, then he'd be reasonable, so reasonable.

If she didn't—he didn't know what he'd do.

"Go to hell," she said.

He averted his eyes. To think Paul Turner believed he had a schoolboy crush on her. The truth was, Dolores reminded him so much of his sister that he couldn't look at her without thinking of what Kris would look like now, of all the years Teddy had taken from her.

His gaze landed on a strip of paper on the ground. Dolores froze. He reached to pick it up—it was the same note she'd had at the party. He remembered now, her fluster as she shoved it in her pocket.

Wyatt let out a chuckle as he read, "The crossroads between Bate Street and Benhill Road. Midnight."

Panic flooded Dolores's face.

"Please," she said. "It wasn't Jacob."

He laughed. He'd heard of women who did this, went out of their way to protect an abuser. A little disappointing, in someone like Dolores.

But the look of distress in her eyes looked real enough.

"You don't understand. He didn't hurt me or Kristen."

"Teddy?"

"*Jacob.*" There was something about how the word came out. Like a choke. Like a prayer. It gave Wyatt pause. "It wasn't him. It was never him. I believed it until I saw him again, until I remembered that it didn't make sense, that it never made sense."

She wasn't making much sense herself.

A blend between pain and rapture beamed on her features. She blurted out stray pieces of information that told him how confused she was. A bullhead mask. A fox smile.

"He was never at the Halloween party. He never laid a finger on me."

"That's not what I heard from your father."

He watched his words land. Dolores stiffened beneath him, and for an instant, inexplicably, she *looked* like her father. Forced to stare into the abyss both of them had spent their lives pretending not to see.

"He believed what he heard from Charlotte," she said. "And Charlotte must have got it wrong, like everyone else did."

"No," Wyatt said, though he wasn't sure why he resisted. It wasn't just that he didn't trust the older, paranoid Jacob he'd interrogated at City Hall. He wished he could say that that's what it was—but something more primal was at work in him.

Teddy Winslow doesn't get to keep his brother, a voice whispered. The voice of Nighttime Wyatt. *He watched your sister die. Why should he be the only one to suffer?*

"I *swear* to you," Dolores said. Wyatt's gaze snapped back to her. The command in her voice grabbed him and in that moment, everything between them vanished, except this appeal. Anger. Violence. Power. They dropped down the hole Dolores had pried open, squaring all their differences. They might have been brother and sister.

"Jacob never hurt me, and he never hurt Kristen. He was innocent."

Wyatt clenched his jaw.

A strange instinct wriggled to life inside him—to be the comforting, cool Daytime Wyatt. To rub the panic out of Dolores's eyes.

But vengeance loomed bright on the horizon. And the night was young.

He said, "Weren't we all?"

Fifty-Five

THE CABIN IN THE WOODS

Kate never thought she'd be grateful for skipping PE in sophomore year to give Jerry Allen a blow job. It had seemed like a good idea at the time—the kind of thing girls talked about in the restroom, and Kate hadn't yet given up on normal. She picked Jerry for his docile temper and his forehead, completely free from pimples.

As it happened, she could hear herself making a joke out of it. *The thing was sooo thin, like Twizzler-thin.* And the first girl she told the next day did get a laugh out of it. Then, for the rest of the year, Kate couldn't open her locker without Twizzlers cascading out of it.

"You're sure you know where we're going?" Paul asked as they ran, their flashlights bobbing up and down.

"For the hundredth time, *yes.*"

After the blow job, she'd left Jerry slouched against a tree with his boxers pooled at his ankles. She had run back in the direction of school and let out a scream, irritatingly girly, when she almost trampled a ten-year-old Junior Horowitz.

"What the fuck!" Kate cried.

He blinked at her, eyes too wide for his face. He looked like a prisoner of war who wouldn't crack under torture.

Kate's heart was racing from what she'd just done with Jerry. Part of her wanted to walk past Junior and go home, to hell with the kid. But what if he ran into an ax murderer or something?

"Damn it, Junior. You can't be in the woods by yourself. It's dangerous."

"*You're* here by yourself."

Kate sighed. "It's dangerous for little boys."

He turned up his nose at her, from his meager height of forty-nine inches. Kate took a step back, and realized Junior wasn't just standing there haphazardly. There was a reason she'd almost tackled him by accident. He'd been standing *in her way.*

She took a look behind him. "Whatcha got there?"

It was almost cute, how he tried to block her vision with his ridiculously small body.

"Nothing."

"Jesus, relax."

"Hey."

Kristen Horowitz's voice killed the smile on Kate's face. She might not like Junior, but she liked him better than his sister. Tall, shaped like she'd come out of a ballerina mold. Her folks had even less money than Kate's mom, yet Kristen got around, in that way beautiful girls do, like their presence in itself had exchange value.

Junior's eyes trained on his sister and he reverted into a normal kid, scared of disappointing the grown-up in the room. "I didn't tell."

Kristen laughed. "It's okay, Junior." She looked at Kate. "We built a cabin back here. Wanna see?"

Kate didn't, but the look on Junior's face was so outraged she found herself saying, "Sure."

For a couple of kids, the Horowitzes hadn't done a bad job. Forgetting her haste to get home, Kate listened as Kristen explained how they'd built the foundations, what kind of nails they'd used. If the girl could score a scholarship, she'd probably grow up to be an architect or something.

"Where'd you get the money for this?" Kate asked.

"You know." Kristen dragged her hand along the wooden walls. "Boys."

"Huh."

The whole time, Junior was looking gravely at Kate, like she was a heretic his sister was treating to their finest rituals.

"It's supposed to be a secret," he said.

Kristen gave him a playful look. "She won't tell. Will you, Butcher?"

And though she jogged past the cabin every day for years, Kate never did tell anyone.

Until tonight.

Until she recognized Wyatt in that picture, and it dawned upon her that Junior had come back to Little Horton under a different guise.

And if he'd taken Dolores, he would need somewhere remote. Somewhere only he knew about.

The beam from Kate's flashlight flickered as she ran alongside Paul, trying to match his pace.

"I sure hope you're not getting us lost, Butcher."

"Hey, I didn't force you to come. You were free to stay at the crime scene doing fuck-all."

"By the way?" Paul said. "I don't believe for a second Wyatt is who you say he is. All you have is a hunch, and a fifteen-year-old picture that kind of looks like him. The man hates violence. Besides, he's an FBI agent. He took an oath of honor. I know you don't like us, Butcher, but that means something. For all we know, he took Dolores somewhere safe."

"Without her phone? Without his phone?" Kate asked over the *slush* of their shoes thrashing through mud.

"There could be a good explanation."

"So, you're here to humor me?"

"I'm here because from what I've seen of the Little H PD, you're the only officer in town who knows your elbow from your ass."

The compliment threw Kate off. She'd hated Paul on sight, because he so obviously hated her colleagues. It hadn't struck her until now to think they had that in common.

By the time the cabin came into view, Kate's lungs were on fire. The structure stood tall, though the forest had begun to reclaim it. Weeds broke out around the foundations, tree branches drew it into a kiss.

She glanced back at Paul, who'd unhooked his Glock. Kate reached for her own weapon with sweaty hands. The cabin door didn't have a knob, but a lock had been drilled in recently. The metal gleamed, brand-new. It wasn't latched.

She gathered her nerve, pushed open the door, and almost dropped her gun in shock.

"Shit."

Dolores sat in a chair at the center of the room, circles of rope coiled around her ankles and wrists. The tape that covered her mouth shimmered when it caught Kate's flashlight.

In an instant, Paul was next to Kate, shoulder to shoulder, as he made a quick scan of the cabin. "Guard the door. The killer could be out there, setting a trap."

She clenched her Glock so hard her knuckles turned white.

Paul ran to Dolores and ripped the tape from her lips.

"He's gone," she said, gasping. "He's been gone for a long time."

Kate's gun turned to lead in her grip. She tried to loosen the bonds on Dolores's ankles, but her fingers were stiff with cold. Paul reached for his belt and a blade clicked into place.

"It's Junior," Dolores said as he sawed through the ropes. "Junior Horowitz. Wyatt–"

"We know," Kate said. She looked pointedly at Paul. So much for Wyatt's oath of honor.

"Wyatt brought you here?" he asked. "Tied you up?"

Dolores nodded.

"You're sure?"

"Of course she's sure," Kate hissed.

Paul shook his head. An FBI agent on a killing spree clearly didn't fit his view of the world. "I mean, maybe it's some kind of ruse. Maybe he was using you as bait–"

"Oh really," Kate snorted, "is that how the bureau does it?"

If it was her sitting in that chair with a man explaining to her she was accusing the wrong person, she'd jump down his throat.

But Dolores only planted her eyes on Paul, so coldly even Kate shivered. "He killed my father. He told me so. He's going to kill Teddy and Jacob."

Paul squared his jaw. Kate's flashlight lowered toward the ground, and landed on a pair of black leather derbies. "Look." Specks of dried blood winked at them under the beam. When they ran the tests, Kate would bet they'd find traces of Gregory's brain ground into the soles.

"Hell." Paul looked back at Dolores, her lips crushed-berry red where the tape had come off.

If he meant to apologize, she didn't give him the chance. "I was supposed to meet Jacob and Teddy between Bate Street and Benhill Road at midnight."

Kate glanced at her phone. Eleven thirty. "We'll never get there in time." She tried to call Nathan, wishing she'd thought to take her radio before she raced out of the house. "Shit. I don't have a signal."

"I'll go," Paul said. "I can make it if I run." His eyes latched onto Dolores. "He won't get away with this."

She nodded, and he dashed out the door.

Kate turned back to Dolores. Her stomach sank—the hate she'd carried, for all these years, shedding its weight like snake scales.

"I owe you an apology. For being an asshole to you."

"You said you were an asshole to everyone."

"Yeah. With most people, I'm not sorry about it."

Kate was hoping for a laugh. But Dolores looked so worried that Kate found herself saying the dumb, empty cop-promise. "I'm sure Paul will get there in time."

"No you're not." The dim light brought out a bruise blooming on Dolores's forehead. "I need to see him," she said. "Jacob."

Kate's gut churned. Dolores had clearly forgotten a lot of things about her teenage years. But this?

"I, uh—" Kate managed. "I don't think that's a good idea."

She cleared her throat under Dolores's stare. The night had been trying enough as it was. But how could she tell her not to go near Jacob without giving her a reason why?

She dragged in a pasty breath. "At your last Halloween party, the one where you invited me, some assholes sent me upstairs. I didn't mean to see anything, I just—the door was open. And Jacob—"

"It wasn't Jacob."

Kate's mouth snapped shut. She stared at Dolores. "You don't know what I'm trying to say."

Dolores's answer was firm, the way she'd sounded when she raised her hand in class, only when she was sure. "I do. It was Teddy."

Kate shook her head. She had seen Jacob that night—or had she just assumed it was Jacob because he was with Dolores?

"Teddy," Kate repeated, as if it would make the information stick.

Everyone's favorite Winslow. Life of the party, always quick with a joke Teddy? "I don't–" Kate started.

After a while, Dolores said, "Yeah. Me either."

They walked out of the cabin and inhaled the night air, purging their lungs of that damp cabin smell. "So you came," Dolores said.

"What?"

"To the party."

"Uh–yeah."

Dolores's voice was strangely calm. "I didn't think you would." A breath almost like a chuckle came out of her. "Isn't it ridiculous, thinking about this right now?"

Kate never needed much prompting to call someone ridiculous. "Yeah. A little."

"Maybe if it hadn't been for Teddy, if the party had gone as planned, you and I would have become good friends."

Kate's tongue stayed glued to the roof of her mouth a while. "I don't know," she said finally. "You're kind of a bore."

Dolores's laughter filled the forest, and for a moment, the prospect of walking back to town through those woods felt slightly less terrifying.

Fifty-Six

MIDNIGHT

The night air lashed against Paul's cheeks as he cut through the darkness. He was a good runner, but this wasn't one of his morning jogs. Trees broke into his line of sight a heartbeat before he had time to dodge. Brambles clawed at his pant legs, branches drew blood from his face and forearms. Paul was no Little Hortoner, and somehow, the forest was letting him know that.

"Hell," he said, as his foot sank ankle-deep into cold mud.

He couldn't shake the ridiculous idea that the woods were alive–that they were *actively* slowing him down. Protecting Wyatt.

Bits and pieces from the past few days clicked into place.

The look on Wyatt's face, when Dolores was handling Kristen's bones–how he took off with the Chrysler, leaving Paul to walk back to town. *There's enough of us watching. Wouldn't you say?* The exhaustion that came off him in waves, the way his face turned feral when Paul touched him.

Visions of dead bodies careened across Paul's mind. Dr. Burke. Gregory Winslow. Alexander Hawthorne.

All this time, had their killer been sitting in his passenger seat, bitching about his smoking?

Maybe there's been a mistake. Maybe Dolores got it all wrong somehow.

The line of trees began to thin on the horizon, until he could make out the glow of streetlights. Finally, he reached the road, treasuring the feel of asphalt beneath his shoes.

Paul took his phone out of his pocket. Ten to midnight. He dialed the address into the app, and ignored the line that read: time of arrival, 12:32.

Wyatt stood with his back against the wall of a toy store, so he wouldn't fall under the headlights of the brothers' car when it came riding in.

The intersection between Bate Street and Benhill Road in LaGrange was an eight-minute drive from Little Horton. And if you thought Little Horton was barely worth stopping for gas in, you wouldn't give LaGrange the time of day. A post office, in front of which the Stars and Stripes hung listlessly, twitching now and then in the breeze. Closed. A café, Mee-Maw's, "Breakfast Special $6, two for $10!" Closed. No shopkeeper had bothered to put a pumpkin on their doorstep. Anyone who wanted to celebrate Halloween would have gone to Little Horton, and the rest had obviously called it a day.

Wyatt checked his watch. Five to midnight.

He heard the car arrive before he saw it. A low purr, coming down Benhill Road. Before long, a dark Toyota came to a stop alongside Mee-Maw's, the hum of the motor filling the air.

Wyatt's heartbeat picked up. If he came out of hiding now, the brothers would start the car and take off. He might have scored some points before, playing the nice FBI agent. But now, ghostly pale, bleeding out of his left eye? He'd look like a phantom—like the Halloween monster he was.

Wyatt forgot to breathe, wiped sweat from his brow. Should he empty his gun into the windshield of their car? His body tensed as he rejected the idea. He wanted to look them in the eye when he killed them. Jacob first, so Teddy would know what was coming, so he would watch his own sibling bleed out in front of him. *A brother for a sister.*

Wyatt cursed under his breath. He should have taken Dolores as bait.

And yet, if he had a chance to do it all again, he knew he'd still leave her in that cabin.

Wyatt gave one last look at his watch. Midnight. Sweat pasted his shirt to his back as he peeled off the wall and stepped out of the darkness.

A shot blasted through the night.

The wind whistled in Paul's ears as he picked up speed. His feet didn't touch the ground so much as stab it, his body grinding with every stride.

When he stopped, all the air in his lungs solidified. Breathing felt like inhaling acid, but he didn't have a split second to waste on his body right now. He drew his gun before he registered what he was seeing.

Wyatt, Wyatt's gun, the car, the shot tire, Jacob and Teddy Winslow with their hands up. The air smelled like a burnt steak. It coated the walls of his throat.

"Drop it," Paul shouted.

Wyatt kept his weapon aimed at the brothers.

Holy hell. The quiet partner Paul had gotten used to these past few days could have stood alongside this mad-eyed killer, and he would not have seen the resemblance.

"Drop it," Paul repeated, the gun moist in his hand. "I don't want to shoot you, Big Guy."

Even as his last efforts to cling to Wyatt's innocence evaporated, he realized he meant it.

Wyatt laughed. "You can lose the radio voice."

"Backup's on the way. In a few minutes, this town will be crawling with police cars. Do the smart thing, Wyatt. Put down your weapon."

Wyatt's eyes narrowed on the hostages. Blood streamed down his left eye.

Paul clutched the Glock harder, his finger tense above the trigger. "Drop the gun."

He fired half a heartbeat before Wyatt did.

Two shots exploded into the night. One of the Winslow brothers screamed, and two bodies thudded to the ground.

Fifty-Seven

SICKLY SWEET

The woods that bordered Little Horton were scary in their own right, but on Halloween night, with a killer in town, they seemed to whisper witchcraft. Dolores and Kate had reached the road about fifteen minutes ago when the motor of an approaching vehicle purred ahead of them. Dolores had never been happier to see a police car.

The window rolled down, Nathan Gunn behind the wheel. Dolores recognized him now, behind his Viking beard. "You girls need a ride?"

Kate sighed, a blend of annoyance and relief. She rode shotgun next to her colleague while Dolores took the backseat.

"So," Nathan said. "Am I taking you home, *Miss Hawthorne*?"

"Yes. Thank you."

Kate feigned looking at her shoes. "You can stay with us tonight. If you want."

Dolores saw her father again behind closed lids. Dead. Alexander was dead, now. His fingers curved inward like bird claws. The bullet hole dripping from his face.

A chill crawled down her spine as she imagined tonight's events, chewed up into a juicy piece of *Little H folklore*.

A year from now, the kids would sing about what had happened tonight.

Her father would be nothing more than a Halloween story–a tourist trap.

"Thank you, Kate," she said. "For everything. I appreciate the offer. But I need to be with my family right now."

When Nathan pulled into the driveway, Charlotte was already on the doorstep. She had changed into a black dress. With her blond hair glowing under the porch lights, she looked like an angel of death.

Nathan followed Dolores out of the car. When they reached the house, he thumped the side of his fist against his mouth and cleared his throat. "Chief asked me to let you know in person—we caught him, ma'am. The man who—Wyatt Holt. He's still in intensive care. That FBI agent, I mean, the other agent, had to shoot him."

"Is he going to be all right?" Dolores asked before she could think.

Charlotte's eyes drilled into her, hard as rubies. She didn't say, *The man killed your father, Dolores.*

There was no need.

"Good night, Officer Gunn," Charlotte said, before Nathan could answer.

He squared his shoulders and pushed up his pecs. "Evening, ma'am."

Charlotte opened the door and Dolores followed her inside.

A hand grabbed her arm, and someone slammed against her like a brick wall. Dolores only knew it was Asher when her fingers sank into golden curls. He smelled like caramel from his afternoon at the apple-dipping stand.

"I was so afraid," he said.

When he drew back, his eyes widened. She had no idea what state her struggle with Wyatt had left her in. Her shoulders felt bruised from his fingers, her wrists burned from the rope. But honestly, that was fairy dust compared with the night cold that had seeped into her bones while she and Kate trudged through the woods. Her feet were ice blocks inside her shoes.

"Jesus." Asher looked horrified. "Do you need a hospital?"

She shook her head. A burning shower and ten hours of sleep. That's what she needed.

It would have to wait, though. Her eyes met Charlotte's over Asher's shoulder.

Her stepmother smiled. "Let's make you a hot drink."

Asher dropped into a chair, but Dolores stood stiffly by the kitchen door, watching Charlotte as she poured water into a kettle.

"Try and keep quiet," Charlotte said. "Josie's asleep."

"Shit, Josie." Asher raked the feet of his chair against the tile. "I'll go get her."

"I wish you wouldn't, darling."

A furrow shot between his brows. "She'll want to know Dolores is okay."

"She's better off getting some rest. Your sister's gone through a traumatic experience."

Asher stared at her, mouth hanging ajar. "Don't you mean my 'sisters'?"

Dolores put a hand on Asher's shoulder. "Can you give us a moment?"

Asher hesitated for a second before he stood up and slid out the door. She waited until she heard his footsteps lumber up the staircase.

"You made me cocoa, too, on my last Halloween here," Dolores said.

Charlotte watched her through long lashes. The kettle started to boil, and she poured three spoons of chocolate powder into a mug. Four spoons of sugar. "What else do you remember?"

"Everything."

In the cabin, as Wyatt repeated her father's confession to her, Dolores had felt like a penny dropped from the top of the stairs. There, in the depths of this bottomless hole, her past was alive and well. She remembered walking out of her bedroom on Halloween night, her hands trailing along the walls, spreading fake Lady Macbeth blood on everything. Wandering to her father's bedroom, even though Alexander was out of town that night. How she had wished he were here, felt certain he would fix everything just by looking at her, that he would lift the curse, free the sleeping castle from its cloak of dreams.

If she had known then that her father would never really look at her after that night, she would have broken into a thousand pieces.

Instead of Alexander, Dolores had found Charlotte, asleep. A look of surprise on her face, then horror. *Dolores, what is it? Dolores?*

"You took me into the bathroom," Dolores said.

"You practically threw up your whole body weight."

Dolores blinked back flashes of her stepmother's face, hanging over her as her cheek rested against the toilet bowl. Charlotte's hand in her hair, curling against her neck. Words that chilled her down to her bone marrow, that sounded almost like a command—*You're going to be okay, Dolores.*

The spoon hummed against the brim of the cup as Charlotte stirred the cocoa. "Milk?"

"No."

Charlotte put the cup down on the table, and it smoldered between them. A smile still etched the corners of her lips. It looked positively deadly. "Well. It wasn't our finest hour, was it? I think I would have killed that boyfriend of yours then and there if I'd gotten my hands on him."

"What made you so sure? That it was Jacob."

Charlotte sighed. "We talked about this. I asked every single person at that party who had taken you upstairs that night. It was Jacob. They all said so. Even your brother—"

Dolores looked up from her mug. This was new. "Asher saw us?"

Charlotte shook her head. "He woke up and needed the restroom. Jacob ran into him in the hall."

"Jacob," Dolores said. "Wearing a mask?"

Charlotte admitted, "Yes. But Asher recognized his voice. He called him 'Ash-Man'—you remember that stupid nickname Jacob used."

A single line creased her stepmother's forehead as Dolores burst into laughter. It sounded, to her own ears, chillingly genuine.

She pictured the scene. Teddy, still in the bullhead mask, rustling her brother's hair. *Hey, Ash-Man. How you doing? Back to bed, now, eh?*

It was so Teddy of Teddy to think of such a detail.

"I didn't think we'd have to go through that conversation again," Charlotte said. "Every witness told the same story. That Jacob carried you upstairs to your bedroom. Those rumors, about you cheating on him—that only came after. The little swine must have denied it all. Poisoned the whole town with his lies. The Winslow golden boy—why shouldn't they believe him? So they all went with it: Jacob wasn't at the party. *You* cheated on *him*."

She put the cocoa back in the cupboard. "All else being equal, Dolores, remember, the woman always pays the price. But we had sway, too, and I told everyone you'd been sick that night, gone to bed early, and I could vouch for that because I'd taken care of you. The poor town was like a ship caught between two winds, blowing in different directions. The

Hawthornes and the Winslows, the oldest families in Little Horton, at each other's throats. The best I could do was convince Gregory to keep up appearances. Pretend the gossip had been born out of nowhere, so you and Jacob could come out clean. A truce, where we didn't accuse the boys of anything–and Gregory kept his sons away from our family."

Dolores licked her lips. "And if I told you it was true? That Jacob was never at the party?"

Charlotte shook her head, adamant. "Everyone confirmed it the next morning."

"It wasn't Jacob."

Her stepmother drew in a patient breath. "Dolores–"

"Teddy tricked them."

Charlotte fell silent for a second.

"Teddy," she repeated thoughtfully.

Light danced over Charlotte's hair as she shrugged.

"Can't say I'm surprised, after what he did to Kristen Horowitz."

Fifty-Eight

GHOSTS AND MILK

Dolores's jaw dropped. The refrigerator hummed. Across the hall, the antique clock struck one.

"You knew. Dad told you—"

Charlotte laughed, that Southern laugh that was all warmth, but her eyes were all ice. "Your father didn't *tell me,* Dolores. I was the one who found them."

Dolores reeled back. The shock felt solid, a fist that had punched her in the stomach. The image sliced into her retina. Of Charlotte, kneeling in the dirt. Ripping Kristen's teeth out.

A voice whispered, *Do you think your father could have gone through with it? He couldn't even stand to clean Asher's scraped knees.*

Then her father's. *If the apocalypse ever happens, Dolores, I want you to go to your stepmother. She is the strongest person in the universe.*

Charlotte's eyes glazed, like she was seeing it all over again. "Teddy Winslow," she said, to no one in particular. "Teddy Winslow. That *boy* had more eyes for girls than he had brains. I'd seen how he looked at Kristen when he dropped by City Hall. A woman notices these things. I'd caught him looking at me, caught him looking at *you.* But that's a far cry from raping or killing a girl."

She shook her head. "He threw himself at my feet that day. There was a girl lying dead on the floor of my workplace, and Teddy Winslow, begging me to understand how *he* was the victim. Rotten to the core, that boy is."

Dolores couldn't will her mouth back shut. If her father hadn't lied to Wyatt and told him he'd been the one to find Kristen that night, would Charlotte have ended up on an autopsy table?

"Did you know he drugged her? That he—"

"What did I know, Dolores? I was barely out of my twenties. I called your father, and we made the best decision we could."

"You took a bribe," Dolores said. How could Charlotte talk about it as if it were just a tough life decision, like quitting your job or leaving your spouse?

Charlotte's face went stiff. "Your father and I needed the money. What happened to Kristen Horowitz broke both our hearts, but nothing was going to bring her back to life, was it? That money built us a future. And it built one for you as well, or do you think you would have gotten through thirteen years of med school any other way?"

"I think if Teddy had gone to trial for what he did to Kristen, I wouldn't have been raped."

Dolores bit down her tongue until she tasted blood.

The words Wyatt had spoken to her in the cabin trickled across her brain. *I felt like the man who destroyed my family had been feeding me my sister's murder in a silver spoon, drowned in sugar.*

"Why did you never tell me?" she asked.

"About Kristen? What would have been the point?"

"About Dad." Dolores heard the cracks in her voice, but she continued. "Why did you never tell me he knew?"

There was no denying, now that the memories had returned, what had really chased her from Little Horton.

His coldness. His silence. The ghost of his love, everywhere in the house. Dolores had made excuses for it. *It's those rumors going around.* Gregory Winslow, telling anyone who would listen what a shameless little slut she was.

As if that would have mattered to him.

She'd told herself her father didn't know about Halloween. About the pregnancy.

But part of her had always known. Or she wouldn't have fled to the other side of the country, all so she could pretend that back in Little Horton, the father she remembered still existed, untarnished. That whenever she was ready to come home, he would welcome her into his arms.

"You made me lie to him," she said. "Appendicitis. You said what he didn't know–"

"Couldn't hurt him," Charlotte finished.

A headache began to throb through her frontal bone, and Dolores tried to stop clenching her teeth. How could Charlotte look at her right now?

Worse than the long years of silence, worse than the lies, was the absence of shame in her stepmother's eyes.

There was no pain on her face. No regret. Charlotte wasn't the kind of woman who looked back. Only ahead.

"It was easier like this," she said.

"Easier?" Rage thickened Dolores's voice. "Easier for whom?"

Her stepmother chuckled humorlessly. "For the both of you, you little fool. You don't think I did it to protect him? To protect *you*? What do you think Gregory would have done, if we'd called his son a rapist? We could not go against him. Dr. Burke was in on the bribe, so I trusted he'd keep his ugly mouth shut about this, too. If I'd taken you to a hospital, and news got around–can you imagine the scandal? If Gregory thought there was evidence of the rape–God, Dolores. Don't you realize that this man had his foot in our faces, all those years?"

Dolores could not help but think of a shoe, crashing down on Gregory's head.

Charlotte smiled. "I knew you'd hate me for it. What difference did it make? You already hated me. You don't think I took the hate so your father wouldn't have to? It was better like this–to tell him you didn't remember what happened, so he had to keep it together. For your sake."

"And to tell me he didn't know, so I'd keep it together. For his sake."

The words shimmered just out of grasp.

Why did you carve this abyss between us? Why did you rip me out of his heart?

"You think I'm the villain," Charlotte said. "In your eyes, I'm still the evil queen who stole your father from you. I swear, Dolores. Sometimes I think the problem at the heart of it all is that because I hated you, you could never bring yourself to get it into your stupid little head that I loved you."

Dolores swallowed a lump of liquid lead. Her lips didn't feel attached to her face, or her thoughts to her brain. There was no room for feeling–the shock of what had just happened in the cabin, of her father's death, took up all the space.

"Then tell me the truth," she managed.

Dolores could see Charlotte's patience wearing thin. "The truth? All right. Your father knew. Of course he knew. Telling him was the hardest thing I ever did. I could have taken a kitchen knife and cut his heart out, and he would have considered it a mercy." Charlotte shook her head. "You can't imagine what it feels like, to see your husband like this. I knew he would trade everything he had if he could take back what happened to you. That he would throw me into a pit of hellfire if he could spare you. And I would have thrown myself into that pit if I could, Dolores. For him *and* you. There were times I wished I'd never told him, that I'd gone to war against Gregory alone."

"So you did the next best thing," Dolores said. "You made us both pretend that nothing happened. You thought if we lied to everyone—*appendicitis*—that we'd forget? That's just what Hawthornes do, isn't it? We decide what we believe, and eventually, reality gives in. You don't think it would have been better if Dad and I had talked about it? That we could have healed?"

"Your father was glad to ignore it. Trust me. He couldn't live with it, Dolores. There are certain things men cannot live with. You want to think I'm to blame? Be my guest. But your father went along with the lie quite willingly. As did you."

The mug of cocoa had gone lukewarm between Dolores's palms. She drew its smell deep into her lungs—too sweet. Charlotte always made it too sweet.

Most things in life don't come with sugarcoating. Might as well sweeten what we can.

The temptation was strong—to paint her stepmother as the guiltiest party. To think she had influenced Alexander, not just to sweep that Halloween night under the carpet, but all of it. That she'd pushed him to take Gregory's deal, to cover up what happened to Kristen. To think he had done it out of love for her. Macbeth and Lady Macbeth.

You just remember the father you know, Dolores.

But a sour taste in the back of her throat knew this was a lie.

Her love for him had been as blind as his was.

How he would let his thoughts wander while Gregory bullied Jacob at the dinner table, flee confrontation—choose the easiest path.

Appearances.

The fact that Dolores could never hate her father for this, could never confront him with his mistakes and let his pain begin to heal hers—

That fact right now seemed injustice made flesh.

Dolores could still taste anger in her ground teeth, but she reined it in. After all these years, she would simply not know what to do with it.

"Did you know that Dad wrote me a letter?" she said. "Before he was taken. He told me how sorry he was for what happened—and that I shouldn't trust anyone. I keep going back to who he was talking about. The Winslows, of course. Maybe the police. But now I think he meant you, Charlotte. That he meant I shouldn't trust anyone, not just in this town—but in this house."

Charlotte held her gaze, silent.

"One thing I can't wrap my head around is why Dad met with Gregory, before he went missing. If Dad had regrets, if he wanted to go to the police—why would he have talked to Gregory? That would be stupid of him, and Dad was a smart man. Did you know that Winslow hired a hit man?"

Charlotte watched her in silence a while. "Why don't you just go ahead and ask me, Dolores."

But Dolores found she couldn't. It was too much of a betrayal. To her father? To Charlotte?

"Did you plan it together?" she said finally.

"You mean, did Gregory and I work together to kill your father."

Dolores sucked in a breath, the smell of hot chocolate turning her stomach. Charlotte loved her father; she knew that much. But if she thought he would dig up the whole Kristen affair, if she thought he was sending them to prison for the rest of their lives? After all, "the rest of their lives" didn't mean the same thing to the two of them. Her father was old. Charlotte had her whole life ahead of her.

"I did call Gregory," Charlotte said, "because I thought if he saw Alexander he could talk some sense into him. That's all I wanted, Dolores. For your father to understand that the rules hadn't changed, that we couldn't go against the Winslows now, any more than we could have in the old days." She shook her head. "Do you know what set your father off? What started all this? You'll laugh if I tell you."

"I doubt it."

Charlotte opened the fridge and pulled out a milk carton. Dolores blinked at a picture of a model with dark hair and eyes. A radiant smile without any tooth missing.

For a second, Dolores felt Charlotte had catapulted them back into the past, that she would read the words "Help us find Kristen Horowitz."

But the text above the photograph boasted, "Happy Wisconsin Milk."

"Ludicrous, isn't it?" Charlotte said. "That damned ad campaign–purely coincidental the girl they cast looks so much like you. And Kristen"–she sighed–"but when your father saw it, he became so still I thought the blood in his veins was freezing over. That's when he started picking up all these strange habits. The lemon pies. The long rants about the past. Until one day, after Josie had gone to bed, we sat in this kitchen, and he told me he wanted to come clean."

Dolores waited, until the ticking of the clock got unbearable. "And," she said, "you tried to talk him out of it."

"Of course I did. It was suicide, Dolores. Not just political suicide. We would have gone to prison; your sister and brother would have to kiss goodbye any shot at a normal life. Alexander said he'd take full blame for everything–but of course, Gregory wouldn't go down without dragging us all into the mud."

Charlotte's hands clutched the edges of the table. "I thought if your father spoke with Gregory, he'd understand that. Then when he disappeared and Dr. Burke died–"

"You thought the Winslows were cleaning house," Dolores let out. "Tying up loose ends. That's what you thought was happening, wasn't it? That all of us were in danger of the Winslows coming after us–that if we acted normal, and just waited this out, Gregory would see we weren't a threat."

"I was hoping he'd only taken your father to scare some sense into him. That he'd come back, a few days later, and we'd act like this was only one of his eccentricities." Charlotte fell silent, eyes drilling into the milk carton. "Then Gregory died, and I didn't know what to think."

She looked up at Dolores. "I didn't understand why your father wouldn't leave all this in the past. That's true enough. But I didn't, I would *never*, let that monster take him from me."

Dolores put the mug down on the table. "You still sent him to see Gregory. Even if you didn't know you were putting his life at risk–you turned on him, when he wanted to come out with the truth."

Charlotte scoffed. "Please, Dolores. What good would the truth have done for this family?"

2 DAYS LATER

Fifty-Nine

HALLOWEEN MONSTERS

Dolores stiffened as smells of cinnamon sweets rose from the hospital's cafeteria, and gift shops dangled rainbow bouquets into her face. She slid into the elevator and went up to the sixth floor. Part of her expected someone to stop her. She walked past room 601, then 602, but couldn't read the number on room 603, because a man shaped like a refrigerator stood guarding it.

"Mr. Winslow isn't taking visitors."

Dolores paused, almost willing to back down. The part of her that had fled her past for two decades certainly wanted to. "Would you tell him Dolores Hawthorne would like to see him?"

The bodyguard cracked open the door. "Sir, a Dolores Hawthorne is here to see you."

"Dolores? Sure, send her in."

Wooden wall paneling greeted her, a plasma screen and a massive window. Only the bed gave away that this wasn't a five-star hotel.

Teddy's leg hung elevated in a cast. His face broke into a smile before he glanced at the bodyguard. "You can give us the room, Mike."

"Considering there was an attempt on your life—"

"The man who tried to kill me is handcuffed to his bed, three floors below. And he's worse off," he said with a wink. "You're not gonna try and kill me, are you, Doll?"

"Not today."

Mike-the-Bodyguard duly retreated outside.

Teddy waved at his leg. "You're gonna laugh, but that's actually not where the bullet went through. Just broke my damn leg when I fell. Here." He guided his palm toward his heart. "Bastard nearly got me. Two inches to the left, and I was a goner. Sorry, I'm being so rude. Sit down." Teddy gestured toward two leather chairs around a table, covered by bouquets. "You like them? Never knew I had so many friends. Apparently, when that lunatic shot at our car, some lady was filming the whole thing through her window. It's on YouTube now. I'm sending flowers away by the ton. Who'd have thought getting shot in the chest turned you into the next Chris Evans. You're sure you don't wanna sit down?"

Dolores stayed silent, waiting for something inside her to snap. She'd scream, she'd hurl a vase at the wall. Instead, an ice lake of quietness entered her bloodstream. Here was the man who had uprooted her life. Because of Teddy, she could never say goodbye to her father or watch her siblings grow up. Here was the man who had kicked open the door of her life with giant boots, and hurled her into a black hole where everything was upside down and her father would never dance with her again or meet her eyes.

Here he was.

Her Halloween monster.

And he was talking to her about YouTube and Chris Evans.

Teddy's brows puckered, then he shook his head. "You heard what they're saying, right? That the fake FBI guy is Junior Horowitz."

Somehow, a lot of people called Wyatt a "fake FBI agent," instead of a man who had gone through all the proper channels, been hired by the bureau, and happened to be a serial killer.

"Apparently he had this obsession with his sister. Like, incest-obsessed. Makes sense he would have targeted you, what with how much you look like her. Kristen. He didn't do anything to you, did he?"

Dolores stared at him, every word in her vocabulary gone. Finally, she said, "You remember Kristen, Teddy?"

"Sure. I'm forty, not a hundred."

Dolores's fists dug into her sides. It was just a façade. If she kept pushing, he would break and the mask would come down, and there'd be the cruel curve of that fox grin slicing into her eyes.

"How many times did you do it?"

Teddy looked left and right, like she was playing a joke on him. "Get shot in the chest?"

"Rape women," she said.

His face caved in absolute shock. "What the fuck did you say?"

A throb of panic stabbed into her. A voice hissed, *See? This is all a big misunderstanding. Maybe you did fuck Teddy or some guy at that Halloween party, but there was no rape. Can't you see that this man wouldn't hurt a fly?*

Dolores couldn't believe how familiar the voice sounded. Like she'd had these thoughts dozens, *hundreds* of times.

She steeled herself against them. "You raped Kristen, Teddy. She overdosed, and you watched her die."

"No, no, no, *come on,* Doll. You know me—we grew up together." His tone was a blend of shock and hurt. Lines furrowed into his forehead. She had never seen him look so old, and so young. "Am I a rapist?"

Dolores's gut, and that voice in her head, screamed: *No.*

"Kris—okay, maybe I did sleep with her, and we did drugs, but she took them willingly. I didn't make her."

"Like you didn't make me?"

He sat back in his bed. "Goddamn it, Doll. What are you saying?"

Dolores tried to breathe past the nail sinking between her ribs. What was she doing here? She had thought she would walk into his hospital room and confront him and—what? What remained of her denial would smash into pieces when she saw the truth in his fox smile?

Instead, his own denial hit her like a brick wall, stronger than hers had ever been.

"I *love* you, Dolores," he said. Blended with the horror in his eyes, there was genuine sadness. "How can you think I'd ever hurt you?"

The ice holding Dolores together snapped. Maybe it was the pain after Halloween, which had followed every footstep for days. How she couldn't get out of bed because to feel it made her want to be dead. Maybe it was the first time she had seen the scar, after the surgery, that clownish grin on her abdomen—thinking it looked just like the smile on a Halloween mask. Thinking she had loved dressing up on this one day in the year, but that now, she would always wear that mask. Sewn to her skin.

"You raped me, Teddy. That night on Halloween, 2003."

Anger flashed through his face, and the ground opened beneath her feet. That word–"rape"–a blaze catching in a pool of gasoline. The air turned, too fast for her to brace herself.

"You are out of your fucking mind. You need help. There's a maniac downstairs who came after my family–and yours. And you think now's a good time to go psycho on me? If it's money you're after–"

"No." She shook her head, her breath running short.

But Teddy wasn't listening. The tango of his words snatched her along. He led the dance, as always.

His hands were fists atop the hospital covers, clenched so tight she could see the veins popping out. "If you come after me, boy, you had better be ready for it. Because I will drag you through mud so filthy your own family will change sidewalks when they see you in the street. I'll tell the story–the *whole* story. You always had a thing for me, even when you dated Jake. What? Did you think we'd be an item after Halloween, that I was gonna be your new lapdog? You were just a kid. I had chicks in Madison lining up at my doorstep. Why can't you let it be what it was? Why'd you have to make things all complicated? I don't wanna hurt you, Dolores." His gaze darkened. The corners of his mouth twitched. "And you sure as hell don't wanna cross me."

Panic thrashed through her chest. *Sphenoid, orbital, lacrimal.*

She planted her feet into the ground, forced herself to meet his eyes. *If he smiles, I'll die.* "I'll see you in court, Teddy."

She spun on her heels, flung open the door, and ran past the bodyguard to the elevator, her ragged breathing beating in her ears.

The elevator dinged as it reached the ground floor, and Dolores dashed out.

"Dr. Diaz?"

Dolores whipped back around. In her haste, she hadn't seen Paul stepping out of the cafeteria. His mouth opened as he took her in, but he closed it politely.

"I'm sorry. I didn't mean to startle you."

Dolores moistened her lips. They were still cracked where Paul had ripped the tape off.

"You're in a hurry. Don't let me keep you."

She appreciated his offering her an out, but seeing him felt good, actually, like running into the last sane person in a madhouse.

Paul glanced at the coffee in his hand. "Look, I haven't touched this, do you want it? It's not exactly how I pictured buying you a drink, but you look like you could use it."

Dolores managed a dry chuckle. Calloused fingers brushed hers as he handed her the cup. "What are you doing here?"

His face turned grave. "I wanted to hear Wyatt's confession. It's–humbling, when you realize your own partner was leading you by the nose."

"I'm sure your ego will recover."

He tilted his head, like he wasn't so confident. "Listen, I wanted to apologize. For my behavior at the cabin. I should have believed you immediately. I just–I couldn't believe that of Wyatt. Part of me still can't, you know. When we got to the crime scene at the Winslows, he was almost sick. It didn't look like he was faking."

"Maybe he wasn't. Killers can be very successful at dissociating."

Paul plunged his hands into his pockets, and she could see the bulge of his fists stretching the fabric. "You aren't here to visit him, are you?"

"No."

Her entire being bristled at the thought. And not just because Wyatt had killed her father.

If she confronted him, his dark eyes would gleam with rage, and it would be the same rage that burned in the pit of her stomach. They would cry out that his killing spree should have ended with Teddy Winslow, the final piece of his revenge–and hers.

Dolores shivered. The blood money that had paid for Wyatt's education had also paid for hers. Everything she owned now might as well have been carved out of Kristen's bones.

And I've paid for it, too.

The crooked scar on her abdomen whispered as much.

Dolores tried to shake the thought. "I suppose you'll be going back to Milwaukee," she said, aiming for a casual tone.

He held eye contact, a wink too long. "And you'll be flying back to L.A."

"After my father's funeral."

His face darkened. "I never got a chance to tell you I'm sorry for your loss. It sounds trite, I know. But I am. Really."

The genuineness in his tone startled her. She couldn't say when she'd become aware of it over the past few days–that there was more to Paul Turner than easy charm and empty flirting. She'd underestimated him. And sensed, deep in her gut, that this was just what the agent wanted.

"I appreciate it."

They went on looking at each other. People bustled in and out of the cafeteria, streamed out of the gift shop clutching helium balloons. That's what Dolores loved about hospitals. They were never silent.

She went for a joke. "Well, I'm glad I ran into you, Agent Turner. It would have hurt my feelings if you'd left town without saying goodbye."

Paul feigned surprise. "Oh, I'm not saying goodbye to you."

"Really?"

The FBI hadn't called her with an offer yet, as Dr. Marley said they would. Dolores hadn't decided what she'd do if they did.

"Really."

She resisted biting her lip, fished for something to say. "Thanks for the coffee."

"Don't thank me. I expect you to buy me one next time we see each other. Sooner, not later, right?" He grinned. "I'm not known for my patience."

Sixty

SHINE

Until the funeral, Dolores found it safer to stay away from the Hawthorne house. She would have checked back into the motel if Kate hadn't asked her over for coffee after she confronted Teddy at the hospital. Kate looked surprised when she learned about her plans to move out. "Don't you want to be close to your siblings?" she asked, scooping sugar into her mug.

"I do," Dolores said. But after everything that'd happened, she simply couldn't go on living under the same roof as her stepmother. She wondered how to put this without having to get too personal.

The look on Kate's face spared her the trouble. "The offer still stands, you know. About staying over with me and Leo."

"I don't want to be a bother."

"No bother. You'll help with the cats."

"What?"

Kate sighed, guiltily. "When I got back to the station, the strays I brought over on my last patrol were still there. I suppose, with everything going on, no one found time to take them to the pound."

Dolores tried to picture the scene. Kate, stepping out of the police station with cat crates in her arms while her colleagues teased and hooted. For a person who had spent so long avoiding being laughed at, it was a big step.

As if reading her mind, Kate said, "Yes, everyone at the station is giving me hell for it—well, more hell than usual." She sighed. "I'm so tired of this place. This life. Busting my ass off to prove myself to people who'll never respect me—people I've never even liked."

"Maybe you should quit."

"Maybe."

A beat of silence settled in. Dolores twirled the spoon in her coffee mug.

"Are you keeping them? The cats?"

Kate shrugged. "I don't know. Who else will take them? Leo says strays should look after each other."

"That's not a bad philosophy."

Her siblings were a little less pleased about the arrangement. Asher didn't prod when Dolores mentioned staying at Kate's house, but Josie dealt her a stony silence that made it plain she viewed the move as a betrayal. "Do you have to?" she finally asked.

"Yes. But I'll just be a few minutes away."

"For how long?" Josie was so solemn, Dolores had to give a serious answer.

"I'm not going anywhere, Josie. Not now. Not ever. Okay?"

Josie held her gaze for a long while, but by the time she acknowledged Dolores's promise with a nod, the coldness had drained from her eyes.

While waiting for the cab, Dolores walked around the Hawthorne house, letting its museum smell soak into her—this house she had left so many times, but never said goodbye to.

The strangest thing was, even though she knew beyond doubt that her father was dead, she could still feel him here. In this house.

She entered his office, where all traces of violence had been erased. The apple-shaped cookie box sat on the mahogany desk, and when she lifted the lid, the crumbly smell of hidden sweets stabbed into her like ten thousand needles. She sank to her knees. Remembered the crisp feel of his hands on her.

But still he was invisible, shimmering out of grasp the way clearness blackens out of burning sugar.

Sobs rocked through her in an avalanche of grief. Alone, in the office where she had whiled away long evenings, Dolores cried like she hadn't cried in years. She cried for her father, and for Asher and Josie, whose childhood had stolen away without warning.

And she cried for hers.

For the girl she had been, who had died one Halloween night nineteen long years ago.

"Dolores!" Asher cried from the ground floor. "The taxi's here!"

"I'm coming!" She wiped her face with the back of her hand. As her father would put it, it was time to face the music.

SHE HAD HALF A mind to be offended when her father's funeral turned into the biggest party Little Horton had ever seen.

"Alexander was the love of my life," Charlotte had said when the local paper interviewed her after Halloween. "And I'll give him a proper parting, like we do in the South. He'll leave this world the same way he lived. With panache."

In mourning, she looked flamboyant, her dress a *Gone with the Wind* costume painted black. Music boomed through the streets. Handkerchiefs wiped teary eyes and greasy mouths, as guests sauntered past buffets gorged with casseroles, corn bread, honey-glazed ham.

The crowd clamored for a speech before Alexander's casket was carried to the graveyard. Cameras flashed, and Charlotte offered her most lenient smile. "This is a time for grief, but it's also a time for joy. A time to celebrate my husband's life, and everything he did for this town."

Asher whispered in Dolores's ear, "Think Mom will be the first mayor voted into office unanimously?"

"What?"

Josie rolled her eyes. "If you hadn't exiled yourself out of the house, you'd know. Jacob resigned."

Dolores looked at her sister, then Asher, who confirmed the news with a nod. "His deputy mayor took over, but elections are coming up, anyway. And if you ask me, Mom is acting *very* much like someone running for City Hall."

Dolores's eyes went back to Charlotte, her teeth unwilling to pry apart. All this talk about her father's achievements, anecdotes about his wits and kindness. She loved her father, of course, but she couldn't stop thinking how wrong this was. What about his part in covering up Kristen's death? The bribe he and Charlotte had taken to bury her and rip her teeth out?

Dolores lowered her eyes. Felt sick at all the food, the crowd, the music. She couldn't see her father in any of this. Not the man who had let Teddy get away with manslaughter, or the wonderful father who had loved her to distraction. If he were here, he'd probably try to slip off, get away from the spectacle. He'd steer her from the crowd, take her by the hand. *Come on, Dolores. How about a dance?*

She shuffled her way out through the crush of people, walked until the music was no louder than the hiss of the wind. But she wasn't alone—not really.

Ghosts filled the air beside her, rising from the few gutted pumpkins left to rot out in the streets. Junior, and Kristen Horowitz.

Dolores dropped onto the edge of the sidewalk, which was mercifully dry. She closed her eyes, but still their presence shimmered all about her. The ghosts were silent, but their eyes whispered, softly, and they smelled like forest fire, like her father's precious box of cookies.

"Mind if I sit with you?"

Dolores looked up, and her heart somersaulted.

Jacob.

He didn't look like the harrowed man who had burst into her house the night Gregory died. Dark bags hung beneath his green eyes, the cut left by Charlotte's knife haloed by a cranberry rash. Dolores couldn't get used to the wisps of silver that glinted in his hair when the sun pierced through the clouds. But he looked quiet again, the madness gone out of his eyes.

"Sure," she managed.

He dropped next to her on the sidewalk and dragged his legs to his chest. The asphalt beneath her suddenly felt warm. Ahead, the hill leading to the graveyard towered in the crisp autumn air. Songs and smells of the funeral rolled down with the breeze, sweet and sorrowful.

Jacob didn't offer his condolences. She didn't offer hers.

Before he had a chance to open his mouth, she said, "Did you try the pie?"

Jacob kept his eyes on the horizon, but the edges of his lips quirked.

Amy was right. Dolores did use humor as a defense mechanism—and so did Jacob. At his mother's funeral, they had done nothing but crack jokes at each other, until they were laughing so hard, Alexander had to sneak them out through the back door.

"Yep," he said. "Charlotte makes one mean sweet potato pie. Must say I missed her cooking this whole time."

"It's the one thing you missed about dinner parties at the Hawthornes', is it?"

"Oh, yeah. The one thing."

Dolores sighed. "Nothing like pie to say, 'Crown me Queen of the Town.'"

Jacob shrugged. "Let her have it. The crown, I mean. It doesn't bring out my eyes as much as I thought."

"Not to mention it makes your brain look terribly small."

In her peripheral vision, she saw his lips stretch into a smile, and couldn't resist looking at him.

And there it was. A pure gem salvaged from the past.

That golden retriever smile, which not even three years of braces had managed to kill.

Even if he didn't say one more word, even if he were to melt into the asphalt, Dolores felt that this, right here, had been worth it. She could leave this town now, and know she had seen him one last time.

This *was* the last time, surely.

The road they'd started on together two decades ago had burned to ash. It didn't matter that neither of them had lit the fire.

And yet–

Dolores bit the inside of her cheek.

Yet she wondered if that place made for her face still existed in the crook of his neck.

She continued, more serious, "You look good."

He chuckled. "Please. If I told people I'd gone to school with you, they'd think I was your teacher or something."

"A very young teacher, then. I meant you look–at peace."

The lines furrowed deeper around his eyes. "Yeah."

"Why did you quit? Really."

He let out a sigh. "When I got into politics, I thought I was cutting a different path for myself. I thought–Jesus, I don't know. That I wouldn't be my father's son. He and Teddy could go on making milk money, but I'd be in the business of making life better for people in town. Sounds stupid now, right?"

Dolores shrugged. "I went to med school because I wanted to save lives, and I wound up dealing with dead bodies. Life's full of surprises."

He shook his head, and she studied him through her lashes. She'd caught the change in his voice when he mentioned Teddy.

"You've been to see Wyatt," she said.

He met her eyes, guilt thick as paint. "I wanted to understand. Why he put Kristen's bones behind City Hall. Why he came after us."

Dolores lowered her eyes to the road. "What did he tell you?"

"Everything. Including what–what he thought I did to you."

Every second stretched into silence. He could not look at her. She would not look at him.

"Did you believe it, Dolores? Is that why it ended the way it did?"

Dolores hesitated. What good would it do to tell him now? That she'd believed he could do something like this to her–the boy who had been her best friend, who would have sawed through his arm before he hurt her.

She closed her eyes.

The truth. You take the truth now.

Even if it hurts.

Every day. Every time.

"Yes," she let out.

The shock in his eyes melted something deep inside of her, something she believed had hardened forever.

He watched her, in silence. In the end, he said, "Teddy?"

Dolores licked her parched lips. She nodded. "Teddy."

A strangled sound came out of his mouth. He whipped around so he was facing the other end of the street, fists pressed to his eyes. The wind carried the faint sound of music from the funeral. They didn't talk when the song ended, or the next one.

Dust smeared on his face from the sidewalk as he wiped his eyes. "God, Dolores. Don't you hate me?"

She met his gaze, surprised. "Hate you? Why? Did you know what Teddy did to me, to Kristen?"

"No. But I didn't put myself through a lot of trouble to *try* to know."

"Jake—"

Somehow, she couldn't find it in her to play the comforter. *You were just a kid. He was your brother.*

"After that night," he said, "I tried to see you again. You didn't go back to school. Didn't return my calls. Nathan said he thought you and I had—" He faltered. "But then when I told him I didn't make it to the party, he said he was drunk, that it must have been some other guy. Everyone started to say it. That you'd cheated on me. Then our parents had this big falling-out, and your family didn't want me within a mile of you. My father said I should forget you existed. All this time, the only person who fought for us was—"

"Teddy," Dolores guessed.

Jacob stared at his hands.

The worst part was, she didn't think Teddy had done it out of malice. "Rooting" for them, as he put it—trying to bridge the gap he had dug between them.

Growing up, she'd been the most important person in Teddy's life, aside from his family. Maybe there was an itch in the back of his head, and he might have wanted to scratch that itch—but not in a way that would jeopardize life as they knew it.

Teddy loved his brother. He never would have wanted to steal her from him.

Bitterness flooded her bloodstream.

At least, not for longer than an evening.

Why can't you let it be what it was? Why'd you have to make things all complicated?

Jacob said, "You know what I can't get over? When I sat with Wyatt—Junior. When he told me what Teddy did to his sister? It's how *fast* I believed him." He chuckled, and it came out perfectly dry, empty as a liquor bottle ricocheting against a wall. "Like he'd just told me the earth was round. He called my brother a rapist, a *killer,* and my mind went: 'Yep. That makes perfect sense.'"

Dolores's palm covered his hand, and he startled. Their gazes locked. Her breath caught in her throat.

Slowly, he widened the gaps between his knuckles so she could sneak her fingers through his.

"What now?" he said.

"I guess we move on."

Cracks splintered into her chest when he laughed.

She remembered the softness of his lips on hers. How easy it had been to love him, to realize she had always been in love with him. Like they were two asteroids, following the same orbit, the fact that they would find their way to each other as inevitable as the pull of gravity.

"That simple?" he said.

"What else can we do?"

He chewed on his lip. "Not together, though."

Though he didn't frame it that way, she heard the question in his voice.

"I don't think we could, after all that's happened."

He nodded. Something filtered out from his gaze–not hope. He couldn't have been hoping for anything. Still she watched as the chance of them ever revisiting their relationship died out. "Right," he said.

"I just–"

"No, you're right. It's been nineteen years. I'm a married man. You're a married woman."

He swallowed. Didn't say the truth, the real reason. *My brother raped you.* That was too unfair. Too unbearable.

"You know what, though?" He bit his lip. His face had never been good at keeping secrets from her. She watched as he fought against the words, decided not to say them, and said them anyway. "I really loved you, Dolores. I loved you out of my fucking mind."

She squeezed his hand. "I know."

Sitting on the opposite sidewalk, at the bottom of the hill, Dolores could see Kristen with her Julia Roberts smile, and Wyatt Jr., looking quiet as he always did. She doubted he felt quiet now, or that he would ever be quiet again–until he had his revenge.

An ice shard sank inside her rib cage.

If she was going to be haunted by the Horowitz family–

No.

She pushed back against the thought. Refused to articulate the desire to see a tall, spectral figure cut out of the horizon.

To see her father again, if only as a dream.

If she couldn't hold him and feel the spell of his arms around her, then she wanted the ice of his absence. For him to haunt her, as guilt had haunted him.

I was a ghost to you. Throughout the house, throughout the town. Won't you be one to me now?

Dolores gripped the edges of the sidewalk.

She understood that her father had let her go to punish himself. That her absence was the price he paid, for what he'd done to Kristen. What he'd let happen to her in the process.

Oh, Dad, she thought.

If he'd only done things differently. If he'd come to find her in Los Angeles. Told her the truth. She could not have forgiven him for Kristen. But she would have loved him, despite it all. Always.

Why couldn't he have chosen that instead?

You just remember the father you know, Dolores.

Her fingers felt frozen around the asphalt, her eyes on the horizon—on the hill that led to the cemetery, where Alexander's body was being put to rest.

Was it worth it? Was it worth losing each other, so he could stay the father she remembered—was it better to have a perfect memory, instead of seeing him, of holding him, real and imperfect?

Her eyelids rolled shut.

Come back to me, she thought. *Haunt me, and I'll carry your ghost for eighteen more years. I'll carry it for as long as I live.*

She opened her eyes again. The Horowitz children stared at her with their abyss-eyes. Unforgiving. Her father was nowhere to be seen. The songs that rode down the hill were not even his kind of music.

And yet—

Yet a glow prickled her skin to life. There, in the sunlight, rising through every pore, every inch of skin—she felt the special shine she always felt when her father looked at her. That cloak of magic, of blinding light, which had seemed the cross-product of herself and his eyes.

Across the street, a cat scrambled from under a car.

Tears spilled down her cheeks. *I love you,* she thought. *I love you, Dad.*

Jacob shook his head. He was crying, too. She could feel it in the way his hand squeezed hers. And she squeezed back.

He said, "I still can't get used to all these damned cats."

Dolores kept silent. She'd have to let go, soon–better sooner than later. Better do it now.

And yet she held on to his hand. For a little while.

"It's okay," she said. "I hear they don't bite."

ACKNOWLEDGMENTS

There are so many people without whom this book would not be possible.

I want to thank my family, who have supported me every second of my life. I'm grateful to my parents, who always encouraged me to write, and whose faith in me has shaped everything I am. I'm grateful to my older sister, who always said I would be a superstar, when she was objectively the one with superstar potential.

My mother in particular has been not only a support but a dedicated beta reader. Mom, you went through this novel at least ten times, and with each reading you provided valuable insight. Especially, you made me feel like you could read it ten thousand more times without getting bored. It was such a pleasure to go down that ride with you. Thank you to the moon and back.

Thanks to my dad, who always made me feel like the most special person in the world (on par with my two sisters and my mother). I literally don't know who I would be without your unwavering confidence, Dad. From the short story you read by accident when I was in my teens, you've been my number one fan. And I'm yours.

In short, thanks a million to my Adams family. Every inch of intense, loving, wonderful-weird that makes us who we are. I love you to pieces.

I'm grateful to my fiancé for providing me with feedback on all my books but especially for bringing joy and peace to me when I get jittery with ideas and enter one of my writing frenzies. My love, you make the real world worth living. If not for you, I'm not sure I'd come out to breathe. Thank you for your inspiring presence, your talent, your strength, and yes, your rugged good looks. All the love stories make sense because of you.

Thanks to my wonderful friends, Anaëlle, Guillaume, Marie (the both of you), MJ, Fleur, Jo, Julie, Jeff, Yann, Eve, Gül, Elisabeth, Nicole, Lisa, Sam, Sarah, Laure, Phéobé, Nolwenn–meeting you is the moment I realized how thrilling and fulfilling human relationships could be. You taught me so much about myself and the variety of shapes that true love comes in. With every conversation, I grow on all levels–intellectual, human, creative. Thank you for being so special and extraordinary and making me remember that there's more to life than ink and paper.

I also want to thank my beta readers, especially Melody from Denmark, who has done much to improve *No Rest for the Wicked* and my prose in general. I'd like to seize this moment to flag that, while I naturally did some research for this book, I was (obviously?) never in contact with FBI special agents or medical examiners, was never able to ask them some of the questions I asked myself or have them fact-check the book. Moreover, I'm not sure I would have wanted the book fact-checked–this is a work of fiction. I took liberties when I felt it enabled me to tell a better story. No, labs don't generally come up with results within twenty-four hours, and a member of a missing person's family would probably never be asked to tag along on an investigation into his disappearance. Everything I got wrong is on me.

Thank you to my wonderful agent, Millie Hoskins, who put work, time, and hope into me at a time when it meant literally everything. A huge thanks to my editors, Sarah Grill, Madeline Houpt, and Rufus Purdy, who helped shape this book into the best version of itself, as well as to my copy editor, Thomas Cherwin, and the whole editing teams at Minotaur and Titan Books.

Two women from different writers' unions, Maïa and Ambre, also deserve a world of thanks. Ambre, especially, for helping me face the intricacies of British tax-exemption laws–which is, this is true, the illustration you get when you type "hell" into the dictionary. Thank you, Ambre, for all the emails we exchanged and all the time you poured into this, even though I wasn't even a part of the union you represented.

Though this will sound surreal, I'd also like to thank two of my favorite actors, Sarah Wayne Callies and Paul Adelstein, who agreed to read my novel and believed in me when all they had read was an old fan fiction of mine. Thanks to Ben Haber, the producer of the *Prison Breaking* podcast, who picked my writing out of a gazillion fanfics on the internet. Thanks to all my fan fiction readers, who helped me grow over the years, and extra thanks to those who took the time to comment and made the writing process less lonely.

A few words of gratitude to two of my high school teachers, Anne Huonnic and Gilles Laugier.

Monsieur Laugier, for being the first person to ask me to give not the least that I could manage, but the most. You set the bar high, and since, I haven't lowered it. It's not been easy every day, trying to live up to those standards. But I would not be who I am, or where I am, without you.

Madame Huonnic, for being the first person outside my twin sister to read one of my stories and tell me I had talent–that 20/20 paper is still hanging on my bedroom wall. You were the teacher of a lifetime. It meant more than you know.

Finally, I want to thank my twin sister, Lily.

You know this, but because it's the only thing I know how to do, I'll put it in writing. Every word is for you. Every line. Every paragraph. Every book. You are the reader I picture perched above my shoulder when I start a story. It is your face, your reactions that I imagine when I finish. Before I could share my stories with the world, I was happy to share them only with you. Thank you for being my kindred spirit, my dark-dreamer soul, my Katherine. Thank you for making every line I write mean anything, and thank you for so much more than that. I've been alive for twenty-eight years, and not a second of them has been lonely. Thank you for your companionship during insomnia, for taking on the night and its demons with me. Thank you for your support and your love. Thank you for your strength and your wits and your defiance. Thank you for always going into the darkness with me–with your hand in mine, your eyes peering as I type, it never feels that scary.

ABOUT THE AUTHOR

Alexis Guegan

Rachel Louise Adams was raised in a small town in Brittany by a French father and a North American mother. After studying literature at university, she wrote her PhD thesis on American fast food and meat eating. When she isn't writing or reading, she can be found advocating for animal rights and spending time with her fiancé, her friends, and her two cats.